Out of Time

Also by Alton Gansky

Finder's Fee

The Prodigy

The Madison Glenn Series

1 | *The Incumbent*

2 | *Before Another Dies*

3 | *Director's Cut*

J. D. Stanton Mysteries

1 | *A Ship Possessed*

2 | *Vanished*

3 | *Out of Time*

J. D. STANTON MYSTERIES

Out of Time

ALTON
GANSKY

ZONDERVAN.com/
AUTHORTRACKER
follow your favorite authors

Out of Time
Copyright © 2003 by Alton L. Gansky

Value Edition, 978-0-310-29218-0

Requests for information should be addressed to:

Zondervan, *Grand Rapids, Michigan* 49530

Library of Congress Cataloging-in-Publication Data

Gansky, Alton
    Out of time / Alton Gansky.
        p. cm. — (J.D. Stanton mysteries; bk. 3)
     ISBN 978-0-310-24959-7
      1. Stanton, J.D. (Fictitious character)—Fiction   2. Naval historians—Fiction.   3.
    Retired teachers—Fiction.   I. Title.
    PS3557.A5195O95 2003
    813'.54—dc21

                                            2003010752

Interior Design by Melissa Elenbaas

Printed in the United States of America

---

08 09 10 11 12 13 14 • 20 19 18 17 16 15 14 13 12 11 10 9 8 7 6 5 4 3 2 1

To Travis Gray and my daughter Chaundel Gansky
in honor of their marriage

Out of Time

The Deep Blue Sea

Not a bad little speech, although I must admit, you looked a little tense."

J. D. Stanton inhaled deeply. The salt air was pleasantly acrid and swirled across the bow of the twin-hulled craft as it motored through the water, its sails furled. The breeze was far cooler than the hot, humid June air they had left behind one hour ago. Above him was a smooth ceiling of cobalt blue, unspotted by clouds. Gulls, white as fresh snow, trailed a few feet above and behind the stern, uttering one piercing operatic caw after another from their yellow beaks. They wanted food, bits of chum thrown over the side, but they were sentenced to disappointment. This was not a fishing trip, at least not at its core. Stanton was fishing for something without scales, but doubt was filling his mind as much as the salt air filled his lungs.

Stanton turned to the man who had tossed the ribbing comment his way. The twenty-two-year old was tall, the top of his sand-colored hair reaching six foot three above the wood-and-fiberglass deck. Mischievous dark blue eyes stared back. Archibald Richmond was a fresh-faced, newly hatched Annapolis grad with a bright future. Biceps bulged beneath the sleeves of the man's tight blue T-shirt as he stood at the starboard helm, turning the steel-and-wood wheel.

"It was that obvious, Richie?" Stanton asked. He felt the heat of embarrassment crawl up his cheeks, and he ran a hand through his close-cut, brown, gray-kissed hair.

"Not really, Skipper," the young man said with a shrug. "I'm just an unusually keen observer."

"You weren't so keen on your history final last year." Stanton returned his gaze forward. The sleek, smooth bow of the vessel plowed easily through the warm Atlantic. In the distance before him and to either side were the multicolored sails of other pleasure craft plying the coastal waters. Most, Stanton knew, would turn back to Miami in a few hours. He, however, and his seven travel companions would continue on as the sun set behind them. If all went well, they would not see Miami for another week.

"Essays are not my strong suit," Richie replied. "I still walked out of your class with an A."

J. D. Stanton, retired captain of the United States Navy, spent his days writing books on naval history and occasionally teaching history at the Naval Academy, Annapolis. As an adjunct professor, he had the pleasure of meeting the best and the brightest the navy had to offer—and it had a lot to offer. It had been in such a course that Stanton had met Richmond and immediately taken a liking to him. He was personable, respectful, and bright and had yet to lose a childlike sense of playfulness.

"I was feeling sorry for your parents, Ensign—you being an only child and all."

"It's true. I am the darling of their eyes. It's a good thing, too; otherwise you'd be undertaking this little mission on a fishing trawler instead of a state-of-the-art catamaran."

Stanton tried to picture Richie on an aged, dingy trawler but the image refused to come, as if merely imagining such a thing were heresy. Richie was from a privileged life. His father, a Harvard graduate, had worked his way up to CEO of one of the early computer firms. He was a man who could predict business futures with almost prophetic accuracy. He had guided the company through rising and falling markets and deflected hostile takeover attempts like a raincoat repelling water. With dogged persistence and unflagging optimism, he had built the third largest computer company in the world and made enough money to buy Montana in the process. It was his boat upon which Stanton stood.

"I have to say it again," Stanton said. "It was very generous of your father to loan the *Tern About* to us and to help with the funding."

"He's a great guy, all right," Richie said. He made no attempt to hide his pride. "Despite the pressures of his business, he always had time for me. He's the one who got me interested in sailing."

Stanton nodded. Richie had won several yachting races and was considered one of the best in the sport. It was one of the reasons why Stanton had asked him to help. While Stanton was familiar with the sea—a long career in the navy had seen to that—he had spent most of his ocean time under the waves as a submariner. He worked through the ranks until he was given command of an attack sub. He had loved the work and loved the life. Four years into retirement now and living in San Diego (when he wasn't teaching at Annapolis), he found himself missing the sounds, even smells, of navy life. There was nothing else like it in the world. Although only in his late forties, Stanton had left the steel hulls of submarines and taken up the pen. He never looked back; he felt no regrets ... but there were moments when he longed to feel the vibration of engines under his feet as his boat patrolled the dark depths of the ocean. He loved the sea but he had never learned to sail, certainly not a half-million-dollar catamaran. That duty fell to Richie and the other member of his crew.

"Dad uses this to entertain clients and friends," Richie continued. "It's a great way to seal deals and negotiate lower prices from suppliers. It's also a pretty nifty tax write-off." Richie paused, then added, "He also believes in what you're trying to do. He has a big heart, my old man. He'd be twice as rich if he didn't keep giving money away."

"Maybe he sees it as an investment in people, and not merely charity," Stanton suggested.

"Don't get me wrong, Skipper; I admire my father more than any son can. It's the world that thinks rich people are stingy."

"Well, I can't thank him enough for his generosity. This boat is great."

"It's a Catana 582," Richie said with pride. "Sixty-two feet of customized luxury and the latest technology. It's a floating palace."

"She handles well."

"Wait until we're in open sea and I raise the sails. You'll think you're flying a foot above the water. Our passengers are in for a treat."

"Let's hope they know how to appreciate it."

"That's what's making you nervous, isn't it? Back at port when you were making introductions and telling everyone what you hoped to achieve, you seemed . . . well, what I mean to say is . . ."

"You said it right before: tense." Stanton shook his head. "In my active-duty days, I played cat and mouse with Russian subs, carried out surveillance missions, and did things that will remain classified long after I'm dead, and aside from a heightened sense of danger, I was never nervous. A short time ago a group of five teenagers put the fear in me. Go figure."

"You didn't mention the other things."

"What other things?" Stanton asked.

Richie flashed his spotlight smile. "How much research did you do on Tenny and me before asking us to come along?"

"A fair amount," Stanton admitted. "It was necessary. I knew you from Annapolis but that was just one class. I'm only on campus a few months a year."

"Well, I did a little research on you too. It's something I learned from my father. Know who you're doing business with and you will save a lot of heartache down the road."

"And?"

"And you're the talk of the navy. The details are fuzzy, but scuttlebutt has it that you did some pretty heroic things on the *Triggerfish*. No one knows how a missing sub from World War II ended up in the Pacific or what happened below its decks when you crawled down the hatch. I don't suppose you want to talk about that?"

"Want to? Yes. Can do? No."

"I assume that goes for Roanoke II."

Stanton snapped his head around. "You know nothing about Roanoke II. Is that clear?" There was no anger in his voice but there was an unmistakable warning. His mind snapped back to late 2000, when he was called upon to investigate a mystery he still could not fully explain—a town in the high desert of California had, in a moment, lost its entire population. What he saw, the danger he faced, still haunted him.

"Aye, Captain. Crystal clear."

Richie turned the wheel and steered the twin hulls starboard a few degrees. Stanton knew it was an unnecessary maneuver but it gave Richie a way out of an awkward situation. He decided to help.

"Why the Naval Academy?" he asked. "Why not follow your father through Harvard?"

"It was his idea. He said Harvard provided a great education and a powerful network of connections, but it didn't teach him to be leader. He told me that the navy would give me something that no university could, and that I could go to Harvard Business School later if I wanted."

"He's a wise man," Stanton commented.

Spanning the twin hulls of the *Tern About* was the sleek cabin that housed the opulent salon, galley, navigation station, and more. The darkly tinted door slid to the side and Rebecca Tennyson emerged, holding two mugs in her hand. Called Tenny by her friends, she was a five foot eight bundle of energy. Her skin was a beautiful bleached ebony and her eyes the darkest brown. Her black hair was trimmed close to the scalp and her lips were as slim as her frame. She was a year behind Richie at Annapolis and had shown an aptitude for engineering. Before entering the academy, she had spent the summer learning to pilot sailboats. It had taken her two years of hard work in a Taco Bell to save the money for the classes. Stanton had learned that she became a sailboat addict after her first trip. Whenever she could scrape the money together, she rented a boat and put it through its paces. When Stanton approached Richie about crewing the excursion, the ensign had suggested that Tenny come along.

"I thought you might want some coffee," she said, walking the slightly pitching deck as if she were strolling down a country lane. "It's a navy tradition, isn't it, drinking coffee while at sea? If you don't want coffee, I can see what else I can find. I mean, the galley is filled with goodies, so coffee isn't your only choice. Do you want me to whip up a sandwich or—"

"Coffee is fine," Stanton said with a smile.

"I don't mind. Really, I don't. I could just zip back into the galley and—"

"Take a breath, Tenny," Stanton said with a chuckle. "We're spending the next week together; no need to use all your words in the first few hours." He took the cup. Richie released one hand from the wheel and took the mug with a nod and a "Thanks."

"Yes sir. Sorry sir," Tenny replied quickly.

"Okay, let me say this again," Stanton began, taking on his professorial tone. "This is not a navy mission. While the three of us are navy personnel and the navy has underwritten this little experiment, it would be better if we tossed rank aside and treated each other as equals. Fair enough?"

"Yes sir," Tenny snapped. "I mean, um, sure, that would be great."

"Fine by me, Skipper, but every boat needs a captain and on this trip that's you. I'm just the hired help."

"Okay, but let's keep it casual. I think it would be better for the kids," Stanton said.

The others agreed.

"Speaking of the kids," he added, "how did the safety lecture go?"

Tenny shook her head slowly. "I talked but I'm not sure they listened. I've been to funerals where people looked happier."

"That's to be expected. These guys are on the edge. You read my report. We have five troubled teenagers, all from navy families. The navy can be rough on kids. Being uprooted and moved every few years, separated from friends and forced to change schools, having a parent out to sea for as long as six months, sometimes longer. The divorce rate is high, juvenile delinquency on the rise. In most cases it can't be helped. Some families thrive despite the pressures; others fragment. We're dealing with the latter. Not one of these kids wants to be here. Two of them are here because a judge gave them the choice of this trip or something worse."

"Do you think this will really help them?" Tenny asked. "It seems like a long shot."

"It is, but it's the only shot we have," Stanton explained. "My hope is that they will see that navy people are just folk who have a job to do. Maybe they can open up to us, and we to them. It's worth a try, long shot or not." Stanton paused, choosing not to mention that he also harbored hopes of sharing his faith.

"You're a brave man, Skipper," Richie said. "Trapped on a sailboat with five angry teens. Sounds like the making of a horror movie."

"Speaking of sailboats," Tenny said to Richie, "when are you going to stop cheating and kill the engines? Sailboats are called sailboats because—"

"They have sails," Richie said, finishing her sentence. "I can think of no better time than now."

When not under sail, the *Tern About* was propelled by a pair of Volvo 105-horsepower diesel engines, so well balanced, sealed, and soundproofed, they were hardly noticeable. The catamaran seemed to move through the gentle swells as if pulled by a magical cord. But Stanton knew the craft would come alive when its white sails rose and billowed with the driving wind.

"Tenny, bring up our friends," Stanton directed. "They might like to see this."

"I wouldn't bet on it," she said with a tilt of the head. "I'll see what I can do."

"Just tell them I want to see them," Stanton said. "Be firm."

"Okay, but if I'm not back in three minutes, call in the marines."

N
Λ

Five teenagers milled around in the open air behind the center cabin. Overhead an aluminum-and-fiberglass cover, called a Bimini top, stretched from just above the main cabin's roof to the stern of the cockpit deck, providing shade. Half the deck was occupied by an L-shaped padded bench and a table firmly bolted down to stay in place on a pitching sea. There was enough room for all five of Stanton's special passengers to sit together, but only three made use of the luxury. The other two stood off by themselves, avoiding eye contact with any other human on board.

Seated around the exterior table were Jamie Penowski, Mary Moss, and Steve Dunlap. Two feet of space separated them, an invisible, inviolable barricade erected by self-conscious strangers. The other two, John Hays and Tony Roscoe, stood apart. John had taken a place by the starboard lifeline and was gazing over the side, clearly lost in his thoughts. Tony leaned against the cockpit bulkhead, his arms crossed before him and his head down. A toothpick was nestled in the right corner of his mouth.

"They were just sitting in the lounge staring at each other," Tenny said as she shook her head. "If I didn't know better, I'd think their best dog just died."

Stanton slipped her a slight smile. It was almost comical. The three adults on board were gathered around the starboard helm, and the juveniles were spread out as far from each other as possible.

"Not a happy ship," Richie commented. "A week of this and I'll be jumping overboard and swimming home."

"Oh no you don't," Tenny said. "You signed on for the whole trip. You're staying with the rest of us."

Stanton sighed. He expected this. Troubled teens, he had been told, tended to isolate themselves until some bond was created. For some, bonding was close to impossible. He stepped toward his young passengers, moving from the narrow area of the pilot's station to the broader aft deck. "Okay, people," Stanton said, then immediately regretted it. He reminded himself that he was talking to a group of teenagers, not a naval crew. "Richie is going to raise the sails in a few minutes. I thought you might like to see that."

There was no response, just the sound of water whipping around the hulls. Stanton studied his new charges. He had never seen an unhappier lot. Steve Dunlap sat on the bench, a headset pressed to his ears, his head bobbing to the beat of music Stanton could not hear.

"Steve." The boy either had not heard Stanton or chose to ignore him. "*Steve*," Stanton called loudly. Still no response. Before he could start forward, Steve jumped, prompted by an unexpected slap to his shoulder.

"Ow, watch it!" Steve glared at Jamie, who had backhanded him. He pushed the headset off. "What do you think you're doing?"

"Earth to whoever you are," she shot back, "someone is talking to you." She jerked her head toward Stanton.

"Just say so," Steve retorted. "Keep your paws to yourself."

Jamie rolled her eyes, then shook her head.

Stanton now had the attention of four of the five passengers. He turned to John Hays, who continued to gaze over the side as if looking for something lost. "Hey, John. How about joining us?"

"I can hear fine from here," he said.

"I would like more than your hearing; I would like your attention."

"I said I can hear you from here."

"And I asked you to join us." Stanton darkened his tone. Before agreeing to head this excursion, he spent some time talking to the youth pastor of the church he attended, seeking whatever advice and guidance he could give. The one comment that had stuck in his mind above all others was, "There can only be one leader in the group and that had better be you. Most young people respond to authority—not always positively, but they respond. They will test you, especially in the beginning. Start strong and you'll finish strong."

John continued his vigil. Stanton glanced at the others and saw them staring, waiting to see what would happen next. Stanton pursed his lips, then snapped a single-word order: "Now!"

John spun and Stanton could see the anger in the boy's eyes. It faded before Stanton's unflinching granite gaze.

"All right, all right," John said. "Ease up, Captain Bligh. Don't have a stroke." He glanced at the others as if to be certain every eye was on him, then stepped away from the lifeline and sauntered onto the main deck and beneath the canopy. "You're not going to give another speech, are you? Two in an hour is too much."

"No speeches," Stanton began. "As I was saying, Richie is going to raise the sails, and I thought you would like to see it. That's all."

"Thrilling," John said. "At long last my life will be complete."

Stanton ignored him. "Before we kill the engines, I thought I would make sure you've all taken the time to exchange names."

No one spoke.

"Okay, I'll take that as a no." Stanton clamped his hands behind his back. "I introduced myself when you first came aboard, and you've already met Richie and Tenny. It's time you told your fellow travelers a little about yourself. Who's going to start off?"

Again silence.

"I know you're not shy, so someone step up to the plate."

Again no volunteers.

"How about you, Jamie?"

Again her eyes rolled. Stanton wondered how many times a day she did that.

"You already know all about me, so what's the point?"

Jamie was a heartbreaker, with deep brown eyes and shoulder-length blond hair. The down-the-middle part revealed darker roots. Her skin was smooth and clean and her lips were full, traced with dark liner and covered in a reddish lipstick. Her mouth seemed unaccustomed to smiling. To him she looked every bit the stereotypical cheerleader, except void of any enthusiasm. She wore jeans and a heavy white T-shirt.

"This isn't for my benefit, Ms. Penowski; it's an opportunity to get to know each other. That will put us on an equal footing."

"What do you want to know?"

"Name, age, and which parent is in the navy should do for starters."

Jamie released an explosive sigh, then spoke with startling speed, as if the words were too hot to hold in her mouth. "My name is Jamie Penowski and yes it's Polish and I've heard every Polish joke in the world so don't bother telling me any. I'm sixteen and my dad is an aircraft mechanic on some aircraft carrier."

"Which carrier?" Stanton asked, though he already knew the answer.

She shrugged. "I don't know and I don't care either."

"I believe it's the *Carl Vinson*," Stanton offered.

"Yeah, that's it."

"And your crime?" John asked.

"That's enough, John," Stanton snapped.

"Oh, come on, Captain or Admiral or whatever you are," John fired back, "we may all be delinquents and losers but we're not stupid. We know why we're here. You're supposed to work some magic to make us find purpose and meaning in life. Maybe grow up and enlist in the navy, fighting to keep home and country free. If we're going to play Biography Channel, then let's do it right."

Stanton started to speak again when Jamie blurted, "I run away. I steal things from stores. I hate school and I hate my family. For that matter, I hate my life. Happy now, pretty boy?"

"Oh, she thinks I'm a stud," John said with a big grin. "Maybe we could rearrange our sleeping assignments—"

"Do you know what a bilge is, mister?" The words came blazing across the deck. Stanton turned to see Tenny stepping forward. Lightning flashed from her dark eyes. "You finish that sentence and I'll make sure you bunk down there. You got that?"

Stanton waited a moment to see what witty comment John would offer, but none came. He took a quick step back. "As you were," Stanton said softly to Tenny.

"Yes sir," she replied but offered no apology.

"Thank you, Jamie," Stanton said as if nothing had happened. "You're up, Tony." Tony was tall with olive skin, black hair slicked back and held in place by what Stanton assumed was a quart of thirty-weight oil. He had a broad forehead and a narrow jaw, making his head look like an inverted pear, except stubble covered this pear. A pair of Oakley sunglasses concealed his eyes. Each ear sported a gold ring, as did his lower lip. He wore all black. Had Stanton met him in the proverbial dark alley, he would have feared for his wallet and maybe even his life.

"Tony Roscoe. Italian. Seventeen. My old man is a cook. I'm here because it's more comfortable than jail." He crossed his arms again and returned to leaning against the cockpit wall.

"Nice," Jamie said with obvious sarcasm.

"Who's next?" Stanton prompted.

"I'll go," Steve offered. Stanton could hear music still playing through the headset that now encircled the young man's neck.

"What say we kill the music first?"

"Oh, okay." Steve fumbled with his MP3 player and the music died a second later. "I'm Steve Dunlap and I'm fifteen years old. I guess that makes me the baby of the group. I don't know why I'm here."

Stanton knew. Steve's mother had died the previous year and he had taken it hard. According to his father, the boy had become more reclusive. Smaller than most fifteen-year-olds and possessing a near genius IQ, he was an outcast at school. Six months ago he dropped out. Whereas once he excelled in his classes and spent his free time reading science fiction, he now spent hours by himself playing video games.

"And what does your father do?" Stanton asked.

"He's a corpsman on the *Toledo*."

"A submariner," Stanton said. "That's something I know a little about. Okay, Mary, your turn."

Mary did not look up, keeping her eyes directed at the smooth laminate top of the outdoor table. Her brown hair was thin, uneven, and hung a few inches below her narrow shoulders. Her mouth was thin with down-turned lips that remained closed beneath a narrow, petite nose. She was what men referred to as cute. She did not possess the kind of face and body that lent themselves to a life of strolling the catwalk with other models, but there was a beauty there nonetheless. Not on the surface, her beauty was concealed under a mask of wariness and introversion.

"Mary?" Stanton prompted softly.

She looked up through eyes that reflected enough emptiness that it made Stanton ache. "Mary Moss, sixteen. Kids at school call me M&M ... you know, like the candy. My father is a chief on the USS *Howard*. It's a destroyer. I'm here because my mom thinks I need time away from home."

"From one prison to another," John quipped. "It's the same with me—except my family needs the time away from me. So here I am. Oh, I'm eighteen and my father is a navy pilot." John was tall, six two in sneakers. His blond hair was cut close to the scalp on the sides but longer on the top of his head. He wore Dockers slacks, Nike sneakers, and a blue polo shirt.

"Eighteen?" Tony asked with surprise. "That makes you an adult, man. They can't make you take this ride."

John shrugged. "It was come along or find a new place to live. I don't have too many of those. Besides, life at home is cheap and the food is free. I can put up with a week soaking up the sun. Beats the alternative—working."

"Okay," Stanton said. "I appreciate your cooperation. I understand that Tenny gave you the in-depth safety instruction and tour. Correct?" Several responded with nods. "I know some of you don't want to be out here, but here we are. I hope we can make the best of it. If things go well, we'll have an adventure. How much fun you have and how much you learn is up to you. Richie and Tenny will teach you as much about sailing as you want—"

"Or as little," Tony interjected.

"Or as little," Stanton agreed. "I suggest you make the best of it. You may be far from home, but this yacht has more luxury than most of us will see in our lives, so enjoy."

"What if we don't like our sleeping arrangements?" Tony asked.

"Hey, I didn't ask to share a cabin with you," John answered hotly. "If you don't like my company, then sleep outside."

"You will sleep where I tell you," Stanton said. His words were direct and pointed but devoid of anger. "Out here we have to depend on each other. That's the lesson, folks. There are several things I want you to take away with you when this trip is over. One of them is the simple fact that we are all individuals, but not islands—we work as a team. If we work together, this trip will be unforgettable." He paused and looked at his charges and imme-diately knew his enthusiasm was wasted. "Okay, then. Richie is going to give you the down and dirty on sailing terms, and then we're going to cut this baby loose to be what it was designed to be—a sailboat."

Stanton replaced Richie at the wheel, and he in turn took Stanton's spot on the deck. "All right, me buckos," Richie said in his best Hollywood pirate accent, "let's raise the mainsail and see how she sets."

Stiff Breeze

The *Tern About* skipped across the small ocean swells, pressing the water into a gentle, flowing bow wake. The white canvas sail which had been neatly stored in the boom now bowed under the constant pressure of the wind. Before, they had motored out of the harbor under the power of the twin engines. The engines were now little more than cargo in the port and starboard hulls. The catamaran was moving as she had been expertly designed to do, its sails engorged with wind and its smooth hulls caressing the surface, running through the ocean like a plane flying through the air.

Even the gulls that had been so insistent before had fallen behind or sought other craft to pester. The wind, self-made by the cat's forward motion, rolled over the cabin in an uninterrupted flow, giving the impression that the boat was flying more than sailing. Stanton found it invigorating; his every nerve was alive with the thrill of it.

"I take it you're having fun, Cap?" Richie asked.

"What makes you say that?" Stanton turned to look at Richie, who stood as erect as a redwood, his hands wrapped lightly around the wheel in the starboard pilot station.

"If your smile gets any bigger, the corners of your mouth are going to meet behind your head."

"And here I thought I was displaying my usual captain's dispassionate exterior."

Richie laughed loudly. "That evaporated the moment the mainsail unfurled and the jib set. I've been waiting for you to dance a little jig."

"No jigging coming, Richie. I have my image to maintain. Let's just keep my little joy a secret. Submariners are supposed to disdain surface ships."

"What's the old quip you guys are so famous for? There are only two types of ships—"

"Submarines and targets," Stanton finished.

"You didn't sink any catamarans while you were prowling the ocean in your sub, did you?"

"None that I'm willing to talk about," Stanton answered.

"It's a shame the kids aren't into this as much as you are," Richie noted. He nodded forward.

Stanton followed the nod. Under the covered deck just behind the cabin sat M&M and Jamie. The latter was working an emery board over her fingernails, and the former stared absently over the stern, her eyes seemingly fixed on the Miami skyline as it receded in the distance. Tony stood nearby, having hardly moved over the last thirty minutes. He remained motionless with his arms crossed in front of him, as if waiting for the next confrontation. John had returned to the starboard lifeline and stared down at the water as it coursed by the hull. Only Steve seemed remotely interested in the goings-on of the trip—he sat on the raised leather chair at the port helm. The catamaran could be guided from either of its two hulls. Identical pilot stations had been built on both sides of the boat. Tenny was in the galley, having offered to make sandwiches for lunch.

"They have an image to keep up too," Stanton said. "Someplace along the short line of their young lives, they have learned that the image they project defines who they are. They're unhappy about life and they want the world to know. Showing excitement breaks the unwritten rule of separation. They've spent a lot of time cultivating the 'I don't give a rip about anything' attitude. It's their shield. They're not going to drop it easily."

"Wow," Richie said. "Retired navy captain, historian, writer, and psychologist—I'm impressed."

"No, you're not," Stanton said. "And I'm no psychologist. I just talked to as many knowledgeable people as I could before coming out here. I want to be as mentally equipped as I can be."

"How about spiritually equipped?"

Stanton made eye contact again. One of the reasons he had selected Richie for the weeklong ocean expedition was the man's Christian depth. He had lived a privileged life of wealth, attended the best schools, and was denied nothing he desired. Yet he was a man of faith, a commitment that was clearly seen by anyone who spent more than an hour in his presence. Not only would he see the *Tern About* through a couple hundred miles of travel up and down the Atlantic coast, but he would help Stanton show the difference belief could make in a person's life.

There would be no forced Bible studies, no "chalk talks," and no tracts pressed into resistant hands, just two men who had learned that Christ made a difference. That would be the strongest sermon they could deliver. Richie brought much more than sailing skills to the expedition.

Tenny was a different matter. Being an able sailor and having a heart for young people had qualified her for the trip, but she had no spiritual definition, at least none that Stanton could find. Faith was not a requirement to crew the boat, only experience, patience, and a desire to help some troubled kids. Stanton had met with her for two hours before inviting her to come along. A fellow instructor at the academy had vouched for her. That, coupled with Richie's recommendation, made her a solid choice.

"Give them time, Skipper," Richie said. "More important, give God time."

"That's the plan, Richie. That's the plan."

Richie turned his attention to Steve, who was still glued to the seat in the alternate outdoor helm. "Yo, Stevie." The youngest passenger turned to Richie but said nothing. "Do you see the compass in front of you?"

Stanton watched as Steve directed his attention to the slender white pedestal just on the opposite side of the wheel. Stanton was standing next to an identical instrument. The white fiberglass base supported a compass protected by a tinted plastic bubble. Steve nodded.

"Speak up, Steve," Richie shouted. "I can't hear your head nod."

"Yeah, I see it. What about it?"

"Do you see where the arrow is pointing?"

He nodded again.

"What?"

"Yeah, I see it."

"Good. I'm going to the head. Keep the arrow right where it is."

"What? You want me to take the wheel?"

"That's the size of it," Richie said with a broad grin.

"No . . . I don't know how . . . I mean . . ."

"Sorry, but nature calls," Richie said. He released the wheel and stepped away. Immediately it began to spin left. Stanton knew that the wheel in the other helm was doing the same thing.

"No, wait!" Steve called.

Richie didn't wait; he just continued on to the cabin. Steve looked at Stanton with fearful eyes. Stanton shrugged and then said, "I just look like I'm in charge. Don't steer us into anything solid." Stanton followed Richie across the deck but not before he saw Steve Dunlap seize the wheel and begin turning it to put the boat back on course.

"I know you know this," Stanton said as he caught up with Richie, "but this tub does have an autopilot."

"Yeah, I know, but this was far more fun, don't you think?"

Stanton had to agree. The look on the young man's face when the wheel began to spin was priceless. "You're a cruel sailor, you know that, don't you?"

"Guilty as charged."

N
↑

Lunch, served in the cabin, consisted of tuna sandwiches, Pringles, and soda. Tenny had made twenty sandwiches, which she admitted "may be too many." It had been. Richie and John downed three sandwiches each; Steve, Tony, and Stanton each consumed two. The girls each nibbled one. The remaining were to be placed in the refrigerator for whoever wanted a snack.

"You could have told me that there's an autopilot," Steve complained between bites.

Richie laughed. "Oh, come on, you enjoyed it. You just spent the last forty-five minutes guiding a half-million-dollar customized yacht through the treacherous Atlantic ocean."

"I know I feared for my life," John said acidly.

"At least he did more than hold on to the guardrail," Tony snipped.

"Lifeline," Tenny said. "The metal cable around the deck is called a lifeline, not a guardrail."

"Whatever," Tony said.

"Oooh, the woman shot you down, tough guy," John said. "But I guess you're used to being shot down by women."

Tony started to his feet but froze when Stanton ordered him to sit. Years of leadership had taught him how to quietly make his point understood. Many of the crew on his submarine had been barely older than Tony and John. Stanton had learned that the right words with the right inflection could diffuse most situations.

Silence filled the ornate salon.

"This place looks like a hotel lobby," Jamie said. "I thought boats were supposed to be cramped."

"Have you been in the bathroom?" Tony asked. "I have to exhale just to get through the door."

"They're not called bathrooms," Tenny began. "They're called heads and—"

Stanton waved her off.

"They're still small, whatever you call them," Tony said.

"Speaking of bathrooms," Steve said, his eyes fixed on Richie, "you sure were in there a long time. You left me out there for almost an hour."

"Oh, didn't I tell you?" Richie replied. "I also took a nap."

"Great," Steve said. "I suppose we're in for a whole week of practical jokes."

"How did it feel?" Stanton asked Steve.

"How did what feel? Being dumped with the responsibility of steering the boat? Did I ask for that?"

"Don't be too hard on yourself," Richie remarked with a grin. "You didn't take us more than a couple of miles off course."

"Don't listen to him, Steve," Stanton said. "We're right where we should be. What I want to know is, how did it feel to have control of the *Tern About*?"

Steve shrugged. "Okay, I guess."

"Just okay?" Stanton probed.

"It was fun," Steve finally admitted. "I didn't know what I was doing, but by keeping my eye on the compass, I was able to go in the right direction."

That was the conclusion Stanton had hoped for. He doubted that the others picked up the point, and he fought with himself not to make this the object lesson it was. "Well, that's one of the things I've learned in life: a person usually ends up going wherever they're looking." He stopped there and took another drink of soda.

"Was that just a lesson or something?" Jamie asked.

Stanton shrugged. "Just an observation, that's all."

"I've got a dumb question," Jamie said. "If we're all down here eating lunch, who's driving the boat?"

"They just said it had an autopilot," John snapped. "Did you doze off or something?"

Jamie's face clouded and she started to say something but caught Stanton's eye. He saw her eyes narrow and her lips purse. He was sure that she didn't take much from anyone.

"Ease up, John," Stanton said. "Who wants to take a turn at the wheel next?"

Silence enfolded the question, and then Tony said, "I'll give it a shot. It sure beats sitting around doing nothing."

"Good," Stanton said. "Okay, here's the drill. There are eight of us on the *Tern About*. As pleasure craft go, she's a big boat, but not so big that we can avoid bumping into each other. To make all this work, we have to pull together. Tenny made lunch, I'm making dinner, and Richie is doing breakfast. We'll take whatever help you're willing to offer. Keeping the boat clean will be your job."

"Wait a minute," John interrupted. "I ain't swabbing no decks. I'm not your slave."

"That's right, but you're not a freeloader either. Just do your part to keep things where they belong."

"What are we going to do out here?" Jamie asked. "I'm already bored."

"Boredom is your choice," Stanton replied. "You can sit in here for a week or you can learn how to sail. We've also brought skin diving gear, fishing poles, table games, books, and movies."

"Movies?" Steve said.

"Yup, the boat has a DVD player and more. There are some video games if you're so inclined."

"How about cards?" Tony asked. "We could play poker."

"Now we're talking," John agreed. "And I know just the kind of poker I want to play."

"It's not going to happen," Stanton said.

"You got that right," Jamie snipped.

"What? You some kind of prude?" John asked Stanton.

"No, but I am a man of principles, and you're stuck with them."

"It's going to be a long week," John said. "Maybe I should swim home."

"I'll give you a push," Tony offered.

"Shut up, druggie!" John snapped. The words that followed went beyond vulgar. A career navy man, Stanton had heard said everything that could be said. His ears had endured curses and vulgarities that seemed capable of staining steel bulkheads. John put them all to shame.

Tony sprang up, fists clinched. John was a little larger and a few pounds heavier, but Stanton had no doubt that Tony was the more experienced street fighter. John was in over his head. Stanton knew this but it seemed John did not. He was on his feet a half second later, ready to let his fist drive home his angry point.

"That's enough," Stanton commanded, placing a hand on John's shoulder. John slapped at it but Stanton's arm didn't budge.

"Let go of me," John snapped.

Instead Stanton pulled him close, turning the volatile youth to face him. "You will not speak that way in my presence again. Is that clear?" His words were calm, even, and weighed a ton.

"Or what? You gonna hit me?" John snarled. "Do you know what assault on a minor is?"

"I thought you were eighteen," Richie said.

John blinked as the ramifications of Richie's comment settled in. Then the anger returned to his eyes. "I can handle myself."

"I'm not interested in a fight, Mr. Hays," Stanton said. "But don't think I walk away from trouble. Now sit down." Stanton released the boy's shoulder. Slowly, and only after a sizzling glare at Tony, John returned to his seat.

"Sit down, Tony," Stanton said.

"I don't have to put up—," Tony started.

Stanton turned to him but said nothing.

"Do as he says," Richie advised, then reached for another half sandwich as if nothing had happened.

Tony did as he was told, but Stanton knew it was a momentary concession. He was locked on a boat with two men who were each three decades his junior. Stanton was fit and healthy, but the last thing he wanted to do was referee a fistfight between these guys.

A discomfited stillness filled the lounge, as if any word spoken in the next few moments would set fire to the powder keg. M&M leaned forward and rested her forehead on one hand. Stanton studied her for a moment. Her smooth face wore a patina of perspiration, and her pleasant skin tone had shifted toward the green end of the spectrum.

"Oh no," she said.

"You okay?" Tenny asked. She leaned forward and laid a hand on Mary's back.

M&M shook her head. She gagged.

"She's gonna hurl," Jamie said and pushed away. The other youths did the same.

A clock tick later the young woman was on her feet, racing from the lounge and out onto the deck. Seven pairs of eyes looked at each other, each set saying the same thing. Stanton glanced at M&M's plate. She had eaten half a sandwich and none of the chips. He motioned to Tenny to follow her. As she rose, a loud retching poured through the open cabin door.

"Oh, sick," Jamie said. "I don't think I'm hungry anymore." Steve and Tony looked toward the door. John chuckled.

"I'm going to go check on her," Stanton said. Making a slight head motion toward John and Tony, he added to Richie, "You might want to stay here a little while longer."

"You got it, Skipper."

Before exiting the lounge area, Stanton retrieved a washcloth from the galley and wet it. He then grabbed a dry towel and headed aft.

The fragrant ocean breeze was tainted with the putrid smell of bile. M&M hadn't gone far. She had bolted from the cabin and found the starboard lifeline. Stanton could see only her back, but her heaving body motions and guttural emanations provided enough information for him. Tenny stood by her side, hand on her back.

"Let it go," Stanton heard Tenny say. "There's no easy way around it. Just let go."

"I . . . I . . . I don't want . . ." More stomach contents were set free in the wind.

Stanton waited a few more moments and when it seemed the convulsions were over, he approached. M&M was leaning over the plastic-coated metal cable that ran the perimeter of the boat. "First time I was seasick, I had two fears," he said, handing her the moist cloth. "My first fear was that I was going to die; my second fear was that I wasn't going to die."

M&M took the cloth and wiped at her mouth. "I'm so embarrassed."

"No need to be, Mary. You're not the first, you won't be the last. I've seen the biggest, strongest, most seasoned sailors doing what you've just done. There's no shame in it."

"I don't think I can go on," she said. "I feel like I'm going to puke my toes up."

"Your toes are safe," Stanton said. "And you'll adjust. It takes a little time."

"I'm no sailor," she said. "The others will never let me forget this."

"They may be next," Stanton said.

Tenny agreed. "I've got a cast-iron stomach and I've still tossed my share of cookies."

Stanton handed her the towel.

"I didn't take the medication you told us to," M&M admitted.

Stanton had sent a letter to each of the kids and their parents, telling them what to bring and what to leave home. He also advised them to get a prescription of scopolamine from their family physicians, recommending the transdermal patch that was applied behind the ear. "That's all right. We came prepared." He reached forward and brushed away a strand of hair that had been cemented to her forehead by sweat. She recoiled and slapped at Stanton's hand.

"Whoa, easy, girl," Tenny said. "He's not going to hurt you."

"I'm . . . I'm sorry," M&M said. "I don't like to be touched."

Stanton nodded. "I understand," he said softly. "I meant nothing by it."

She cut her eyes away.

"Tenny, I think we need to get some fluid replacement going. Would you bring up some Gatorade and the scopolamine gel?"

"Will do," Tenny replied quickly, then started for the cabin.

"When Tenny gets back, drink some of the Gatorade, but drink it slowly. It will help in several ways, including replacing electrolytes. You may feel like vomiting a few more times. If so, then just go with it, but keep replacing the fluids. You'll feel better soon. Also, stay on deck as much as possible, look at the horizon. Don't try and read right now. It will just make things worse. Take in the fresh air, look out over the ocean, and move around some. Soon all this will be just a memory."

"Okay," she said weakly. "I'm sorry about slapping your hand. I just—"

"You owe me no explanations, Ms. Moss. I'm just here to be your friend."

M&M nodded, turned pale, spun on her heel, and leaned over the lifeline once again.

N
Λ

Tenny emerged from the cabin with two large cups of coffee in hand. Steam danced off the hot fluid, rising into the cooling night air. Richie had steered the catamaran a few miles off the coast and turned her south. Actually, Tony worked the wheel, with Richie on his shoulder. Despite his best efforts, Tony could not completely conceal his pleasure. At first he had stood as rigid as a board, following Richie's direction with all the enthusiasm of a ten-year-old stepping into the dentist's chair. Stanton had watched from a few feet away, trying not to stare. When the wheel pulled against the young man's hand, he responded immediately, correcting and then redirecting the wheel to its proper position.

Richie was the consummate teacher, pointing out the gauges, the compass, and giving a quick lecture in boating terminology. Tony's face was a concrete mask of indifference but his eyes told a different story. The hours passed as each of the students took their turn behind the wheel. Only John refused to participate, preferring to sit in the lounge drinking soda. M&M remained too queasy to stand on the moderately pitching deck.

When darkness moved in like a fog, Stanton took his turn in the pilot's station, the others having gone below. He would stand watch until after midnight, then be relieved by Tenny. Since she was going to be on deck through most of the wee hours, he was surprised to see her pass through the cabin door. Music poured out from the opening behind her. Apparently, the kids had found the CD player.

"You being a diehard navy man, I assume coffee doesn't disrupt your sleep," Tenny said. Her voice was direct and seasoned with playfulness.

"The elixir of life," Stanton said. "But that doesn't look like navy coffee."

"What do you mean?"

"First, it's staying in the cup instead of crawling out under its own power, and second, it's covered in froufrou."

"Froufrou? That's a nautical term I'm not familiar with."

Stanton took one hand from the wheel and pointed at the cups. "Froufrou—foam and milk and stuff."

"They're lattes, Skipper. Since the designers thought to include an espresso maker on board, I made use of it. Surely you've been in a Starbucks before."

"Star-whats?"

"I'm not buying it, Cap. Everyone in the universe knows what Starbucks is. They've taken over the planet. Soon they will join forces with McDonald's and we will all go happily to an early grave on Big Macs and double lattes. Join the hordes, sir. Be seduced and come over to the European coffee side."

Stanton took the cup and sniffed the rising steam. "It smells like vanilla."

"Flavor of the gods," Tenny said.

"I'm pretty sure there is only one God," Stanton said.

"And he created vanilla. Give it a try."

Stanton was a straight-coffee man. In his mind, coffee should be blacker than coal and as thick as warm maple syrup. Raising the cup to his lips, he drew in a sip. It was hot, sweet, and far tastier than he expected. "It's like drinking dessert," he commented.

"That's nothing," Tenny said. "Next time I'll make a white mocha coffee with raspberry."

Stanton shuddered. "At what point does it cease to be coffee and become something else?"

"Coffee is in the mouth of the beholder," Tenny quipped.

"You know that sentence makes no sense, don't you?"

"I'm being poetic," Tenny rebutted. "You want me to take that back to the galley and whip up a straight, boring, uninspired cup of Joe?"

Stanton took another sip. "No need. I think I can keep this down."

"Hah, another convert!"

"Speaking of keeping things down, how is young Ms. Moss?"

"Better, I think, but I have a sweater the same shade of green that she's wearing on her face. She went to bed about thirty minutes ago. I made sure the port was open for fresh air. I also gave her a plastic bowl to sleep with. She named it Ralph."

"Ralph? I don't get . . ." Stanton made the connection. "Ah, as in—"

"Yes sir. She seems to be keeping down the Gatorade. I also gave her a few crackers to nibble. She'll be okay. I think she's responding to the scopolamine gel. She should be up and around tomorrow."

"Let's keep a close eye on her. Seasickness can turn bad, even deadly. She needs to force liquids."

"She's a tough girl. I think she'll recover nicely."

Tenny moved to the side and leaned against the lifeline, which moved only slightly under her diminutive weight. Gazing up, she sighed.

"It's beautiful, isn't it?" Stanton said, adding his gaze to hers. Away from city lights that washed out the night sky, the black dome of night was alive with flecks of brilliance that stared back as if they were countless eyes, each fixed upon the sailboat bobbing in the ocean.

She agreed. "The first time I saw stars like this, I was ten. It was on the water. My father had taken me on an overnight deep-sea fishing charter. The boat was loaded with people, each trying their best to outfish the others. But not my father. He took me to the bow and began pointing out the constellations and naming some of the stars. I'll never forget that." Her expression soured.

"Your father sounds like a good man."

"He was," she said softly. "We lost him last year. Prostate cancer. Like many men, he avoided the doctors. He avoided them too long."

"I'm sorry," Stanton said.

"No one gets out of this life alive," she replied. "I just wish he could have seen me graduate. He worked as hard as I did to get me into the academy."

"If you're any reflection of him, then he must have been a great man."

"He was," she said immediately. "He spent some time in the navy, too. He enlisted during the Vietnam conflict and was assigned to one of the carriers."

"Career man?"

"No. Not many opportunities for an enlisted black man in those days. He used the GI Bill to go back to school. Took a degree in electrical engineering from San Diego State."

"San Diego," Stanton said. "My hometown."

"He and my mother moved shortly after he graduated, and settled in Rhode Island. He worked for a small aerospace firm. We didn't have a lot of money but we weren't poor. The worst times came during the layoffs. Aerospace is very cyclic. He would work for three years straight, then be unemployed for six months. He taught me that tough times make tough people."

"He was right about that," Stanton said.

"He also taught me to make my own way in life. When I wanted to take up sailing, he made me earn the money for the lessons. I thought he was being stingy. He wasn't."

"He sounds like a man worth missing. How about Mom?"

"She's still in Rhode Island. Took up real estate when Dad died. His insurance carried her for a while but it wasn't going to last forever. She's dating again."

"Really? How do you feel about that?"

"Okay, I guess. I don't know the men she's seeing. I worry about her."

Stanton chuckled. "It always comes full circle, doesn't it? I bet your mom worries about you, too."

"This is different."

"Really? How so?"

Tenny fell silent, moving her eyes from the black of the heavens to the brown of her coffee. She raised the cup to her lips, took a sip, then said, "I don't know. It just is." A moment later she asked, "How about you, Skipper? You got any kids?"

Stanton shook his head. "It was never meant to be. At first we held off. I was worried that having children early would be difficult with a navy career. Later we learned that children were out of the picture."

"Regrets?"

"I suppose, but I try not to dwell on those things I can't change. We're fine with it. My wife has her moments but she has accepted it as God's will."

Tenny seemed surprised. "God's will? Do you think God cares whether you have kids or not?"

"I think God cares more than most people know. I'm not saying he caused the infertility. Life is life and it isn't always fair. What he cares about is how we deal with what life throws our way."

"Like my father's death?"

"As you said, none of us gets out of this life alive. We enter the next life sooner or later."

"Next life," Tenny mumbled. "It's a quaint idea."

"I think it's more than that."

"Perhaps," Tenny said. She turned her face skyward again. "'When I consider your heavens, the work of your fingers, the moon and the stars, which you have ordained; What is man that you take thought of him, and the son of man that you care for him?'"

Stanton snapped his head around to face the cadet. "I'm impressed—Psalm 8."

"My father was very religious. He used to read from the Psalms before supper." She pushed away from the lifeline, turned to face the dark water running by the hull, and poured out the remainder of her coffee. "He died anyway." A second later she said, "I'm going to check on the kids. I left Richie in there alone. He may need backup."

"Very well," Stanton said. He wondered what other pain Tenny was hiding beneath her cheerful veneer.

The call was clear. Every unspoken word was understood, tattooing its intent on the mind. The water rushed by. Cool. Salty. Deep. Inviting. Darkness covered it and darkness was familiar, welcome. What was blue was now black, like flowing, pulsating, liquid asphalt. It glittered and shone where hull slipped past the silky ocean. Phosphorescing as if the ocean were alive—a giant firefly. That's where the message was, in the glitter and sparkle, the spangled sea, and the message was in the sound of a caressed, sleek, smooth hull. Those things spoke in hot whispers, in breathy melody murmured in the ear by a mouth that was much too close.

The ocean was attempting seduction: gently, softly, irresistibly.

How easy it would be. At the right moment, at precisely the correct instant, to choose to fall into the reaching arms of the sea, to surrender to its embrace, to allow it to flow by, flow over, and flow in.

The darkness would come then. The peaceful darkness. The pain would be gone; the fear would evaporate under the steady heat of death. It wouldn't take long but care was needed. The others must not see. They didn't understand—couldn't understand. In some noble effort they would try to stop what must take place. It was beyond their comprehension. They would only see the end. It was the beginning that mattered. The beginning of nothingness . . . blessed nothingness.

It would have to be done at the right time and in the right way. Not a jump. No, too noisy, too noticeable. Gentleness would work. A simple act of slipping over the side and letting the ocean enfold, encase, caress until there was nothing.

It would be easy. No pain. That's what the voices promised—ease, relief, and no pain. That was the treasure, the dream, the compelling vision.

Water. Cool and complete, able to do what desperately needed to be done. Death in the ocean couldn't be bad. Millions of fish and whales and whatever else lay beneath lived their lives and embraced their deaths in the aqueous womb. This would be no different.

The voices said so. They had always said so. They were saying so now.

Efforts to push them away had failed. Years of secret battles had proved the point: they were here to stay. There they were, wriggling in the brain like worms, rubbing the soul like sandpaper. Nothing quieted them. Nothing stilled them. Nothing was powerful enough to evict them. They could only be tolerated, listened to, and obeyed.

They were speaking now, painting images on a canvas of gray, tightly packed cells, images impossible to ignore no matter how garish and ugly they became. Hating the sights only made things worse. The only defense was acquiescence. It was a defeat, but defeat was the companion of the hopeless.

The voices said so.

Doldrums

Stanton emerged from his stateroom and found the lounge filled with the thick aroma of coffee. The smell of it made him instantly thirsty. Since most of the boat's inhabitants were still fast asleep, he moved quietly, being certain not to bang coffee cups and decanter. He poured the liquid into a mug that bore the logo of Richie's father's firm. It smelled fresh and the heat of it radiated through the cup. Turning, he let his eyes take in the opulence of the salon. Most of his seagoing experiences were on small boats or long nuclear submarines. Neither was known to have handcrafted teak floors, supple leather seats, and a high-end entertainment center. Everything about the *Tern About* was designed to impress. *A man could move into this place and finish out his days in luxury*, Stanton thought. *And all it would take is the income of a large corporation.*

As he took in the lavishness, a movement caught his eye. The lounge was furnished with a curved, padded white leather bench wrapped around an oval table. It served as a dining room, game room, or general place to relax. Someone was sleeping on the bench. Quietly Stanton approached and saw Jamie curled up on her side, still dressed in the clothes she had been wearing when she boarded. Her blond hair draped her face in a cascade of shiny strands. Quiet and still, resting in the arms of slumber, she seemed anything but a troubled teen with a sharp tongue and the warmth of a concrete block. In the stillness of sleep she seemed innocent and frail.

Stanton shook his head in wonder. The catamaran had four staterooms; three were roughly the same size, the master's quarters a little larger. With eight people on board, quarters had to be shared two to a room. After years on submarines of various sizes in which the crew slept inches apart, the arrangements seemed spacious to him. Jamie was assigned to share a room with M&M. Apparently, she found the lounge more to her liking. Perhaps she wanted to give the room to the seasick girl. It was a nice thought, but Stanton, who had lived too long to believe that every person possessed a noble nature, had doubts that Jamie was the sacrificing kind.

Leaving the cabin, Stanton emerged on deck. The air was cool and sweetened by the ocean. A gentle white mist hovered just above the surface. Stanton was thankful that it was not fog. Always an early riser, he had come topside to watch the sun rise. A slit of red that looked every bit like an open, bleeding gash hovered above the horizon. The sky was bleaching from black to gray and soon would diffuse the new light into the cobalt blue they had seen the day before. Stanton knew this because he had checked with the marine weather bureau before leaving port and again before retiring for the night.

"Good morning, Skipper," a voice said. Stanton directed his eyes to the speaker. Richie stood behind the wheel, one hand fixed to the twelve o'clock position and the other holding a mug of coffee identical to Stanton's. Next to him stood Tenny. She rounded out the coffee club.

"Good morning," Stanton said as he approached.

"Everything's shipshape, Cap," Tenny said. "An uneventful night."

"And a long one, I imagine," Stanton replied. "You got the short end of the stick, pulling the graveyard watch."

"Not at all," she replied. "I don't sleep as much as others. Never have. I enjoyed the alone time. It was just me, the stars, and a gibbous moon."

"Since we're still afloat, I assume that we didn't run into some tanker," Stanton said with a smile.

"Didn't see another vessel all night," she said. "Seems kinda odd. I thought surely I would spy lights of fishing boats, cruise ships, or tankers, but I didn't see anything."

"We didn't drift off course, did we?" Stanton inquired.

"We're right where we should be," Richie said. "I verified that when I took the helm. It must just be a slow seafaring night."

"The bunk is free," Stanton said to Tenny. "You have to be exhausted."

"Not at all. Like I said, I don't sleep much. I'll hit the sack after the sunrise. No sense in being out here without seeing the sun come up over the Atlantic."

"Amen to that," Richie said. "So you're going to fix breakfast before catching your winks?"

"Hah, rich boy," she shot back, "I made lunch and dinner. Someone else is cracking eggs today."

"I'll do it," Stanton said. "I make a mean ham-and-cheese omelet."

"Ooh. I may have to stay up for that."

"I'll make yours first." Stanton turned his gaze east. What had a few moments before looked like an open gash in the sky had blossomed into a pink, red, and purple tapestry. Distant strips of cotton clouds glowed as if powered by a nuclear plant and filled with mile-long neon lights.

"Wow," Richie effused. "I hope I never get used to seeing that."

Stanton started to make a quip but stifled the urge. When creation spoke, it shouldn't be interrupted. Silence was the only appropriate response. Three sailors stood on the gently swaying deck, their eyes fixed on the ballet of color, their thoughts their own.

When the whole solar disk had laid itself bare to the new day, Tenny said, "I wish the kids could have seen this."

Richie laughed. "When I was their age, I only got up before nine if I had to. I used to clock some serious bedtime before I entered the academy. My sleeping-in days ended there."

"The military does tend to cut into such luxuries," Stanton agreed. With the sun now on duty, he looked around the boat, letting his gaze rise up the composite mast. The sail hung limply, like a handkerchief held by one corner at arm's length. "We're not going to make much headway with a wind like that."

"It's been dead most of the night," Tenny said.

"It'll pick up soon," Richie said with confidence. "The sun will warm the air and we should get enough breeze to move faster. Not that it matters. We don't have a destination; we're just cruising the coast."

"Actually, we do," Stanton corrected. He reached into his pocket and pulled out a piece of paper and handed it to Richie. "We need to be at those GPS coordinates by 1030 hours."

Richie studied the paper and then looked at the GPS reading on the helm's instrument panel. "Well, the good news is that we're not too far away, but I may have to crank up the diesels if we don't get some air soon."

"Do what you need to do," Stanton said. "We don't want to miss this."

"Miss what?" Tenny asked.

"It won't be a surprise if I lay it all out now. I suggest you let me whip up some breakfast for you so you can snag a little sleep. I'll wake you twenty minutes before you need to be on deck."

"Hey, it's a little early but if you're feeling culinary, I'll take my omelet now," Richie said. "I'd also like a side of hash browns. Oh, and if you could top off the omelet with a little Tabasco, that would be great."

Stanton looked at Richie and narrowed his eyes.

"Hash browns aren't necessary," Richie stammered. "Anything you've prepared will be fine. Really, anything."

"Shall I prepare the yardarm, Captain?" Tenny asked with a smile broad and bright enough to intimidate the sunrise.

"I was thinking of a simple flogging."

"Hey, the kids would love to see that," Tenny said.

"Thanks for the support," Richie grumbled.

"Tabasco it is," Stanton said, ending the joke. He raised his coffee cup. "To the sunrise."

The others followed his example, raising their mugs in an early-morning toast.

"What's so special about this place?" John Hays asked with irritation. "It ain't nothing but water."

"You weren't planning on staying below the whole day, were you?" Richie asked.

"As a matter of fact, I was," John shot back. "I can be bored inside as easily as I can outside. And why do I have to wear a life jacket?"

"You'll notice that we're all wearing vests," Richie said. "Stanton must have his reasons."

"Well, if something doesn't happen soon, I'm heading back in."

"Your pasty skin could use a little sun," Tony said. There was a challenge in his voice. Stanton, who stood near the port rail, lowered his binoculars and turned toward his gathered charges. Each wore an orange life vest and none seemed happy about it.

"Shut up," John snapped.

"At ease, gentlemen," Tenny said firmly. "Let's see what our fearless leader has in store for us."

"It better be more than some whale watching," John said.

Stanton raised the binoculars to his eyes again and scanned the sea. Richie had powered up the engines and gotten them to the site just ten minutes early. They were in the right place at the right time. That meant he should see it anytime.

"Thar she blows," Stanton said loudly. The binoculars allowed him to see what the others could not. Three hundred yards away a small white wake moved through the water.

"Great. It is a whale," John snipped. "I did the whale-watching thing in junior high."

"All right, folks," Stanton said. "I need all of you to do two things. First, find something to hold on to—and get a good grip."

"Why?" John asked.

"Just do it," Richie said. "I think we're in for a show."

"What kind of a show?"

"Just grab something," Richie ordered.

"Hop to, guys—we only have a couple of seconds." Stanton watched crew and passengers take hold of lifeline or pole. Several were wise enough to spread their feet. "Now look this way." Stanton pointed a finger east. "Keep your eye on the surface. Company is coming."

"I don't see anything," Jamie complained.

"Stand by, Ms. Penowski," Stanton said. "Patience is a virtue."

"Hah," John said. "As if she knows what virtue is."

Stanton was about to chastise John when the surface of the sea exploded a hundred yards off the port side. Water bellowed up, then cascaded down in sheets and spray. A large black cylinder followed the water like a whale breaching, then slammed to the surface and disappeared beneath churning foam.

"Whoa!" Steve shouted. "Way cool! A submarine!"

Stanton turned to see the wide eyes of the youth. Richie and Tenny were no less impressed. "Hold tight, we're about to get rocked."

A wave, propelled by hundreds of tons of steel, rolled toward the *Tern About.*

"Bring it!" Tony exclaimed.

The wave decreased in size as it moved from the black hulk in the distance to the white hulls of the catamaran, but it was still enough to repeatedly seesaw the large boat. The impact of the wave against the port hull sent spray into the air, raining down on those who stood near the edge.

Stanton's heart was tripping like a sprinter's at the end of a hundred-meter dash. Seeing the submarine breach and settle had stirred up the old excitement, a bright thrill that time could not dim. It had been several years since he had seen such a sight. In his career he had made the maneuver several times, but seen from outside the hull, it was a thing of glorious beauty.

"Ladies and gentlemen, may I present the USS *Virginia.*" Stanton made no attempt to conceal his pride. "She's new, she's lean, and she's mean. You're looking at 377 feet of 'Don't mess with the U.S.,' in-your-face technology."

"Oh, baby," Richie said. "How did you get them to meet us here?"

"The Department of the Navy owes me a couple of favors," Stanton said with a grin. "What do you think?" There was a hush as the cat settled in the water; then voices began to chatter.

Stanton let it go on for a few minutes, then said, "She's a beauty, isn't she?"

"Is that your boat?" Tony asked. "I mean, the one you were on?"

"No," Stanton admitted. "The *Virginia* didn't set sail until this year. She's brand-spankin'-new. Not many people have seen what you just saw."

The submarine lay still in the small swells, as if the ocean itself were intimidated by her size and power. Her black sonar-absorbing hull glistened in the sun as seawater rolled off her deck. The sail rose into the sky, a rigid black obelisk, intimidating in size and shape.

"Look," Jamie said, pointing. "Someone is coming out."

At the top of the sub's sail, a man appeared, then two others. One raised a megaphone to his mouth. "Ahoy, catamaran off our port side. . . . Is Captain J. D. Stanton aboard?"

Stanton cupped his hands to his mouth. "I'm Captain Stanton."

"Captain Vincent wishes to know if cheeseburgers are acceptable."

Stanton turned to his crew. "You guys like cheeseburgers, don't you?"

"They brought lunch?" Steve asked, breaking his stunned silence.

"Actually, you're having lunch over there," Stanton explained. "Your dad ever give you a tour of the *Toledo?*"

Steve shook his head. "He offered once but I turned him down."

"Well, you can't turn this one down. I've cashed in all my markers to get this meeting. I now owe some very powerful people a ton of favors."

"We're really going over there?" Jamie asked.

"Absolutely. I didn't ask them to come to meet us here just so they could splash us with water."

"How are we going to get there?" Tony asked.

Stanton motioned to the aft of the *Tern About*, where a Zodiac YL 4.2 DL rigid inflatable boat rested between the stern hull projections, on a hydraulic lift. "The dinghy," he replied. "It only carries five, so it will take two trips to get seven across the water."

"Seven?" Steve said. "There are eight of us."

"Someone has to stay with the boat," Stanton explained.

"I sure do envy you guys," Richie said.

"No need for envy, Richie," Stanton said. "You're going too. I'm staying behind."

"That doesn't seem fair, Cap," Tenny said. "After all, you're the one who took the trouble to arrange this."

Stanton cut her off with an upraised hand. "Don't feel sorry for me. I toured her before her sea trials. I've already seen all there is to see." Turning to Richie, he said, "Okay, here's the drill. You'll take the first group over. Tenny will be in that group. You'll pick up a passenger and bring him back here; then you take those who are left to the sub. You'll be over there for sixty minutes. No more. Clear?"

Richie's face broke into a broad grin. "Aye, aye, Captain." He snapped a perfect salute. "Oh, who am I bringing back?"

"The *Virginia*'s skipper. Be nice to him. He may be your commanding officer someday."

Richie swallowed hard, then barked, "Will do."

"All right, everyone, listen up," Stanton said. "That submarine is the best the navy has. To step foot inside is an honor reserved for her crew, admirals, and key members of Congress, so please act accordingly. There are some rules. First, you will treat your hosts with the highest respect. If they give their rank, then please address them by that rank. Second, you will not go anyplace without an escort. Some places are off limits and they are very serious about such things. Third, you will see that some of the gauges and equipment are covered. They are concealed for a reason. Do not peek under the covers. Questions?"

There were none. Stanton looked at each teenager and smiled. "It's a great experience. Enjoy it as much as possible." His eyes fell on M&M. Her skin was pale and her shoulders stooped. "You feel up to this, Ms. Moss?"

"My stomach is still a little unsettled but I'll be okay."

"If it's any comfort, the submarine should rock less than our boat."

"That would be great."

"Okay," Stanton snapped. "Let's make this happen. Richie, lower the Zodiac. Let's not keep Captain Vincent waiting."

Ⓝ
Λ

Captain George T. Vincent was five foot eleven when he wore his shoes, and stood ramrod straight. His head was as bald as river stone, and his azure eyes seemed capable of cutting holes in the steel hull of any ship that crossed his path. His jaw was square, and rigid as concrete block. At forty-one, his shoulders had lost none of their square set, but his belly was rounder than Stanton remembered.

He stood in the dinghy piloted by Richie, who had formally pronounced, "The USS *Virginia* arriving."

Vincent stared at the *Tern About* for a moment, then addressed Stanton. "Permission to come aboard."

"Permission granted," Stanton answered quickly. "Get yourself up here, Captain."

Vincent wasted no time stepping from the bobbing Zodiac to the built-in steps at the stern of the catamaran. A moment later he bounded onto the deck. He snapped a salute at Stanton.

"No need to salute me, Captain. I'm retired."

"Not in my book. You were my first and best CO."

Stanton returned the gesture, then shook hands with his old friend. "It's been a while since we were on the water together, George."

"That it has, and the one hour we have together will not be enough to catch up on things."

"In a few minutes we'll have the boat to ourselves and you can tell me all the trouble the navy is causing you." Stanton watched like a worried father as Richie piloted the Zodiac across the safe expanse of ocean that separated the *Tern About* from the *Virginia*. Once Richie and the others disappeared down the submarine's forward hatch, Stanton led his longtime friend into the salon.

"So this is how the retired live," George Vincent said. "Pretty posh for an old salt like you."

"Who you calling old, sonny?" Stanton quipped. "I took early retirement. I was little more than a babe when I enlisted."

"Hah!" George bellowed. "Your kiddy crew might buy that, but I served too long with you to not know that's a lie. Those gray hairs at your temple bear witness."

"Age is a mental thing," Stanton rejoined. "I still think I'm thirty. Want some coffee?" He moved into the galley.

George followed. "I'll bet the java is as fancy as your boat."

"It's not my boat. It belongs to Richie's father. He's the young man who played taxi driver for you."

George nodded. "Seemed nice enough. Handled the Zodiac well."

"He should. He's been sailing since he was in grade school. Dad owns a large tech company. It was through Richie that we were able to borrow the *Tern About*. If you like him, you should see about getting him assigned to your crew."

"He's navy?"

"Yup, just out of Annapolis. He was one of my students last year."

George stepped to one of the narrow counters and found a shiny bag of coffee. He raised it to his nose. "Whew, rich stuff." He read the package label. "Ethiopian coffee? You gotta be kidding. You haven't become one of those snooty double-shot-half-caff-half-milk-no-foam coffee guys, have you?"

"At home it's straight Yuban. My wife won't buy anything else."

Stanton started a fresh pot of coffee brewing and then took a seat in the lounge. George joined him, leaning back and stretching. "Subs are a lot bigger these days," he said, "but they're still as cramped as an overstuffed closet."

"You should have asked for a boomer," Stanton stated, "then you would have enough room to stretch your legs."

"Not me, buddy. I'll let people crazier than me carry missiles around. I prefer playing cat and mouse and chasing down unsuspecting foreign subs. It keeps the mind sharp."

"How do you like her?" Stanton asked, keen with interest. He wanted to quiz his friend about every detail of her engineering and electronics but reined in his curiosity. Stanton knew that George was limited in the details he could give. The navy had her secrets. Like a Russian doll, those secrets contained other secrets. George might grant him a little leeway, but not much. Stanton was determined not to put his friend in an awkward position. "She looks beautiful on the water."

"She's a peach, J. D., a real peach. We're just doing another shakedown cruise to test some electronics and do crew training. If we were doing anything else, we wouldn't break surface. Of course, you know that."

Stanton knew it well. "I take it she's everything the navy promised."

"And more. More speed, faster electronics, and a few other things."

Things you can't talk about, Stanton said to himself.

"For the most part she's been perfect," George continued.

"For the most part? Uh-oh, glitches already. You didn't ding the paint or anything, did you?"

"Of course not. You know me: slow, cautious, reserved."

Stanton laughed. "Cautious I'll agree with; slow and reserved is too much of a stretch."

"So my carefully sculpted image has a few cracks in it, eh?"

"We served together, remember. I used to write your fitness reports. All of them excellent, I might add."

"Don't think I don't appreciate it, J. D. I took your place when you retired, and I know you were the one who made the recommendation."

Stanton shrugged. "I wanted someone to take care of my boat. But now look at you. A brand-new sub all your own. I bet it still has the dealer sticker in the window."

George laughed. "You look great, J. D. Your wife must be taking good care of you. How long have you been married?"

"Close to twenty-two years, all of them happy ones. Not everyone can say that."

George's face clouded. "That's true."

"Did I blunder into something, George? How's Jen?"

"Last I heard, she's fine. She left me about a year ago. Got tired of being a navy wife and got interested in a stockbroker. Can you believe it? A stockbroker!"

"I'm sorry. I didn't know."

"No need to be sorry. It's my own fault. I paid more attention to my career than I did to her. She deserved better than me."

"I don't buy that," Stanton said. "There's no such thing as a perfect husband, but I have to believe you did the best you could."

"Sometimes our best isn't good enough," George said. "I can't blame her. The guy she's with makes more money than I do and comes home every night. He doesn't disappear beneath the waves for six months at a time."

"So she filed for divorce?" Stanton probed. An empathetic ache spread through him. He and George had been more than fellow officers; they were friends who shared meals, laughs, and trust. Retirement for Stanton and George's reassignment to the Atlantic fleet had put physical distance between them. The friendship remained but the three-thousand-mile separation had diluted the contact. Over the last two years only a handful of calls had been made. Beyond that, communication had been compressed to Christmas cards. Stanton felt guilt percolate in the mix of emotions bubbling inside him.

"No, not yet, but I expect to see papers soon. To make matters worse, after these sea trials are over, I'll be shipping out with the *Virginia*. It's a short tour, just three months, but I'm sure it will be the final nail in the marital coffin."

Stanton was unsure of his next step. Like the high-wire acrobats he had seen in the circus as a child, he felt as if he stood on one foot, arms out to his side, trying to recover his lost balance. Too little would lead to a fall; overcorrection would bring the same plunge.

"Do you want me to talk to her?" Stanton asked after an eternally long second. "We used to get along pretty good. Or maybe my wife—"

"No," George said with a barely perceptible shake of his head. "I'm afraid we're past the talking stage. We tried the base counselor but he wasn't much help. Jen felt he was siding with me. She refused to go back after the second session. A week later she took up with this stockbroker in shining armor. The guy's ten years her junior, drives a hot BMW, and knows all the party spots. The best I can offer her is a short tour of a submarine on family day and dinner at the officers' club."

Stanton rose and walked to the galley. He did so under the pretense of fixing the coffee, but what he really wanted was a moment to pray for wisdom. The coffee was rich and aromatic—Ethiopia's best mountain-grown. He was sure it would taste better than any coffee he had ever purchased, but knew it would do little to help his friend. With mugs in hand Stanton returned to the lounge. "Let's take this topside," he said. "Conversation is better under a blue sky."

They moved out of the salon, each with his coffee and silent thoughts.

Seated on the wraparound bench at the deck table, Stanton asked another question. "How is your boy dealing with all this? Mark is what . . . sixteen now?"

"Seventeen. He's not taking it well," George admitted, raising the coffee to his lips. He drew a sip of the hot liquid but gave no indication that he tasted it. He was in automatic mode. His body did what it was supposed to do with a cup of coffee, but Stanton could tell the captain's mind was several miles west of the catamaran. "Our relationship was strained to begin with; this hasn't helped. I think he's counting the days to his eighteenth birthday. You've seen it before. Guys like us get to play with multimillion-dollar toys because we have proved that to us the most important thing in life is the navy. Everything else slips into the wake. How many sailors do you know who have family woes?"

"Too many to count," Stanton replied. "It doesn't have to be that way, but it takes a special couple of people to make things work. That's true in any marriage, but even more so in the military. We do things that can't be discussed, disappear for six months at a time, and our loved ones have to sit at home and wonder where we are. It's needed, but patently unfair to our families."

"It can't be any other way," George said defensively.

"I know that as well as anyone, George. That's one reason I'm out here with five teenagers. Their families have more problems than Swiss cheese has holes."

"So you've become a family therapist," George said. "I suppose I should admire that."

"I'm no therapist, George. I'm just a guy who felt led to make an effort. The idea was my brother-in-law's. He deals with these families all the time."

"The chaplain? What's his name again?"

"Jim Walsh. He's a good man." Stanton let the conversation lull while he studied the coffee in his cup. The liquid seemed to move from side to side as if trying to shinny out of the cup. Stanton knew it was the cup that was moving in step with the rolling ocean. The liquid was the stable substance. "He thought that if the kids could see navy personnel in a nonmilitary environment, they might discover that sailors are just ordinary people in uniform. He hoped that if they were confined with others like themselves, they might see that they are not alone in their hurts. I volunteered to lead the first expedition."

"I wish there were something like that for Mark. He could use the help."

"We all need help," Stanton said. "Have you talked to the base chaplain?"

George shook his head. "You know me, J. D. I'm not a very religious person. It doesn't make much sense to me. God talk makes me nervous." Stanton started to suggest that the nervousness he felt might be better described as conviction, but George continued, "Besides, you weren't always that religious."

"*Religion* isn't the right word. *Faith* is the preferred term, and you're right—I've changed over the last couple of years. I've always felt that faith was important, but I let it sit on the back shelf. Then something happened and I needed my faith more than any other time before. I was glad it was there."

"I'm happy it worked for you, buddy, but it's not for me."

"How can you be sure?"

"I know two things," George said. He had fallen into captain mode. "I know submarines and I know myself."

"That's not enough, George. Trust me, it's not close to being enough."

"That's the way I like it."

His words had an edge. Stanton was moving too close to private thoughts. Stanton said nothing but he did stare deep into the eyes of his longtime friend, then leaned back in his seat.

"I'm sorry, J. D. I didn't mean to snap at you like you were some wet-behind-the-ears ensign." George shook his head. "The irony is biting. I can lead a submarine crewed by scores of sailors to any place in the world. I can make the tough decisions and wouldn't hesitate a minute to fire off a couple of Mark 48 torps at an enemy ship, but when it comes to keeping the rudders of my personal life amidships, I'm incompetent."

Stanton chuckled at the metaphor. It was one he understood thoroughly. "The problem with life is that none of us have enough experience to live it right. By the time we gain the experience, we're too old to do anything about it."

"You got that right."

One moment followed another as the two men, each seasoned by events in life, gazed at the undulating ocean. Stanton broke the silence with a question. "What was the hardest thing we ever had to do when we served together?"

"Bobby Teller," George said immediately.

"Doesn't take much thinking to come up with that one, does it?"

George closed his eyes and blew out a steady stream of air. "I hope I never have to do that again. I was ready to toss my dolphins on your desk and walk away."

"You can't walk far on an Ohio-class sub," Stanton said.

"Still, I was tempted."

Just the thought of the incident sent bile burning into Stanton's stomach and made his heart trip unevenly. Bobby Teller had been a sonar operator on a mission to the South China Sea. Stanton was leading a covert intelligence mission, monitoring Chinese military radio broadcasts. It was a touchy mission, since relations between the U.S. and China had become as strained as a rubber band stretched around a battleship. Most military experts expected the relations to break down completely. If Stanton and his crew had been discovered prowling off the Chinese shore, the overstretched band could break. What would happen after that was anyone's guess, and the professional guessers painted a bleak picture.

Radio communications were kept to a minimum, confined to "flash messages" received and sent at prescribed times. One flash message chilled Stanton's blood more than did the dangerous patrol he was conducting. Bobby Teller was twenty-six years old, a husband of three years with a two-year-old baby girl. On July 15 a sleepy truck driver drove his heavily loaded semi through a red light. Michele Teller and her baby were killed immediately, their bodies burned beyond human form in the conflagration that followed. The trucker walked away with only a concussion.

The message from headquarters left the announcement to "your best discretion." After consulting with George, who served as XO, or executive officer, Stanton decided not to tell Bobby his family had been killed. The decision had sickened him. It was unfair at every level and in every way. Bobby Teller went about his duties oblivious to the sorrow that awaited him. He wrote letters that would never be read, showed pictures of a wife and baby who no longer lived, and dreamed of stepping into their outstretched arms when they pulled into port.

The problem had been clear. The mission was not over and his commanders had not ordered Stanton and crew home. If Stanton told Bobby the hideous truth, he would still be able to do nothing about it. The submarine would cease to be a vessel at sea and become a submerged prison. Such things had happened before, and the corporate experience had been that it was better to keep the tragedy secret rather than have a grieving sailor on board who could do nothing but disrupt the mission.

Every day, Stanton would pass the young man at his station and his heart would melt like wax in an oven. Only two men on board knew the truth that Teller had every right to know but was being deprived of. It would be two months before he would return home, and by that time his wife and child would long be in the grave. Other family members would be weeks farther along the trail of tears. Bobby Teller would live through the experience alone and spend the rest of his life hating the navy in general and Captain J. D. Stanton in particular for doing the horrible thing that had to be done.

One week out of port, Stanton called Teller to the officers' mess. George was with him. Stanton remembered shaking inside like a bird trapped in a hunter's hand. Not prone to emotionalism of any type, Stanton felt as if he would vomit at any moment. Every second of that meeting was branded into his brain. The night before, he had a nightmare about the meeting. The nightmare would become his companion. Everything around him seemed amplified. For a moment he believed he could hear the water rushing past the hull, and the waves that were four hundred feet above him.

"You asked to see me, Skipper?" Teller had said.

"Have a seat, son," Stanton said. His words stuck in his throat like a fish bone. Stanton had to repeat the comment. George closed the door behind the young sailor.

"Have I done something wrong, sir?" His blue eyes were wide with anxiety.

"No, son. I have."

"I don't understand."

Stanton inhaled as much air as his lungs allowed, then fired off the message like a torpedo from one of the forward tubes. "I want you to pack your gear, son. At 0930 we are going to surface and rendezvous with a frigate. A helicopter is waiting to take you back to base."

"I'm not arriving in port with the crew? But my wife is supposed to meet me and—" The truth of the words not yet spoken exploded in the sailor's mind. "Oh, God. Oh, God, no. What happened?" He sprang to his feet. George reseated him with a hand on his shoulder. "Tell me what happened!"

Stanton did, fighting back boiling tears and volcanic nausea. The words came quickly. There was no easy way to deliver a message sure to rip the heart out of any man. Say it. Say it fast and without emotion. Say it clear and direct, then deal with the fallout later. He did.

"Two months ago? Two months ago! Why didn't you tell me! Why? *Why?*"

"You know why, son, but that doesn't make it any easier—"

Teller launched himself at Stanton, wrapping his hands around his throat. Stanton was knocked from his seat and landed on his back, Teller on top of him, squeezing with hands made superhuman by grief. Just as Stanton felt his trachea pinch shut, Teller was gone. There was a loud thud followed by another impact. From on his back Stanton saw George toss Teller into the bulkhead as if he were a rag doll, then press him on the metal table where the officers ate their meals.

"Easy, son," George said with even, unemotional words. "It's not the skipper's fault."

"But—"

"There are no buts about it, sailor. He is not God. He didn't make this happen. He didn't like what he had to do, but he did his duty. Now do yours."

Bobby Teller dissolved into convulsive sobs. Slowly George released the crewman. Stanton rose.

"You okay, Cap?" George asked.

"I'm fine."

"I'll write this up and—"

"No, you won't, XO," Stanton snapped. "This never happened. Is that clear?"

"Yes sir."

"Stay with him while he packs. I'll be on the bridge." Stanton started for the door, then stopped. He placed a hand on Teller's shoulder. "I would give my right arm for this all to be a bad dream."

Teller jerked away from Stanton's touch.

The scene that replayed in Stanton's mind was one that had come to him many times before. He had done his duty, he had made the right decisions, and someone still got hurt in the process. The event was a burn to his heart which left a blister that would never heal.

"As bad as that was," George said, bringing Stanton back to the present, "this separation is worse—at least emotionally. I could rationalize away the pain we caused young Mr. Teller, but I can't seem to do the same with my wife. Teller lost his wife to an accident. I let mine slip away through inattention."

"Don't give up," Stanton said.

"I can't look past the fact that she's seeing another man," George said.

"Yes, you can," Stanton replied. "It won't be easy but you can. If I can help, I will. I'll also make it a matter of prayer."

"Thanks, buddy. I appreciate it." George sighed, took a long drink of coffee. "Enough of this open-wound stuff. Let's talk of happier things."

"Like life below the waves?" Stanton suggested.

"Yeah. I want to ask you something. Have you ever heard of a total power outage on a sub?"

"Not a contemporary sub, no. Why?"

"Strangest thing," George said. "We were running a drill yesterday, a few miles from here. Everything was humming just the way it should. Suddenly everything blinked out. I mean everything. Engines ground to a halt, all electronics died, even the lights went out."

"Good thing there are redundant systems," Stanton said.

"Those failed too," George said. "It was as dark as a tomb. Do you remember all those blindfold drills we used to have to do to earn our dolphins? We were reduced to that, operating in the dark."

"What about lanterns—"

"That's the weird part. We couldn't even get those to work. That lasted about two minutes; then everything came back on like nothing had ever happened."

"What did you do?"

"I raised her to the surface and started diagnostics. Didn't find a thing, not a single thing. Weird, huh?"

"Let me get this right," Stanton said. "You suffered a catastrophic failure of all electrical systems and then suddenly everything came back on. No shorts, no fire, just a full power outage."

"More than just electrical—mechanical too. I've never seen the likes of it. Everything's been fine since, and engineering tells me we're good to go."

"I assume you made a report."

"I did. I played it by the book. We're headed back in for a full in-port diagnostic. Maybe the engineers who designed her can figure out what caused the hiccup. I want to know that everything is tip-top before we head into blue water."

"You got that right. I'd hate to be at depth when that happened," Stanton said. "It's enough to give an old salt like me the chills."

"You and me both, brother. You and me both."

Late Watch

Night had rolled in from the east, leaving only a sliver of red and purple in the western sky. A breeze, little more than a whisper, had risen, and Stanton used it to push the *Tern About* farther east. *Push*, he decided, was too strong a word. The breeze barely filled the sails, which could catch enough air to move the boat a few hundred yards, then drop flaccid against the mast. It was a pathetic sight. The catamaran was not designed to be a racing yacht, but it was meant to do more than mosey on nearly flat, lifeless water.

"Come on," Stanton said to the open air. "Give me something to work with."

The engines were available, but Stanton wanted to spend his watch skipping across the swells and practicing his tacking skills. Yet the weather was uncooperative. Only his resilient optimism kept him topside while the others were watching a movie in the main cabin.

Stanton and Captain George Vincent had talked away the single hour they were allowed. Their serious conversation had turned light, neither wanting the short time together to be remembered as a counseling session. Talk of past difficulties, family concerns, and navy irritations blossomed into stories of the old days and jokes each had learned since they last saw each other.

The conversation ended when the little Zodiac made its first trip back, loaded with teenagers. Another trip was made to bring the final passengers back aboard and to return George Vincent to his boat. Stanton and the others watched as the *Virginia* slowly pulled away, then descended beneath a mildly pulsing ocean. For a moment, a long wistful moment, Stanton wished he were aboard. His ears filled with the unique sounds known only to those who ply the oceans beneath the shipping lanes.

Stanton had asked each teenager how he or she enjoyed the tour. Each replied nonchalantly that it was "all right, I guess." The only enthusiasm was shown by Tony and Steve, who mentioned being impressed with the size of the torpedoes. John maintained his tough-guy image; Jamie cultivated her "nothing impresses me" persona. M&M said very little. She worried Stanton. Her skin was pale and looked moist and she seemed to have trouble standing erect. Pleading seasickness, she took to bed again.

The cabin door opened and Richie strolled on deck. "Having fun?" he asked.

"The night is warm, the stars are bright, and we're moving like a bar of Ivory soap in a bathtub."

"Does seem a tad still," Richie said. He sipped a can of Dr. Pepper.

"Tad still?" Stanton shook his head. "This gives *doldrums* a new meaning. I expected far more breeze than this. The sun is dropping, the temperature changing; we should be getting something but we're not. A good sneeze would propel us farther than the wind we have."

"There are always the engines."

"Nah, I want to sail, not motor around."

"You are a true sailor, Skipper. You would have been happy on some nineteenth-century schooner, ordering lowly hands to their knees to scrub the deck they had scrubbed the day before."

"Now there's an idea."

"Sorry I mentioned it," Richie added quickly. "Can I get you anything? Soda?"

"No, I'm fine. How are the kids doing?"

"Fine. The movie is pretty good, although buying the DVD of *The Abyss* was an interesting choice. You know, a lot of people die underwater in that show. Worse, the bad guys are navy personnel."

"It's called 'ironic humor.' If you can't laugh at yourself, then who can you laugh at?"

"I can think of lots of people. Anyway, everyone is eating popcorn, candy, and chips. I figure they should be sick by sack time."

"Don't count on it. When I was their age, I could eat anything. Junk food never bothered me."

"They had junk food when you were their age?" Richie raised a whimsical eyebrow.

"So we're back to deck scrubbing again."

"Just a little high seas humor, Cap. That's all. Sure I can't get you something?"

"Wind, we need wind."

Richie looked around. "I'm good but I'm not that good. You'll have to talk to someone with more seniority than me."

"I have been. I've been begging for wind."

"I'd be careful praying for wind, Skipper. Every time wind and a boat are mentioned in the New Testament, there's a storm. I don't think our crew is ready for that."

"No need to worry, weather reports are good." Stanton gazed ahead into the darkening horizon. Even he was getting bored.

"I can't believe you arranged a tour of one of the navy's newest subs," Richie said. "If I weren't already in the service, I would have enlisted."

"It all worked out. The odds of being able to do that again are astronomical—" Stanton's heart turned a somersault. Richie caught his expression.

"What? Did you see something?"

"Take the wheel," Stanton ordered. "Better yet ..." He switched on the autopilot. "Everyone is below, right?"

"Yeah, why?"

"Go around the port side of the cabin; I'll go starboard. I thought I saw something ... someone."

"You saw one of the kids?"

Stanton didn't answer. He wasn't sure what he saw. Something gray, something tall, something moving had appeared on the bow. It was just a glimpse, something seen from the corner of his eye, but it made his breath catch. Whatever it was, it didn't seem right.

Not easily startled, Stanton was embarrassed by his thumping heart, which beat at double time. Willing his heart to slow, he took a deep breath and moved forward, one hand on the lifeline and the other against the smooth fiberglass cabin. He rounded the front of the salon the same instant Richie did. No one was there. Nothing was there except the flat deck forward of the cabin, and the mesh trampoline that spanned separate hulls.

"I don't see anyone," Richie said with a shrug.

Stanton squeezed his eyes shut, then opened them again. "The sea must be having fun with me. Sorry."

"No sweat. It's better to be safe than sor—"

A loud snap cracked behind them. Stanton spun, his eyes searching the streamlined form of the boat. Another snap, this time above them. The mainsail that had a moment before been drooping like a wet bedsheet hung out to dry bowed to life. Spreading out its 1,238-square-foot triradial form, it gorged itself on the sudden wind like a baleen whale feeding on a cloud of krill. A half second later the triangular jib inflated like a balloon.

The *Tern About* lurched forward with such unexpected abruptness that Stanton lost his footing. The deck shot forward and Stanton went backward, falling to the textured surface. Pain blazed up his hip and into his back, but he had no time to complain. Despite the nonskid surface, he was moving backward, rolling on his side. He reached out to steady himself, and his right hand found one of the stainless steel uprights supporting the lifeline that ran the perimeter of the boat. His knee slapped against one of the deck cleats used to tie the boat while in dock. The pain ricocheted up his leg.

Snap. Snap.

The sails sagged momentarily, then immediately refilled with wind. Again the lightweight yacht surged forward, and Stanton felt his weight shift sideways. The sudden motion and the unexpected force rolled him to one side. He felt the toe rail pass beneath him; his shin struck another stainless steel upright. The boat bounced once, then again, and Stanton felt the deck disappear as he slid overboard.

Abject fear strengthened him as adrenaline pumped through his veins. His feet plowed the water. He clung to the upright with his right hand, squeezing it so hard that he expected it to crush at any moment. Stanton's feet hit the water again, water that was racing by. A moment ago the *Tern About* could not make enough speed to pass a walking man, but now it was skipping across the surface as if jet-propelled. Stanton had no idea how this could happen, but he didn't take the time to figure the physics. If he didn't get back on deck in the next few seconds, he would be in the drink, in the dark, with the catamaran racing away from him.

Blindly he threw his left hand up, reaching, grasping for any-thing that would help hold his weight. He had a vague sensation of pain in his hip, leg, and right shoulder, but his mind was too occupied with survival to take much notice.

"Skipper?" It was Richie. "Skipper, where are you? Stanton!"

"Here, Richie! Over the side." Stanton looked up to see Richie's eyes widen. A half second later the younger man was on his knees, reaching down to grasp Stanton's collar.

"Tenny!" Richie called. "Man overboard! Tenny, I need you!" Stanton heard a thumping and pulled himself up just enough to see Richie kicking the side of the salon. "Come on, Tenny, come on!"

A moment later the sound of the salon door slamming open penetrated the wind. "Where are you?" she shouted.

"Here!" Richie called.

Tenny rounded the corner and said something Stanton couldn't make out, but he did feel her hand take hold of his shirt. "Your arms are longer than mine," she said to Richie. "Grab his belt."

Richie complied. "On three," he said and began to count. The moment three passed his lips, Stanton felt himself rise. He kicked, he pulled with all his might. Three people grunted and groaned until Stanton felt the blessed firmness of the deck beneath him.

"What is going on?" Tenny demanded. "I thought we hit something." The boat lurched forward again. Then suddenly the wind changed directions, hitting the sails from the side. The *Tern About* creaked as the carbon-fiber mast fought back against the onslaught. The sea was no longer flat. It churned and roiled. Whitecaps danced like tiny white witches, jumping and reaching for whatever was nearby.

"I don't know," Stanton said, lying on the deck, catching his breath. "One second we're near dead in the water, and the next . . . I'm near dead in the water."

"How did you get over here?" she asked, but Stanton didn't answer. He was looking at the sails and his eyes drifted skyward. Three minutes before, the night dome had begun to dress in its nightly sequins of stars, but things had changed. Clouds rolled in. Not moved in, not pushed in, but rolled in, as if being swept by the broom of God.

Stanton struggled to his feet. "Tenny, secure all the hatches and ports. Get inside and make the kids put on PFDs. Batten down everything you can. Richie, drop the sails. I'll crank the engines. This doesn't look good."

"Where did this come from?" Richie shouted over the wind. "Storms don't come up this quickly."

"Nature seems to think otherwise," Stanton said. "Let's move. Everyone move!"

The engines fired up. Ports and hatches slammed shut. In less than two minutes Stanton had donned a padded safety harness lashed to the starboard steering station with a six-foot tether. The harness was designed to serve as a PFD, or personal flotation device. Richie was tethered to the port helm. At least they wouldn't be washed overboard. Stanton had released all boat control to him. Stanton had more experience under the water, but Richie was the master sailboat racer. It made sense that he should guide them through the storm. Already he had changed Stanton's original order to drop the sails. Instead of retracting the canvases completely, he reefed them, lowering them so less surface area was before the wind. Fortunately, the Catana catamaran came equipped with an automatic reefing system that Richie operated from the steering station. A Harken hydraulic winch shortened the sails. Using both the lowered sails and the diesel engines, he had been able to present the ideal profile to the wind, running ahead of it. They would have reefed the sails earlier had there been any warning of the gale. An old sailor's maxim said, "If you're thinking about shortening sail, you probably should have already done it." They had not had the privilege of thinking about the procedure.

The multihull accelerated at an alarming speed.

Every sailor knew that the ocean was unpredictable, mysterious, and fickle. Those who had spent their lives on the seas had scores of stories to tell. This would be one more. Stanton was thankful for several things. First, Richie was a highly trained sailor, which meant he had spent hours sailing in adverse weather. Good sailors, especially those who raced yachts, as Richie did, often chose to sail in inclement conditions to improve their skills, racing before the wind or sailing into it, what some sailors called the "hard chance."

Stanton did what he could: hold on and pray. He did one other thing. He wondered where the storm had come from. The wind was blowing and increasing in force. Both steering stations had an instrument panel, and atop the mast a Windex weathervane measured the true wind speed. Stanton read the indicator every few moments, unable to believe the numbers he was seeing. A microburst storm could whip up winds of twenty-five knots in just a few minutes. This had to be a microburst. It was the only kind of storm he knew of that came out of a clear sky. The starry expanse had been gobbled up and digested by clouds that appeared from nowhere. And the wind was beyond what he would expect in a microburst. Thirty-eight knots and rising. Once wind speed rose above forty-one knots, it would be a force-nine gale. Even in a sixty-two-foot-long, fifty-eight-ton vessel, these were survival conditions.

Stanton turned to see Richie working the wheel, his eyes fixed forward. Through the deck lighting and the dim light that poured from the salon, Stanton could see that Richie was enjoying himself. The young sailor glanced his way, flashed a huge smile, then released the wheel with his right hand, whooping and thrusting a fist in the air. *The man is crazy*, Stanton thought.

The wind speed moved up another couple of knots. They were now in a strong gale. The wind shrieked past the mast, whistled through the lifelines—banshees demanding to be heard. Something else bothered Stanton—the waves. The wind was capable of creating surface waves. The longer the winds stayed, the higher the waves would become. Stanton had seen seas that could drop tons of water on a tanker. A low-to-the-surface vessel like the *Tern About* could easily be hammered by ten-foot seas.

There were three great dangers that Stanton could see. Each chilled his blood. First was taking a wave over the stern. The wind-aided waves pushed the catamaran faster and faster as they grew in size, but there was always the danger of a wave breaking over the back of the boat. The *Tern About* was steered from the stern. Any wave crashing down on that section would crash down on Richie and Stanton. Both were tethered to the boat, but being smashed to the deck and tossed around like a sock in a washing machine was an adventure Stanton could do without. Waves over the stern also carried the danger of flooding. Tenny had locked down every hatch and closed every port. That should keep them safe, but bigger boats had been sent to the bottom when a hatch had given way.

Another fear was broaching. If Richie lost control of the helm and the boat suddenly veered into the wind, she would expose her side to the waves, making her all the more vulnerable to the crushing force of the waves. The *Tern About* was a multihulled boat and almost impossible to capsize, but the ocean specialized in the impossible.

Then there was pitchpoling. The waves came faster and were becoming larger, which meant that Richie had to steer up the back of a wave and then "surf" down the face of it moments later. If he did not control the boat's speed, he could drop too fast, driving the bow of the boat into the back of the next wave. The forces would be immense and boats were known to pitchpole, to tumble over their own bow. Stanton didn't want to imagine what would happen next.

The waves rose and Stanton had to look up to see their crests. All communication with Richie and the others was impossible. The shrieking of wind filled Stanton's ears and echoed in his brain. Holding on to the metal guardrail that surrounded the steering station, he focused on seas ahead, analyzing everything the experienced Riche was doing. If something happened to him or if the storm continued too long, Stanton would have to take the wheel. Tenny could take a turn, but just making the distance from the cabin to either of the two helms was treacherous. At the moment, Stanton knew, she had her hands full securing anything that could fly around the cabin—the coffee pot, books, even the case from the DVD they had been watching, could become dangerous.

If Richie harbored the same apprehensions, he didn't show it. The display of bravado given a few minutes ago may have been for Stanton's benefit. He admired Richie for that. He also admired the way he skillfully piloted the boat in heavy seas.

Rain began to fall in sheets, as if the heavens themselves were flooded to overflowing. Stanton was thankful that the wind had come first. The sailor's rule of thumb was that rain then wind meant a more difficult and enduring storm. A sudden onset of wind was often considered a good sign. Old sailors had a saying: "The sharper the blast, the sooner it's past." He hoped they were right.

The waves continued to grow at stunning speed. At times the boat was high on a crest and Stanton was looking down into the watery trough before them. An unsettling moment later he was looking up at saltwater mountains threatening to pound down on them, leaving only splinters and corpses in life jackets floating on the surface.

The *Tern About* slipped off the crest of an eight-foot wave and skated down its face. The wave before them seemed taller by a yard.

The wind screamed. The waves piled upon themselves. The rain shot down like pellets from a gun. Stanton studied every maneuver Richie made and prayed between each one.

He was not terrified. Stanton had faced death on several occasions, and the thought of leaving this life caused him no discomfort. His concern was not for himself but for those below deck. Five teenagers had been entrusted to him. Five sets of parents expected their children back, and the youths were caught up in high seas and gale-force winds.

A wave ran over the port stern, slamming into Richie like a linebacker. The force knocked his feet from under him. He seemed to hang horizontally in the air, then crashed to the deck, awash in foam. The wheel before Stanton began to spin and the boat heeled to one side. Stanton seized the control and instinctively cranked it in the reverse direction to counter the action of the waves against the hull and of the water against the rudders. His quick action and Richie's earlier deployment of the dagger boards, keel-like units that could be moved up and down through the hull to keep the catamaran from side-slipping, straightened the craft.

A quick glance at Richie showed that he was uninjured. Scrambling to his feet, he retook the wheel, placed a hand on the throttle levers, and sent more power to the engines. Another wave broke over the stern but with much less force. Richie was now running slightly ahead of the watery attackers. It was a delicate procedure that required a sharp eye and a practiced hand.

Too slow and they would be awash in churning water and run the danger of downflooding—water pouring into the boat. Already the unyielding ocean had filled the cockpit, making it look like a child's wading pool. The light from the canopy pressed through the spray and danced on the roiling water.

A pounding caught Stanton's attention. Through the screeching gale a dull thump-thump added a base line to the storm's tune. It took only a second for Stanton to identify the source of the noise: the mast was pumping, moving forward when the short sails filled with wind, then snapping back as the wind was hindered by a rising wave or forced change of direction. Forward then back. Forward then back. The mast was made of the strongest carbon fiber, Stanton reminded himself, not like the old masts, which were crafted from weathered wood. Still, the sound made him uneasy. Storms had done unbelievable things to ships in the past. Even on the Great Lakes, a tanker could be sunk by a sudden blow. The *Edmund Fitzgerald* was sent to the bottom of Lake Superior when the cargo ship was driven bow-first into the trough between waves, plowing into the lake bottom and springing all her hatches. All hands died not far from Whitefish Bay that day in 1975. If weather could sink a ship that size, it could certainly have its way with a sixty-two-foot catamaran.

The *Tern About* climbed the back of the next wave, slowing as physics and gravity did their work. Richie powered up the engines to compensate, but sailing uphill seemed a losing battle, and Stanton knew there was always the danger they might slip backward, sliding under the wave behind them, its tons of angry salt water cascading down upon them in an avalanche of destruction.

The wave they were climbing was the largest they had seen yet. But more disturbing than the size of the waves—rogue waves, driven by wind, had reached heights far greater—was the speed at which they were growing, making the storm all the more unbelievable.

The boat slid port as Richie aimed for the crest's "flat spot," the place where the wave was less intense. He found it, and boat and crew surfed down the leading edge of the wave, dropping at roller-coaster speed into the open maw of the trough. For a moment Stanton was sure the bow would be forced so far beneath the surface that the boat would somersault. But the *Tern About* was made of sterner stuff. Her designers had created a water warrior that refused to succumb to the noise and bluster of the gale.

Stanton looked at Richie. Across the darkness they made eye contact. He seemed less thrilled than before. This time there was no whooping, no pumping of fist in the air. He showed no fear, but even separated by over thirty feet, Stanton could see the stress on the man's face and in his posture. This was no longer fun, no longer a sought-after adventure; it was becoming a struggle for life.

Thump . . . thump.

Richie's head snapped up as he looked at the mast. The light atop it jerked back and forth, not merely swaying but moving in an exaggerated motion, like a whip antenna on a car.

The mainsail began to move, shrinking in size. Richie was reefing the sail again, shortening it so less wind could fill it. He was exchanging control to ease the pressure on the mast. On some boats this had to be done by hand, requiring that someone tie down the unused portion of the sail. In this case that would have been Stanton, but Richie could do the reefing from where he stood at the helm. Stanton could not have been more relieved.

The waves continued. The wind increased squealing like a tortured animal. Stanton's ears were becoming numb. The storm had come upon them so suddenly that neither he nor Richie had been able to don their foul-weather gear. Strapping on the safety harnesses and tethering themselves to the boat had been chore enough. The harness rubbed against the back of his neck and chaffed his underarm, but no discomfort would be able to persuade him to part with it.

Soaked to the skin, salt water stinging his eyes, his legs and back aching from fighting to remain erect on a pitching deck, Stanton wondered how a storm could come upon them so suddenly. All the marine weather reports had been clear, not just for today but for the rest of the week. The sea was surprising, even mysterious, but it was not magical. Weather was a function of physics. Experience told him that they should have had some warning, seen something in the sky, but there had been nothing. One moment the seas had been calm, the next they were possessed by an evil intent on drowning them all. It made no sense. It was irrational. It was impossible. Yet no amount of disbelief could dispel the reality of what he was enduring.

Steadying himself against the guardrail, he wished he could do more, but the only actions available to him were vigilance and prayer. He would have to be content with that.

Minutes stumbled by like hours. Time seemed to slow as the waves rose higher, the wind blew harder, and the boat rocked and pitched and bounced. Stanton could feel it all: the wind, the water rushing along the hulls, and the vibration of engines working hard to fight a foe much larger than they.

Suddenly Stanton's heart seized, quick-frozen by the abrupt realization that something had changed. What was there a moment before was now gone. It was not something he could hear but something he had been feeling. It took a second for him to isolate the missing element that chilled him several more degrees.

The engines. The powerful diesel engines that had been valiantly straining against the churning ocean had quit—suddenly, unexpectedly.

Stanton turned to see Richie struggling to restart them. Nothing. Richie shook his head and worked the controls to raise the mainsail. They had to maintain forward motion and control; otherwise they would be little more than a sixty-two-foot cork bobbing in the Atlantic.

Directing his attention to the mast, Stanton saw the sail begin to rise, when another motion caught his eye. A form was gazing at him through the tinted glass of the cabin door. It was Tenny, bathed in light from the salon and dressed in a life jacket. Her face was draped with fear. Had she noticed the loss of the engines? Was she looking for direction, action to take? Or was something else wrong?

She disappeared. The lights of the salon, the lights of the canopy, the navigation lights—all of them blinked twice and went out.

No power. No light. They were sailing in a malevolent storm that grew more evil with each minute.

The rain turned icy. Stanton stood in the dark, unable to see anything or anyone. It was as if he and everyone on board had been swallowed by a Jonah-esque creature, a leviathan who found the *Tern About* an irresistible snack.

Stanton continued to stare where a moment before he had seen Tenny. He thought of Richie on the other side of the boat, battling heroically against an ocean which cared nothing about the heroes now fighting to save their lives in the dark; he thought of Tenny with still a year to go at the academy and a whole life ahead of her; he thought of the five teenagers who came on board, each against his or her will but trusting him to keep them safe.

"What have I done?" he asked.

The wind answered with a demonic cry.

Darkness

"What's happening?" It was Jamie, and Tenny recognized the fear in her voice—it matched her own.

"Take it easy," Tenny said, attempting to exude a confidence she didn't feel. She could see none of her charges. When the lights failed, the salon had plunged into sepulchral darkness. Outside the wind whistled, shrieked, and moaned menacingly. Tenny's mind filled with images of disembodied faces with tortured expressions hovering above the boat. There was a rushing, crashing sound, and Tenny knew another wave had come over the stern. She felt the boat rise and slow and in her mind she could see the catamaran crawling up the back of a wave. She waited for what she knew would come next: the sudden drop down the wave's face. "We've lost power for a moment. Just hang on to something and stay calm."

"Why is it so dark?" Jamie cried.

"Because we lost power, you idiot. She just said that." John's words were harsh, sharpened by the terror Tenny knew he felt.

"No," Jamie protested. "When we first came on board, she gave us the safety lecture. She said the boat had emergency lights. Why aren't they working?"

It was a good question. The boat's electrical system was state-of-the-art, with a Northern-Lights generator and ten Sonnenschein house batteries. Even if the generator cut out, there should be enough juice in the batteries to power the lights for hours. There were also emergency lights designed to come on in a power outage. They were lifeless—every one of them lifeless.

"I don't know," Tenny said. "Just sit tight for a moment. They'll bring the engines on line in a minute."

The boat shook; cabinets that had been locked down rattled as if their contents wanted out. Tenny could feel the bow begin to rise again. The roller-coaster movement made her stomach turn.

"What if they don't?" Steve asked. His voice was calm but punctuated with tension.

"We all drown, stupid," John snapped in the dark.

"That's enough!" Tenny ordered. "You're not helping."

Tenny was confined in the salon with four of the five teenagers. M&M was still in her bunk and, Tenny assumed, terrified. If she had been seasick before, she must certainly be wishing for a speedy death now. And she was not the only one sick. Jamie and Steve had both vomited, filling the confined space with the stench of bile. That had led to more nausea. Tenny's first desire was to open one of the ports and let out the odor, but that was far too dangerous. While it might release the fetid air, it could just as easily let in a ton of water. There had been complaints but Tenny held her ground.

Forcing herself to think, she tried to remember where the emergency flashlights were. Once aboard, she had committed the layout of the boat to memory and opened every locker to examine its contents. Captain Stanton had charged her with the task of teaching safety to the teenagers, and she took that order seriously. She was grateful she had. When the gale descended—and *gale* was the only word Tenny could think of to describe the sudden onslaught—she had ordered the kids to strap on the PFDs. Since she had taken the time to drill them in the procedure when they first arrived, they were able to locate and don the life jackets with only a little trouble. They had done better than she expected. She had taken one flotation device to M&M, who was sitting wide-eyed on the bunk. She put the device on without hesitancy but refused to leave the cabin. "I'm too sick," she complained. Tenny didn't have time to argue.

Sliding away from the glass door, where she had been looking out to see how Stanton and Richie were doing, she sidestepped to the left. The *Tern About* had lockers everywhere. Some contained tools, others held life preservers, flares, and everything else a sailor might need, including battery-operated lanterns. One such locker was on the wall to her left. She could see nothing. It was as if she had been blindfolded, her head had been covered with a blanket, and she had been dropped into a deep well—a well that pitched and yawed violently.

"I'm trying to find a flashlight," she explained, knowing that the others could not see her. "I know there's one on this wall somewhere, but I'll have to find it by touch."

A dim light came on, flickering yellow against the white plastic-laminated wall. Tenny turned to the source and saw John with a wry smile. He was holding up a lighter. His face seemed to float in the air sans body. The pale illumination gave him a ghostly appearance. "Who's your hero now?"

"I could kiss you," Tenny said.

"I get that a lot," John replied.

"I'll bet," Tenny said, trying not to sound too sarcastic. "I won't ask why you brought a cigarette lighter on board." The boat shuddered and moved to the side. She didn't like the feel of it. Turning back to the locker, she found the handle and popped it open. Inside, lit by the soft, inconsistent light, was a large lantern. She seized it. It felt heavy in her hand and she was grateful, knowing the weight was due to the large battery. She fumbled with it until she found the switch, then clicked it on.

Nothing.

"I can't burn this thing all night," John complained. "Turn that thing on."

"I've tried," Tenny said. "Something's wrong. The battery must be dead." But she didn't know how. Surely Richie wouldn't overlook something so fundamental as checking all the emergency gear before leaving port. She flipped the switch again and again. Nothing.

The light went out.

"Hey," Tony said. "Flick that Bic again, man."

"It was getting hot," John said.

"Don't be a sissy," Tony admonished. "Turn it back on."

"Use your own," John sneered.

"I don't have one."

"Precisely," John said smugly.

"Why doesn't the flashlight work?" Steve asked. He sounded sick again. Tenny hoped he could hold his stomach down. Another round of vomiting and she would become a retching contributor. The thought embarrassed her, but she knew that even hardened navy chiefs had been known to toss their cookies in bad weather. Still, she expected more of herself.

"I don't know," she admitted. This was too weird to believe. The sudden onset of the storm, the engine failure, the power loss, and now a flashlight that was useful only as a paperweight. "Hey, hero, give us some more light. There's another lantern mounted in the galley."

There was a soft click and gentle effusion of light. The single flame was small, but in the absence of any other light it did an admirable job. Tenny moved to her right, toward the kitchen, which lay a few steps to the side. She struggled to keep her footing, leaning as much as possible on the wall and the galley counter.

"Can't we light a candle or something?" Tony asked.

"Not in rough seas," Tenny replied. "That's just begging for a fire and as bad as a storm at sea is, a fire is worse. The last thing I want is to be left floating in a life raft in these waters." The thought chilled her. Staggering to the side, just a slip away from stumbling, Tenny squinted in the dim light, searching for the wall-mounted lantern. She found it and quickly pressed the plastic-covered switch. It clicked but no light came out. "I don't believe this!" she snapped in frustration.

The light went out again. "Is this what my dad means when he says 'shipshape'?" John quipped. "I always thought it meant everything was where it was supposed to be and in working order."

The boat dropped precipitously and Jamie screamed. Tenny felt herself go weightless and thought for a moment that she would float to the ceiling. A second later the weight returned and the hull popped and vibrated as the boat hit the bottom of the trough.

"What are they doing out there?" Tony shouted.

"Keeping us alive," Tenny snapped back. She shook the flashlight. "Why doesn't this work?" She banged it on the galley counter and tried the switch again. Nothing changed.

"I want to go home," Jamie said. "I didn't sign on for this."

"None of us signed on," John said. "We were forced to come."

"You weren't forced," Tenny replied. "You came of your own free will."

"Yeah, right," John said in the darkness. "Did anyone here say, 'I wanna go to sea for a week with a bunch of sailors'?" He paused. "I don't see any hands. . . . Okay, I can't see anything, but

I don't hear anyone saying, 'Yeah, I did.' Not even Tony the Tiger."

"Shut up, John-boy." Tony's words cut through the darkness.

"Knock it off, guys," Tenny demanded. "You can show off when you get home. Right now we need to keep our emotions in check and our heads screwed on tight."

"You sound like my dad," Steve complained.

"Even dads can be right sometimes," Tenny said. She spoke with confidence and courage. Inside her guts had long ago turned to overcooked oatmeal, but that wasn't something the kids needed to know. "Okay, listen up. I don't know why the lanterns aren't working. I know they were operational before we left. Our power may come back on line in a few minutes or we may have to wait until the sun comes up. In either case we need to work as a team. That means no bickering. Keep your opinions to yourself."

"Keep your puke to yourself too," John added.

"You're just not clear on the concept, are you, John?" Tenny remarked. "Of course, fear makes people act out."

"I didn't say I was afraid," John countered.

"Then stop acting like it," Tenny demanded. "We're going to come through this fine. Just fine. But we might as well use this time to talk about what to do if we have to . . . need to . . ."

"Just say it," Tony said.

". . . if we need to abandon ship. There are some things you need to know about the life raft and floating in the ocean."

As if on cue, the boat rose, then dropped like a free-falling elevator. A wet retching sound rumbled through the darkness, followed by another. A few seconds later Jamie said, "I'm sorry."

"Gross," John said. The pungent odor was sickening.

"I said I was sorry."

"Leave her alone and listen up," Tenny said. "There is a life raft stowed below the deck of the cockpit. Richie made sure it was big enough to hold all of us, but I imagine we'll make use of the Zodiac too."

"We have to leave the boat?" Jamie asked, her voice raspy and tremulous.

"No," Tenny said. "I'm just trying to make sure we're all on the same page should the worst happen."

"I don't want to leave the boat," the young woman complained.

"We're not leaving the boat unless we start sinking," Tony said. His tone was softer than the tone he used with John.

"I'll be responsible for pulling and inflating the raft. Captain Stanton and Richie might be able to help, but if they can't, I will have to depend on some of you to step up. Once the raft is inflated, the wind will try to snatch it from our grasp. We can't let that happen. No matter what, we can't let that happen."

"How do we get in it?" Steve asked.

"That's the . . . fun part. We'll try to jump in, but there's a good chance that some of us will hit the water and need to be pulled in," Tenny said.

"Uh-uh, no way. Not me," Tony said. "We wouldn't last two minutes in the water. The waves would separate us."

"We'll tether ourselves to it. No one gets lost. Not on my shift." Tenny spoke bravely but she knew that Tony was right. Eight people trying to mount a raft in survival-condition seas was tough even with the best and most experienced sailors. A group of kids attempting it was a terrifying prospect—one more likely to fail than fully succeed. Anything less than full success meant someone died.

"How long is this storm going to last?" Steve asked. He was sounding woozy.

"It came on quick; it will probably pass quickly."

"But it could go on for much longer, right?" Tony asked. "I mean, my dad said he was in a storm that lasted two days."

"I'll die," Jamie said. "I don't think I can take two more hours."

"You'll do fine," Tenny said. The boat slid sideways and Tenny could hear water crashing down on the deck outside. "Think of the stories you'll have to tell."

There was a scream. Loud. Piercing. Sharp. It was terror amplified in the smooth cocoon of the boat. The cry came again, louder this time.

"Give me some light," Tenny demanded, and immediately the flickering flame erupted from John's hand. Tenny stepped, hopped, then slid on the rolling deck to where John was sitting. She snatched the lighter away without comment. He made no protest. Striking the lighter again, Tenny worked her way toward the scream, toward the cabin where M&M was holed up alone.

N
⋏

The *Tern About* had four designated staterooms with plenty of room in the salon to sleep several more. M&M was in the aft room on the port side. The constant motion of the boat made it impossible for Tenny to cross the salon, pass the open galley, and descend the four steps to the port hull without accumulating a few bruises. She steadied herself with one hand and clung tightly to the lighter with her other. If she were to drop it, she might not find it until sunrise. The lighter couldn't provide much light but it was all she had available. She had no intention of losing the one small advantage she had.

She moved slowly, testing each step before she placed her weight. A fall in the wrong place could mean anything from a bump on the head to a broken ankle. She wanted none of that.

A screech bounded down the passageway, bouncing off the hard surfaces like a ball. It was not a cry for help. It was not a shriek of pain. It was unmitigated terror given flight by voice. The scream was hot with fear and it froze everything inside Tenny. Ill-defined horrors began to race in her mind, cinematic horrors seen lived out on the silver screen. What was behind the wood door? Demons? Monsters? Trolls with sharp axes? Flesh-eating—

"That's enough," Tenny whispered to herself. "Let's keep this in the real world."

The boat rocked and heeled, then rocked some more. The sound of weeping, deep and volatile, rolled through the solid door as if it weren't there.

Tenny paused, her heart beating rapidly.

Taking the handle of the door, she plunged into the tiny room. The pent-up air was fetid from M&M's unrelenting seasickness, causing Tenny to gag. "Mary?" she said softly, not wanting to add to the young woman's terror. "It's me."

There was no response, just the heart-soaking sobs of the horrified teenager. "Mary, it's Tenny." Tenny raised the lighter and the soft yellow-white light flickered in the cabin. "What's wrong? What's the matter?"

"There! There! It was there!" M&M's voice was raspy from the day's vomiting. The screaming could not have helped any.

"What? What's there, girl?"

"It was there. I swear it. It was there."

Tenny glanced around the room. She could see the two narrow beds that took up almost all the deck space. M&M was on the inboard bed. She was curled up like an adult-sized fetus. Even in the indistinct light, Tenny could see she was trembling. Tenny forced her eyes to trace the details of the cabin. The room was no larger than a good-sized walk-in closet. To her left was a small closet for hanging clothes, to her right another narrow bed. Her eyes followed the room's perimeter, searching for the terror in the darkness. Her spine tingled, her heart trembled. A desk was just a step to the right, and above it—

Tenny inhaled involuntarily, gasping and stepping back. Above the desk was a face, dark and undulating in the flickering light. Its eyes were wide and white and its mouth hung open in a wide gape. "Oh my . . ." Then she stopped. There was a familiarity about the face. She squinted through the artificial twilight. Tenny closed her mouth and the face mimicked the motion.

A mirror. A mirror above the small desk. Tenny's heart, which had been rolling like a boulder down a steep hill, slowed, and she forced herself to take several deep breaths, forgetting the rank air for a moment. She chuckled to herself as if she found the whole thing humorous. She didn't.

"You saw it!" M&M said. "You saw it too."

"Girl, all I saw was my ugly face in the mirror."

"Not in the mirror. By the door. By the door. It was there, by the door."

"What was there?" The lighter was getting hot in Tenny's hand. She approached the bed and sat on its side. Standing was too difficult in the pounding seas.

"A man . . . but not a man. He was there but wasn't there." Her voice cranked up several decibels. Tenny knew she was on the verge of hysterics. "It was a ghost." She sat up.

Tenny put an arm around the girl and pulled her close. "It's all right. Nothing happened and whatever you saw is gone. I'm here now." The light went out and Tenny felt M&M tense like a clock spring ready to break. "The lighter was getting hot. I was burning my fingers. I'll turn it back on in a minute."

"How come the lights don't work?" M&M whimpered, like a toddler who had awakened from a bad dream.

"The engines died and the generators went out. As soon as the sun comes up, we'll fix them. Until then we all have to stay calm and wait." Tenny saw no reason to bring up flashlights that didn't work. That would just fuel the girl's fear.

"I really saw it, you know. I'm not making it up."

"These are weird conditions," Tenny said. "Sick as you've been, in a storm, no lights, it's a wonder you haven't seen more."

"It was real."

Tenny gave her a little squeeze. "How's your stomach?" she asked, hoping to switch the topic from hobgoblins.

"It still hurts."

"You've been throwing up a lot. I imagine your muscles are sore. Mine always are when I have the flu."

"I think something's wrong with me."

"You'll be fine. I want you to come out into the lobby with the rest of us. There's no need for you to be alone."

"I've been sick again," she said sadly. "They'll laugh at me."

Tenny chuckled. "You should see them. Everyone is sick out there. Almost everyone has tossed their cookies at least once. Those who haven't will soon. Very few people can get bounced around like this and not feel the need to upchuck. You're in good company, girl."

"Really?"

"Truth is, I've come close several times myself." Truth was, she was close at that moment. She needed to exchange this putrid air for some less putrid. "Come on. Let's get out of this cubicle and spread our wings a little."

"I don't have wings," M&M said. "Angels have wings. I don't have wings."

Tenny started to ask what she meant by that but decided against it. Better to face one problem at a time. Flicking the lighter, Tenny waited for the flame to settle. "Come on. I'm springing you from this prison cell." She rose, took M&M's

hand, and led her toward the salon. "Kinda like walking on the back of a whale, isn't it?"

"I guess," M&M said. She seemed so fragile, so delicate, like crystal glass cut too thin and set near the edge of a table. It was going to be broken sometime but no one could predict when.

Mary Moss followed, slowly and with uncertain steps. She was leaning forward as if she had just been punched. *This is one sick girl*, Tenny thought.

Tenny found an empty space on the curved bench of the salon and guided M&M to it. Once the girl was seated, she joined her.

John was the first to speak. "So what happened?"

"Bad dream," Tenny answered before John could press the issue.

"Boogie man after you?" John teased.

Jamie took the lead. "No, she dreamed she was on a date with you. That's enough to make anyone scream."

The others laughed. Tenny was sure she detected a little chortle from M&M.

"Oooh, you've been burned bad," Tony said in the dark. "Shot down in a storm. It must be the story of your life."

"Shut up," John fired back. His words seethed with sudden anger.

"Or what, big guy?" Tony said. "You gonna bust a move on me?"

"Nothing like a happy crew," Tenny said. Her sarcasm was firm, loud, and carried the point. "You guys can duke it out later. Right now we're in a storm and we need to keep our wits together. This ride isn't over yet—"

As if to put an exclamation point on the statement, the boat tipped forward and dropped as though it had just sailed off the edge of the world. Tenny had no way of knowing if the others noticed, but the drop seemed longer than any one previous.

The waves were getting higher.

Exhaustion

Every part of Stanton's body hurt. The rising, falling, slipping, pitching, heeling of the catamaran had bounced him around, his body hitting the padded chair behind him or the metal rails around him or the wheel in front of him. His legs ached from standing and constantly shifting his weight, but sitting on the elevated chair was out of the question. The boat gyrated so much that he needed his legs planted beneath him. So Stanton stood for the third straight hour, balancing the best he could on a deck that constantly changed beneath his feet. He felt like the circus acrobats who adroitly worked their way around the ring while walking on a giant ball or standing on the back of a trotting elephant. The performers had the advantage of being under the big top, in a controlled situation. Stanton had no mastery over the deck upon which he stood. It moved as if alive, with a mind of its own and a determination to send him crashing down ingloriously.

Another glance toward Richie at the port helm revealed a focused man who must be close to exhaustion. Anytime, Stanton expected the signal that would mean it was his turn to take the wheel and try his hand at avoiding destruction. It was not a job he wanted.

The rain fell harder; drops the size of gravel pummeled skin made raw by wind and salt water. Stanton's eyes stung and his muscles threatened to surrender to nagging fatigue. And he had not been fighting the wheel or bearing the mental pressure of steering a boat with no engines or electrical power. Richie must have felt as if he were in round fourteen of a fifteen-round heavyweight match. *To be that young again*, Stanton thought.

Again, for what must have been the hundredth time, Stanton wondered about his young charges below deck. They had never been sailing and certainly had never been in a sudden storm like this. For that matter, Stanton had never been in such a storm. They must be frightened, he reasoned, scared out of their young minds. And it was his fault for bringing them out here.

He corrected himself. There was no fault. There had been no indication that the gale was brewing, no foreshadowing. It just suddenly appeared like a rabbit out of a magician's hat. It made no sense. Nothing was making sense. A storm with this kind of power took time to develop and should have been seen long before it arrived, but it had dropped upon them as if it had fallen from space. The engines suddenly cutting out bothered him, too. He knew that in some boats engines could overheat if the boat heeled to one side too long, lifting out of the sea the water intake used to cool the engines, leaving them nothing to suck in but air. But that failed to explain what they were experiencing. It was understandable that the engines might overheat and cut out, but that would not explain a full electrical failure. The *Tern About* was equipped with batteries. They should have power for hours without a generator running.

Then there was the thing he had seen. The image of it was still fresh in his mind, although it remained indistinct. It had appeared as a dark-gray blob, an amorphous something that was clearly there, then immediately gone, as if it had descended through the deck to the compartments below.

Stanton forced the image from his mind. Clearly, he had imagined it, or seen some common thing in an uncommon way. The sea could play tricks on the mind. Stories of mermaids, sea serpents, and more had their origins in the minds of weary sailors whose eyes had endured too much glare from the sun. Stanton was the victim of an optical illusion. That had to be it. No other explanation fit the bill. He wasn't the first sailor to see the unexplained, and he knew he wouldn't be the last.

The ocean had grown angrier, offended by the small boat that sailed its surface. The wind, rain, and waves made the sea a writhing monster intent on devouring everything it touched. To Stanton it seemed as if they were not sailing the ocean's surface at all but navigating a gigantic pot of boiling water that bubbled and roiled around the hulls as though trying to cook the boat and everything it held.

The waves grew into swollen, surging mountains. Stanton had stopped estimating their height. He just knew they were too large for the situation and that they were real and dangerous and capable of destroying them. An inkling of fear swirled within him. So far he had kept it at bay, but the image of bodies—young bodies of teenagers—floating in the debris of what had once been a half-million-dollar boat played in his mind. He closed his eyes and willed the projector of his subconscious to end the movie. It worked—at least for now.

A motion to his left caught Stanton's eye. He snapped his head around to see Richie pointing at him. As soon as their eyes met, Richie pointed at the wheel. The squalling, screaming wind made voice communication impossible. This was all they had and it was enough; Stanton got the message. It was his turn to fight the wind and waves. His stomach dropped and he felt all his courage and resolve tumble after it like dirt in a mud slide, burying his bravery in thick wet debris. For half a second Stanton struggled with his emotions. More than anything he wanted to shake his head, to indicate that he lacked the experience and the practice to safely steer through the waves that sought to ruin them.

Instead he nodded, shifted his weight forward, studied the wave before them and the trough they were about to slip into, then grabbed the wheel so hard that he was certain he had left the whorls and ridges of his fingerprints embedded in the grain of the mahogany wood decorating the rim of the carbon-fiber wheel.

"Guide my hands, Lord," Stanton said into the wind. He was unable to hear himself but trusted that God had been able to hear the plea.

The boat plummeted down the face of the wave like a body-surfer. Before him was the back of another wave. Keeping the bow pointed at an angle up the wave, Stanton steered for the closest flat spot. He set his jaw, steeled his spine, and maintained his viselike grip on the wheel. He then glanced at Richie, who had turned around and was bent over the seat, his head resting on the cushion. Stanton knew Richie had worked to the point of collapse. He guessed it had been close to three hours that Richie had kept them afloat. Now it was up to Stanton, who knew he would never last a three-hour watch. Still, he was determined to do everything he could. He would find a way, with God's help, to get his charges home again.

The twin bow cut deep into the watery trough, like a pair of knife blades, and the boat slowed. Then, as it had uncounted times before in the storm, the bow came up. Water crashed around them, thickening the rain. It was like walking under a powerful waterfall that threatened to beat them down. Stanton cranked the wheel starboard and hoped they had enough momentum to carry them up the back of the wave looming before them. The catamaran slowed even more as it climbed skyward, its bow now pointing to where stars should be instead of a swollen, bruised sky. From trough to crest the wave had to measure fifteen feet, and Stanton felt they weren't going to make it.

The boat's momentum flagged as it neared the top of the wave. "Come on, baby, come on," Stanton coaxed the craft. It approached the crest and the bow went airborne for a moment, then settled back down on the churning cushion of water.

Stanton's ears began to hurt. Something had changed. So sudden was the wind's departure that his mind struggled to believe it. The gale-force winds had ceased—suddenly, unexpectedly, impossibly. A moment before, the air had whipped around the rigging, roared over the deck, pushed and pulled Stanton from side to side, but now it was gone. It was as if somewhere a switch had been thrown, cutting off power to the storm.

While Stanton allowed himself the luxury of noticing the change, he kept his eyes dead ahead, plotting the next wave. The boat passed over the crest and began its descent, skipping along the wave's sloped surface, plunging into the trough. Stanton steeled himself for the bow's impact into the water, but it never came. The seething waves that surrounded them petered out, like balloons slowly releasing air. What had been a mountain of boat-crushing water in front of them a moment ago was now merely a mound, a hill that deflated with each passing second.

Stanton craned his neck to look behind him, measuring the size and speed of the wave off the stern. It too simply melted into the depths.

The wind was gone and the reefed sail hung flaccid on the mast. The rain had stopped also. No wind. No waves. No rain.

"How did you do that?" a very tired-looking Richie asked. "I knew you were good, but I didn't know how good."

"It's . . . it's weird," Stanton replied, glad that he could now communicate with Richie. "It just all went away."

"Storms don't do that, Skipper." Richie looked skyward.

"This one just did," Stanton said. "It left faster than it came . . . not that I'm complaining. Someone must have been praying."

"I know I was," Richie said. "That's all I had left." He eased himself into the chair he had been bowed over a minute before. He looked like a rag doll, his limbs hanging loose, his head tilted back. "I really, really need a nap."

"I don't get it," Stanton said. "It's unnatural."

"There was nothing natural about that storm, Skipper. Nothing. I say we chalk it up as a miracle."

Stanton was for that. Miracles were welcome, especially in this case, but it didn't feel like a miracle, although he wasn't sure he knew what a miracle felt like. He looked around. The engorged clouds overhead dissolved before his eyes, leaving a cottage cheese sky behind. He couldn't see the stars—

"Wait a minute," he said. "The sky is light."

Richie looked up. "That's fine with me. I've had my fill of darkness."

"You don't get it. It should still be night. At best we should see stars, but it looks like the sun is shining behind those clouds."

"Maybe the storm lasted all night. Time flies when you're being beat to death in a gale."

"Three or four hours," Stanton said. "That's all the storm could have been. Three or four hours." He looked at his wristwatch. The second hand was frozen in place. "My watch isn't working."

Richie looked at his own watch. "Mine either. It stopped at 2110 hours."

Stanton examined his watch again. "Mine too." He checked the pedestal next to the wheel. "My compass says we're thirty degrees off magnetic north."

Richie leaned forward to see his compass. "Mine's different. We're at least eighty degrees off north."

"The storm knocked our compasses out of whack?" Stanton wondered aloud. "How can that be?"

Richie was back on his feet. "I don't know. The sky is getting brighter, too. A sudden storm that leaves as fast as it came, dead watches, and disparate compass readings. That's one for the books."

"Add to that the sudden loss of power and electricity—all electricity." Stanton released the harness that kept him tethered to the boat. "Are you okay?"

"I'm a train wreck, Skipper. That thing beat me to the core."

"Get below and get some rest," Stanton said but Richie shook his head. He reached for his harness and released the line. "Damage assessment first, then sleep."

The salon door opened and Tenny emerged on wobbly legs. A sharp odor followed her. "What happened?" she asked.

"I wish I knew," Stanton said, "I really wish I knew. How are the kids?"

"Shaken but alive. Everyone's seasick. It's pretty nasty in there."

Stanton nodded. "I'll help you clean up in a minute. First, check everything below. See if the hull maintained its integrity. Richie and I are going to check above deck."

"Tell me I can open the ports," she pleaded.

"Please do."

"Can the kids come out?" she asked. "They've had a rough and dark trip."

Stanton looked around, but there was little to see except a sky that was lighter than it should be and a thick mist rising off the water. "Yeah, let them get some air."

A half second later four teenagers streamed out onto the cockpit deck. To Stanton they looked haggard and battered, a group beaten by the rising, falling, shifting, shuddering boat. Each seemed relieved to be in the fresh air.

"What a ride!" John exclaimed, throwing his arms wide. "It was better than a roller coaster." No one else seemed to agree with him.

"A real E-ticket," Stanton said.

"A what?" John asked.

"An E-ticket," Stanton explained. "You know . . . Disneyland . . . the best rides used to require an E-ticket."

"I don't get it," Tony said.

"When you went into Disneyland, you used to have to buy tickets for the rides. They gave you a booklet of tear-out tickets labeled A through E and . . . You know what, it doesn't really matter."

"Was that before or after World War II?" John asked with a smirk. He was the only one with enough energy to smirk.

"Cute," Stanton said. "Since you're so full of enthusiasm, John, why don't you go below and help Tenny open the portholes and hatches."

"No way. It stinks down there."

"That's why she's opening everything up."

John frowned and Stanton expected another excuse or even a flat refusal, but the boy surprised him. With a sharp turn he reentered the salon.

Stanton moved forward to the bow of the boat, to the starboard peak. Both starboard and port hulls were equipped with Swedish pulpits, metal guardrails over the leading edge of the bow. Each pulpit had a teak seat for passengers to sit and enjoy the ocean before them. Stanton wanted nothing more than to collapse in the chair, stretch out his legs, and surrender to the warmth and comfort of sleep. The chair, however, had been rendered suitable for nothing more than kindling. He took hold of the metal railing and leaned over it. Below was the ocean that had minutes before been a pulsating monster doing its best to gobble down the *Tern About*. Now it was as smooth and settled as bathwater. For hours he and Richie had battled growing, malevolent waves, all of which had been replaced by swells that measured mere inches. It was impossible, but Stanton had just lived through it.

The white hull was made in a "vacuum-bagged sandwich" fashion, making the boat durable but not impervious to structural damage. The boat had taken a beating far greater than it had been designed for. After this it could be the poster boat for the designers. The starboard prow seemed undamaged, something for which Stanton was thankful. The stainless steel rail, however, had been twisted and its fastening plate had pulled loose. He would hate to depend on it to hold his weight.

"How bad is it?"

The voice came just over Stanton's right shoulder and startled him. He jumped and instinctively spun around. Steve was facing him. "You scared me," Stanton said with a laugh.

"Sorry. I just wanted to see if there was something I could do to help."

"No need to apologize," Stanton said. "I'm a little jumpy after the storm."

"You have a right to be." Steve paused. "You kept us alive."

"Actually, Richie gets the credit for that. I was just his backup. He stayed at the helm for almost the whole thing. I think we owe him lunch."

Steve's face tinged green. "Please, let's not talk about food. I may never eat again."

"It must have been rough in there," Stanton said.

"We all hurled . . . except John and Tenny. Tenny's tough. John is just too stupid to know when to be sick."

"Don't let him get under your skin," Stanton said, then leaned over the edge.

"So, we gonna sink or something?"

"Not today, Steve. Outside of this rail and the chair, things look fine." Remembering Steve's offer of help, Stanton said, "I'm going to work my way along the side here. Why don't you check out the mast? Look for cracks or anything that doesn't look right. Be sure and check the bottom of the mast. It was pumping like crazy in the storm."

"Pumping?"

"Snapping back and forth. I want to make sure it hasn't worked up an opening or cracked the deck. Check the salon windows too."

"Got it." Steve wasted no time in starting his assignment.

Stanton methodically worked his way along the side of the boat from prow to stern, examining every inch of deck and hull. To his relief he found no breaches, cracks, or other damage. As he continued his inspection, he heard hatches and portholes opening. The boat had twenty-four opening hatches of various sizes. Some hatches provided ventilation, others led to storage lockers, others were escape hatches. Stanton wanted all the hatches opened, not just to provide ventilation but to inspect for damage and see what cargo, equipment, and supplies might need to be resecured.

Richie met Stanton at the stern. "My side looks pretty good. The port pulpit is banged up pretty good but nothing structural. A few thousand dollars should fix it up just fine."

"The starboard side is in the same condition. Everything looks good on the outside."

"I need to run the sails and check their integrity. I see you put Steve on the mast. I think I'll need to double-check him."

"We need to double-check each other. I'll take the port side now. You take the mast and Steve can retrace my steps."

Steve stepped quickly to the two men. "Hey, guys, there's something you need to see."

"The mast?" Stanton asked. He didn't like the look on Steve's face.

"Yeah, I'll show you." He bounded off, Richie and Stanton close behind. "There," he said, pointing a finger.

Richie groaned. A crack ran around a third of the mast's circumference. To Stanton it looked as if someone had drawn a chalk line along the base. "At least it's not clear through," Stanton said, wanting to sound an optimistic note.

"The result is the same," Richie moaned. "If we operate under full sail, we run the risk of bringing the whole thing down. The boat's tough but it doesn't need that kind of beating. The carbon fiber is lighter than aluminum but the mast is still heavy. I wouldn't want to try and catch it."

"What now?" Steve asked. "Can't we use the front sails . . . the whatchamacallit sail?"

"Jib," Richie said as he shook his head. "They're supported by the mast, too. There is no way for me to know how deep this fracture is, but I'm betting it's bad."

"So we're stuck with no engines or sails?" Stanton asked.

"The engines were next on my list," Richie said. "We'll just have to get them going."

"Tony is a gear-head," Steve said. "We were talking earlier. Maybe he can help."

"I'll take whatever help I can get," Richie said.

"Okay," Stanton said. "Steve and I'll try to get the electronics working."

"The batteries are all dead," Steve said. "Tenny tried several flashlights and none of them worked."

"Well, we have plenty of light now," Stanton said. "The batteries in the cell phone should work, and if I can't connect with that, we'll break out the satellite phone."

"Once we have power, I'd like to spend some time at the navigation station. I have no idea where we are," Richie said.

"It sounds like we have our work cut out for us," Stanton said. "Richie, you've done enough for now. Maybe you should grab some shuteye. Tony and I can take a stab at the engines after I make contact with the Coast Guard."

"I don't think I could sleep right now. Not after seeing the mast. Let's get things operational; then you can steam us in to Miami. I think this outing has come to an end."

"Unfortunately, I agree," Stanton said. He looked around. The gray mist continued to rise, obscuring everything more than fifty yards away. The sky had retained its unusual texture. "We're going to need the navigation station. With no compasses and no horizon, I'm as lost as a toddler in the woods."

Richie looked around. "I can't say I've ever seen anything like this before. It reminds me of something from a Stephen King novel."

"I hope not," Steve added. "Someone always dies in his books . . . and they die badly."

Stanton felt unsettled.

Silence

*T*he opportunity was missed. The sea had made the effort, issued the call, but its appeal had gone unanswered. The welcoming pleas had been clear enough, the prospect recognized, but still it lay out of reach. How easy it would have been. A simple step, a slight leap, and the ocean would have spread wide its strong arms and taken in the one longing for its embrace.

Sinking.

Down.

Peace.

The call was refused but not by choice. Too many stood in the way. The ocean was angry. It raised its waves, it sent its wind, but the one being wooed remained distant. Then it stopped like a suitor rejected one too many times.

The sea was angry.

The voices were angry. The gift of opportunity had been given, the promise of sweet oblivion proffered. Death would have sponged away the unending pain and quieted the yammering, jabbering voices.

Yammering.

Jabbering.

Constant noise. Hot evil words.

*No more opportunities must be wasted. Death was a fickle suitor,
an impatient companion. "Travel with me now or stay in your miserable life. Freedom in death or confinement in life; you choose."*

The choice had been made.

N
Λ

"The cell phone is dead," Stanton said with disgust and surprise. He was seated at the gray navigation counter. He had tried
the radio, cell phone, and satellite phone to make a distress call,
but nothing worked.

"Everything is dead," Tenny said, putting away the mop she had
been using to clean up the mess left by the seasick teenagers. Jamie
lent some help but seasoned every effort with, "Eww, gross, gross."

"Every flashlight, radio, phone, nav system—everything is
dead," Tenny continued, "even my watch quit."

Stanton raised his arm to check his own wristwatch. The second hand still hadn't moved. "This is shaping up to be a real
mystery. All we need are aliens and a slick-looking UFO and we
could make a television special."

"This is the Bermuda Triangle, you know," Steve said.

"Yeah, I know," Stanton admitted, "but I'm sure there's a reasonable explanation for all this."

"You trying to convince us or yourself?" Steve asked.

"Anyone who will listen."

Richie and Tony stepped into the salon. They had spent the
last half hour examining the engines. "Any luck?" Richie asked.
His voice was steady and optimistic but his face and posture
revealed the weariness he felt.

"No," Stanton blurted. "I've tried every piece of electrical
equipment we have and not a single one works. Not even those
with their own batteries."

"We didn't fare any better," Richie admitted. "Tony and I examined both diesels and can't find any reason for them not to run. They should each be chugging out 105 horsepower for us, but they won't fire up."

"Diesels aren't my thing," Tony said, "but I can't see any reason for them being dead. I checked all the wires from ignition to glow plugs. Nothing, and I mean *nothing*. We both checked the batteries. All the connections are clean and locked down. It's weird, man. It's like something just sucked all the electrical power out of the boat."

"Dee dee dee dee . . ." John was standing in the doorway between the cockpit and salon. "Just like *The Twilight Zone*," he said. "So, fearless leader," he said to Stanton, "how are you going to get us home?"

"You're welcome to swim for it," Tony said.

"Nah," John said. "They brought us out here to scare us straight or save our souls or something. They're responsible for us. I think I'll let them figure out how to get us home."

"You got any ideas?" Tony asked. "Or do you just got lip?"

"I'm a lover, not a mechanic."

Jamie whispered something Stanton couldn't make out and he was glad for it. "We'll get you home, John," Stanton offered. "We just have to figure out the problem, and if we can't, then someone will come upon us soon. These waters are some of the busiest in the world."

"You don't find it odd," John said, "that we haven't seen any other sailboats or military ships? I haven't heard the sound of a motor, foghorn, or anything else. Why is that, Captain?"

"It's a big ocean, John. If it were too crowded, people would be bumping into each other. We'll see another craft soon."

"You had better hope so," John said, "because she's looking pretty sick to me." He pointed to the padded bench next to the salon table. M&M lay on her back. Stanton had assumed she was sleeping off her seasickness, but now he saw that her forehead was dotted with perspiration and that she was holding her stomach. He rose and approached but Tenny beat him there. He stared over Tenny's shoulder. M&M was pale and clearly in pain.

"What's the matter?" Tenny asked gently.

"My stomach hurts." Her voice was strained and tinted with a sob.

"How does it hurt?" Tenny inquired. "Do you feel like you need to throw up?"

She shook her head.

"Where does it hurt?" Stanton asked.

She pointed to her right side, just above her hip.

A sharp and terrible thought occurred to Stanton. To Tenny he said, "Raise her shirt a little."

Tenny reached for it but M&M pushed her hand away. "No. Leave me alone."

Stanton looked around the salon. Everyone had their gaze fixed on Mary Moss. "All right, everyone, we need some privacy here. Richie, take everyone topside. Tenny and I need to talk to M&M."

"You heard the skipper," Richie said. "Everybody outside."

When the cabin was empty of all but Tenny and M&M, Stanton kneeled beside the sick girl. "Mary, we need to see your stomach for a moment. Tenny is going to pull your shirt up, but just a little."

"No, I don't want her to."

"Mary," Stanton said firmly, "it needs to be done." M&M was wearing a teal T-shirt with an orange cartoon drawing of Garfield the cat. He nodded at Tenny, who gently took the bottom hem of the garment and raised it just underneath the girl's first rib. Her jeans had been unsnapped. Stanton saw her smooth milky skin. He also saw a yellowing blue bruise the size of a grapefruit on her left side. It was at least a week old, Stanton judged, but not old enough to have escaped notice. Tenny looked at him.

"Show me where it hurts," Stanton said. Again Mary pointed at her right side, a few inches above the hipbone. She looked frail and skinny, almost anorexic. He reached forward. "I'm going to press gently—"

"No! Don't touch me!" She tried to get up.

"Stay still," Tenny ordered. "No one is going to hurt you." Mary settled down.

"Can Tenny touch you?" Stanton asked.

"I . . . I guess so."

Stanton nodded and said, "Go ahead. Press lightly over the area where she said it hurt. See if it feels warm."

Tenny did as instructed. "The skin feels normal."

"Press a little harder, then quickly release the pressure."

Tenny did.

"Ow!" M&M cried. "Don't. Stop. It hurts."

"Okay," Stanton said. "We won't do that anymore." To Tenny he added, "Feel her forehead. Is she feverish?"

Tenny placed the back of her hand on the girl's damp forehead. "Yes. A little."

Stanton inhaled deeply, then blew out a long stream of air. "Mary. There's a bruise on the left side of your stomach. How did you get that?"

"I don't know."

That was doubtful, Stanton decided. The bruise was large and looked deep. "How long have you had it?"

"I don't know."

"Mary," Tenny said, "we're here to help you. Did you fall into something?"

"I said I don't know!" A tear squeezed from her closed eye and trickled down her face until it was stopped by her delicate brown hair.

"Okay," Stanton said. "We're done." He watched as Tenny pulled the cotton top back down, concealing the bruise. "Would you feel more comfortable in one of the cabins?"

"I don't know . . . I guess so."

"Okay, Tenny is going to help you. I'm going to see what's in our med kit. Maybe it has something for pain. In the meantime try and rest as much as you can."

"Okay."

To Tenny he added, "Once she's settled in, come see me."

"Aye, aye, sir," Tenny said. Stanton could see the concern etched into her face. She was thinking the same thing he was.

Stanton moved from the salon to the cockpit. Jamie was once again seated at the exterior table, as was Steve. Tony stood nearby. "Where's John?"

"Up front," Tony said. "Probably looking at his reflection in the water."

"What's wrong with M&M?" Jamie asked. Stanton heard a hint of concern in an otherwise cold and detached question.

"I'm not sure," Stanton admitted, then walked aft to the port helm, where Richie stood at the wheel, his hands to his side.

Richie spoke first. "It seems odd to be standing in the steering station with nothing to steer. We are truly dead in the water, Skipper. No engines, no electricity, and no wind. A butterfly could create more breeze than we have here." He shook his head. "Tell me something, Cap. You ever been at sea when there wasn't at least a small breeze?"

"No. Never."

"This isn't right," Richie said. His normal jocular spirit had given in to concern. "I've seen some weird weather before, storms, fog, rain—I've even seen a waterspout, like a tornado at sea—but I've never, never seen anything like this. I mean, look at the sky. I've never seen a sky like that."

The cottage cheese sky had lightened another shade but had taken on a new texture that reminded Stanton of a television screen filled with static and white noise. It roiled and moved as if alive. "The clouds don't look normal, that's for sure," Stanton admitted.

"Normal? They don't even look like clouds. And this fog or mist or whatever it is, it's almost tangible, yet it's like it's not even there. You can feel a fog; even a dry fog is composed of water vapor, right? Then why can't we feel this fog?"

"I don't know," Stanton said. He looked at the deck. It was dry—bone dry.

"Ah, you noticed that too. We were covered in water, Skipper. It would have evaporated eventually but not this fast. It's been less than an hour since the storm stopped, best I can tell anyway, and all the water that was sloshing around on the deck is gone. I even checked the mainsail, which I know should be wet; it's as dry as overcooked toast."

"I've never seen anything like this," Stanton said. "I've never even read about anything like this."

"I've got more questions," Richie went on. "Why is it light at all? When we were in the storm, time seemed to stop, but that's to be expected. Every second in a storm seems like an hour, but I know, I mean I know, Skipper, that we didn't fight that storm all night. You said it yourself: three, maybe four hours tops. Even if I'm way off base and we were pounded for six hours, it should still be dark, but it's not. Unless that gale pushed us all the way across the Atlantic, we should be stumbling around in the night."

"I have no answers, Richie. I can't explain the engine loss, and I sure can't explain why every battery on board is as dead as a stone."

"If this were some plywood tub and our equipment had been purchased from Uncle Barnacle's Bottom of the Barrel Boat Shop, then maybe I could believe it. But this is a state-of-the-art craft, handpicked and customized. It doesn't get better than this. The only way everything could die on us like this is sabotage, but that's out of the question because—"

"Because you, Tenny, and I checked everything twice before we left," Stanton said. "Someone might be able to trade out a few batteries, like those in the lanterns and maybe even the cell and satellite phones, but some pieces of equipment have sealed cases to make them watertight. You'd have to tear them up to yank the batteries out."

"John's mean enough to do something like this," Richie reasoned, "and Tony has the mechanical skills to make it possible. And Steve . . . well, Steve is smart enough to figure it all out, but it doesn't fit. They might have motive—although I don't know what that would be—they even have means, but they certainly haven't had opportunity.

"And even if that were possible," Richie continued, "it wouldn't explain why our ten storage batteries have stopped producing power. How would they pull that off? I suppose it could be done by someone with a sick enough mind, but I can't imagine how."

Stanton was at a loss to explain their situation. "We have another problem."

"M&M?" Richie guessed.

"Yes. She's bad and I think she's going to get worse."

"Hey, guys," a voice said behind Stanton. He turned to see Tony, Steve, and Jamie. "We need to talk," Tony said.

"I'm listening," Stanton said.

Tony stepped forward. "Is this some kind of test or something?"

Stanton was puzzled. "A test? I don't follow."

"Oh, come on," Jamie said. "I mean, this is all pretty whacked—the storm, the weather, the batteries getting fried or whatever happened to them."

"I can tell you that this is no test," Richie said. "Controlling the weather is a little beyond our reach."

"Then what's going on?" Tony asked. "There's nothing wrong with the engines but they don't work."

"The truth is," Stanton said, "we don't know. We're as puzzled as you. Don't be afraid, though. We'll figure something out."

"We're not afraid," Tony replied. "We're . . . we're something, but not afraid."

"Concerned," Steve interjected. "Something weird has happened and we're concerned you're going to send us to our rooms or something while you try and figure out the problem. We think you should include us. We're not stupid. We might even be able to help."

Stanton raised an eyebrow. Yesterday they wouldn't talk to each other; now three of the five had teamed up to make demands. "I have never thought you were stupid, and I'm happy for any help I can get. I don't know what is going on, but we need to figure it out and soon. If you're serious about helping, then I welcome it."

"We're serious," Tony said.

"Is that true for all of you?"

They nodded their agreement.

"What about John?"

Tony grimaced. "Who knows about him? He lives on his own planet. I wouldn't turn my back on him."

"Let's keep the door open on that one," Stanton advised. "He may come around."

"Fill us in," Tony said. "We know about the storm and we know the engines and electricity are out."

"And the mast is broken," Steve added.

"That's right," Stanton agreed. "All our radios, phones, navigation systems, and beacons are out of service. We don't know why."

"What's wrong with M&M?" Jamie asked. "She looked pretty sick, and I mean more than seasick."

"I was just getting ready to tell Richie about that," Stanton said. "I think she may have appendicitis."

"Really?" Tony asked. "That's bad, isn't it ... I mean, it can be bad."

"I'm afraid so. If we were back in Miami, it would be easy enough to get her the help she needs." Stanton looked up and saw Tenny approaching. "How is she?"

Tenny looked at the teenagers, then back to Stanton. The question was written on her face.

"We're in this together," Stanton informed her. "They want to be part of the solution."

"She's resting. The bed is more comfortable and since the boat is stable, she's not as sick. I'm afraid she's a little dehydrated." Tenny paused, then added, "It's her appendix, isn't it?"

"Most likely," Stanton replied. "I had the same symptoms when I was twenty-two. A quick surgery later I was good as new."

"But there are no doctors here," Jamie said. "Can't appendicitis kill you?"

"If the appendix bursts, it can," Stanton said. "A ruptured appendix leads to an infection called peritonitis. That can be deadly. Sometimes, though, the inflamed appendix can settle down on its own. That's what I'm praying for."

Jamie looked stunned. "So she may die?"

"Not if I can help it," Stanton said immediately. "This is one place you can help, Jamie. M&M is a little sensitive about being touched. She seems more comfortable about Tenny. I assume that's because she's a woman."

"She's been abused," Jamie said matter-of-factly. Stanton immediately thought of the aged bruise. "It's obvious."

"Why obvious?" Richie asked.

"Oh please," Jamie retorted. "She's quiet, standoffish, dresses like a bag lady to make herself unattractive, doesn't like to be touched, seldom eats. I bet you tried to touch her and she went ballistic."

The last comment was addressed to Stanton. He had rationalized the behavior as a young woman's shyness around an older man.

"She doesn't dress like a bag lady," Steve said.

"Get real," Jamie chided. "Wake up and smell the cappuccino."

"I think she's right, Skipper," Tenny said just above a whisper, as if her voice would filter down into the cabin where M&M lay. "I'm no expert on this, but I've known sexually abused women and they sometimes act that way."

"You may be right," Stanton said, feeling certain that Jamie had hit the nail on the head. A fire began to rage in him, a fire fueled by the knowledge that came to him like a slap from a sandpaper glove. The thought of such an atrocity perpetrated on someone as young and vulnerable as Mary infuriated him. His heart marched double-time, his neck tightened, and his stomach pulled into a tight knot. The only outward expression of fury he allowed himself was the momentary shutting of his eyes.

"I bet it's her old man," Jamie said as if discussing a school dance. "It usually is. Do you remember what she said when you were forcing us to introduce ourselves? 'My mother thought I needed to get out of the house for a while,' or something like that. I bet her old man is a perv."

The comment stoked the fire that was boiling Stanton's blood. If Jamie was right, he would make sure the navy and the police knew about the matter. The offender's house of cards would fall around his ears, even if Stanton had to knock it down himself. "As horrible as that is—assuming it's true—we have to set it aside for now. First things first: we have to get her to a hospital, which means getting her off the boat."

"How?" Steve asked. "We have no radio, no power, and no wind. I'm not a sailor but I've got a feeling we're stuck here."

"We keep trying to get our communications to work," Stanton replied. "We listen for passing ships or other boats. We also listen for aircraft. Richie, let's get flares ready. Fire one off. There may be someone close and we can't see them because of the fog. The others we keep ready for when we do hear someone."

"Got it."

"Is there any way to strengthen the mast?" Stanton asked. "If we do get a breeze, I want to be able to use it."

"I'll think of something," Richie said with a confidence Stanton didn't feel.

"Jamie, are you willing to keep an eye on M&M? I think she'll relate to you better than to any of us. It would free up Tenny to help Richie with the boat."

"I guess, but I ain't no nurse."

"You don't have to be. Just be there for her. Be a friend. Lend an ear. Let me know if she gets worse."

"What do we do?" Tony asked.

"You help Richie. I don't know how he's going to strengthen the mast, but I know he's going to. He'll need someone who knows how to use his hands. And if you can think of a way to get the engines going again, you'll be my hero. Steve, you're with me; let's see if we can't jury-rig a radio."

Stanton turned to Richie. "I don't suppose the med kit has antibiotics."

Richie shook his head. "We have a trauma kit that has some painkillers, bandages, and the like, but no heavy-hitting antibiotics, not what you'd need for peritonitis."

"Then let's pray we're successful getting under way. Mary's life may depend on it."

Sargasso Sea

S tanton snapped the plastic back of the emergency beacon in place and refastened it with its factory screws. He frowned as he did so. He had examined it thoroughly. Removing the batteries and looking for corrosion, he searched for loose wires, but unlike the electronics of two decades ago, there were very few wires, just a circuit board that appeared intact, as if it had just come straight from the factory. He and Steve had checked not only the emergency beacon but also every radio. Nothing worked. They had systematically looked at every battery on board, exchanging them when possible, but all were as dead as driftwood.

It was beyond logic, out of reach of reason. Such things could not fail in unison. He had even caught himself hoping to find signs of sabotage. While the thought of a saboteur back on shore or even on board was unsettling, it would at least be an explanation that Stanton could wrap his mind around. He found no indication that the equipment had been tampered with. The waterproof seal on the beacon had been in place until he cracked it open to examine its electronic guts.

"Now what?" Steve asked. There was a tinge of fear in the question. The young man was bright, perhaps the brightest mind on the *Tern About*, and it didn't take a genius or a seasoned sailor to know that the world had, in an instant, gone wacky, leaving them as powerless as a cork in an undulating sea—if the ocean were undulating instead of lying flat like an undisturbed pond.

"We've done all we can here, Steve," Stanton said. "The electronics have no obvious problems, other than the fact that they don't work."

"I've seen electronics go bad but never a bunch all at once," Steve complained. "I thought you were onto something, linking several batteries together to try and get enough juice to make a quick radio call."

"It was an act of a desperate man," Stanton admitted. He and Steve had taken several batteries from the flashlights, joined their contact points with wire cannibalized from one of the larger lanterns, and held them in place with medical tape taken from the trauma kit. It failed.

"You're not giving up, are you?" Steve wondered.

"The phrase isn't part of my vocabulary," Stanton replied. "But this is a dead end." He rose from the leather seat and stepped away from the navigation center, where he and Steve had been working, using the center's counter as a workbench. "Let's go topside and see how Richie and Tenny are doing with the mast." Without waiting for a response, Stanton turned and headed for the door to the cockpit. Steve followed a step behind.

Things outside had changed slightly. The sky was a shade brighter but as opaque as clam chowder and about the same color. The ocean was as flat as a painter's pallet, and the water remained dark and foreboding. Any darker and it would seem they were afloat in a giant well of India ink. The air was as motionless as the inside of a tomb. The scene unsettled Stanton to his sailor's core but he pretended not to notice. Instead he strolled through the cockpit onto the deck and around the streamlined, swept-back salon cabin. Instinctively he reached for the coated lifeline that ran the perimeter of the boat. The gesture was meant to steady him on a constantly swaying deck, but the deck didn't move beyond its reaction to his weight.

The boat's mast rose to the sky just in front of the salon's forward windows, a graphite gray tower that poked seventy-five and a half feet into the air, a finger attempting to tickle the unhappy heavens. Stanton traced the sleek form until his eyes rested on the weather instruments securely fastened to the top. The wind vane was unmoving and the anemometer was paralyzed in place, its spinning cups, which measured wind speed, frozen. It was a sensitive instrument that could dance in the slightest breeze, but the atmosphere played no music for the instrument to perform to. The air was dead.

Three people stood at the base of the mast: Richie, Tenny, and Tony, each staring down at the result of their handiwork. Forward, standing at the port pulpit, stood John, staring into the distance. He hadn't moved since Stanton saw him there ninety minutes ago.

"How goes it?" Stanton asked as he and Steve joined the small group.

"It goes," Richie said. "We had to get creative, since we're hamstrung by the lack of tools and building supplies."

Stanton looked at the base of the mast, where he had seen the white line that indicated the stress fracture the mast had suffered in the storm. The damage was now hidden by teak slats and a tightly wound halyard. The rope and wood slats made Stanton think of a splint for a broken arm. It seemed an apt image.

"Are those what I think they are?" Stanton asked, directing his attention forward to the pulpit areas, where once teak lounge chairs had been bolted to the deck.

"Yup," Richie said. "We won't be sunning ourselves on the way home."

"That would require sunshine," Tony said. "We haven't seen much of that over the last couple of hours."

"It was Tenny's idea," Richie continued. "We dismantled the chairs and used the narrow slats as supports for the base of the mast, wrapping them with the rope. I think it looks pretty good."

"Ingenious," Stanton said. "Good thinking, Tenny. Will it work?"

"In this weather?" Tenny said. "Sure. But then again, in this weather bubble gum would have worked."

"How about under sail?" Stanton pressed. "When we get some wind, will the mast hold until we get to Miami?"

"Depends on the wind," Richie said. "We'll have to keep her reefed to keep the sails low enough to minimize the moment arm."

"Moment arm?" Steve said. "What's that?"

"It's an engineering term," Stanton explained. "The mast is almost seven stories high and when something pushes at the top of it, its natural tendency is to tip forward, pivoting on its base. The twisting force at the base can become enormous. That's why the mast cracked low, near the base, and not higher up."

"So if a wind comes up and we raise the sails, that force is transferred down the mast and into the boat," Steve said thoughtfully.

"Exactly," Richie said. "That's the problem. The damage to the mast is very low, except at the base. To keep the forces down, we'll reef the sail, keeping the pressures away from the top, where the twisting force originates."

"Okay," Stanton said, "bottom line, guys: if we get into another blow, what happens to our mast?"

Richie shook his head. "I don't know why it's still standing. It shouldn't have fractured in the first place. This is the top end in materials design. It should have weathered the storm better than it did."

"And . . . ," Stanton prompted.

"Our patch job will hold up for now, but in a strong wind with sails up . . . well, what we've done won't be much help."

"All right," Stanton said. "Then we pray for a gentle wind."

"You might want to pray for the engines too," Tony said. "I checked them out again. They're in perfect order, the best I can tell. The batteries are useless."

"I take it you had no luck with the electronics," Tenny said to Stanton.

"Same problem there. Dead batteries. I have no idea why."

"Guys," a distant voice said.

"I've studied naval history since high school," Stanton said. "I've never come across anything like this."

"So we'll be famous when we get back," Steve said with a forced smile.

"If we get back," Tony said. His expression was dour.

"Um, guys," the voice said. It was John. "You might want to see this."

Stanton had trouble understanding the words, since John continued to face forward, sending his voice out over the ocean and not at them.

"Speak up, John," Stanton said, projecting like a man calling across a football field.

John turned and pointed in the direction he had been staring. "I said you might want to see this. I think we have company."

Stanton moved from the mast toward John. As he did, he gazed through the mist, which seemed to thicken in the distance. At first he saw nothing and assumed John was passing the time playing the prankster. He expected to hear him say, "Made you look!" But he didn't.

"Where?" Stanton asked, straining his eyes.

"There, man." John pointed again. "In the fog. It's big. It looks like an iceberg."

"Not many icebergs off the coast of Florida," Stanton commented.

"Does the sky look like we're off the coast of Miami?" John shot back. "Come on, man, you know we're in deep—"

"I know the situation we're in, Mr. Hays," Stanton said. "And your point is well taken." Stanton narrowed his eyes, as if the act would improve his ability to see through the sickly fog that hung over the water. It took several moments before his older eyes could see what John had spied.

It was big and pale and slow. It seemed to be moving toward them, crawling through the water, angled toward the *Tern About*'s stern. He could determine no color and only a general shape. "You're right," Stanton said. "It does look like an iceberg."

"Told you."

"But it's not," Stanton added. "Whatever it is, it has too many straight and vertical edges to be something natural." He turned to the others, who remained huddled around the mast. "Richie, I need the binocs."

"Binoculars coming right up." With no hesitation Richie bounded down the boat to the cockpit, where he disappeared from Stanton's sight. Fifteen seconds later he reappeared with a large pair of binoculars in one hand and a smaller pair in the other. He moved effortlessly along the deck until he joined them at the port pulpit. "Here you go, Skipper. What are we looking at?"

"I don't know; let's find out." Stanton raised the large glasses to his eyes and rolled the focus knob with his index finger until the distant object became as clear as he could expect in the foggy conditions. Nestled in the gray-white mist was something far more substantial. He had been right about the straight lines indicating something manmade. The object in view was huge.

"Is that what I think it is?" Richie whispered.

"I think so," Stanton replied.

"What?" John asked impatiently. "What do you see? What's out there?"

"A ship," Stanton said but he offered nothing more. There was little else to offer, since the vessel was wrapped in the foggy shroud.

"A big ship," Richie added. "Here." He handed the small binoculars to John. "You spotted it; you deserve a look-see."

Stanton kept his sights trained on the looming dark form. "How far do you make her to be?" he asked Richie.

"A hundred yards tops, Skipper. It's hard to tell in this soup. If the fog would lift, I'd have a better idea."

"I make her to be less than that but not much," Stanton said. "She's moving but not fast."

"More like a caterpillar," John remarked. "It looks weird."

"What do you mean, weird?" Stanton asked.

"I don't know. It looks different than other ships I've seen."

"Let me have another look, John," Richie said. There was eagerness in his words.

Stanton lowered his glasses and watched Richie raise his. He waited for the sailor's reaction. "I can't be seeing what I'm seeing."

"Um, Skipper," Richie muttered. "I can see it a little better and . . . well, this is more up your alley. I can't tell you what I'm seeing. It's an odd design."

"It's odd because it's old . . . very old." Stanton raised his glasses again. "I can only see the bow and the anchors but unless I've lost my mind, we're going to see something even more amazing."

"I don't care how old it is," John said. "At least we'll be able to get off this tub."

"At the very least we can get Mary help," Richie added.

"I hope so," Stanton said.

"You don't sound too confident," Richie commented.

"I take it you haven't noticed." Stanton lowered his glasses and turned to Richie, who continued to fix his gaze on the behemoth emerging from the fog.

"Noticed what?"

"What do you hear?" Stanton asked. Richie pulled the binoculars from his eyes and looked at Stanton.

"Nothing."

"Precisely."

"So what?" John asked. "So it's a quiet ship."

Stanton pursed his lips. "I hope you're right, buddy," he said. "But a ship that big is driven by large engines. We should hear something. There are no crew sounds either."

"Maybe they're too far away for us to hear anything," John said, furrowing his brow.

"Maybe," Stanton admitted. "Richie, let's give them a blast from the air horn. Also, bring the flare gun forward. Let's see if we can get someone's attention."

Richie wasted no time. Handing the binoculars to John, he moved aft and then reappeared a minute later with two objects in hand. The first looked like a large can of shaving cream with a blue horn attached to the top. Stanton easily recognized the SeaSense air horn. It was a can of compressed air that bellowed an eardrum-piercing blast which could be heard a mile away.

"Shall I?" Richie asked.

"Watch your ears, John. Let her fly, Richie."

In the muffled environment in which they had floated for the last few hours, the air horn sounded like the sonorous call of some dinosaur. The noise of it rolled along the flat sea. Richie sounded it again, then waited for a reply. Nothing. He sounded several more blasts, then waited. Again nothing.

"I know they can hear that," John said. "Why aren't they responding?"

"I'm going to put up a distress flare," Stanton said. The flare gun was bright marine orange with a black handle. Several flares—a white nonemergency flare and three red distress flares—were attached to the handle of the gun by a metal bandolier. Stanton loaded one of the twelve-gauge red flares into the breech and snapped it shut. Stretching out his arm and aiming high and in front of the ship, he pulled the trigger. Instantly the flare was airborne and burning, leaving a trail of red smoke. Six seconds later the flare blinked out. Stanton waited for a response: the sounding of a horn, a sailor's voice calling, "Ahoy!"—anything that would indicate that their signal had been seen. All he heard was his own breathing.

"They can't just leave us out here," John snapped. "Aren't they required to help? Isn't that like a Coast Guard or navy or international law? They can't just cruise by."

"I don't think they're cruising by," Stanton said. "I don't think they're operating under power."

"What do you mean?" John asked.

Richie answered, "They're just as dead in the water as we are."

"I'm not buying that," John protested. "They're moving. Look, you can see they're closer."

"You're right," Stanton said, "but as you noted, they're moving as slow as a caterpillar."

"So what? Maybe we're closer to shore than we realize. The storm could have moved us toward land as easily as away. Maybe they're moving slowly because they don't want to run aground."

"Good point," Stanton said, "but I don't think that's the case. I think their engines are out, like ours."

"So you're going to give up," John said.

"Oh no," Stanton replied. "I'm not giving up. As soon as I get a better look at her, I'll decide what to do next." He raised the binoculars again. The ship had moved ten yards closer. If it stayed its course, it would pass within twenty yards of the *Tern About*.

All Stanton had to do was wait.

Minutes before, J. D. Stanton had been pressing down a rising sense of disquiet. He made a point to appear calm, confident, and self-assured to the others; inside the vault of his mind he was disturbed, uncomfortable, and on edge. Their situation was not a worst-case scenario. They were still afloat, had plenty of food and water, and couldn't be more than ten or fifteen miles from shore—at least he couldn't see how they could be any farther out. His logical mind told him that all was well. Sure, they had some problems to deal with. The loss of power and electricity made the voyage interesting, but it could be dealt with. Sooner or later someone would come along and lend a hand. The greatest concern was M&M. Stanton could not be certain that her appendix was indeed inflamed, but all the signs were there. He knew that these things sometimes reversed themselves, but not often. In a few hours she could be feeling much better. Of course, he also knew things could get worse, much worse. A ruptured appendix was nothing to dismiss.

This last concern was the one that ate at him the most. Drifting for a few days might be a little uncomfortable but it would be manageable. They had food to feed eight people for more than a week. Some of it required refrigeration and would go bad, since the electric refrigerator could no longer function. They would first eat as much of the perishables as they could. After that they would turn to the canned and preserved foods. He could not imagine a circumstance in which they ran out of food.

Water could be a problem. The *Tern About* came equipped with a Sea Recovery electric water maker capable of making seawater drinkable, to the tune of thirty-two gallons an hour. The problem was that it was electric and nothing electric was operating.

Water and Mary Moss. Those were the immediate concerns, and since they had over a hundred gallons in two onboard water tanks, they were fine for now. Of course, showers were out for a time, but that was a small price to pay.

Water and Mary. Those two needs pressed upon Stanton like an unrelenting vise. Surely someone would come along before water became critical, but Mary ... who could know? The thought of the abuse she had endured wrenched his gut. His emotions swung wildly from seething anger at the perpetrator to a deep, icy ache of sorrow on her behalf.

When the bow of the large ship had first pushed through the fog, Stanton felt a rush of relief. A ship that size would have some medical help on board—if not a doctor, then certainly a crewman trained in shipboard medicine. The weight that had come to rest on his shoulders evaporated. He could feel it leave as if the load had been nothing more than a pile of feathers and leaves, now blown away by the breeze of certain rescue.

That was when the ship first appeared. That was when the fog-veiled bow implied rescue. That was when he saw the approaching vessel as a solution. Instead it proved to be another mystery, and Stanton's plate was already overloaded with enigmas.

He stood near the damaged metal rail that defined the port pulpit. He leaned over the rail—careful not to press his weight against it—as if doing so would make the binoculars pressed to his eyes stronger, able to pierce the misty curtain with X-ray-like power.

Slowly the hulking mass of steel approached. There were no sounds of engines, no voices of crew members snapping to their duties, not even the muffled noise of a steel bow pressing back the water by its forward progress. It was as if Stanton had suddenly gone deaf. But he hadn't. He could hear his heartbeat and his uneven breathing.

"Why don't they answer?" Tenny called from her place by the mast.

"I don't know," Stanton admitted. For the last five minutes they had sounded the air horn repeatedly and received no reply. Before them was a ship as silent as a coffin in a tomb.

"Sargasso Sea," Richie said. "Do you know anything about it?"

"I do," Stanton replied, then quickly added, "but I'm not buying it. Not for a minute. It's nothing more than tales of superstitious sailors. Besides, we're too far away."

John had remained close, as if the ship were his discovery and therefore he could make claim to it as his own. "Sargrassy Sea? What's that?"

"Sargasso," Richie corrected. "It's named after a type of brown seaweed. *Sargassum natans*—brown gulfweed."

"So," John said, "it's got a lotta wet weeds."

"It has more than that, laddie," Richie said, affecting an Irish brogue. "The waters of the Sargasso Sea are calmer than the rest of the Atlantic, and the ocean is saltier there than anyplace else. Some think the fabled *Atlantis* went down there, and there are many stories of lost vessels, ghost ships, and crews who abandon their boats for no reasons."

"You mean, the waters are weird like here?" John pressed.

Stanton lowered his glasses and turned to Richie, offering a disapproving smile. "The waters are calmer because the Sargasso Sea is bordered by four major currents: the Gulf Stream, the North Atlantic Current, the Canary Current, and the North

Equatorial Current. The currents flow clockwise around the region. The waters are saltier because the evaporation rate is higher there and the rainfall less. As far as missing and abandoned ships, you can find stories about them in every ocean and even the Great Lakes." Stanton returned to monitoring the approaching ship. "Besides, the Sargasso Sea is a long way from here. Unless the storm blew us hundreds of miles northeast of where we were, we're probably safe."

"Just trying to pass the time," Richie said. "I like a good ghost story."

"I don't believe in ghosts," Stanton said.

"I don't either, but I still like ghost stories."

Stanton had to admit to a certain fascination with the subject. Sailors told wonderful tales of mysterious adventures, bizarre storms, and of course ghost ships. The hulk before them was the perfect candidate for such stories. Still, he was a man who preferred simple, reasonable answers, although on two prior occasions he had faced the impossible. For now, he could not force himself to think in those terms. Until the supernatural presented itself, he would pursue natural explanations.

"Someone needs to talk to the captain about his maritime manners," Stanton said. "Give them a few more blasts."

Richie raised the air horn and pressed the trigger. Three long blasts that sounded like something from *Jurassic Park* skipped across the distance. The *Tern About* waited silently for a reply to its doleful cry. None came.

Stanton could see more of the ship now. He was thankful for one thing: it was moving so slowly that it would leave very little wake to buffet the catamaran. He studied the ship's lines, looking for a name or a standard by which to identify her. Minutes slogged by at glacial speeds and Stanton's impatience grew. He felt like a child forced to open a Christmas present with a tiny pair of tweezers. He could not make the ship move faster and he could not move the catamaran closer. All he could do was wait and hope that the vessel didn't come to a full stop.

The ship moved toward them at an angle. All Stanton could see was the port side of the bow and more of that side of the ship as it inched closer. He could make out the stem, the upright leading edge of the bow. It was slightly convex, the ocean edge protruding more than the edge at the main deck. A single, large anchor was fitted tightly to the ship, tucked in a cavity designed to keep the heavy object from impacting the hull during sailing. A pair of lifelines ran along the main deck.

Two lines of portholes ran the length of the ship, at least as far as Stanton could see. There was something unusual about the ship, but Stanton couldn't put his finger on it. Ships came in various sizes and configurations, but function dictated their basic lines. Through centuries of development, marine engineers had learned and implemented many things. Stanton had seen hundreds of ships but this one was somehow different.

The dense fog released more of the ship. As he watched it slowly emerge, Stanton saw something that made his gut twist. "This can't be," he said.

"What?" Richie asked, raising his own binoculars.

"Yeah, what?" John repeated. "What do you see?"

"A gun," Stanton stated flatly. "A very big gun."

N
Λ

It had taken another thirty minutes for the full length of the unexpected vessel to show itself, as if the ship were embarrassed to be uncloaked, to have its hull laid naked before hungry eyes.

"Unbelievable," Stanton said.

"More like impossible," Richie corrected. "Am I seeing what I think I'm seeing?"

"What?" John asked. "What is it? It just looks like a big boat."

"Hey, Skipper," Tenny cried. "Am I hallucinating or is that a battleship?"

"If you are, then we all are," Stanton shouted back.

"Okay," John said. "So it's a battleship. So what? That's as good as anything else."

"It's not just any battleship," Stanton explained. "It's an old battleship."

"You mean, like from your day?" John snipped.

"No, wise guy," Richie said. "Old like a hundred years ago."

"What?"

Stanton was looking at a gray-white battleship, the kind that had ceased sailing three-quarters of a century earlier. "It's a dreadnought." He turned and made his way to the mast to get a different angle on the ship.

"What's a dreadnought?" John asked, following him.

Once Stanton, John, and Richie had joined the others, Stanton saw that Jamie had come topside. She answered the question in his eyes. "She's sleeping. I don't think she's in as much pain as before. She's not puking anymore, either." It was a direct answer if not a delicate one. "What is that?" She asked, pointing at the battleship.

"It's a very old battleship," Stanton said. "Ships like her were called dreadnoughts, after the first of their kind. If I didn't know better, I'd say that was the original *Dreadnought*."

"Maybe it is," Tony suggested.

"No way," Stanton said. "The *Dreadnought* was built in 1906. Her hull was laid down in Portsmouth dockyard in England. She was a remarkable boat. They built her in a year and a day. She was a historic ship, but that didn't keep her from being dismantled in 1923."

"She doesn't look dismantled to me," Steve said.

"That's the point," Stanton explained. "That can't be the *Dreadnought*. It must be one of her sister ships." He raised his glasses again and scanned the hull. The ship was closer now, and without the gossamer veil of fog obscuring his vision, Stanton quickly found what he was looking for, on the port side, just above the anchor: HMS ARCHER. "The *Archer*," he said.

"You know her?" Richie asked.

"No," Stanton admitted.

"I thought you taught this stuff at the Naval Academy," John said.

"I do, but I don't know this ship." He paused. "There's a rumor that gets bounced around among naval historians, that there were really two original dreadnoughts built. The man behind the ship was First Sea Lord Admiral John Fisher—Sir John Fisher. He proved that a big battleship could be built in short order. The *Dreadnought* was that ship. His purpose was to have a ship with guns all the same caliber—in this case, twelve-inch guns. It made spotting and firing much more accurate. It would be several years before America, Germany, and others caught up. Some say Admiral Fisher hedged his bets by building an identical ship at a rival shipyard—maybe Devonport or one of the other ten shipyards in the British Isles—but building it much more slowly to avoid mistakes. He built the *Dreadnought* in a year and a day but its twin supposedly didn't arrive until months later."

"You think the *Archer* is that ship?" Richie asked.

"I don't know what to think," Stanton said. "There's no extant record of her construction, service, or destruction. It's just a rumor."

"But why would the admiral do that?" Tenny asked.

"Lots of reasons, I suppose. One might have to do with the pending war with Germany. The *Dreadnought* gave the Brits a huge lead. Imagine the psychological advantage if the Germans were to suddenly discover that there were two such ships and more on the way."

"So others were built?" Steve said.

"Only one dreadnought—at least officially. There were other battleships: the *Bellerophon*, the *Superb*, the *Temeraire*, and others. The Brits went on to develop the Invincible class of battle cruisers. Three ships—the *Invincible*, the *Indomitable*, and the *Inflexible*—were as heavily armed as the battleship but were also faster. They carried less armor than the *Dreadnought*. That gave them greater speed but less protection."

"So what's a century-old battleship doing out here?" Tenny wondered.

Stanton shrugged. "Now, that is the twenty-four-thousand-dollar question, isn't it? Maybe she's a floating museum."

"Or a movie prop," Steve suggested.

"She's too well built to be a movie prop," Stanton said. "I think we're looking at the real thing. Some history books are going to have to be rewritten."

"What are those things on the side?" Tony asked. "They look like poles dangling against the hull."

Stanton studied the objects. Thirteen "poles" ran at a forty-five-degree angle from the line of the main deck to just above the waterline. They looked like a fence pushed to the point of collapsing. "Booms," Stanton answered. "They're booms for the torpedo nets."

"You can stop a torpedo with a net?" Tony said. "That doesn't seem likely."

"It isn't now," Stanton explained. "A hundred years ago torpedoes were relatively new. It was thought that if you extended a steel-mesh net down and away from the ship and sunk it to the depth of the keel, then torpedoes would blow up the net and not the hull. It wasn't long before the drive mechanisms of torpedoes became too powerful for a net to stop them. The torpedo nets were abandoned a few years after the *Dreadnought* was built. You can see them rolled up along the edge of the main deck."

"So that means this is from the earliest days of the battleship," Richie said.

"That's right," Stanton said. "Who would keep such a ship afloat? The money needed just to keep her paint fresh would break most budgets."

"The real question is," Tenny said, "why are they ignoring us?"

"Maybe they're all sleeping below," Steve suggested.

"Someone would be on watch," Stanton said. "Something is wrong with her. There's no smoke from the stacks. Ships of that day were steam-driven. They used coal to fire the boilers, which turned the steam engines. Unless she operates under some other kind of power, she should be blowing smoke into the air. And if they have refitted her with diesel, then why isn't she moving faster? She can't be doing more than two or three knots—if that."

"You think she's dead in the water?" Richie asked.

"Yes," Stanton replied.

"Then why is she moving at all?" John wondered.

"Momentum," Tenny said. "She's big. She's gotta displace . . . what . . . ten thousand tons or more."

"Eighteen thousand tons," Stanton corrected. "In her heyday she would have been crewed by over seven hundred men. No matter what they use her for now, there has to be someone on board. We're going to try and contact her one more time. Hit the air horn, Richie."

He did. Jamie and Steve put their fingers in their ears. After three more blasts Stanton cupped his hands around his mouth, inhaled deeply, and called, "Ahoy, ship off our port bow. Ahoy!"

Nothing.

"Ahoy, *Archer*, this is the *Tern About*. We are in need of assistance."

Nothing. Stanton set his jaw tight and mumbled, "That's it." He turned and started for the stern.

"Where you going, Skipper?" Richie called.

"To crash a party."

Aboard

Whoa, whoa, hang on, Skipper." Richie was on Stanton's heels. "What do you mean, you're going to crash the party?"

"I'm going over to the *Archer*." Stanton spoke as if he were announcing a quick trip to the hardware store. He moved past the salon and into the cockpit, opened one of the lockers, and retrieved a life vest.

"You can't be serious," Richie said, then added, "sir."

"I'm dead serious," Stanton barked as he handed the PFD to Richie. "Put this on." He removed another vest. "You're going with me."

"And how are we getting there?"

"The Zodiac, of course."

"The engine doesn't run, Skipper. Remember? We tried every motor on board, including the Zodiac's. Nothing works."

"That's why you're going with me," Stanton replied, buckling the nylon straps of the vest across his chest. "I can't paddle that thing alone." Stanton gave a quick look at the inflatable dinghy that rested securely on its hydraulic lift. Richie was right: the forty-horsepower Yamaha outboard motor was as lifeless as an anchor.

"No disrespect intended, Skipper, but have you thought this through?"

"What's going on?" Tenny asked as she and the others joined them in the cockpit. "You're not thinking of—"

"I am," Stanton said, "and to answer Richie's question, yes, I have thought it through."

"I don't see the logic," Richie said. "We can't just stroll over there because they don't answer our hail. For all we know, their engines and power are as dead as ours. She's drifting."

"I am aware of that, Richie," Stanton said, "but this needs to be done."

"Why?" Tony asked. "It seems kinda stupid to me."

"Okay, let me break it down for everybody," Stanton replied. "First, she's an old ship, long past her days of military usefulness. But there she sits. Either she's some kind of floating museum or someone has converted her to a tourist vessel. Either way, she must have modern communication and navigation on board. Maybe it's working. Even if it isn't, they may have a better med kit than we do. Mary is my first concern right now."

"But—," Tenny began.

"I'm not finished," Stanton snapped. "There are other reasons. If my first two hopes are groundless, the *Archer* can still help us. I'm assuming that sometime the fog is going to lift and we'll be able to see other boats in the area. The *Archer* rides higher in the water than we do. A signal sent from her upper deck or even from that massive tripod mast you see over there would be much more easily seen and over a greater distance. And if we're out here past our in-port arrival date, the Coast Guard will be sent looking for us. The *Archer* presents a much bigger radar image than the *Tern About*. Most likely, we'd be spotted from the air first, but we need to work every advantage we can. Look at the ship. Tell me what you see."

"A big old ship," Tenny said.

Stanton stepped out of the cockpit and took another long look at the battleship. To him she was a work of art, sleek by the definitions of her day, broad across the beam, and over five hundred feet in length. Her bridge was boxy and her two stacks towered above the deck like grain silos. A three-legged mast was planted amidships and looked like a giant teepee without its covering. "Look harder."

"Boats?" Richie said.

"That's right, boats," Stanton said. "If memory serves, the dreadnought carried about a dozen boats of various sizes, from fifty-foot pinnaces to a thirty-foot gig."

"A what to a what?" Tony asked.

Stanton explained, "That ship over there is still carrying original lifeboats and service boats. They vary in size. A pinnace is a boat carried on a larger ship. A gig is a type of rowboat. What I'm trying to say is that one of those boats may be able to help us if we need it. If we can crank up the engine on one of the larger boats, we could tie off the *Tern About* and tow her back to Miami."

"But you said their engines aren't running," Tony protested. "Richie may be right. Their engines may be dead like ours. No juice to crank them over. Nothing electrical working. What makes you think their engines will fire when ours won't?"

Stanton couldn't help smiling. "Because, my young mechanic, ships of that age didn't use gasoline or diesel engines. Unless they've refitted everything, some of the boats will be powered by—"

"Steam!" Richie said, slapping his head. "I should have thought of that."

"That's right," Stanton said. "We don't need electricity to fire up the engines; all we need is fire and water: fire to bring the small onboard boiler up to pressure, and water to convert to steam. And even if that doesn't work, the smaller boats are designed to be rowed, and rowing one of them will be far easier than paddling a sixty-two-foot catamaran."

"Shouldn't we just, like, wait for help?" Jamie asked. "This all seems a little extreme."

"If M&M weren't sick, I'd agree," Stanton replied. "But if she truly is in the throes of appendicitis, we need to get her medical help ASAP."

"But you're taking a big risk," Jamie said. "Couldn't going over there be dangerous?"

"Yes," Stanton said. "But Mary is worth it. All of you are worth it."

"It's too big a job for two people," Tenny said. "I'll go with you."

"Negative," Stanton said. "I need an experienced hand to stay on the *Tern About*. Once on board, we need to tie off and take the cat in tow. The *Archer* is still moving and we're not. I'm assuming she's moving under inertial momentum—she was under steam, then cut power. Her forward momentum continues to push her along, albeit at a snail's pace. That will run out sometime, but not before she's out of our reach."

"Wait a minute," Tony said. "If that thing is powered by steam, why aren't her engines running now?"

"That's a good question," Stanton answered. "And I know of only one way to find out. If they won't talk to us, then I'm going over there to talk to them. Tenny, get some line and tie us off at the bow. Richie, lower the Zodiac; we have some paddling to do."

"I still think you're undermanned," Tenny said.

"She's right," Steve said. "I'll go with you."

"It might be dangerous—," Stanton started.

"So what?" Steve countered. "You brought us to be part of the crew. Am I part of the crew or not?"

Stanton looked at Richie, who shrugged as if to say, "He's got you there." Truth was, Stanton needed at least one more pair of hands. He had a plan but it was going to be difficult for two people to pull off.

"If Steve goes, I go," Tony said flatly, as though no one could raise a successful argument against his logic.

Stanton hesitated and Steve used the moment of silence to press home his point. "We've been in the Zodiac before. You didn't have a problem with us going over to the sub on it."

"This is different," Stanton said. "Once we get to the *Archer*, we'll need to get on board, and that's going to be a whole lot tougher than being helped onto a sub."

"We'll manage," Tony said. "Let us help."

Stanton exhaled loudly and let his mind grapple with the idea. "Okay, put on some vests, but first the ground rules. You will do exactly as I say and if for some reason I'm not around, you take your orders from Richie. Got it?"

"Got it," Steve and Tony said in unison.

N
Λ

Not the ocean. After all, not the ocean. The call, the soothing beckoning to find rest in the saltwater folds, had been the lesser choice. Attractive as the liquid tomb was, the New Thing was more so. Although an undeniable longing to step from the deck to the deep had been a companion since the beginning, and despite the desire to embrace the nothing that waited at the end of this life, the New Thing was a stronger attraction. It was alluring. Enticing. For unknown reasons its silent siren call filtered through innate mental defenses, as if the New Thing held out welcoming arms like those of a mother extended to a hurt child.

It was beautiful: long and sleek and untroubled by its environment. It sat upon the water like an emperor upon a golden throne. Its presence insisted, demanded, that all eyes be fixed upon it. The strange sky, the peculiar ocean, the mist—all seemed subservient to the captivating mass of steel that rested upon the surface like a feather upon a grand bed.

It remained silent, apparently feeling no obligation to reply to the call of the others. Because it was there, it was not constrained to answer the puny things living on the small boat nearby. Perhaps it would answer soon. Perhaps it would condescend to notice them, like an elephant taking notice of a flea.

Grand. It was as grand and powerful as it was large and strong. And it was magnetic, drawing attention, drawing thoughts, drawing desire. Like a magnet that pulls iron filings to it by the mystical laws of physics, the New Thing drew minds.

There, a short distance away, was a gray-white creature formed of riveted steel, an iceberg of engineering that had become greater than its designer's intent, more powerful than their calculations, more enduring than their expectations.

It had done nothing but it was doing something—something beyond observation and definition, something that was not readily seen with the eyes but clearly felt in the heart. Tendrils of inducement reached out from its metal carcass, enticing, baiting, inviting . . . beguiling.

In the present, unexplained, confusing world so different from a day ago, the New Thing seemed to belong. This was its place, this was its natural environment; everyone and everything else were interlopers tromping through a private world, trespassers with self-invitations and no regard for the majesty that loomed before them.

"It's wrong," the voices said. "It's improper and uncivil. No right. They have no right."

The voices were correct.

N
∧

"Um, I hate to be the downer on this trip, but how are we going to get on board?"

Stanton sat forward in the skiff, holding a black paddle. He didn't pause as he considered Tony's question. The teenager was seated on the wood bench next to him, pushing his paddle through thick water in perfect time with Stanton's. Directly behind Stanton sat Steve, and behind Tony, Richie worked his paddle.

"With the help of the crew," Stanton said. "They should be able to lower a ladder over the side."

"Have you forgotten?" Tony said. "We haven't seen any crew."

Stanton kept his eyes focused on the ship. Each stroke put them a few feet closer. Once they had hand-lowered the Zodiac to the water, the four entered the boat and Richie tried to start the outboard motor but, as expected, the Yamaha refused to kick over. After five minutes of pressing the starter and pulling the manual cord, Stanton told him to stand at ease. He was sure they were going to have to paddle the distance between the *Tern About* and the *Archer*. There was no sense in delaying the task. Each second the ship moved a short distance farther. It was slow, very slow, but it was still pressing forward under its own inertia.

"There must be a crew," Stanton said. "Maybe they didn't hear us, maybe they're all playing cards, I don't know, but I can't believe that a ship that size and in perfect condition is out here without the help of a crew."

"Maybe it's a ghost ship," Steve suggested.

"I repeat," Stanton answered, "I don't believe in ghosts."

"It's that Christian stuff, isn't it?" Tony said.

Stanton was nonplussed. It had been his hope to share his faith with his young crew but he had yet to mention anything of a spiritual nature.

"Don't look so surprised," Tony added. "I had it figured out the moment I stepped off the dock. I can smell you guys a mile away."

"That obvious?" Stanton said.

"Like stink on a skunk," Tony said, then quickly added, "No offense meant."

"None taken," Stanton replied. "I think."

"I take it you don't much care for Christians," Richie said.

"I can take them or leave them, as long as they leave me alone and don't try to stuff a tract down my throat. And yes, I know you're one of the Bible toters, too."

"Guilty as charged," Richie admitted.

"Tenny, now, she's different," Tony continued. "I don't know what to make of her. You guys are obvious, but not her. Is she part of your group?"

"Group?" Stanton asked.

"Yeah, you guys teamed up to convert us or something, right?"

Stanton shook his head. "No group, Tony. I haven't spent much time with Tenny. I met with her during the planning stages. Richie knows her better than I do. He recommended her. As far as her faith goes, I couldn't comment."

"So this isn't some kind of take-the-rotten-kids-out-to-sea-and-get-them-saved thing."

"No," Stanton answered. "I had hoped to share my faith with each of you, but that was a personal decision. This is a pilot program for the navy. I love the navy, but it's not known for its deep spiritual qualities."

"You got that right," Richie said.

"Wait a minute," Steve said. "Because you're a Christian, you don't believe in ghosts? I don't get the connection."

"Ghosts are supposed to be the disembodied spirits of the dead," Stanton explained. "I believe that the human soul continues to live on after death. Because of Christ's work, the believer's soul goes to heaven. To be absent in the body is to be present with the Lord, to paraphrase the apostle Paul."

"And the unbeliever?" Tony asked.

"It is appointed unto a man once to die, then the judgment," Stanton said. "That's from the Bible book called Hebrews. Again a paraphrase."

"Does the Bible say anything about this weird water and sky?" Steve asked.

Stanton looked over the side again, something he had done more times than he could count. The water remained inky and seemed thicker, as if some alchemist had changed its viscosity with incantations and the wave of a wand. The sky above remained the color of translucent cottage cheese. Only the mist had changed, slowly withdrawing to reveal more of the strange-looking sky. The sights troubled Stanton. No matter what his eyes told him, he had trouble believing what he saw. "No, it doesn't," he admitted. "At least, nothing comes to mind." He thought he heard Tony snicker.

They paddled on in silence for several minutes; then Steve asked, "Just for the sake of argument, what if there is no crew to help us on board?"

This was a question Stanton had been asking himself. He was less concerned about getting safely on the *Archer*'s deck than he was about explaining how a five-hundred-foot-long steel juggernaut could be floating empty in the Atlantic Ocean. "Believe it or not, I have a plan."

Each orchestrated stroke of the paddles propelled them closer to the battleship, and with each stroke the metal sides seemed to loom ten feet higher. As warships went, the *Archer* was small. A Nimitz-class aircraft carrier was twice as long and supported a crew of 5,500. Still, being afloat in a rigid-hull inflatable dinghy powered only by human muscle made Stanton feel as if he were approaching the Cliffs of Dover.

The four continued their rhythmic stroking in silence. Only the sound of plastic paddles striking the velvet surface of the ocean could be heard. Nothing came from the ship. Stanton glanced over his shoulder and saw Tenny, John, and Jamie watching intently from the catamaran. Redirecting his attention to the battleship, he said, "We'll approach amidships."

"Where?" Tony asked.

"Do you see the tripod mast?" Stanton asked. Tony said he did. "There's a large panel just below the deck. These old ships were often coaled while at sea. A coal ship, which was much smaller, would approach and coal could be loaded over the side. The same was true for other supplies. It seems the logical place to start."

"You find logic in this situation?" Steve asked. "I don't see anything close to logic."

Stanton didn't answer but he agreed. Ten yards from the hull Stanton stopped the paddling. "That's far enough now," he said. "We can be seen more easily if we stay some distance away." Tony and Steve drew their paddles in; Stanton and Richie let theirs drag in the water until the Zodiac came to a stop.

"Shouldn't we see people on the deck?" Tony asked. "Because I'm not seeing anyone."

Stanton raised his hands to his mouth. "Ahoy, *Archer.*" As before, it was a call that returned unanswered.

"Spooky," Steve said.

"Ahoy, *Archer!*" Stanton bellowed, his eyes fixed on the bridge, searching for some movement. His voice seemed to die a short distance from the boat. "You brought the air horn with you, Richie. Give it a blast."

Richie did as he had done several times before. Three sharp blasts from the can of compressed air sliced through the stillness like a scalpel. The sound was piercing enough, loud enough, to be heard by anyone on board the battleship, but no faces appeared in the windows of the bridge or peered at them from decks above.

"I'm telling you," Tony said, "we have a real live ghost ship on our hands."

"Don't you mean a real dead ghost ship?" Steve asked. "Hey," he said suddenly, "isn't there something about salvage rights? I mean, if no one is on board, can't we claim it as our own?"

"I'm more concerned about getting Mary to a doctor than about staking a claim to an old battleship," Stanton said.

"What's next, boss?" Tony asked. "We can't sit here all day making noise."

"You're right," Stanton said. "Let's circle around her and see what there is to see. Maybe we'll get lucky and find an easy way on board." He pointed to the back of the ship. "We'll start aft but we'll keep some distance. We'll see more that way."

"This line is going to play out soon, Skipper," Richie said. "I've got a hundred feet of this nine-sixteenth utility braid. We have enough to reach the ship but not to go around her. Besides, the rope might get fouled."

Richie was right. Since the ship was moving slowly past the *Tern About*, they had decided to tie off the catamaran to the *Archer* if necessary. Stanton had doubted that it would be necessary, but he was a cautious man. He could not bring himself to believe that the *Archer* was an empty ship, but he wanted to be ready just in case. He was hoping the crew would take them in tow until help could arrive.

"Okay," Stanton said. "Let's move aft a little. We'll tie off the Zodiac and the *Tern About* on the torpedo net booms, but not in the same place. I don't want the Zodiac interfering with the tow-line. We'll tie the yacht off first, then move forward along the hull a ways and tie off the dinghy."

"And how do we get on board from there?" Tony wondered.

Stanton studied the booms. Thirteen thick poles were fastened to the side of the ship, each hinged at the bottom so they could swing free from the deck and away from the hull, the metal torpedo nets hanging from their ends like a steel curtain. "One of us is going to climb up one of the booms. Once on deck, he can search for help or, at very least, a ship's ladder."

"That sounds like a job for super-Richie," Richie said with a flourish.

"You get my vote," Tony said. "But I got five bucks that says you don't make it first try. You're gonna get wet."

"We have a doubter on board, Skipper."

The light banter was a stress reliever and Stanton recognized it as such. He welcomed it. "I wouldn't bet against Tony," he said.

"That's it. After my daring circus act, I will expect full apologies from everyone."

They tied the towline to one of the aft booms, then paddled forward until they were near the middle of the ship's port side. They pulled close to the vertical wall of steel that composed the exterior hull. A metal boom swept back at a forty-five-degree angle, its lower end just above the waterline. Stanton tied the Zodiac to it with a polyester line and pulled the small boat close.

"It's steel," Richie said with surprise, fingering the thick pole. "I don't know why, but I was expecting it to be made of wood. Silly me."

"It's only six or seven inches in diameter," Stanton said, "but it appears to be in perfect condition. No rust and the connections look sound. It should hold your weight just fine."

"Famous last words," Tony said.

"Your cheerfulness has made this trip worthwhile," Richie said to Tony. "I would have succumbed to depression and terror had it not been for your steady optimism."

"My sarcasm alarm just went off," Tony said.

"I wonder why," Richie said.

Stanton watched the young man study the boom, its supports, and the guy wires attached to it. He offered no suggestions. Since it was Richie who would be doing the acrobatics, he left it to him to decide on the best way to proceed. Steve and Tony remained silent also. Everyone understood that the task before Richie was a difficult one.

"Okay," Richie finally said, reaching into his pocket and removing a small folding knife. He then retrieved the paddle he had been using and began cutting a notch into the hard plastic blade.

"What are you doing?" Steve asked, puzzled. Stanton wanted to know, too.

"The pole is certainly wide enough to stand on," Richie explained as he continued whittling on the paddle. "The problem is that it is very close to the hull. If I just try to stand on the boom and tiptoe my way up to the deck, I'm bound to fall backward into the drink. As much fun as that might be for you guys to see, I would prefer to avoid it. I'm going to have to press myself against the hull, but there's nothing for me to hold on to, at least not at first." He pointed up with the knife. "You see the guylines up there, just a foot or so below the deck, the ones running horizontally between the booms? Once I get a hand on those, I'll be okay. It's the first few steps that are going to be tough."

"So you're putting a notch into the paddle so you can hook it on the metal wire that runs between the poles," Stanton said.

"I assume those guylines are used to pull the booms into place. They need to be pretty strong to do that. They should hold a little extra weight—my weight. If I can hook the paddle on the line, I can use it to steady myself as I work my way up the boom. Genius, eh?"

"If it works," Tony said.

"It will work, pal," Richie said. "Mrs. Richmond raised a real smart boy." Richie stood, taking hold of the boom to steady himself. "How high do you make the lines to be, Skipper?"

"Twelve to fifteen feet above the waterline," Stanton said. "The Zodiac gives you a couple of feet above the water. You should be able to reach it with the paddle." Stanton watched as Richie stretched his six-foot-three frame, extending his arm over his head. The four-foot paddle barely reached the boom's guy wires, and the notch carved by Richie slipped over the metal line.

"Here goes nothing," Richie said. "Watch yourselves."

As if he did this on a routine basis, Richie raised a foot and planted it on the steel boom, yanked on the paddle that served as his only handhold, and pulled himself up onto the boom. The Zodiac bounced and rocked with the sudden motion and shifting weight. Richie immediately pressed himself against the hull and paused. A moment later he slid his left foot a few inches up the boom and then followed with his right, all the time using the hooked paddle to steady himself. He repeated the motion, then paused to reposition his hand on the paddle. Slowly, like a tightrope walker, Richie inched his way along.

"You should be able to reach the line with your hand," Stanton said calmly. He didn't feel calm.

Richie had his face pressed against the side of the ship. He allowed himself to tilt his head back just enough to get his bearings, then slowly raised his free hand, feeling for the wire that was above his head. He found it. A second later he released the paddle, which continued to hang from the cable, and grabbed the wire with his other hand. Stable with feet on the boom and hands on the guy wire, Richie continued his climb until he was able to take hold of the deck's edge.

"He'll have to reach the lifeline, then crawl through," Stanton said to the others. "There should be a large roll of torpedo net not far from the edge." Stanton was holding his breath and his heart was rattling in his chest.

Inch followed inch until Richie was able to reach the lower of two lifeline cables that ran the perimeter of the deck. Stanton watched, his eyes glued to each of Richie's movements until he was high enough to crawl onto the deck. He disappeared and remained missing for long minutes.

"Richie, you okay?" Stanton called. Nothing. "You still with us, buddy?"

He waited for an answer and was about to call out again when Richie peered over the railing. "Hey, that was too much like work."

Stanton released a small cheer. Steve applauded and even Tony raised a triumphant fist.

"Way to go," Steve said.

"Hey, Tony," Richie called down. "You owe me five bucks."

Empty

Tenny stared across the table-flat sea and held her breath as Richie began his climb up the torpedo net boom. The binoculars she held to her eyes allowed her to see each painfully slow movement. The distance between the vessels had begun to widen as the battleship slipped slowly forward. With all her heart she wished she were in the Zodiac, helping the others. She understood why Stanton had left her behind. A portion of her had screamed, *It's because I'm a woman*, but Tenny quickly silenced that nonsense. An experienced hand had to stay on board the *Tern About*, and with an ill girl sleeping below—a girl who recoiled at the touch of a man—Tenny was the sensible choice. Still, as illogical as it was, she felt cheated.

"That guy's crazy," John said. He had moved from his perch at the front of the boat and joined her and Jamie near the port steering station.

"Which guy?" Tenny asked. "Captain Stanton or Richie?"

"Take your pick, but I was talking about Richie climbing up that pole thing. I was waiting for him to do a back flip into the water."

"Waiting or hoping?" Jamie asked.

157

"Sheesh, chill out, woman," John shot back. "Man, did you wake up on the wrong side of the web."

"Knock it off, you two," Tenny said, her eyes still fixed on the scene playing out a short distance away. "We've got people over there busting their rumps to try and get us back to Miami. The least we can do is give them our attention."

"Yeah, whatever," John grumbled.

"What's going on?" a voice asked from behind them. Tenny turned to see Mary standing in the cockpit. She steadied herself with a hand on the outdoor table. Her skin was pale but had regained a touch of rose at the cheeks. The translucent green that had accented her skin was gone. She had changed clothes and was wearing a fresh blue T-shirt and a pair of loose-fitting jeans. She was barefoot.

"You shouldn't be up," Tenny said. She could see that M&M was bending forward slightly. She also held one hand to her stomach.

"I'm tired of lying down and I'm feeling a little better."

"Better?" Tenny asked, uncertain that she was hearing the truth. "Are you sure?"

"A little. My stomach still hurts but I don't feel like vomiting anymore." She looked around. "Why is the sky so weird? Where is everyone?" Her eye caught sight of the *Archer*. "What is that?"

"It's a long story but I'll give you the *Reader's Digest* version," Tenny said. She did, explaining the damage to the catamaran, the unusual weather and water conditions, and the sudden appearance of the old battleship.

"It doesn't look that old," Mary said.

"And that's just the beginning of the mysteries," John said. "Apparently, they don't talk to the likes of us."

M&M looked at Tenny inquisitively. Tenny explained. "We've hailed them several times and no one responds. Nor have we seen anyone on board."

"Isn't that kinda weird?" the girl asked.

"Yeah," Tenny admitted. "It's way weird. Are you sure you don't want to go back to bed?"

"No," M&M protested. "I really do feel a little better. Besides, it stinks down there."

"I wonder why?" John said. "I've seen more—"

"Not like that," M&M shot back. "It's a different stink."

Stink? Tenny was puzzled. She and Jamie had cleaned up the "contributions" made by the seasick teenagers. She had even made sure that the cabin where M&M had been resting was free of anything foul. The ports had been opened to let fresh air in and to vent any lingering smells. Tenny sniffed the air and noticed a faint but familiar odor. Stepping from the side of the boat and down into the cockpit, she noticed that the odor was stronger. Her mind raced to recognize the scent but it lay just beyond the grasp of recall. It was familiar but smelled in no way organic. The refrigerator had ceased to run, like everything else electrical on the boat, but they had not been without power so long as to cause spoilage.

Tenny walked into the salon. There the odor was stronger but not unsettling. It was pungent and very familiar . . . "Oh no," she whispered and jogged through the salon to the sleeping areas, opening each door. She then raced back topside, through the cockpit, and to the starboard steering station. In the teak floor was a hatch that led to one of the two diesel engines. Tenny popped the hatch and was greeted with the slight smell of oil and diesel fuel, but it was not as strong as she'd expected. She secured the hatch and darted to the twin station and opened the hatch over the port engine. Again the smell of diesel and oil, but it too was not as strong as she'd anticipated.

"What are you doing?" Jamie asked.

"There's a diesel smell below," Tenny answered.

"Ya think?" John spouted off. "They're diesel engines. Of course they smell like diesel fuel."

"I'm smelling it inside the cabin areas, not in the engine bays," Tenny replied.

"A gas leak?" Jamie said. "You mean there could be a fire or an explosion? You guys really are trying to kill us."

"Settle down," Tenny said firmly. "Diesel fuel is safer than gasoline. It doesn't ignite as easily. I don't think we're in any danger. At least not right away. The smell, however—that is a different matter."

"If the engines are in the back of the boat," John began, "how come the smell is up front?"

Tenny thought for a moment, then let the hatch fall shut. She moved forward urgently around the cockpit and salon until she stood near the mast. John and Jamie followed. On the deck before her were four hatches. She knew that two of the hatches were lockers for ground tackle, lines, and other things a yacht might need on a trip. The other two hatches opened to the fuel tanks, one on each side of the boat's median. Kneeling, Tenny opened the port hatch to see the fuel compartment. She was assaulted by the thick smell of fuel. "Oh, great," she said. "Just what we need, another problem." Leaving the compartment open to vent, she moved to the other hatch and opened it. It too reeked of diesel.

"What now, coach?" John asked.

Tenny looked up and saw John peering down at her. Jamie stood several feet back, apparently uncomfortable with the smell and situation. "We let it vent into the open air," Tenny replied. "That should alleviate some of the smell."

"I guess they just don't make yachts like they used to," John remarked. "Engines that don't work, electrical systems all down, a broken mast, and now leaky fuel tanks. If I were Richie's old man, I'd ask for all my money back."

Tenny rose and faced her smart-aleck charge. "She's been through a rough storm, John. The bow dug deep several times. This boat weighs nearly sixty tons. That's a lot of weight to send slamming into ocean troughs. I would have bet the farm that the composite mast was beyond the ability of any storm to break. Mother Nature proved me wrong on that. My guess is, the tanks were damaged when we were getting bounced around. They've been leaking slowly ever since."

"Are you sure it can't blow up?" Jamie asked.

"I'm sure," Tenny said with confidence. If she had told the entire truth, she would have mentioned that diesel fuel explosions had occurred but were so rare that few knew of them. Still, she was in no mood to take chances. "I want everyone to stay topside until all the fumes are gone. We'll see what Captain Stanton wants to do when he gets back."

"I'm no sailor," John said, "but if the tanks are leaking, the fumes won't go away until all the fuel is gone. Right?"

He was right and there was more to the question than he could have realized. Tenny didn't know from where on the tanks the fuel was spilling. Her best guess was that the fuel lines had been split or even severed by the multiple impacts the boat had endured. That could mean that the fuel was leaking from the bottom of the tanks, filling the well in which the tanks had been installed. There wasn't much room between tank and well wall. She had no fear that the fuel would spill out. It was a fluid and the leak would stop once it reached the same level as that in the tanks. Assuming, of course, it didn't find another way to seep out.

"You take that side," she said to John, pointing starboard, "and see if you can see any fuel floating in the water. I'll take the other side." John shrugged and started for the boat's edge. Tenny worked her way along the port side of the boat, looking for anything floating on the surface. She saw nothing but she felt no relief. There was another possibility that concerned her. The fuel tanks were positioned forward of the salon. This helped to offset the weight of the engines in the stern. Next to each tank, in each of the tapering hulls, were cabins. On the starboard side was the owner's stateroom, on the port side another cabin. M&M had been in the cabin closest to the port steering station and not in either of the forward cabins near the tanks. Her new fear was a breach in the bulkhead that would allow the foul fuel to seep into the boat's interior. While she hoped against hope that she was worrying about nothing, she felt an overpowering disquiet. The smell below had been enough to drive the ill M&M topside. How had the thick oily smell made its way to her stern cabin?

There was only one way to find out. "I'll be back in a minute," she said and bounded for the salon door. Again Tenny started below. Earlier she had done little more than notice the odor and open the doors to the sleeping areas. Now she wanted to take a closer look.

"What are you doing?" John asked.

"Just sit tight," Tenny called over her shoulder, then plunged into the spacious lounge. The odor was stronger than before. Moving quickly forward, she charged into the forward port cabin. Dim light drifted from a bleak sky, pouring through the open window. All the windows had been opened to vent the acrid smell left behind by several seasick teenagers. It was a good thing, since the fuel odor was far more pronounced than she had first noticed. Before her was the bed. To her right was a small closet which abutted a vertical locker. The back of the locker and closet shared a wall with the fuel compartment. If fuel was leaking inside, it would have come from a crack in that partition. Tenny stepped to the closet and pulled open its thin double doors.

Nothing. The closet was empty except for a few shirts and pants hung there by Stanton and Richie, who shared the room. Sliding to her left, she took hold of the locker's shiny metal latch and gave a tug. It opened freely. Tenny gasped and took a step back.

Dark fluid spilled out of the locker's base and onto her feet. Diesel fuel.

Tenny swore under her breath, then pulled the locker door open as far as it would go. The only light available to her came begrudgingly through the window and over her shoulder. She squinted and leaned forward. Halfway up the rear partition was a vertical crack wide enough to insert a dime, and a half foot in length. Brown fluid dripped like molasses from the bottom of the crack. The rising fuel spillage from the tank into the fuel compartment had reached the bottom of the crack and was now seeping inside.

"Swell," Tenny said to herself as she gritted her teeth.

Richie had talked her into coming along. "What could be better than sailing the Atlantic on a yacht?" he had asked. "You can build up the ol' sailing résumé."

"Let's see, baby-sitting seasick kids, enduring a storm, fixing a battered boat, and now watching fuel flood one of the cabins. Yeah, this has been great." Tenny walked from the cabin through the salon and poked her head out the door. "Hey, John. I need you for a minute."

"No way," John said. "It reeks down there."

"I need your help," Tenny pleaded.

"Sorry, I'm not the helpful type."

"Get your butt down here, mister—*now!*"

John said something Tenny had only heard longshoremen say, but he appeared in front of the door. "It's time for you to earn your room and board. Come with me."

Tenny led the reluctant teenager to the galley, released the latch on one of the cabinets, pulled out a box of trash bags, and handed it to John. She then opened one of the drawers and removed a butter knife. "How can you stand the smell?" he asked.

"Don't be a wimp," Tenny retorted. Her patience had reached its limits and was teetering on the edge of fury. John must have sensed it, because he kept any smart remarks locked away. "Follow me." She led him to the forward cabin and marched in. He held back a step, stopping at the threshold. "The longer you delay, the longer we have to be down here, so I suggest you step lively, mister." John entered the room, but unhappily.

"What do we need trash bags for?"

"Get one out and open it."

John did, pulling the thin plastic from the roll of bags in the cardboard box. He dropped the box on the carpeted deck and struggled to unfold and open the clinging material. Clearly, it was an act he was unfamiliar with. Tenny frowned, turned to the bed, and grabbed one of the two pillows. Deftly she stripped away the pillow cover and threw the pillow back on the bed.

"Do you mind telling me what we're doing?" John finally asked as he snapped the bag up and down.

"There's a breech in the partition behind that locker," she said, motioning with her head. "Fuel is spilling out of the tank into the compartment that houses the tank. The fuel level has reached the bottom of the breach and is leaking into the cabin. We're going to stop the leak."

"How?"

"Hold the bag open," Tenny ordered as she stepped close. She took the pillow cover and slipped it into the open plastic trash bag. It fit as if it had been designed for that purpose. Tenny took the bag from John, pinching the opening closed on the edge of the cloth case. "We're going to plug the leak. I need you to hold this in place while I force it into the crack. Open the locker."

John did and then took a step back as stronger fumes assaulted him. "Lovely," he said sarcastically.

"Just be glad it's not gasoline," Tenny said. "Here, take the bag and hold it over the crack, but hold it loosely. I'm going to use the butter knife to press as much of the bag into the breech as possible."

"Why not just stuff the plastic in?"

"Because the fuel will make it slippery and it won't provide much of a seal. The pillow covering will provide the thickness we need, and the trash bag will keep the diesel from saturating the cloth. At least until the fuel eats the plastic away."

"It can do that?"

Tenny shrugged. "I have no idea," she admitted, "but everything else has gone wrong, so I'm assuming the trend will continue. Now let's do this."

Echoes

When Richie had finally pulled himself onto the deck of the *Archer*, he felt two emotions. First, relief coursed through him like a cold brook through a dark forest. He had exuded every bit of confidence he felt, which wasn't much. The rest was show, bravado for Stanton and the others. From the moment the notched paddle hooked onto the guy wire of the torpedo net boom, he was sure he was going to fall. It wasn't the narrowness of the boom or its proximity to the nearly vertical hull of the battleship that eroded his confidence. It was the very idea of the act. It was incomprehensible to think that one could paddle up to a battleship and crawl on board. Of course, he reminded himself, this was not just any battleship. It was from an era long past. The torpedo net booms were proof of that. Still, scaling the cold hull of the ship had proved easier than he expected.

That first emotion of relief was welcome. He had to muster some discipline not to leap in the air and shout, "I did it!" The second emotion, however, dampened the first. Where relief had cooled his anxiety, apprehension chilled his bones. Richie stood alone on the wood deck. Alone. That was the source of the frost in his blood. Someone must certainly have seen him climb aboard. A ship this size could carry a crew of several hundred. Where were they? It was one thing to ignore a call from another vessel, but Richie could imagine no situation in which officers and crew would allow a stranger to simply climb on board. He should be facing the business end of a gun.

But no one greeted him or assaulted him or seized him or anything else. He stood in the open, in full view of anyone looking his way, and was ignored. The still air, the muted light, the strange sky, and now this—Richie was at a loss.

From his spot on the deck, the *Archer* looked even larger. Wide planks of wood covered the steel below from stem to stern. He was on the main deck that ran from fore to aft. Several other decks, smaller and higher, ran down the middle of the ship. Richie tried to take everything in, but his mind was reeling from all there was to see. His impression was that the ship had been built within the last year. The paint was fresh and he could see no rust. "Whoever keeps this tub afloat must have sunk a fortune in renovating her," he said to himself.

He turned in a full circle, letting his mind absorb as much as it could. Something wasn't right.

"Hello!" Richie called, then waited for a response. None came, just the simple, muffled echo of his own voice. "Anybody aboard?" Again nothing.

Richie stepped to the rail and leaned over. Below he saw the anxious faces of Stanton, Tony, and Steve. "Well?" Stanton prompted.

"Nothing, Cap," Richie replied. "The ship looks sound from here, but I can't see anyone on board."

"You're kidding," Tony said. "No one? Not one, single person?"

"Not yet," Richie said.

"How about a ladder?" Stanton asked.

"Not yet, Skipper, but I'll find one soon enough . . ." Richie's voice trailed off as he heard another voice. At first it sounded as if it were behind him, and he turned, hoping to find a friendly face. Instead he just saw the metal bulkhead that rose from the main deck and supported the upper decks of the superstructure. He redirected his attention seaward. The *Tern About* lay a short distance off. He could see four people standing near the edge of the boat. Tenny was waving her arms over her head and shouting. Richie looked down and saw that Stanton had heard her call.

Stanton cupped his hands to his mouth. "What's wrong?"

"Fuel leak." Tenny's voice seemed weak, too weak for the distance. Richie wondered if something was wrong with his hearing. "No danger. Just be advised."

Stanton lowered his head for a moment, then looked back up at Richie. "I'd better check that out," he said. "We'll paddle back while you look for a ladder."

"I don't think you should leave him alone," Steve said. "I can't be any use back there, but I can help Richie look around. Tony can help you paddle back, and he knows more about engines than I do."

"I don't know," Stanton said. "Watching Richie scale the boom was hard enough on my nerves."

"Not a problem," Steve said. "I'm lighter than Richie. I can do it. Besides, he's already on the ship and can help me up."

"It's a good idea, Skipper," Richie said. "I'll keep an eye on him."

"Very well," Stanton said. "Just look for help and a ladder. Don't do anything wacky."

"It's the world that's gone wacky," Steve said, "not me."

"It's just my way of saying be careful," Stanton answered.

"I will," Steve said. "Hey, Richie, how about handing me your paddle?" Richie took the notched paddle from where it hung on the metal boom line and tossed it down to Steve's waiting hands.

Steve then took hold of the same boom Richie had used moments before and began his ascent.

N
Λ

"You did everything right," Stanton said, emerging from the thick, sour air of the *Tern About*'s interior. He was glad to be in fresh air again. Tenny had given him a tour of the problem areas, pointing out the open hatches over the fuel tanks and explaining her theory that the fuel lines leading from those tanks had been sheered off in the storm or at least worked loose from their fittings. She had also taken him below and showed him her "finger in the dike" solution to stem the steady flow of diesel fuel into the cabin.

"We didn't see the crack in our first damage survey because it was hidden behind the locker," Tenny had explained. "I should have thought to look behind every door and in every locker."

"Don't beat yourself up," Stanton said. "It didn't occur to Richie or to me. You've done a great job."

Now outside and free of the stink, Stanton worked his way forward of the salon and found Tony on his belly looking into the open fuel hatch. Tony heard them coming and pushed himself to his knees. "I found the leak," he said. "It's hard to see but the fuel line is bent where it meets the tank. The fuel isn't gushing out but it's flowing enough."

Stanton bent over and looked in. "We can't fix it, can we?"

"Not easily," Tony replied. "We'd have to drain the tank and the fuel compartment. With the right tools we could make some repairs, but the tank really needs to be hauled out of there and replaced."

"What about the second tank?"

"It's leaking, too," Tony said, "just like Tenny said. Same problem."

"Except it's not pouring into the sleeping quarters," Tenny added.

"That's one good thing," Tony said. "Bottom line: the boat is seriously broke." He rose and stretched his legs.

Stanton took a deep breath and let it out slowly. One problem upon another. It was remarkable, unsettling, and frustrating. Never had he imagined that so many things could go wrong so quickly. He looked around at the others who had joined them forward of the salon.

"You know, Captain," John began. He was leaning against the mast, his hands thrust into the pockets of his jeans. "I'm beginning to think that our parents paid you to bring us out here and bump us off."

"If I was going to do that," Stanton said without emotion, "I would have tied you to an anchor and pushed you overboard, then enjoyed a leisurely sail to South America. But you're still here."

"Will we get any help from the crew of the *Archer?*" Tenny wondered. "Certainly, they're not going to leave us adrift."

"We haven't seen any crew," Stanton answered. "We hailed her from a few yards out and got no response. Richie was able to climb up one of the torpedo net booms and board her. No one tried to stop him. In fact, he still hadn't seen anyone by the time we left. He hadn't had much time to look, but you'd think that someone would be on deck somewhere. He's making a search now. Steve's helping."

"Little Stevie?" John said with a laugh. "He's probably more a hindrance than a help."

"Well, he had the guts to go over there, didn't he, Johnny-boy?" Tony snapped. "All you've done is sit on your skinny little butt."

"How about if I come over there and knock you on your butt?" John started forward, his jaw clamped down like a bear trap.

Stanton stepped in front of him and stopped him with an out-stretched arm. John slapped it away viciously and took another step. It was the last step. Stanton extended the arm again, this time grabbing the front of John's shirt and yanking him forward. He saw the teenager's eyes widen. Before John could do anything about it, Stanton was nose to nose with the troublemaker.

"Here's the deal, Mr. Hays," Stanton said in iceberg-cold words. "We have a bit of a crisis here and you're not helping. I'm a patient man, very patient, but there's an end to it. You have reached it." John pushed away, grabbed Stanton's wrist, and tried to force himself free. Instead Stanton snapped him back so they were eyeball to eyeball. "As I was saying, we have a bit of a crisis, and because of that I need people who are going to work their minds more than their mouths. Is that clear?"

"Let me go. You can't touch me."

"It looks like he's touching you pretty good," Tony said with a laugh. Stanton snapped his head around and met Tony's eyes. "Um, sorry, Captain."

Redirecting his attention to John, Stanton repeated, "Is that clear?"

"Yeah . . . whatever . . . just let me go."

Stanton did and the young man stumbled back a step. He started to speak but bridled the impulse. Instead he straightened his shoulders and smoothed out his shirt with exaggerated motions. He was furious and Stanton knew it.

Silence filled the moment, like the diesel fumes that filled the cabins below.

"I saw crew."

It took a moment for Stanton to process what he heard. M&M had said something that didn't make sense. "What?"

M&M inhaled, then said, "While you and Tenny were below. I saw crew on the ship."

Stanton looked at Jamie, who shook her head. "I didn't see anything," she said.

"What about you, John?"

"Don't talk to me," John snapped. "I'm just the troublemaker, remember? I'm not to be trusted."

Stanton frowned. "What did you see, Mary?"

She shrugged. "Just some people, moving around."

"Are you sure it wasn't Richie and Steve?" Tenny asked.

"The ship's not that far away," M&M replied. "Besides, I saw more than two people."

"Finally, some good news," Stanton said. He stepped to the port side and looked back at the husky battleship. He saw no one, not even Richie and Steve. "Where did you see them?"

Mary joined him and pointed. "On the back part of the boat. It looked like they were working … sweeping or mopping or something. They were wearing dark-blue uniforms and had blue and white caps on their heads." She paused. "I … I don't see them now."

"What now, Skipper?" Tenny asked.

"I want to see what's on that ship," he answered. "The plan hasn't changed. I'm glad Mary's feeling better, but that might be temporary. I'd still like to get her to a doctor as soon as we can."

"The diesel leak has made it impossible to spend much time below," Tenny said. "It can't be healthy, breathing those fumes."

"I was taught that diesel fumes contain something like forty toxic chemicals and fifteen carcinogens," Stanton said. "It'd be best if we got everyone off the boat."

"No argument here," Jamie said. "I'm ready to gag."

"So we paddle the dinghy back to the ship?" Tony asked, glancing at the Zodiac, which was floating beside the *Tern About*. "It's going to be crowded."

"I have a better idea," Stanton said. "The water is as flat as a pond and now we're tied off to the *Archer* by the utility line. We have enough muscle on board to pull ourselves close. It won't be hard."

"I like it," Tenny said. "It makes more sense than using the Zodiac."

"I'm in," Tony said.

"Okay then, let's do it," Stanton said.

He took the lead, walking to the bow, bending over the lifelines, and taking the braided rope in hand. The line was still limp in the water. The *Archer* continued to move past the sailboat but at very slow speed. At some point the line would become taut and the *Tern About* would be under tow. The tow wouldn't last long. Stanton could tell that the battleship had used up all but the last traces of its inertia. It was close to being fully dead in the water, a cork measured in steel tons.

With Stanton in front, Tenny behind him, and Tony behind her, they pulled the line, leaning back carefully so as not to let their feet slip. If ancient Egyptians could pull stone blocks weighing fifteen metric tons across desert sands, Stanton reasoned, then a few people should be able to pull a sleek catamaran across glasslike ocean. Each tug moved them a little closer and the work became a little easier. Once the resting inertia was overcome, the labor became almost effortless.

"Easy now," Stanton said. "We don't want to build up too much momentum. Stopping may prove more difficult than starting."

At first the process was awkward, but by the fifth pull the team was working in unison. Water from the wet line rained down on Stanton's pants and shoes. Inch by inch, then foot by foot, the yacht closed the distance to the battleship. The gray-white block figure of the *Archer* dwarfed the sailboat. The *Tern About* was by no means small but size was relative. The battleship seemed to do more than float; it loomed, foreboding and eerie. It was a ship out of place and out of time. Stanton wanted to admire it, to take in its classic lines and appreciate the craftsmanship of workers who riveted, cut, wired, and constructed her a century before. But every feeling of admiration cowered before the stronger, dominating emotions of confusion and uncertainty. There was another feeling Stanton struggled to suppress: dread. Before the others he appeared confident, even bold, but deep inside, where emotions were forced to be honest, he was afraid.

Under their joint and purposeful work, the *Tern About* moved smoothly across the surface, her bow bearing on the battleship's stern.

"Easy does it," Stanton said and slowed his pace. Time trick-led by, each second bringing them closer to the ship. "Tony, you spent the most time at the wheel. Do you remember how to steer the boat?"

"Yeah, sure."

"Good. Take the wheel on the starboard side. We don't have engines but the rudders will still work. Take us just along the ship's port side."

"Wait a sec," Tony said. Stanton could hear the confusion in his tone. "You want me to steer toward the left side of the ship, right?"

"That's right."

"I'll never get this port, starboard, aft, forward, jib-this, boom-that stuff," Tony replied, dropping the rope. "Left oughta be left and right oughta be right."

Stanton chuckled. "Yeah, but then anyone could do it. Hurry up. I don't want to smack into the back of the ship."

"Don't you mean the stern?" Tony asked as he hustled away.

"Kid's got a sense of humor," Tenny said.

"Let's hope he has depth perception," Stanton added.

Tony did. Slowly the catamaran moved alongside the larger vessel, close enough for Stanton, who had moved to the starboard side, to touch. Tenny had moved starboard and aft; she leaned over the lifeline and pushed against the vertical hull, preventing the yacht from scraping along its side.

"Did you guys remember to bring the chips and dip?" a voice said above them. Stanton looked up to see the smiling faces of Richie and Steve.

"Did you remember to find a ladder?" Stanton asked.

"Of course," Richie called down. "What kind of host would I be without one? You'll find a rope ladder just another dozen feet forward."

Stanton pushed against the torpedo net booms along the ship's side until the *Tern About* reached the spot where Richie had dropped the folding ladder. It took a little effort but Stanton and Tenny were able to bring the forward motion of the yacht to match that of the *Archer*.

"Tenny, grab some line," Stanton called. "We need to tie her off temporarily. We'll slow faster than the ship." Tenny moved smoothly to one of the many lockers in the cockpit and came back with some line and handed one end to Stanton, who fed it through the space between a torpedo net boom and the hull. Tenny tied it to one of the *Tern About*'s deck cleats.

"We shouldn't leave her tied this close, Skipper," Tenny said. "If the ocean picks up any, she'll be slammed against the battleship. She's a tough craft but that's one wrestling match she would lose."

"Agreed," Stanton said. "Since she's still tied off at the bow, we can release her once the others are up the ladder."

Tenny laughed.

"What's so funny?"

"I was just thinking that that would make her a dinghy to the *Archer*—a half-million-dollar dinghy!"

"After what she went through, she'll never be a dinghy. We're just keeping her close by. I would hate to get back to Miami and have to explain to Richie's dad why his yacht is still floating somewhere in the middle of the Atlantic."

Stanton took a moment to tie off the Zodiac's shorter line to the nearest torpedo net boom, in case they needed it to return to the catamaran later.

"Now what?" Jamie asked.

"We climb," Stanton said. "It's not far and Richie will help you at the top."

Jamie frowned and looked up. "My mom said this would be an adventure. I didn't believe her."

"None of us had this in mind," Stanton admitted. "So who's going to show us how it's done?"

"I'll go," Tony said.

"Let me go first," Jamie said. "I hate climbing things. I just want to get it over with." The ladder hung limply to the side. It was made of rope and wood slats.

"Whoever kept this beauty in shape is a nut for detail," Stanton said. "That's a real hemp rope, not one made of synthetic fibers."

"No offense," Tenny said, "but only you would notice something like that."

"I'll take that as a compliment," Stanton said. "My point is that synthetic fibers are stronger, don't absorb water, and don't shrink or stretch like rope."

"Like you said, the owner must be a nut for detail." Tenny placed a hand on Jamie's elbow and guided her to the ladder. "Just take one step at a time. Believe it or not, you'll be more secure if you lean back from the hull a little. It's not far; you can do it."

Jamie sighed. "I'd better not break a nail." She took hold of the ladder and placed her foot on one of the wood slats, then paused. "I was kidding about the nail," she said. "I'm really not that shallow."

"We know you're not," Stanton said. "Now up you go. Let Richie help you at the top. It makes him feel useful."

Her ascent was slow and awkward and Stanton was sure she was going to fall back on the deck or, worse, between the battleship and the yacht. He positioned himself to catch her. It was an unnecessary precaution. The *Tern About* rode much higher in the water than the Zodiac, so the distance to the main deck was several feet less than what Richie and Steve had to negotiate. It took less than two minutes for the slow-moving, uncertain Jamie to climb the twisting, swaying ladder. Topside, Richie took her arm and helped her over the edge.

"Next," Stanton called. Tony was there in a second and fearlessly took hold of the ladder. Its unstable movement seemed not to bother the youth. He was up and on deck in a few seconds. "Your turn, Mr. Hays. Adventure awaits." Stanton heard him mumble something but the words were too indistinct to understand.

John approached. Looked at the ladder, then up at the ship. "This is worse than gym class, but it beats sitting around in this reeking tub."

"Do you know what a Pollyanna is?" Stanton asked.

"No."

"I didn't think so. Up you go."

If the climb bothered John, he didn't show it. He frowned, mumbled to himself, then started up. Unlike Tony, he didn't sprint up the ladder, but he didn't linger either. Richie reached to lend a helping hand but John knocked it away, almost losing his footing.

"Pride goes before destruction, and a haughty spirit before stumbling," Stanton said softly.

"What's that?" M&M asked.

"A Bible verse," Stanton said. "One that young Mr. Hays could benefit from."

M&M moved forward timidly, like a cat uncertain of its footing. She studied the rope, then raised her eyes to the deck above. Several faces were staring back down.

"What do you think, Ms. Moss?" Stanton asked. "Are you strong enough to do this?"

She shrugged. "I don't know. Maybe. I've never climbed a ladder like this."

"We can climb it together," Stanton suggested. "I'd be right behind you."

She took a half step away and Stanton realized his blunder. He was awash in emotion: profound sadness for her, and simmering fury for whoever had crushed her spirit.

"I'll follow her up, Skipper," Tenny interjected. "Ladies first, you know."

"Of course. Good idea. Just take your time and everything will be okay."

"Okay," M&M said. Her voice was almost childlike, like that of a toddler trusting her mother not to let the doctor hurt her. Another part of Stanton's heart broke off.

The climb was grueling for Stanton. He stood on the deck of the catamaran and tried to steady the ladder so it didn't twist with each step. M&M had started up and Tenny was right behind her, her arms forming guardrails for the sick girl. If M&M slipped, she would fall back into Tenny, who would become a human safety net. Whether or not Tenny could support her was another matter, one Stanton hoped would not be tested.

With every step they took, Stanton tensed more. A silent prayer floated from his lips. He was relieved to see them helped over the edge and to see Tenny reappear, flashing a thumbs-up sign.

"All right," Stanton said to the ship, as if it had ears. "Let's find out what you're doing out here." He uncleated the line that had kept the *Tern About* close to the barely moving vessel while they climbed aboard. Placing both hands and one foot on the ladder, he positioned his other foot on the edge of the catamaran's deck and pushed. He hung on the ladder for a moment, watching the yacht drift away from the ship's hull. It would continue to drift, Stanton knew, as the *Archer* inched along, and once the line that joined the two vessels became taut, it would then follow dutifully.

Step followed step until Stanton reached the main deck and crawled between the lifelines. He found himself standing on a ship that should have been dismantled three-quarters of a century ago. Instead it seemed brand-new, as if it had only been to sea for a week.

"Did you learn anything while I was gone, Richie?"

"Just one thing, Skipper. Steve and I checked the bridge and several other places where people should be and found no one. Best I can tell, sir, HMS *Archer* is completely deserted."

"But I saw crew," M&M protested. "I know I did."

Richie tossed Stanton a puzzled glance. "Ms. Moss says she saw sailors on deck," Stanton said.

"I did," she asserted.

"Imagined it is more like it," John said.

"No, I didn't," M&M protested. "I saw men in blue uniforms and white hats."

"Sounds like old British navy," Richie said, "but I haven't seen or heard a soul."

Stanton pursed his lips, then nodded. "There was no one standing watch on the bridge?" he asked Richie.

"That's the first place Steve and I went. No one there, Skipper. It's like she's been out here alone for decades."

Stanton shook his head. "Not in this condition," he said. "Look at the deck. The wood looks as if it were laid less than a month ago."

"It's a mystery, all right," Richie said. "So what do we do now?"

"First priority is communication. Steve, you and John are with me. We're going back to the bridge—"

"I don't know anything about electronics," John said. "Why me?"

"You have eyes and I need all the eyes I can get. This is unfamiliar territory to me. I know something about these ships but only from reading. I've never walked around on one. There aren't many alive who have. You can help us find our way around. Richie, you and Tony check out the lifeboats. At least one of them should be powered by a steam engine. You'll have to find it and see if you can figure out how to get it in the water. Tenny, you and the girls see if you can't find a decent first-aid kit. Whoever refurbished this thing made her seaworthy. They must have a med kit of some sort. Look for antibiotics."

Stanton looked at M&M. Her posture was a little better and her pale skin was showing a touch of pink. "Do you feel up to staying with Tenny? We can try and find a place for you to rest."

"I'll stay with Tenny," she answered.

Stanton nodded. "Let's meet back here in thirty minutes. Since none of our watches are working, we'll have to judge time the best we can. Everyone got that?"

Each acknowledged understanding. "Be safe, be smart. Let's get to work." Stanton turned and walked aft briskly along the main deck. Steve and John followed. Stanton knew the direction he wanted to go: up. But getting there was going to be like moving through a maze. He had studied the history of ships and naval warfare since high school, but that was a far cry from knowing his way around a century-old battleship from another navy. "You've been there, Steve; lead the way," Stanton said.

They were walking along the port side of the main deck. There were two noticeable decks above them: an upper deck and a flying deck. The latter was his destination. He had studied the lines of the ship from the moment it first pressed through the mist. The bridge was easy to identify, stationed before the massive tripod mast and forward stack. It was the place he expected to find a working radio.

Driven by curiosity and a need to put an end to the avalanche of problems and setbacks that had put an end to their trip, Stanton moved with long, powerful strides. Moving aft a short distance, Steve led them to a pair of metal doors opening to the inside of the boxy superstructure. Without hesitation Stanton swung open the doors, which moved effortlessly on their hinges. He had expected the heavy armored doors to squeak in protest, but they moved in silence, a testimony to the detailed upkeep of the vessel.

Through the door waited a thick darkness. No lights burned. The only illumination came through several widely spaced, eighteen-inch-diameter portholes. The muted light trickled in as if intimidated by the darkness inside.

"Hello," Stanton called. "Anyone aboard?"

Only his voice answered back, in a hard echo.

"Odd," Stanton said, more to himself than to John and Steve.

"What do you mean?" Steve asked.

"The portholes are open," Stanton answered. "The same storm that pounded us must certainly have hit this ship."

"So?" John asked.

"The first thing you do in a storm is close all ports, scuttles, and hatches so water doesn't pour in. Tenny did that for us on the *Tern About*. Water inside a boat is a bad thing. These portholes are open."

"That doesn't mean anything," John argued. "The storm was yesterday. Someone must have opened these after the storm."

"So where are they? And why are there no lights on?"

Neither boy responded.

"Upward, gentlemen. Let's keep moving." Stanton stepped into the steel-plated, sepulchral darkness.

The Wide Empty

It was the silence that bothered Stanton the most. A ship this size should be filled with the noise of engines, the talk of sailors, the commands of officers, and other clatter of human activity. There was none of that. The air remained dead still, and the ocean flat as a mirror. They had found a set of stairs that led to the upper deck, and from the higher footing of this deck Stanton surveyed the ocean, hoping to see signs of some other craft, to catch a glimpse of whatever ships were out there. He saw nothing. No matter how hard he looked, he could see no ships on the ocean, no planes in the air, not even the distant horizon. The gray mist that clung to the ocean surface like a carpet seemed to rise skyward in the distance, making a backdrop of gray-white that merged with the cottage cheese sky.

Other things ate at him. Mary Moss had been adamant about seeing a crew on deck. It was not Richie and Steve, whom she might confuse with battleship sailors; there had been more than two. What had she seen? And she had seen things before, causing her to cry out in the darkness of the cabin where she had rested. Then there was the "whatever" he himself had seen—the indistinct, unidentifiable something.

"I don't think we're in Kansas anymore, Toto," John said. "I like the spooky as much as the next guy, but this is over the top."

"You'll get no argument from me," Stanton said. He led his small team to a metal ladder. They had more climbing to do. "One more level and we'll be on the flying deck. There's got to be some answers there," he said and started up.

Anger welled up in him as he trotted up the metal rungs. The unresponsive nature of the crew was more than rude; it defied the laws of the sea. Stanton was determined that there was going to be captain-to-captain conversation—assuming he could find the ship's skipper.

The ladder led from the upper deck to the flying deck, two levels above the teak-covered main deck below. The interior portion of this deck was also lit only by the sunlight that pressed through portholes. Had the ship been docked in some city and open to the public as a museum, Stanton would have taken time to observe the ship's details, her construction, her rooms. But he had other things on his mind. He wanted help for his crew and answers for himself.

Another ladder led to a semi-open area with a clear view over the bow of the ship. As with the main deck, wood lined the floor. Five large windows were situated forward of the deck, but there were no side walls. Wind could whip through the area—if there were any wind. The shape of the deck reminded Stanton of the wings of a small jet. Both port and starboard portions of the deck were open to sky and air. The middle part had the window wall before and a heavily windowed room behind. Metal beams and decking formed a ceiling overhead.

"What is this place?" John asked. He was breathing hard. The climb up the stairs and two sets of ladders had tired him.

"Navigation platform," Stanton replied. "It's the pilot's station," he added, pointing at the wood-and-brass ship's wheel.

"Or I should say it's one of the pilot's stations. These old ships usually had four or five places from which to steer the ship. There are probably one or two wheels below us and maybe one or two in the signal towers."

"You're confusing me," John said. "All this boat talk means nothing."

"A ship this size is a complicated beast, John," Stanton explained. "It was designed for war and had redundant systems in case parts of it were hit." Stanton stepped forward and studied the wheel. It was beautifully constructed, its wood smooth and finished, its brass brightly polished. All it was missing was a pilot. To the left of the wheel was the ship's compass, sitting motionless in its binnacle. Stanton tapped the covering but the compass remained fixed. "Electric," Stanton said. "I had forgotten."

"Forgotten what?" Steve asked as he stepped to Stanton's side.

"The *Dreadnought* was the first British ship of the era to be fitted with an electric compass. It appears the *Archer* shares that distinction."

"It looks stuck," Steve said, "just like ours."

"No lights, no compass, no power." Stanton's frustration grew a notch. He spun around and marched to the back wall. A heavy, antique-looking phone hung on the wall. Stanton snapped up the bulky hand-piece and pressed the receiver to his ear. He heard nothing. A small crank was situated to the side. Stanton turned it several times, then listened for a response. Again nothing. Several switches were mounted on the phone's base, each paired with a metal tag identifying the place being called: signal tower, capstan, torpedo rooms, signal offices, and more. He tried them all but each effort was futile. Slowly Stanton returned the receiver. "This is nuts."

"She's dead, isn't she?" John said. "Just like our boat. No power. No engines."

"Engines!" Stanton said. "Good thought. Someone must be in the engine rooms." Stanton stepped across the deck again, to the right side of the steering wheel. There he found the engine room telegraph. "Just like the movies," he said. The telegraph was a round-faced dial with a large brass handle above it. It rested on a metal pedestal that seemed to rise out of the deck like a small tree. The white face of the telegraph was marked with black letters. The brass handle and its pointed indicator rested a few degrees from the vertical. The pointer indicated "Dead Slow." Stanton seized the handle, ran it all the way to the right, then all the way around to the left, only to bring it back to perfect vertical. The indicator now pointed at "Stop." He waited.

"What are you doing?" Steve asked.

"See this small arrow?" Stanton said, pointing at a red sheet-metal pointer. "Whoever is down in the engine room should reply by working his telegraph so it matches this one. In other words, this arrow should move to 'Stop' to match where I put the indicator."

Stanton waited. Nothing happened.

"The electric is dead on that, too," John said. "You should have thought of that."

"It doesn't operate on electricity," Stanton answered. "It's purely mechanical."

"Then why aren't they responding?" Steve asked.

"Because there is no one on board to respond," John snapped. "Mr. Captain Sir here doesn't want to admit it, but this is a ghost ship. You're not afraid of ghosts, are you, Stevie-boy?"

"There are no such things as ghosts," Steve said without conviction.

"They believe in you," John said. He raised his arms in zombie fashion and slowly approached Steve, rocking from one leg to the other as if his knees had been welded tight. "Join us,

Steve," he said eerily. "Join us. We've been waiting for you. There's room for one more."

"Stow it, John," Stanton ordered. "You can practice your comedy routine later." Moving back across the navigation deck, Stanton approached the back wall, where he had stood a moment before. There was a door to his right. Stanton opened it and peered inside. The room was small, seven by nine, he judged. Along the wall to Stanton's right ran a padded bench. Toward the back of the room, on his left, was a wood kneehole desk. "Captain's room," Stanton muttered. He turned to see Steve's inquisitive face. "It was where the captain worked while on the bridge."

Stanton stepped in. The room's several large windows overlooked the pilot's station, letting in much-needed light and making the space very unlike the tomblike superstructure below. Stanton studied the room for a moment. It was Spartan in appearance and function.

"He didn't sleep here, did he?" Steve wondered.

"No, he would have quarters elsewhere." Stanton began to say something else when something caught his eye. The desktop was free of papers and books but it did display a large dark stain. Stanton approached and studied it closely. It was dark brown and seemed to have worked its way through the lightly varnished surface and into the wood grain. Stanton touched it, then rubbed his fingers together. It felt moist. "Tea," he said. "Fresh tea."

He began to look around. The chair to the desk was against the wall that separated the room from the navigation deck. Stanton looked at the chair, then at the desk. Stooping, he peered into the kneehole. It was there. Stanton reached into the space and removed two white porcelain fragments. He rose and set the pieces on the desk.

"A cup," John said. "Big deal."

"It looks new," Stanton said. "The stain on the desk is fresh and the cup is new. Does that sound like something you'd find on a ghost ship, Mr. Hays?"

"Maybe."

"What's in there?" Steve asked, pointing at another door.

"Let's find out." Stanton knew that another room lay on the other side of the door. The captain's room couldn't take up more than a third of the windowed area they had seen from the navigation platform. He approached the door. It opened easily and Stanton crossed its threshold. This room was larger but similar. To the right, at the aft wall, was another padded bench. To the left, a wide table. On the floor, large sheets of paper rested in crumpled masses, like collapsed sails. Stanton stooped and gathered up the papers. He laid them out on the table and studied them for a moment. "Charts."

"What kinda charts?" Steve stepped forward.

"Ocean charts, shipping lanes, the usual." Stanton spread one large sheet out on the table. "See, that's England, Ireland, Scotland, and the North Sea. There are more detailed charts, too." He flipped through the pages.

"So why are they all over the floor?" Steve wondered.

"The storm, I imagine," Stanton said. "Same thing with the teacup. This ship is a lot bigger than the *Tern About*, but it would have been knocked around nonetheless. The ocean doesn't care what size you are."

"Wouldn't someone have bothered to pick up the charts?" Steve wondered. "I mean, they're pretty important."

"That they are." Stanton studied the charts for a moment. "Strange," he muttered.

"What's strange?" Steve asked.

"The charts are all for waters near England," Stanton replied, his eyes fixed on the papers.

"So?" John commented. "You said the ship is British."

"We're off the coast of Florida, not England," Stanton explained. "I would expect to see something showing the shipping lanes for the whole Atlantic." He studied the documents more closely. "Not only that, these charts are nearly a century old."

"They don't look that old," Steve said. "The paper looks new."

"Reproductions," Stanton declared. "These guys didn't miss a trick. If you're going to have a floating museum, you might as well have authentic-looking charts." Stanton paused for a moment and wondered who he was trying to convince.

"I thought we were supposed to be looking for a radio," John said. "I don't see no radio in here or anyplace we've looked so far."

"You're right," Stanton said. "I'm getting distracted. I thought there would be a radio up here, but there's not." He also thought there would be, at the very least, a modern intercom system, but he chose not to mention that.

"Maybe they keep the modern radio where they used to keep the old one—in the old days, I mean," Steve said. "If that makes any sense."

"It makes perfect sense," Stanton said. "In the early nineteen hundreds, radio communications was confined to telegraph signals. There was a room aboard ship called a wireless office. That's what we need to find."

"Where is it on this ship?" Steve asked.

Stanton shook his head. "I don't know. Things are very different now. My guess is that it is somewhere up here on the flying deck. That way, the transmitter would be close to the antennas. To be honest, though, I'm guessing."

"Your guess carries more weight than ours," Steve said. "Where do you want to start?"

"I saw a couple of rooms that are likely candidates. They're farther back. Let's open doors until we find the right one."

"We should split up," John said. It wasn't a suggestion.

"We should stay together and we will," Stanton replied. His was even less a suggestion. "Let's do this, guys."

"Just watch out for ghosts," John added. "They might be right behind us."

Λ

"The dark is creeping me out," Jamie said. "And it's cold."

"Stay close and move slow," Tenny replied. She was thankful that the skylights in the deck above were open, although that same fact puzzled her. Certainly the ship had endured the same storm, had been slapped by the same waves. Everything should have been battened down. But they weren't, which meant someone must have opened the ports, the upper hatches, and removed the watertight covers from the skylights. She had opened the hatches of the *Tern About* after the storm. The act was not unusual. But where were the sailors who had done that work on the *Archer?*

"It's cold," M&M moaned. "I've got goose bumps."

"Me too," Jamie said, "but it's got nothing to do with the cold."

Tenny knew exactly what Jamie meant. They had come down a level from the exposed main deck, and with each step along the steep, curved metal stairway, she felt she was descending into a steel cave, like spelunkers probing the chambers of a massive cavern. Their footfalls echoed off the hard deck and bulkheads. Light sifted through the skylights and open hatches, piercing the darkness like glowing stalactites that melted on the deck into noncorporeal puddles of illumination.

Tenny was a young sailor, but she had learned enough to know that ships don't sail themselves—especially ships this size. She had also learned that leaders were unemotional in crisis, focused on the task before them, and certain in their speech. So she spoke with confidence and moved with assurance, appearing unfazed by the enigma they strolled through. Beneath her own hull of flesh she felt as cold and empty as the battleship.

"We won't be able to search every room," she said. "We've tried every light switch we've come across and nothing works. The ship is as powerless as the catamaran. The skylights can't illuminate the whole deck. Rooms that run the perimeter of the hull will have portholes. That will help. Any rooms in the middle of the ship will be too dark to investigate. If we have to go down another deck, things will be even darker."

"If it gets any darker, we won't be able to move," Jamie said.

"I know. Let's hope we find what we're looking for on this deck."

Tenny had found an early-twentieth-century storm lamp mounted on one of the bulkheads and removed it. It was heavy and bulky, little more than a large battery, a single bulb, a lens surrounded by a tin case. She flipped the switch several times but the lamp refused to release any light. It was as useless as the flashlights on the *Tern About*.

"You'd think they'd have one of those 'You Are Here' signs around," Jamie said. "You know, like they have at the mall."

"This is a warship, Jamie, not a Mervyns," Tenny said.

"I was kidding," Jamie said. "I'm not that stupid."

Tenny stopped and turned to the girls. "I'm sorry," she said. "I'm a little on edge and when I get nervous, my sense of humor goes into hiding. You keep joking, Jamie. We need it." She resumed her march through the gloomy passageway. She had no idea which way to go. The ship was huge. Small, perhaps, when compared with a modern aircraft carrier, but to three women feeling their way along dim corridors, it seemed mammoth. Even choosing a direction was little more than a flip of a coin. Tenny had decided to move forward and search the smaller area, hoping they would be lucky enough to find a medical dispensary.

They had come down the curved stairs into a large open area. Just behind them was a series of metal walls and wood doors. Each wood door rested in a track and hung from an overhead support. It took a minute for Tenny to realize that the doors were meant to slide, not swing on hinges. She approached one, then hesitated. In the stillness and tomblike quiet of the ship it seemed a ridiculous act, but she did it nonetheless. She knocked on the door. Had someone answered, Tenny was sure she would have died of shock. No response came. A U-shaped metal tube served as the door's handle. Tenny took it in her right hand. It felt cold, as if it had been stored in a refrigerator. She started to pull the door to the side but hesitated. Images, garish and ugly, filled her mind. For a moment she was certain the room beyond the door was occupied by the skeletal remains of some sailor long dead and left moldering in the solitude of his cabin.

Closing her eyes for a moment, she inhaled deeply and then pulled the door open with a flourish. It slid easily on its track. Tenny's intuition had been correct but, to her relief, only partly so. She had assumed that the door led to a crew member's cabin, which it did. Fortunately, there was no skeleton, moldering or otherwise. She crossed the threshold.

The room was small, no larger than a child's bedroom in a middle-class home. What little space there was, was well used. A porthole let pass enough light for Tenny to see the crowded space. Just below the opening was a bunk composed of a thin mattress dressed in a dark wool blanket. The bunk was elevated on what reminded Tenny of kitchen cabinets. She estimated the sleeping surface to be three feet off the cork-carpeted floor. Four cabinet doors opened to the space below the bunk itself. To keep anyone sleeping in the bed from rolling off its narrow surface was a metal railing, similar to those on hospital beds. To her left, pressed against the metal partition, was a chest of drawers. Opposite that was an oak desk and chair. Suspended from the walls were a mirror, bookshelf, hat pegs, bottle rack, and curtain rod. A plain curtain hung next to the porthole, and several books populated the shelf.

"Anybody home?" Jamie asked.

"No," Tenny said. "The room is empty."

Jamie came close and peered over Tenny's shoulder. "It's not very big."

"Officer's cabin," Tenny said. "Regular sailors should be lucky to have this much space."

"You're kidding," Jamie said. "I've seen bigger closets."

"Life on the sea can be hard. That was especially true a century ago." Tenny stepped to the desk and, feeling like a nosy guest who can't resist looking in her host's medicine cabinet, opened the top drawer.

"What are you doing?" Jamie asked. Tenny turned and saw that M&M had joined her at the door.

"Looking for anything that can help us."

"Like what?" Jamie pressed.

"I don't know. I'll recognize it when I see it." The drawer held a few sheets of paper, thin envelopes, and a leather pouch half filled with tobacco. Tenny picked up the small bag and opened it, bringing it to her nose. She sniffed.

"Eww," Jamie exclaimed. "What are you smelling?"

"Tobacco. Pipe tobacco, but I can't smell anything. It looks fresh." She returned the pouch and opened another drawer. Inside she found a fountain pen and a bottle of ink, its rubber stopper firmly in place. She lifted the bottle to eye level and shook it gently. The black fluid inside flowed evenly, coating the glass sides of the container, then slowly settled back to the base.

She studied the rubber stopper, running her finger over its surface. It was smooth and pliable. "This looks new," she said. "If it were as old as this ship, the ink would have dried up long ago and the rubber should be cracked and flaky." She replaced the ink bottle.

The next drawer was nearly empty, holding only a black-and-white photo of a man, a woman, and a small child. All looked happy, the woman pleased, the man proud, the child tickled. The man was thin and wearing what Tenny assumed must have been his Sunday best, a stiff-looking coat, white shirt, and thick tie. His hair was curly and his eyes light; Tenny assumed them to be blue. She turned the picture over and found the inked words "Rebecca and Ian, March 1905."

"Okay," Tenny said, "this is getting too bizarre for me." After returning the picture to the drawer, she closed it, turned to the bed, crouched, and opened one of the doors to the storage space below the raised bunk. The thin wood door opened easily and noiselessly. Beneath the bunk were two pairs of shoes and an empty ditty bag used to carry personal goods.

"Should you be rummaging through someone else's things?" Jamie asked. "What if he showed up right now?"

"I'd kiss him full on the mouth," Tenny said. She rose and quickly went through the chest of drawers, finding only blue uniforms, underwear, and a hand-carved chess set. "There's nothing here to help us. Let's keep moving. There has to be a sick bay around here somewhere."

"Which way do we go?" M&M asked. Even in the dim light she looked pale, but her voice was stronger than before.

"It's a toss-up. I say we go forward."

"But doesn't the ship get narrower the farther forward we go?" Jamie wondered. "I mean, wouldn't a place for sick people be larger than one of these cabins?"

"There's still plenty of space forward . . ." Tenny's voice trailed off. Jamie had a point. The ship was large enough to hold a crew of six or seven hundred men. In battle any number of them could be injured. Large ships meant large sick bays. And the sick bay would be the place to find the medical dispensary. "I think you're onto something, Jamie. Good thinking. Let's move aft along the starboard side and see what we see." Jamie seemed pleased with the compliment.

"What's that?" M&M asked, pointing at a large curved wall. "Why is it round?"

"It's one of the barbettes," Tenny said.

"What's that?"

"Remember the big guns you saw on the main deck?" Tenny replied. "The mechanism that moves the shells up and down goes through most if not all the decks. All of that has to be protected. A barbette—at least on this ship—is the armor protection for the guns and their supports."

"Oh," M&M said. She looked confused.

"They teach you all that in the academy?" Jamie asked.

"That and a whole lot more," Tenny answered. "I still have a year to go, so I imagine I'll learn more. I hope to, anyway."

"You really like all this stuff," Jamie said. "It seems so . . ." She didn't finish.

"Unfeminine?" Tenny prompted.

"No offense," Jamie answered, "but yeah. It's so guylike. All the machinery and metal and stuff."

"There's more to the navy than that. Still, I like all that stuff. Don't get me wrong. I enjoy a night on the town as much as the next girl. My closet has a few nice things hanging in it. You should see me in heels."

Jamie laughed. There was a sweet musical nature to the chortle.

"What? You don't think I can wear heels? Girl, you haven't seen anything until you've seen me dressed to the nines."

"The what?" M&M asked.

"The nines," Tenny answered. "Don't they teach you anything in school? It means dressed up in formal wear. You know, fancy-dinner-go-out-on-the-town kind of stuff."

"For some reason, I can only envision you in sailor whites," Jamie said.

"The navy has made me a sailor, Jamie, not a man."

"So you really like it?"

"The navy? So far it's been great. The academy is hard—it's even harder for a woman—but I love it. It makes me feel good to be part of something bigger than me. They make demands of me. I have to think. I have to perform. I have to learn. It sure beats beautician school—for me, at least."

They rounded the armor-plated barbette and found a door to another room. Without hesitation Tenny opened it, forgoing the ritual knocking. Inside they found it similar to the officer's cabin they had explored a few moments before, except this cabin had a wash basin.

"Commander's cabin," Tenny said.

"How do you know that?" Jamie asked.

"What? You don't think I can deduce that fact from the evidence in this room?"

"There's a brass plate on the door," M&M said with a nod. "It says, 'Commander's Cabin.'"

"Okay," Tenny said, "that may have helped a little."

"You gonna rifle through this one too?" Jamie asked.

"No. Let's keep moving."

A few steps farther Tenny stopped. Mounted on the wall was a rack with several rifles in it. Each rifle looked new, the wood stocks showed no cracks, and the barrels were free of rust.

"What's with the guns?" Jamie asked.

"I imagine they're for the British marines who would have been on board," Tenny said, "but you'd have to ask Stanton that question. Wait, the marines came later—a little before World War II, I think. I'm over my head here. I suspect we'll see these racks throughout the ship." The sight of the weapons unsettled Tenny. While it was not unusual for such weapons to be found on a ship, it was the type of rifle that bothered her. While not an expert on firearms, she could distinguish between a modern rifle and one designed a century before. Most unsettling, however, was the fact that they were there at all.

The next two rooms were officers' cabins, but the third caught her by surprise. Like the others, it was an officer's cabin, but a large wood cross was fixed to the bulkhead. On the desk rested a Bible. It was opened to the Psalms.

Tenny read aloud: "'They that go down to the sea in ships, that do business in great waters; These see the works of the LORD, and his wonders in the deep. For he commandeth, and raiseth the stormy wind, which lifteth up the waves thereof. They mount up to the heaven, they go down again to the depths: their soul is melted because of trouble. They reel to and fro, and stagger like a drunken man, and are at their wits' end. Then they cry unto the LORD in their trouble, and he bringeth them out of their distresses. He maketh the storm calm, so that the waves thereof are still. Then are they glad because they be quiet; so he bringeth them unto their desired haven.'"

"A religious sailor," Jamie said. "Who would have thought that? Not the image I have of sailors."

"I think this is the chaplain's quarters," Tenny said. Next to the Bible were three pieces of paper, two blank, one with writing. "It looks like he was working on a sermon." Tenny closed the Bible and walked for the door.

On her second step, Jamie and M&M backpedaled suddenly. M&M gasped and raised her hands to her mouth. Jamie let loose a small scream.

"What?"

Jamie raised her hand and pointed past Tenny. "The Bible . . . ," she began, but the words caught in her throat.

Tenny snapped her head around and felt her heart stumble. The Bible remained on the desk right where she had left—right where she had closed it.

Now it lay open again.

Cut Off

Does this mean what I think it means?" Steve asked. His mouth was pulled back into a tight line as he studied the device in front of him.

To Stanton the boy seemed to have aged several years since coming on board the *Tern About*. It was something Stanton understood; he felt a decade older himself. The sudden onset of the gale, its peculiar behavior, his fall on the deck, and his near-tumble overboard had left him stiff, sore, and bruised. He had not slept in well over twenty-four hours. Weariness dogged his every step and fogged every thought. Those were annoyances he had to ignore. Food and rest would come later.

Stanton sighed. He, Steve, and John had, after crossing steel decks and opening doors to nearly every compartment on the superstructure and flying deck, found the wireless room just forward of the towering aft funnel. This was the room from which all electronic communication with the outside world took place. It was natural to assume that a radio transmitter would be located here—natural but disappointing. Stanton expected a variety of electronic gear but found something far less impressive. Before him, securely attached to a wood table, was a Tune C, Mk II wireless set—a hundred-year-old telegraph. He knew its make and model because a thin brass plate attached to the face of its wood case identified the contraption.

"That doesn't look like any radio I've seen," Steve said.

"It's not a radio," Stanton said. "It's a wireless telegraph. No voice, just dots and dashes."

"We could send out an SOS," Steve suggested. "I mean, that's what it's here for, right?"

"We could if we had power," Stanton answered. "Look, the power switch is on but the set is dead." Stanton found the light switch on the wall and flipped it several times, but nothing happened. He was being forced to face a truth he had been keeping at arm's distance, a truth that would not be ignored or denied: the *Archer* was a lifeless hulk, powerless, empty, abandoned, and it offered very little help.

"So whatever sucked the power from the sailboat did the same to this ship," Steve said.

"Maybe," Stanton said. "It's possible that the generators are shut down. We know the engines aren't running. Maybe everything has just been turned off."

"Do you really think that's the case?" Steve asked. Like Stanton, he was staring at the century-old electronics.

"That's what I want to believe," Stanton admitted. His optimism was cracking and flaking like an old plaster wall. It seemed the world had been turned upside down. Reason, logic were now abstract philosophies, not the expected norm: the sudden storm, the damage to the *Tern About*, the sudden appearance of a ship that should have been scrapped three-quarters of a century earlier, a ship that was empty, lifeless. "I suppose we could find the generators and see if we could get them going again, but that won't help our communications. We might be able to send an SOS, but the Coast Guard doesn't monitor those types of distress calls anymore. Not much need to with all the modern communications available. I think our best bet is getting one of the larger lifeboats going and towing the *Tern About* back to Miami . . . or to the closest ship that will help."

"Maybe Richie will have some good news for us," Steve said. "I'm ready for some good news."

"Me too," Stanton agreed. "Let's head back to our starting point. Our half hour must be up. We don't want to keep the others waiting." Stanton turned for the door and then stopped short. "Where's John?"

Steve shrugged. "I don't know. I was looking at the gear with you."

Stanton marched from the small office in quick steps. He emerged through the metal door and onto the open flying deck. "John!" he called. "Hey, John, where are you?" There was no reply. Leaning over the metal rail, Stanton peered down to the deck a level below. "I don't believe this," he said to himself. "That kid is making me old."

"He's a bad one," Steve said.

"He's just young and rebellious," Stanton replied, but the words didn't ring true in his heart.

"It's way more than that," Steve said. "No offense, but it's been a long time since you were our age. I don't know what high school was like in your day, but I go to a school where someone gets expelled every week for toting a gun to school. Survival for small guys like me requires identifying who the bad guys are and staying out of their way."

"That's a harsh assessment, Steve."

"Yeah, well, it's an accurate one."

Stanton chose to let the conversation die there. John was a problem, that much was certain. The sudden disappearing act was just additional proof. Still, Stanton wasn't ready to sign off on him yet. It was part of his faith to believe that all people are redeemable, no matter how far gone they might seem. After all, the apostle Paul had persecuted the church and imprisoned many believers. John Newton, who wrote the hymn "Amazing Grace," had been a vicious slave trader in the eighteenth century. If God could redeem the likes of them, surely he could find a way to turn around a disgruntled eighteen-year-old.

"John," Stanton called again but received the same silence as before. "Come on," he said and started off. The flying bridge was half the width of the ship and covered an area nearly one-third its length. Its exposed deck ran the perimeter of the ship's superstructure and was cluttered with boiler-room vents, deck pipes, hoists, and winches. Stanton moved quickly around the deck, rounded the aft funnel, and peered down the stairs that led to the deck below. A few moments later he was back at the door of the wireless room. He had made a complete circle of the deck and found no sign of John.

"He's not up here," Steve said. "He must have gone down one of the stairways. He could be anywhere."

"Let's hope he's with the others."

"You can hope, Captain, but I wouldn't put any money on it."

"Let's find out." Stanton moved to the nearest of four curved stairways that led to the enclosed superstructure below their feet. They descended, exchanging the open air for the confined space marked off by thick, steel, rivet-pimpled walls. "We'll check each of these rooms. You take those," he said, pointing to the starboard end of the large room. The area contained a series of rooms set side by side, like pearls on a necklace, including the ship's bakery, rooms used by the ship's carpenter, and ones for other ship services. The rooms that most interested Stanton were the twelve small bathrooms. Perhaps John had felt nature's call and found his way to one of the heads. That would make sense. Just leaving would not. Stanton knocked on each door and called John's name. If there was no answer, he opened the door and looked inside.

It took five minutes to check each room, but John was nowhere to be found. Stanton then heard muted voices. He led Steve out of the structure and back to the deck, where he found the rest of his crew. Richie stood erect, as if unfazed by the grueling past hours. Tony stood at his side, a thin sheen of perspiration on his dark brow, his breathing slightly labored. "He made me run," Tony explained, motioning to Richie. "He's hard to keep up with."

"Better you than me," Stanton said.

Richie looked around. "Wait a minute. Aren't we missing someone? Where's John?"

"I don't know," admitted Stanton. "He was with us in the wireless room. I turned around and he was gone."

"Maybe John is in the john," Tony said, "if you get my drift."

"I checked the heads on this deck and he wasn't in any of those."

"Great," Tenny snapped. "Things are bad enough. We shouldn't have to play hide-and-seek."

Stanton looked at Tenny, whose ebony skin was a shade lighter. Next to her stood M&M and Jamie. Both girls looked rattled. "What happened?"

There was a moment of silence before Tenny explained. She started several times before finding the right combination of words. "We . . . we searched part of the lower deck. But just the lower one. We didn't have time to move farther down."

"I didn't expect you would," Stanton said.

"We found several rooms . . . officers' quarters, I think. We also found the chaplain's quarters. There was a Bible there." She stopped. "This is going to sound too weird, Skipper. I don't want you to think I've lost my marbles."

"Everything about this trip has been weird," Stanton said evenly. "Just say it."

Tenny took a deep breath and explained what had happened.

"Whoa, that is weird," Steve said. "Sounds like something from a ghost movie."

"You must have only thought you closed it, Tenny," Stanton said softly, making sure his voice was free of accusation.

"With all due respect, Captain," Tenny said, her jaw stiffening. "I'm in the top ten percent of my class at the academy. I've got a good brain and a great memory. I know I closed that Bible."

"She did," Jamie interjected. "I saw her do it. I really did."

Stanton raised his hands as if surrendering. "Easy, folks, I'm not saying you're wrong, just trying to understand what happened."

"The Bible opened itself," M&M said. "That's what happened."

"Just because you didn't see it happen doesn't mean it didn't." Jamie's word came like bullets from a machine gun.

Richie spoke before Stanton could get his words out. "Ease up, ladies. No one doubts what you saw. There's enough strangeness here for everyone to enjoy."

"I'm not enjoying any of this," Jamie fired back.

"Did you find any antibiotics for Mary?" Stanton asked.

"No," Tenny admitted. "We need more time . . . and more light. The lower decks aren't going to have portholes and skylights to help us."

"Agreed," Stanton said with a nod. "How are you feeling, Mary?"

"About the same," she replied. "Maybe a little better."

"Is your stomach still tender to the touch?" Stanton probed.

"A little, but it's not getting worse."

"That's good." She still looked pale to Stanton but her appearance had improved. "Fever?"

"I don't think so. I don't feel hot."

That was encouraging. Maybe M&M's problems were caused by something other than appendicitis. However, he could not take that chance. It was still imperative to get her to a medical facility as soon as possible.

Turning to Richie, Stanton asked, "What did you find out? Any luck with the boats?"

"Some," Richie said. "We found fifteen boats of various lengths—actually, fourteen boats and one wood raft. There are two forty-five-foot steam pinnaces and one steam barge. The rest of the boats range in size from about sixteen feet to better than forty feet and are all sail- or human-powered—no engines."

"So there are three steam-powered boats," Stanton mused aloud, turning his attention to the various boats hanging from the superstructure. "How about lowering them? Any problems there?"

"Shouldn't be," Richie replied. "They're secured to davits. It's just a matter of extending the arms and winching the craft down to the water. Of course, we'll need to stoke the boiler and all that."

"Coal is already on the pinnaces?" Stanton wondered.

"Yup, just like the old days, or so I read in books." Richie paused, then asked, "What about a radio? I don't suppose you found something useful."

Stanton shook his head. "Wireless telegraph, and that's all. That really puzzles me. The ship is in great shape. In fact, she looks like she's less than a year out of the shipyard. If she had been restored to sailing condition, she would have modern electronics. Every maritime nation has safety rules. How could they pull into port without a radio to talk to the harbor master or to any tugboat hired to ease her into dock? The only thing I can think of is that she's a museum piece being towed from one port to another."

"Maybe she broke away in the storm," Richie said.

"Or was cut loose," Stanton added. "I sure wouldn't want to be tethered to this thing in a gale."

"It can't be a floating museum," Tenny said. "Everything we saw below speaks against it. The rooms are open. We just walked into the officers' quarters and rummaged around. We found personal effects in the chest of drawers and in the desk. What museum would allow such unrestricted access? It goes beyond that. There are no signs indicating public rest rooms, no plaques describing interesting details about the ship, and no barricades to keep people away from potential hazards."

"What kinds of hazards?" Tony asked.

"All kinds," Tenny said. "A ship can be a dangerous place. Take the stairs. Some are fairly wide and easy to negotiate, but others are very steep and narrow. A fall could easily break a leg, an arm, or even a neck. I've toured several shipboard museums and they always have areas that are off-limits to tourists. For example, there's an American-made World War II submarine in San Francisco called the USS *Pamanito*. It served in the Pacific during the war. It's a self-guided tour. People just walk up and down the thing like they're moving through their own living room. Still, certain areas are off limits. You can't go into the conning tower, because the access ladder is too steep for inexperienced visitors. Other areas are sealed off with Plexiglas partitions. You can see in but you can't touch. This ship is much larger and much more dangerous, yet I haven't seen a single sign or warning."

"Leaving us with what?" Richie asked.

"With the truth, the hard truth. This is really HMS *Archer* as she was in the early nineteen hundreds."

"Complete with Bible-reading ghosts," Tony quipped. Tenny shot him a hot and hard look. "Just trying to lighten things up a little," Tony said quickly.

"What now, Skipper?" Richie inquired.

Stanton looked over the expanse of ocean. The ocean was never this still. The waters acted more like a lake than the Atlantic. The sky had remained unchanged. It was no brighter than before, nor was it dimmer. The white fog also seemed unchanged. It rose in the distance, erasing the horizon line and nearly obscuring the sky overhead. Even more disconcerting was its uniformity. No matter where Stanton looked, the haze seemed the same. Experience had taught him to expect some variation. No fog was so homogeneous and unvaryingly consistent.

"We stay the course," he finally said. "You and Tony prep one of the steam pinnaces for departure. I've never fired up a boiler before and I doubt you have either, so there will be a learning curve. Figure out how to get a fire going in the boiler and how the engine works."

"Aye, sir," Richie said with formality. "What are you going to do?"

"Look for our missing boy," Stanton said darkly. "I want him found as soon as possible."

"That may not be so easy," Tenny said. "We searched only a portion of one deck, and even then there was a lot we must have overlooked. If he's hiding from us, we may never find him. There are a thousand places to hide."

"Still, we have to try," Stanton said.

"He's just trying to get attention for himself," Jamie opined bitterly. "He's probably just showing off. He's so ... so ... needy."

"Maybe he'll just show up on his own," Tony said. "Not that it matters to me. You can leave him here, for all I care."

"We have to look for him," Stanton insisted. "Like Tenny said, a ship can be a dangerous place, especially if you're not familiar with it."

"Tony and I'll have the boat operational ASAP," Richie said.

"I know you will." Stanton wanted to say more but decided to keep the last thought to himself, at least for now. Even if everyone was present and the pinnace was ready to steam off, Stanton would still hesitate. Again he looked at the distant milky mist, knowing that he had no idea which way led back to Miami.

Hide-and-Seek

Stanton's mind accelerated like the engine of a race car, each piston a different emotion. He was angry with John, worried about M&M, puzzled by Tenny's account, and confused by the mysterious ship he now searched. After he sent Richie and Tony back to the boats hanging from the *Archer*'s superstructure, Stanton and the others plunged into the metal-cased twilight of the ship's interior. It was exactly as Tenny described it—the dimness made seeing difficult.

"How long ago did you search this deck?" Stanton asked Tenny.

"We searched for about thirty minutes, then went back to the rendezvous point to meet you. We waited for you about ten minutes."

"I don't know when John wandered off, exactly," Stanton admitted. "It took us about twenty minutes to search the bridge, pilot station, and chart room. It took at least another five minutes to find the wireless room. That's twenty-five minutes. If John left as soon as we entered the last room, he's been gone for ... what? Five or ten minutes?"

"Longer," Tenny replied. "You were a little late getting back and we spent another five minutes or so talking outside."

"Okay, then he may have disappeared fifteen or twenty minutes ago."

"That's what I make it," Tenny said.

"Why can't we just leave him here?" Jamie asked. "He's been nothing but a problem."

"You know I can't do that, Jamie," Stanton said. "I'm taking everyone home, including John."

"He's the one who ran away," Jamie protested. "If he wants to be alone on the ship, then let him."

"Maybe he's just playing a little game," M&M suggested.

"I'll tell you one thing," Jamie said, "if he jumps out of the shadows and yells 'Boo!' I'm personally going to throw him overboard."

Jamie's tension was palpable and Stanton dismissed her comments as an attempt to expel fear. "Let's just find him as quickly as we can." He turned to Tenny. "This is the deck you searched, right?"

"Right," Tenny replied. "We didn't have time to check every room. We didn't make a complete search. We could spend the day just looking in each of the rooms. I'm guessing there are at least three more decks below this one."

"Maybe one or two more than that," Stanton said. "And you're right. There's not much light. At least at this level we have some light from portholes and skylights." He paused and looked through the dim room. They were standing next to a curved stairway. It was far more ladder than stair and was made of cold, unbending steel. It was one of two in the large space. A companion stairway stood a few steps port. Stanton clenched his jaw and squeezed his eyes shut. The ship was a maze of metal rooms, companionways, ducts, and pipes. He estimated that there were hundreds of rooms in which a young man could hide, and perhaps thousands of lockers and spaces. If John truly wanted to remain hidden, there was no stopping him. Twenty people could, with a little planning, live on this ship and never see each other if they didn't want to.

"Okay," Stanton finally said, raising his head and opening his eyes. "John is going to have the same problem we do. If he goes deeper into the ship's belly, he will have less light—"

"He has the lighter," Jamie said.

"What lighter?"

Tenny explained about the lighter and how they used it during the storm.

"That gives him the advantage," Stanton said, "but the lighter has limited fuel. He can't use it for long. We search up here again, at least at first. If this deck checks out, then I'll see if I can't rig up some light source."

"Like what?" Tenny asked.

"I have no idea. Some kind of torch maybe."

Tenny led the way, pointing out the rooms they had examined and giving a brief account of each survey. When they came to the chaplain's quarters, Stanton marched in, looked around, then let his gaze settle on the open Bible. "This is it?"

"Yeah," Tenny answered. "That's it."

Stanton looked up and saw that Tenny stood by the door but still outside the room. Jamie and M&M were several steps back. Only Steve had followed him in. Stanton looked back at the Bible. It lay open. Next to it were three sheets of paper. The top sheet displayed a fine cursive writing. "Is this the page the Bible was open to previously?" He watched as Tenny blinked several times, then crossed the threshold into the room. Stanton knew she did so only after commanding her fear to take a backseat to duty.

She looked down at the Bible. "Yes. Psalms. The one about sailors."

Redirecting his eyes to the pages, he read aloud one of the verses: "'They that go down to the sea in ships, that do business in great waters; These see the works of the LORD, and his wonders in the deep.' Psalm 107." He touched the book. "The Bible is in good shape. It looks almost new. Just like everything else."

Stanton stepped from the room and started aft again, opening every door and peering inside, hoping to find John. A part of Stanton was enjoying the expedition. If he hadn't been worried about M&M's health or concerned about John's whereabouts, he would have wanted to examine every inch of the old battleship. What a great adventure for a naval historian. The opportunity to explore a ship made nearly a century ago was too good to be true. That's what he had to keep reminding himself: too good to be true. Not one thing since the storm seemed logical.

"This was as far as we got," Tenny said. "We spent too much time looking in the officers' quarters and other rooms." She sounded disappointed in herself.

"You did fine, Tenny. Let's push farther back."

The next few doors opened to cabins of various sizes. "Junior-grade officers," Stanton said. "Higher-ranking officers would be forward."

Stanton limited his time in each room. John was his concern right now. He had to stay focused on finding him. He swung open another door, expecting to see a small cabin. Instead he was greeted with a long room. Four portholes and one loading hatch dotted the exterior wall. Beds with tubular metal head frames and foot rails stood in two rows to Stanton's left. Porcelain sinks were spaced along the near wall. The center of the space was dominated by a large table. Benches with locker space below framed the table.

"Sick bay," Stanton announced. He entered. "You got close. Another ten minutes and you would have found it." The others followed him in. "This way," he said and strode across the metal deck to what appeared to be a smaller room within the larger expanse.

"This looks like a hospital," Jamie said. "A really old-time hospital."

"That's what sick bay is," Stanton said. "Be glad you live when you do. The early nineteen hundreds were not a good time to get sick. Until the late eighteen hundreds, surgeons performed their operations with bare hands and in their street clothes. Germ theory wasn't developed until nearly the turn of the century. X-rays weren't discovered until 1895. A few years later they were used to find foreign objects, like bullets, in the human body. It was all pretty crude stuff."

"It smells weird," M&M said. "Yuck."

"You're probably smelling the soap they used to keep the place clean—that and the medications."

"What 'they'?" Jamie said. "There is no 'they,' remember? It's just us on an empty ship."

"I meant back in the day when this was a new ship," Stanton said.

"I thought it was a new ship," Jamie pressed.

Shaking his head, Stanton said, "I can't explain it, Jamie. I wish I could. It makes no sense. The ship should not be here, it should not be empty of crew, and it shouldn't appear as new as it does, but here it is . . ." Stanton's voice trailed off. Jamie was right. The room did smell odd. Why did that seem strange? "Have any of you noticed odors before?"

"The sailboat reeked pretty good after our all-night vomit session," Jamie answered.

"I mean since we've been aboard the *Archer*."

They thought for a moment and Tenny shook her head. "Not that I can remember." The girls agreed. "Why?"

"I hadn't thought about it before," Stanton said. "But this ship should be filled with smells, even if it's just a floating, empty shell. Yet everything we see tells us it's in its original condition. I can't explain that, but everything around us contradicts logic. So if the ship is what it appears to be, why don't we smell coal, oil, bread, and a thousand other smells? Why is this the first time we notice any odor?"

No one answered. Stanton didn't expect a response—he had no explanations to offer. Opening the door to the smaller room, he found what he expected. "Dispensary," he explained. "This is where the medications and narcotics would have been kept . . . are kept and dolled out by the ship's doctor."

"This room stinks more than the big one," Jamie complained.

The smells were getting stronger. The air was becoming thick with sweet odors punctuated by sour aromas, reminding Stanton of a pharmacy. Ahead, several large wood cabinets lined the walls. Each was painted white and had doors with panes of glass, like a French door. The glass was wavy, not smooth like those in a modern window. Through the glass he could see row upon row of large bottles and paper boxes. Most of the bottles were brown glass, a technique still used, Stanton knew, to limit the access of light to the medicine within. Light would break down certain chemical compounds. For some medications to remain fresh, they had to be stored in dark glass. Each package and each bottle bore a label. Some of the labels were crooked, a reminder that the job had been done by hand.

Quickly Stanton read the labels. Most were compounds he didn't recognize. He was hoping to find an antibiotic he could identify by name. At the very least he hoped to find penicillin. He worked quickly but not hastily, reading each label before moving on to the next bottle or box. He searched every cabinet, until he finally unchained the truth he had been keeping prisoner in the back of his mind.

"With all these medications," Tenny said, "you'd think they'd have at least some kind of antibiotic."

Stanton shook his head. He was convinced now that they would never find antibiotics on this ship. Everything he had seen was indeed original. He had hoped that the *Archer* was an old ship made seaworthy for the twenty-first century, but the truth had begun slamming against the locked door of his mind when he and Steve first saw the wireless telegraph. No matter how much or how often Stanton dismissed the notion, it came roaring back. The *Archer* was a dreadnought, a ship built a century ago, and everything on board, no matter how new it looked, was from a different era.

"No antibiotics," Stanton said. "We won't find any here or anywhere else on this ship."

"You sound sure," Steve said.

"I am. I should have realized it sooner. Antibiotics weren't discovered until 1928," Stanton explained. "That's when Alexander Fleming discovered penicillin. This boat was nearly a quarter of a century old by the time penicillin was in wide use." He let his eyes trace all the open cabinets. "All this is from a time before modern medicine." He turned his gaze to M&M. "I'm sorry, Mary."

She shrugged. "I'll be okay. Don't worry." She offered an uncertain smile.

"Wait," Steve said. "Did you hear that?"

"Hear what?" Tenny asked.

"I thought I heard a . . . a rumbling."

Stanton froze in place, closed his eyes, and listened intently, as if he could make a muted sound louder by sheer willpower.

"I hear people whispering," Jamie said.

"Maybe it's Richie and Tony," Tenny suggested.

"No way," Jamie shot back. "I'm hearing more than two voices."

"How can that be?" Tenny asked. "We know there's no one on board—"

Light flashed through the room.

The metal deck vibrated.

Stanton was hurled backward, his feet losing their purchase on the deck. Before he could speak, he felt himself lifted into the air and slipping back toward the open cabinets. He slammed into Steve and both tumbled hard to the deck. Jamie and M&M screamed as they too were forced backward. Fortunately, they had only been a foot or two away from the wood cupboard. Both clawed the furniture to keep from being slammed to the ground. Tenny was not so lucky. Stanton watched helplessly as her feet slipped away as if on ice and her head bounced off the steel floor.

Lights in the room blazed and Stanton was sure he heard the guttural rumbling of steam engines. The deck pitched up slightly, then came back down. It repeated the motion several times. Instantly Stanton recognized the movement. It was the action of a ship sailing through an active sea.

Through the partially open door, he heard a voice—a strange voice—say, "Did you hear that?"

"I should say I did," said another stranger. "It sounded like a crash in the dispensary."

Stanton looked to the door and tried to get to his feet. He heard footfalls, then saw two men. For a long second Stanton's heart stopped beating. Not only did he see two men—he saw through two men.

As quickly as they had come on, the lights went out, the engine noise died, there was another violent lunge, and the translucent strangers disappeared.

Questions

In any other situation, Richie would have taken a step back and leisurely admired the boat before him. It was forty-five feet long and made of wood. No, Richie corrected himself. It wasn't "made" of wood, it was "crafted" of wood. The hull was smooth and coated with thick marine paint that looked as if it had been applied only a week before. The boat hung from gooseneck davits and was suspended by cable and tackle that had yet to see any rust. Richie could see the craft from stem to stern and from keel to the top of the single metal stack that rose from just before the middle of the boat. Farther back and piercing the low-slung cabin were two hunchback-shaped funnels, proof that the pinnace was steam-powered. Stamping an amen to that truth, Richie could see a single propeller and shaft below the stern. The stack would vent smoke from the coal-burning furnace that would fire the boilers, which would in turn drive the steam engine. "Old-world construction," he murmured.

"What?" Tony asked.

They were standing on the starboard side of the deck above the flying bridge—the boat deck. It was one of the highest decks on the battleship. The only higher vantage points were the compass deck above the bridge and a small searchlight platform on the towering foremast—the crow's nest. Few things caused Richie pause, but the thought of climbing the tripod mast structure and standing on that small platform gave him the shivers. He was glad such an effort was unnecessary.

"The pinnace," Richie explained. "It's beautiful; true old-world craftsmanship. They knew how to make boats back then."

"If you say so," Tony said. The boy seemed uncomfortable. "What now?"

"First we climb in and check things out. I'm hoping everything we need will be on board."

"Like what?"

"I can tell by the funnels and the propeller that it's a powered craft." He pointed at the roof of the boat. "The two small funnels are for the engine room and the boiler room. The tall, straight funnel vents the coal smoke."

"How do you know all this?"

"Simple deduction, my good Dr. Watson. Good deduction and sheer genius on my part."

"Okay, Sherlock, if you're so smart, then lead on. I don't want to stand in the way of genius."

"You just want to see how high I'll bounce off the deck if I fall," Richie quipped, giving Tony a friendly punch on the arm.

"Yeah, well, there is that."

The pinnace was secured in place over the main deck by the bent, tubular davits that acted like small cranes, able to extend over the water to lower and raise the boat when needed. Guy wires kept the craft from swaying in heavy seas. Since the ocean was as flat as a butcher's block, the guy wires had little to do.

Two steel ladders bridged the vertical gap between the boat deck and the pinnace. "Should be easy enough," Richie said. "A little climb and then—bingo—we're aboard a boat that is aboard a boat." Richie paused. "Get it?"

"I get it," Tony said with a sigh. "I don't want it but I got it."

"You didn't know you were partnered with a man of wit as well as skill, did you?"

"I still don't. Start climbing, O fearless leader."

"You seemed a little frightened. I'm trying to lighten the moment. You know, lift your burden and all that."

"I'm not frightened, I don't have a burden . . . unless you count that thing you call a sense of humor. Do you want me to lead the way?"

"Lighten up, my man," Richie said, his tone more serious. "You're acting like a kid who didn't get his nap. We've worked well together so far; let's not flush that now."

"I have a low tolerance for the bubbly optimist."

"Bubbly optimist?" Richie asked as he took hold of the ladder.

"Yeah. I see them all the time. Guys like you and Stanton. Religious types. The world is coming apart at the seams, and guys like you skip off to church to sing songs and say amen."

"You're saying Christians are oblivious to their problems?"

"I'm saying we should stop working our jaws and start climbing the ladder."

"There's more to faith than church songs, Tony. Much more. You're being critical of something you don't understand."

"Yeah, well, it's in my genes. It's just the way guys like me are. We tread water in school until we turn eighteen, and then we go out and get meaningless jobs, buy beer, and drink ourselves to sleep so we can start it all over again."

"Who have you been watching?" Richie asked.

"My dad. My friend's dad."

Richie had climbed three treads. He stopped. "Your dad comes home and gets drunk every night?"

"Not drunk," Tony corrected, "but he has a good buzz on by bedtime."

"Your father is the—"

"Cook," Tony finished. "I'm sure he doesn't drink when on ship, but he makes up for it at home."

"Is he—"

"Violent? No, which is a good thing for him. There are days when I wish he would take a swing at me. That'd give me the excuse I need." He paused just a second, then added, "I've been through all this with school counselors and every other bleeding heart. I don't want to go through it again. Just climb. I'll be right on your heels."

Richie continued up the ladder. One more riser and he would be able to reach over the gunwale and then step aboard the boat. He stopped. Something caught his attention. A noise. A sudden smell. A vibration. Then—

The ladder was jerked out of Richie's hand and he fell to the side, the solid support of the steel ladder now gone. He reached, grasped, clawed for any hold and found himself hanging from the edge of the pinnace. The ladder he had been standing on was suddenly three feet to his left—an impossibility. It was as if the entire battleship had shifted forward and his inertia had kept him in place.

Strengthened by the sudden rush of fear-induced adrenaline into his blood, Richie kicked, pulled, worked, and shinnied up and over the gunwale and onto the boat's deck. A half second later he was on his feet, looking down to see Tony flat on his back. The boy cursed loudly and then struggled to his feet. "You all right?" Richie asked.

"Yeah," Tony said, then punctuated the affirmation with a hot stream of curses. "What happened?"

"I don't know," Richie admitted. "It's as if—" He stopped. Movement caught his eye. Looking up, he saw a thick, wide stream of black smoke climbing high into the air from the ship's forward stack. "That's impossible," he said, more to himself than to Tony. Snapping his head around, he looked aft over the stern of the ship. A long white river of foam trailed after her. It was at least a mile long. That made no sense to Richie. It was one thing for someone to fire up the steam engines and set the ship moving, but there was no way the ship's wake could be that long in the few seconds that had just elapsed.

Other things were different. The sky was a crystal blue, not the milky white it had been since the storm. Three-foot swells undulated along the ocean's surface. Everything was alive again. Turning his attention forward, Richie watched in stunned horror as a man exited the sheltered navigation deck of the flying bridge and scanned the horizon. The act itself was not startling—what shocked Richie was that he could see right through the man.

N
⋏

John could hear their voices. He could especially hear the tone of that self-righteous Stanton. They were searching for him and they weren't being very clever about it. Every time they spoke, their voices echoed off the steel walls. Avoiding them should be easy. All he had to do was listen and they would give away their location.

He felt proud of himself. He had slipped away unnoticed and avoided contact with the others as easily as if they were blind. His first plan had been to descend into the deepest part of the ship, but the darkness drove him back to the main deck. The lighter was useful but limited. The longer he let the flame flicker, the hotter the lighter became. Then there was the matter of fuel. The lighter was cheap, something he had shoplifted a week earlier. He hadn't needed a lighter then but he had wanted the thrill of the theft.

John had moved with the stealth of a cat, always keeping Stanton and the others in sight. That was dangerous. Hiding in some dark cubbyhole would be better and there were many of those, but there was no excitement in that, no drama. And so what if he were caught? What were they going to do to him? Nothing. They could criticize, ridicule, yell, whatever; it didn't matter. They might keep a closer eye on him, but they didn't have what it took to force him to do anything. None of them did. No, they would have to play his game, his way. Once again he was in control.

He watched as Stanton led his little party of kiddies into the sick bay. He himself had been in there a few moments before, slipping out just in time to avoid detection. Moving back through the ship, he went through an open door, being careful to step over the bulkhead sill, and found himself in a large room filled with long tables and benches. He estimated that there were twenty tables. Mess hall, he thought. A small room was situated to one side. John approached and peered in. Inside were shelves and dressers holding food stuffs. Turning, he saw a large open area with a cooking range, a boiler of some sort, and several other appliances he couldn't identify. John knew he was looking at the ship's open galley. It made sense. Benches, tables, cooking appliances—he was in a sailor's favorite part of the ship.

He moved back to the door and quickly peeked around its edge. There was no sign of Stanton and the others, but he knew it wouldn't be long. Stanton seemed to be an organized, logical man. That meant he would set up a plan and follow it. It made sense but it also made him predictable. The mess space would be Stanton's next stop, and it was much too open an area in which to hide. John supposed he could conceal himself under one of the many tables, but Stanton was no dummy; he'd look.

It was better to move farther along and see what lay beyond the next bulkhead.

John stepped lightly but quickly passed the tables and benches and racks that filled the room. He was coming to the very back of the ship. He knew this because the distance between the left and right hulls was diminishing. He might be cutting off an escape route but he wanted to take the chance. So far the game had been too easy. Eluding the others was meant to be fun, but there was no fun if there wasn't the risk of being caught. That's what motivated him. At school, at home, in stores, it didn't matter. If others were around, that was the time to misbehave. Such antics were useless when alone. It was impossible to annoy people who weren't there, and if they weren't annoyed, they ignored him. He hated to be ignored.

John slipped through the door.

Compared with the mess area, this room was smaller by half. Several rows of racks, the kind he had seen elsewhere in the ship, stood in the middle of the space. Each rack held scores of canvas bags. When he first slipped away, John had gone to one such sack and rifled through it. It was filled with underwear, shaving kits, and the like. Personal effects of some missing sailor, he decided. None of it interested him. At least not then. If he weren't hiding, he might have gone through the bag in detail, but the game was more important. He had placed the bag back in the rack. There had been hundreds of such bags and this room sported more.

The room was different in another way. To his right was a row of seven toilet stalls. That was one thing that hadn't changed since the ship was built. People still needed a place to go to the bathroom. More interesting were the small, divided spaces to his left. These too were easily recognizable. The giveaway was the iron bars at the front of each cell.

"Cool," he whispered and took a step toward them.

The lights came on, which would have stunned John had he not been thrown head over heels and heels over head toward the back of the ship. He landed hard on his back and slid several feet. The deck was moving up and down and rolling back and forth. The floor vibrated from what John assumed were the engines. He sat up and shook his head. Pain rolled down his neck and back. "Who started the engines?"

Then he heard the voices. He sprang to his feet and turned toward the sound. He looked. He saw. He stumbled back in fright.

Before him were two men, one older and one about John's age. Both were nearly transparent. The voices were clear but hollow and echoey, as if the words were being uttered inside a tin can. The older man had his back turned to John. He was big and round like a barrel and his arms were so thick, they strained the shirt of the blue uniform he wore. The younger man was the antithesis: rail-thin, dark eyes, coal black hair. John could see all these things and make out all the details, but the people were still see-through, like the ghosts depicted on television.

The younger man's blue uniform hung limply on his narrow frame. He stood with his hands clasped behind his back, as if standing at ease, but his posture beamed apathy. He was looking at the bigger man, who was doing all the talking. John recognized the posture and the expression; the young sailor could care less about what he was hearing.

". . . you got that, lad?" the older man said. He had an accent that reminded John of something he had seen and heard on television. Years ago he had watched a TV show on the history of rock and roll. At the time, he was entertaining the idea of being a rock and roll star, but then he found out how much work was involved in learning to play the guitar. He gave up within a week.

The show highlighted the Beatles. They were from Liverpool, England, and talked funny. The big sailor spoke the same way. "You might think that because your uncle is high up in the Royal Navy, I won't ride you, but you're wrong. I know your kind, boy, and I know how to fix the likes of you. Do you understand me?"

The young man didn't answer.

"I asked you a question," the big man bellowed but the kid remained silent. A small smile crossed his face. A second later he was on the deck, blood trickling from his mouth, where his tormentor had cuffed him with the back of his hand. "I'll be taking no disrespect from you, boy. Now get up and start cleaning them toilets. When you're done with them, go aft and clean the urinals. And they had better be clean enough to eat off, because if you give me one second more of grief, you'll be eating all your meals out of them. You better clean the prisons while you're at it." He pointed to the barred cells. "You might be spending the rest of this tour in one of them." Then he laughed. He pointed to the portholes along the hull. "I wants them side scuttles cleaned too, boy. Hear that, do ya? Clean, and I mean glass and the deadlights."

The boy started to rise, then looked in John's direction. He froze and tilted his head to the side, as if uncertain as to what he was seeing. Then he winked.

Everything fell silent and John went sliding forward along the floor. The lights had gone out and the deck no longer pitched and rolled.

The two sailors were gone.

"What . . . what happened?" Steve asked. He was sitting on the deck. He looked stunned.

Stanton struggled to his feet. "Is everyone okay?" He held out a hand to Steve and helped the boy up, then hurried to help the others. Jamie was lying on the floor, a red rivulet running down the right side of her forehead. Stanton could see a small gash just south of her hairline.

"My head," she moaned. "I hit my head on something."

"Let me see," Stanton said, crouching beside her. He examined the wound closely. It seemed superficial. "There's a little cut," he said.

"Little?" Jamie complained. "Look at the blood." She drew her hand across her forehead, lining it with a streak of sticky crimson.

"Scalp wounds always look worse than they are," Stanton said. "There are a lot of tiny blood vessels in the skin there. Let me see your eyes." He studied her pupils and was relieved that they were the same size. "How's your vision? You're not seeing two of me, are you?"

"Oh, please! One is enough."

Stanton laughed lightly. "Apparently, your cynicism is intact." He turned to Steve. "See if you can find some bandages or gauze," he said. "There should be plenty in here." Steve immediately returned to the cabinets. "How's your neck?" Stanton asked Jamie.

"Okay, I guess. It doesn't hurt or anything."

"Let me see your ears." Gently Stanton turned her head from side to side, looking in each ear. No blood. No cerebral spinal fluid. "I think you're going to live."

"Try to act more pleased," Jamie quipped, sitting up. Her tone was much softer and Stanton thought he detected a note of appreciation.

"How about you, Mary? You okay?"

Mary was seated, leaning against one of the storage cabinets. One glass panel, the one behind her head, was shattered. She was motionless, eyes wide and mouth open. She was staring at the door. When Stanton saw the shattered glass, his stomach twisted into a tight knot.

"Mary?" Stanton moved to M&M and knelt by her. "Talk to me, Mary."

"Did . . . did . . . I mean . . . they were right there, but . . . they weren't there."

"Take it easy," Stanton whispered. "Let me have a look at you."

"I'm not crazy," Mary said as if each word weighed a ton. "I saw them."

"Me too," Stanton said.

"Really? You're not just saying that?"

"I really saw them," Stanton said. "Kind of took the wind out of me. Lean forward."

"Why?"

"You hit your head; I want to see if you're bleeding." He reached forward and she pulled back. Stanton withdrew his hand. "Mary, listen to me. I know you've been mistreated, but it's time you started trusting me. If we were in a normal situation, I'd give you all the room you need, but we're in . . . whatever it is we're in. Now lean forward . . . please."

Stanton watched as M&M cut her eyes to Jamie. From the corner of his eye he saw Jamie nod. As reluctant as a novice tightrope walker, M&M leaned forward and turned her head so he could see the back of it. He was relieved to find no matting in her straight brown hair. He touched her hair and she started to pull away. Gently he felt the back of her head. There was a small knot but nothing more. He repeated the same exam he had given Jamie. He was no paramedic, but he knew enough to look for obvious signs of head trauma. He found nothing of concern.

"It looks like you'll live too," he said.

"Mr. Stanton," Steve said. "You'd better look over here."

Turning, Stanton saw Steve standing with an empty box in one hand and a white gauze bandage in the other. He was looking across the dispensary, where Tenny lay facedown, unmoving. Rising, Stanton strode calmly across the floor, fighting to keep his fear in check. He hunkered down by Tenny but didn't touch her. He held his breath as he watched her back rise and fall, then rise and fall again. She was breathing. Stanton took a much needed breath and held it for a moment, then let it out slowly.

Tenny lay on her belly, her head tilted awkwardly, allowing Stanton to see the left side of her face. Tenderly he touched two fingers to the side of her neck and felt for a carotid pulse. It was strong and even. Another good sign. Pulling down her collar, he examined her neck. He feared seeing an uneven line of bumps, indicating a broken spine, but her neck too seemed normal. Still, there could be a break he couldn't see.

"Tenny," he said softly, but there was no response. "Tenny. You with me?" His words were louder. This time there was a moan. "Tenny," Stanton repeated.

The one eye Stanton could see opened, closed, then opened again. He watched as she blinked several times.

"How are you feeling?" Stanton asked. She rolled over. "Easy does it, sailor."

"Ow." She raised a hand to her head. "Who hit me?"

"I think you hit the deck." Now that Tenny was lying on her back, Stanton could see the other side of the woman's face. It was swollen just above the cheekbone, and the ebony skin under her right eye had darkened. "Take it easy for a moment and let me look at you. Does anything hurt?"

"My body," she said.

"Can you be more specific?" Stanton asked as he examined her eyes and ears.

"I'm okay, Skipper. Just took a knock on the noggin. I've received worse horsing around with my brother." She sat up. "Whoa, who's spinning the room?"

"Go slow," Stanton ordered. "You don't want to go dribbling your head on the deck again."

"Will do," Tenny said. "Does anyone know what happened?"

"Not really," Stanton said. "It was as if the ship suddenly came alive, then died again a moment later."

"Why did we all go bouncing around the room like pinballs?" Steve asked. He was putting the gauze bandage on Jamie's head. To Stanton's surprise, Jamie was allowing it.

"I have no idea." Stanton rose. "I think we'd better check on Richie and Tony. If we got banged up, they must have, too."

"What about John?" Tenny asked.

"We don't know where he is. As soon as we're sure the others are all right, I'll start looking again."

"Don't you mean 'we'?" Tenny asked.

"I think you guys have been banged up enough. I can search faster by myself."

"I'm not banged up," Steve said. "You shouldn't go alone. I'll go with you."

Stanton studied the boy for a moment. It was as if he were changing right before his eyes. "Thanks, Steve. I'll take the help."

"I must have really whacked my head," Tenny said, blinking several times.

"Is there something wrong with your vision?" Stanton worried aloud.

"There must be, because I thought I saw something before I went under. Of course, I couldn't have. I must have been dreaming."

"Transparent men?" Jamie asked.

"How did you know?" Tenny shot back.

"We all saw them," Jamie answered. "Even Captain Cool."

"You saw them, sir?" She held out a hand to him.

Stanton nodded and helped her to her feet. "I sure saw something."

Reasoning

Stanton led the others back the way they had come. He moved as quickly as he could, not wanting to leave anyone behind. One missing charge was enough. Aches and pains erupted in his body with every step. The latest physical abuse reawakened the bruises he had received while on the *Tern About*. The pain was secondary. No matter how much his body complained, he pushed it forward, making one foot follow the other. What he really wanted to do was sleep; even more so, he longed to wake up from the nightmare he was living. He hoped it was a nightmare. Bad dreams required no explanation, no logic. Everything he had seen on the battleship lacked those two elements; therefore all this had to be a long, convincing, Technicolor dream. But the sound of his sneaker-clad feet treading a metal deck, the throbbing pain in his body, the pounding of his heart, and a hundred other indicators told him that the nightmare was real.

Moving past the officers' quarters, to the spiral stairway, and up to the main deck, Stanton finally burst from the twilight interior to the muted, milky exterior. The deck below his feet was the familiar wood-over-steel he had seen when he first climbed aboard. He hustled to the rendezvous point, hoping to see Richie and Tony waiting for him. They weren't. Stepping to the life-line, Stanton directed his gaze upward to the boat deck. Richie was supposed to be preparing one of the pinnaces, but Stanton didn't know which boat that was. Some of the boats were easy to see, hanging from their supports, but others were hidden by parts of the tripod mast, the superstructure, and other boats. From his location, Stanton could see only a few of the fourteen boats Richie said he had found. Stanton didn't even know if the boat they were readying was on this side or the starboard side. He wished he had asked for more details. Good command required good information, but he had failed to ask the pertinent questions. He grew angry with himself about the oversight but pushed the feeling away. Emotion seldom helped.

Stanton waited for the others to catch up to him, then announced, "Tenny, keep everyone here. I'm going up to the boat deck and see if Richie and Tony are okay—"

"No need," came a voice from behind Stanton. He turned to see Richie hobbling quickly along the deck. Tony was right behind him. "We were going to look for you."

"You're hurt," Stanton said.

"Not really," Richie replied quickly. "I just barked my shin when I fell from the ladder."

"Fell?" Tenny said with concern.

"I was just about to enter the pinnace when . . . whatever happened, happened. I lost my footing but was able to catch the side of the boat and pull myself up. I'm okay."

"You should have seen it," Tony said, "a real circus act. He should play Vegas."

Richie's eyes narrowed as he gazed at the others. Stanton could tell he had noticed the bumps and bruises. "It looks like you guys took a bigger beating than we did," Richie said.

"Jamie cut her scalp; everyone else got knocks on the head for souvenirs," Steve said. "Except me. Years of riding skateboards paid off."

"I guess I'll be part of the ugly young mutants," Jamie said. She was touching the bandage on her head. The white gauze had a red stain in the middle.

"No one can ever call you ugly," Tony said. There was an uncharacteristic gentleness in the words. Jamie picked up on it.

"Um, thanks," she replied.

To Richie and Tony, Stanton said, "Tell me what you saw."

Richie shook his head. "You wouldn't believe me if I did."

"Right now I'd believe just about anything."

"Okay," Richie conceded. "Like I said, I was climbing one of the ladders into the pinnace when suddenly everything began to move. I slipped sideways off the ladder but was able to grab hold of the gunwale. I hung there for a moment, then pulled myself up. At first I was confused . . ." He stopped. "Actually, I'm still confused. Everything had changed."

"Changed how?" Stanton prompted.

"First, the sky was blue, not this misty white surrounding us. I could see the sun and the clouds. The ocean was a proper blue. And—this is really weird—there was black smoke coming out of the forward stack, pouring out big-time, like the ship was under full power." He paused and Stanton let him collect his thoughts uninterrupted. "I looked aft and saw the ship's wake."

"Wake?" Stanton said. "You're kidding."

"Yeah, wake. A long, wide, white ribbon of foam. The propellers must have been churning pretty good."

"That can't be right," Stanton murmured, more to himself than to the others, but Richie heard it.

"It may not be right, sir, but it is what I saw," he intoned seriously.

"I don't doubt you, Richie," Stanton said. "I'm just trying to get the pieces to fit."

Tony laughed. "Yeah? Well, wait to hear what else he saw. I'd like to see you fit that piece in."

"Give me the rest of it, Richie."

Richie was instantly nervous, shuffling his feet. He even took a step backward. "I don't know, Skipper. I mean, I was pretty shook. For a moment I thought I was going to drop headfirst to the deck below."

"Come on, Richie Rich," Tony prodded, "tell it. You weren't hanging by your fingernails when you saw them."

"Cut me some slack, will ya, Tony?" Richie snapped.

"Ghosts," Tony whispered and rolled his eyes. "He saw ghosts."

"He's not alone," Steve said.

Stanton looked Richie hard in the eyes. "I need your report."

Richie sighed. "First of all, I wasn't hanging by my fingernails. And it's not 'them,' it was just one person. After I was on the pinnace, I looked toward the bridge. I saw someone step out and survey the horizon . . . except . . . well, he wasn't all there. He was . . . I could see through him."

Tony made ghost sounds. "Hey, this would make a great movie."

"Back off, Tony," Steve said with more authority than Stanton had heard from him before. "We saw the same thing."

"Wait a minute," Richie said. "You saw the guy too? How could you? You were below deck."

"We didn't see what you saw," Stanton explained. "We saw something similar. We were in the ship's dispensary when the"— he struggled for the right descriptive word—"event happened. We heard voices, then two men appeared in the doorway. A moment later there was another lurch and the men disappeared."

"You could see through them?" Richie wondered.

"Oh yeah," Steve answered. "Big-time."

"Ghosts," M&M said softly. "Just like what I saw in my cabin."

Stanton recalled what Tenny had told him about Mary's hysteria. He also recalled what he had seen on deck of the *Tern About*.

"If I weren't so scared, I'd be excited," Steve said. "How many people get to see real live ghosts? Real dead ghosts—whatever."

"Can they hurt us?" Jamie wondered. "I mean, they're just ghosts, right? They can't really touch us or anything."

"They do in the movies," Steve said. "Do you remember that one flick with—"

"Enough, people," Stanton said firmly. "There are no such things as ghosts."

"You said you saw them yourself," Jamie protested. "You can't back off that now."

"I'm not backing off anything," Stanton replied. "I don't believe in ghosts."

"So you've said before," Steve said. "That doesn't change what we know to be true."

"You don't know that ghosts are the truth, Steve. We've all seen something we can't yet explain, but I'm convinced there are no ghosts."

"So you're just going to deny what you've seen?" Jamie said. "So much for logic."

"That's precisely the point, Ms. Penowski," Stanton said. "Everything we've seen is contrary to the idea of ghosts and ghost ships."

"I don't follow, Skipper," Tenny said. "Either we're all suffering from some mass hallucination or we saw two ghosts standing in the doorway looking at us."

"Oh, let it go," Tony said. "This is one of the Captain's go-to-church-every-Sunday things. You can't talk to people like that."

"That's right, Tony," Stanton answered, "my opinion is based on what I read in the Bible. It hasn't been wrong so far."

"The Bible says there's no ghosts?" Jamie asked.

"Not specifically, but it does teach us about the soul," Stanton began. "Students of the Bible know that every person is composed of two parts: the physical and the spiritual. The physical is the body, but the body is just part of the story. We also have souls. Some say we all have three parts: body, soul, and spirit. That's fine; the point is that there is a material and immaterial part to each of us."

"Isn't that what a ghost is?" Steve asked. "A disembodied spirit of a dead person?"

"Yes, but that implies that the soul can be separated from the body and wander around. In the book of Hebrews is a verse that reads, 'It is appointed for men to die once and after this comes judgment.'"

"Hebrews 9:27," Richie said.

"Exactly," Stanton said.

Tony groaned. "Here comes the sermon."

"No sermon, Tony," Stanton said. "Just a point. A person's soul is not free to run around after death. It has to go someplace. The believer's soul goes to be with the Father after death."

"And the unbeliever's soul?" Jamie asked.

"I've heard this before," Tony complained.

"God has a place for them as well, where they wait for the judgment."

"You really believe all this?" Tony said. "I don't buy any of it. I didn't see ghosts or souls or anything else. As far as I'm concerned, you're all nuts."

"Let's think about this for a second," Stanton said. "When did these ghosts appear?"

"After the event," Richie said. "After the ship suddenly came to life."

"That's right," Stanton said. "Why not before? Why only after the event? And there's another thing to consider. Remember what Richie said he saw? The sky was different than it is now, as was the ocean. What do ghosts have to do with that?"

No one answered, so Stanton went on. "More shocking than the see-through man Richie saw was the smoke and the wake. Richie, you said the wake trailed the boat for quite a ways."

"Yeah. I don't know how long it was but it was substantial."

"And what about the smoke—did that trail behind the ship?" Stanton inquired.

Richie thought for a moment, then replied, "Yes, but not straight behind. It trailed off the starboard stern. I'm assuming the wind was off the port bow."

"And it was thick and full?"

"Just like you'd expect from a coal burner," Richie said. "I'm not seeing where you're going."

Stanton ran a hand through his hair. "That would explain why we went sliding around. We didn't move, the ship did."

"Wait a minute," Tenny said. "You're saying that the ship suddenly shifted places?"

"Close. The trailing wake, the full plume of smoke from the stack—all indicate that the ship had been moving for some time. If the ship had just suddenly gotten under way, Richie wouldn't have seen a wake, at least not a long one, and the smoke indicates that the engines had been running awhile. It takes time to get enough coal burning to get the boilers up to steam, yet everything came alive in a moment. Now we're back where we were."

"Stuck motionless in the fog," Tony said.

"Right," Stanton said. "If it is fog. But I have another concern."

"Goodie," Jamie snapped. "More to worry about."

Richie frowned at Jamie, then asked Stanton, "What's on your mind, Skipper?"

"The things you said about the smoke and wake. Did you get any sense of how fast the ship was traveling?"

"I didn't have time. I would guess it was running close to top speed, but that's just a guess. Why?"

"Like I said, when the event happened and we all went bouncing around on the deck and against the bulkheads, it wasn't us moving, it was the ship. Somehow, for a brief moment, we caught up to it."

"We're already on the ship," Steve said. "How can we catch up to it?"

"I don't mean we caught up to it in space, but in time." Stanton's comment was met with puzzled looks. "Everything we've seen here looks new, right?" They all agreed. "The paint can't be more than a few months old; the gear, everything looks like it's less than a year old. Even the wireless telegraph that Steve and I saw is very old technology but it looked new—the case, the signal key, everything. The medications in the dispensary looked genuine and untouched by age. I've been fighting this idea since we first saw the *Archer*. It's too much to believe but the facts won't go away. This ship looks new because it is. Freshly made in 1906."

"But that was almost a hundred years ago," Tony protested.

"Precisely. We are sometime between then and our now." Stanton felt frustrated. He was trying to explain the impossible. "For some reason, the *Archer* is in both the past and our present. What happened a few minutes ago was that we caught up to its place in time."

"That would mean we went backward in time," Tenny said. "That's not possible."

"Not backward in time but to a different place, a place where the past and present can meet, but they can never meet fully."

"How?" Jamie asked. "How can that be?"

Stanton shook his head. "I don't know, but I think there's a more important question: why? And there's a great danger."

"I don't like danger," Mary said weakly. She was holding her stomach again.

"Me either," Stanton admitted. "But we have to face this."

"Face what?" Tony pressed.

"A few minutes ago we were tossed around like rag dolls. That's because we were near dead in the water and all of a sudden the ship was moving. Not picking up speed. One moment she's still, the next she's chugging along with a full head of steam."

"So our inertia kept us in place while the ship moved under us," Richie said.

Stanton agreed. "And when the event ended, we were thrown the other way, because we were then traveling at the same speed as the ship."

"It's amazing there weren't more injuries," Tenny said.

"That's what I'm afraid of," Stanton said. "I don't think we were fully in the *Archer*'s time. That's why the people we saw seemed transparent. We weren't in sync with the past. We just got to see it and partially experience it for a moment—and it's a good thing."

"I don't think I like where this is going," Richie said.

Stanton made eye contact with the young sailor and saw the fear in his eyes. He wondered if the same fear shone in his own. "Richie's description of the smoke and wake tells me the ship was traveling near top speed. I don't know exactly what the *Archer*'s top speed is, but boats this size could do something close to twenty knots. That's around—"

"Just under twenty-five miles per hour," Richie interjected.

"That's not all that fast," Jamie said.

"Maybe not for freeway travel," Tony said. "But imagine stepping off the back of a truck going twenty-five."

"It's worse than that," Steve corrected. "It's like stepping in front of a truck going twenty-five."

"Wait a minute," Tenny said. "You're saying that if what happened before happens again, we could all go flying into steel bulkheads."

"Yes," Stanton said. "We were spared last time because we didn't align completely with 1907. Next time we might."

"So we all end up busted up or dead," Tony said.

"Maybe, or thrown into the ocean," Richie added.

"This just gets better and better," Jamie said.

"So what do we do?" Richie asked. "We can't sit around here waiting for physics to catch up to us."

"We get everyone off the ship," Stanton said. "I want everyone back on the *Tern About* as soon as possible."

"What about John?" Steve asked.

"I'll stay behind and find him, then join you."

"Why don't we all just leave?" Jamie asked.

"Because John might be hurt," Stanton answered. "Each of us got banged up. He probably did too. Maybe more so."

"It's his own fault if he is," Jamie protested.

"No, Jamie. I'm not leaving him or anyone else here." Stanton turned to Richie. "Did you get to examine the pinnace?"

"I took a quick look, since I was on board, but didn't do a detailed survey. I wanted to make sure you guys were all right."

"What did you find?"

"She's plenty big enough for all of us. She's definitely steam-driven and has a good supply of coal on board, probably enough to get us to Miami—however far that is. Lowering her to the water will be easy. It's just a matter of using the winches on the davits. Getting her started will require a heat source."

"There must be a lot of kit bags one deck below," Stanton said. "That's what the sailors kept their personal belongings in. There are bound to be matches in some of them."

"The first cabin we investigated," Tenny said, "I found tobacco in one of the drawers, and a pipe. I wasn't looking for matches but I bet there are some there."

"Good thinking," Stanton said. "I'll start there. In the meantime you get the girls back on the Zodiac. Steve and Tony will go with you. You should be able to paddle back to the *Tern About* without too much trouble."

"No way," Steve said. "I'm staying here to help you look for John."

"Can't do that," Stanton replied immediately. "I'm responsible for your well-being."

Steve shook his head vigorously. "No sir. You brought us out here to teach us responsibility and teamwork. Now is my chance to prove I know what that means."

"Steve, I appreciate your courage—"

"It's not about courage, Captain; it's about proof. Kids like me . . . kids like us are the way we are because no one trusts us. We make a few bad decisions, do a few stupid things, and trust is gone forever. We always have to prove ourselves but no one will let us. Now is my chance to prove I'm not worthless."

"No one ever said you were worthless," Stanton said.

"They don't have to," Tony said. "Unspoken words are louder than spoken ones. The little guy is right. I'm staying too."

"Guys, if we shift time again, we're going to be little more than ugly ornaments on steel walls. If I'm right, we might all die next time."

"You don't know that for a fact," Steve said. "You're just floating a hypothesis. I'm willing to take the chance."

Stanton closed his eyes and inhaled deeply. "All right. You've made your case. Let's get going. Tenny—"

"I'm staying too."

"Will someone please let me lead?" Stanton said with exasperation. "I want Jamie and Mary off the ship and that's final."

"But sir—"

"That's an order," Stanton snapped.

"Hey, Richie, can a retired captain order a midshipman around?" Tenny asked.

Richie didn't answer. He was looking over the lifeline.

"Richie?" Tenny said.

"It may be a moot point," he said. "The Zodiac is gone."

A second later Stanton was peering over the side, his eyes tracing the waterline at the hull. He could see the ladder that Richie and Steve had lowered so the others could climb aboard. He could also see a small piece of line hanging in the water where the Zodiac had been tied off.

"The sudden movement of the ship must have broken the line or torn off the cleat on the dinghy." Richie shook his head.

Stanton was starting to feel as if he were sliding down an icy slope. No matter how hard he tried to change the circumstance, he continued down.

"I thought those lines were unbreakable," Tony said.

"No such thing," Richie replied. "Anything can break. Still, it should have held. I don't get it."

"The motion was sudden," Stanton said. "Maybe the abrupt force undid the knot on the Zodiac—or, like you said, it may have snapped off the hardware."

"The event was strong, but I didn't think it was powerful enough to do that," Richie said. "A force strong enough to do that should have worked us a lot harder than it did."

"Maybe it's because we're on the ship," Steve suggested. Stanton turned to him. It was a good point.

"You mean that the Zodiac experienced a greater force because it wasn't actually on the *Archer?*" Stanton asked.

"Could be." Steve shrugged.

"He's got a point," Richie conceded.

"He does," Stanton agreed. "Of course, that would mean . . ." His voice trailed off and his eyes met Richie's. "The catamaran!"

Stanton led the rush to the stern of the battleship, passing the large turrets with their twelve-inch guns pointed menacingly at the distant mist. Stanton reached the rail and searched the water. His eyes hungrily consumed every inch before him, but he saw nothing but off-color ocean and gray-white mist. Looking straight down, he saw a segment of towline floating on the surface, one end still tied to the lower end of one of the torpedo net booms.

The *Tern About* was gone.

Phantasm

John had no idea what he had just seen. He remained seated on the deck, where the sudden movement of the ship had thrown him. He had stayed there, looking through the dim light of the room. A moment ago he had not been alone. The lights had come on, noises had filled the compartment, and the angry voice of the uniformed toad had ricocheted off the hard walls. The object of his wrath had been a skinny, black-haired young man who could not have been older than John himself.

John shook his head. Had he really seen it? Had he really heard the hot words? And did the sailor look at him and wink? Transparent sailors. Not something one sees every day. By reason he should have been terrified. Wasn't that the natural response to seeing ghosts? Screaming, shaking, blood-chilling fear? But John felt none of those things. Instead he felt an odd kinship with the young sailor. After all, he was clearly an outcast and a troublemaker. The very identity John cultivated and enjoyed. He was at his happiest when those around him were miserable. It was an odd entertainment but he found some satisfaction in it. His school counselor had suggested psychiatric treatment and his parents had made the effort. He went to six sessions before refusing to go again. Seeing the frustration on the doctor's face and the disappointment in his parents' eyes filled John with a sense of self-determination. No one could make him do what he didn't want to do, or be what he didn't want to be. *The young sailor,* John reasoned, *he's like me.* He could sense it, and the sailor must have sensed it also—hence the wink.

John had no friends. At school there were the good kids, those who excelled, worked hard, made high grades. He was oil to their water—no matter how much stirring occurred, they would never mix. He was as smart as they and he relished proving it from time to time. In class he would often ace a test, getting every answer correct; then, for the sheer fun of it, on the next test he'd purposely get every answer wrong. None of his teachers were clever enough to realize what he was doing. It was easier for them to assume he cheated on the tests on which his answers were correct. It was a game. All of life was a game. Power resided with those who could control others without their knowledge.

There were bad kids at school, too. Those who defaced the walls, fought with teachers, tormented other students, and felt more empowered every time they broke a rule. John didn't fit in with them either. They were stupid, mindless, little more than untrained dogs who did bad things and felt they had accomplished something. They were jail-bound and were too dumb to know it. No, John had no interest in their type. So he was always in the middle, too bad for the good kids, too smart for the bad ones.

Things might be different if he knew how to feel, but John realized that such sentimentalities had never been wired in his brain. Whatever it was that caused people to respect others was absent. John didn't miss it. In fact, he considered his lack of feeling to be one of his strengths. Emotion was a waste of energy and caused more pain than joy.

When he was nine, John had come home from school to find an ambulance in front of his house. The door to the home stood open. Rather than go inside, he stopped by the front curb and watched. A few moments later his mother was carried out on a gurney; a white sheet covered her form, and three wide nylon straps held her in place. The ambulance attendants moved quickly, clearly with urgency. His father was gone, floating on some navy boat in the ocean. Gone when his wife needed him.

He had watched as they loaded her in the back of the ambulance, pushing the gurney with its collapsing legs into the void of the open vehicle. For a moment he considered dropping his bike on the side of the road and racing to the ambulance before they could close the door. He could go to the hospital with her. She would like that. A moment later he dismissed the idea. His favorite cartoon was due to start in ten minutes. He didn't know much about hospitals, but he was sure it would take more than ten minutes to make the round trip.

The ambulance had taken off, its emergency lights flashing against the houses. John pulled his bike up on the lawn and then let it drop to the green blanket of grass. He walked into the house and shut the door. He remembered hoping that his mother had been considerate enough to leave a snack for him before becoming ill.

While aunts and uncles had worried, John remained cold and distant. It was easier that way. Mom returned a few days later, minus a gallbladder, and things returned to normal. In the interim, Aunt Cleo had moved in, and she stayed for a week to care for him and his recuperating mother. He was pretty sure she was glad to leave.

John rose to his feet and straightened his clothes. Falling was undignified, but at least no one had been around to see it. His mind ran back to the black-haired sailor. The young man's tormentor, someone John assumed was a superior, had smacked the kid a good one. He had hit him hard enough to spin him around before he collapsed to the floor. Even then, he showed no pain or emotion. John admired that.

The question was, what to do now? He was still hiding from Stanton and the others and was not ready to end the game. They still had buttons to push, a nerve or two he could frazzle. At some point he would either be found or grow tired of the game and simply make himself known. But that time wasn't now.

John crossed the room and entered one of the small cells. Even though the iron-bar door was wide open, he still felt uncomfortable being in a jail. Each of the five cells had a porthole, or what the toad had called a "side scuttle." A round metal plate with a rubber ring was raised above the opening, like a garage door. John studied the porthole for a moment, then realized that the metal plate was meant to be lowered to cover the glass. This must be the deadlight the sailor mentioned. A little more study revealed that the porthole's glass pane was fixed in a brass frame and could be swung to the side on a hinge. Three bolts with what looked like wing nuts were pressed back against the wall. It didn't take an engineer to realize that these bolts were used to fasten down the deadlight when needed.

John brought his face close to the glass and peered outside. He could see the pale ocean, the gray-white mist, and the indescribable sky. He could also see the cable safety rail at the deck's edge. He looked right, then left, but saw nothing more. Gently he pulled the brass-framed glass back and listened. He heard voices. He moved closer and strained his ears to hear.

"So what do we do?" It was Richie. "We can't sit around here waiting for physics to catch up to us."

"We get everyone off the ship." Stanton's voice was easy to recognize. "I want everyone back on the *Tern About* as soon as possible."

Steve: "What about John?"

Stanton: "I'll stay behind and find him, then join you."

One of the girls, most likely Jamie: "Why don't we all just leave?"

Stanton again: "Because John might be hurt. Each of us got banged up. He probably did too. Maybe more so." *Ah*, John thought, *he really cares for me. Isn't that sweet.*

Jamie again: "It's his own fault if he is." John whispered a slur.

Stanton: "No Jamie. I'm not leaving him or anyone else here...."

John gently closed the glass and moved back to the middle of the cell. They were planning on leaving the ship. They were afraid. Whatever happened might happen again, and Stanton thought it could get worse.

"Interesting," John murmured. "Really interesting."

$$\overset{\text{N}}{\wedge}$$

Since the storm, the sea had looked unusually empty, like a blank canvas waiting for the artist's brush. Now it looked even emptier. The Zodiac was gone and so was the *Tern About*, presumably snapped from their moorings by the sudden movement of the ship. Stanton corrected himself. The ship did more than move—it was transported through time. The catamaran and the much smaller dinghy must have been left behind.

"This isn't good," Richie said.

"That may be an understatement," Tenny added.

"Boy," Tony said, "your dad's going to be ticked when he learns you lost his pretty, pretty boat."

"My father is very understanding," Richie said.

"Have you ever lost a half-million-dollar yacht before?" Tony asked. "He might not be as understanding as you think. I don't want to be there when you tell him."

"We won't be anywhere unless we figure out what is going on," Tenny said with exasperation. "We must decide our next step."

Stanton turned and looked up toward the boat deck. "We can still lower the pinnace and get everyone off the ship. If we get the boiler working, we can use it to head toward Miami."

"Bad idea," Steve said. "Real bad."

Stanton turned to him. "You have a reason for the pessimism, son?"

Steve seemed to shrink under everyone's gaze. "Um . . . I was just thinking . . ." His voice trailed off.

Stanton smiled. "Steve, we're in this together. Your opinion matters, so don't be shy. We need to hear what you have to say."

"Yeah," Richie added. "Spit it out."

Steve pushed back his reluctance, drew in a full breath, then said, "I've been thinking about what you said earlier." He was speaking directly to Stanton. "You said something about the battleship slipping back in time and that's why there was the sudden motion and why we saw people as ghosts. Right?"

"Right," Stanton said. "Go on."

"If we get tossed around when the battleship slips back to its own time, what's to say the same thing won't happen in the pinnacle?"

"Pinnace," Richie corrected.

"Yeah, whatever," Steve said. "The boat is as much a thing of the past as the battleship. If it shifts from wherever we are . . . or whenever we are . . . the same thing will happen."

Stanton shook his head. "Good thinking, but you're overlooking something. We went skidding around because the *Archer* is under steam. It went from dead in the water to full speed. Our bodies kept their standing inertia while the ship went to its forward motion. The pinnace will just be bobbing in the water, not traveling at any speed."

"Excuse me, Mr. Stanton," Steve replied, "I think you're missing something. If you get the boat up to speed and we're in it, we'll still go slamming into walls because the lifeboat, or whatever it is, is still moving at the same speed as the *Archer*; it's just being *carried* at that speed. The fact that it's not moving under its own power is irrelevant. In the past it's still moving."

"This is making my brain cramp," Tony said. "Can anyone talk English?"

Steve sighed and rubbed his temple. "I don't know how to explain it. Let's try this. Tony, you're a gear-head. You work on cars. Say you're driving in your hot rod or whatever you drive—"

"A '68 Camaro, baby," Tony said with pride. "It's cherry, too—"

"Okay," Steve said with an upraised hand. "That doesn't matter. Let's say you've just driven through the Jack-in-the-Box and have a bag of burgers and a Coke sitting on the seat—"

"Not on my leather—"

"Tony, shut up!" Jamie snapped. "Let him talk. He's trying to tell us something."

Steve seemed surprised by who came to his defense. "Okay, you have the burgers in a bag on the seat. A car pulls out in front of you. You hit the brakes. What happens to the burgers?"

"They slide off," Tony said.

"Why? The bag has no power. Why does it keep going?"

"I know what inertia is, man," Tony said. "I'm not stupid."

"I'm not saying you are," Steve shot back, his words more bold than any Stanton had heard from him. "The point is this: the bag keeps going because the brakes can stop the car but not the bag. Now imagine that the bag doesn't hold burgers but it holds people—us. If we were in the bag, when you hit the brakes, what happens to us?"

"We slide off the seat with the bag," Tenny answered.

"Exactly," Steve said. No one responded. "The pinnace is Tony's Camaro; we are the burgers. The reverse is true. If the bag is on the dashboard and you floor the Camaro, it all comes back in your lap. That's what we're facing. If we get in the boat and it slips back to nineteen-whatever, then the boat will be traveling at the same velocity as the ship. Granted, it will slow down quickly, since it has no power of its own, but that's after we play human Ping-Pong ball."

There was a few moments of silence, and then Tony said, "You're pretty smart, buddy."

"Is he right, Captain?" Tenny asked.

Stanton nodded slightly. He should have thought of that. "He's right."

"There's more," Steve said.

"We're not going to like this any better, are we?" Jamie said.

"No," Steve intoned flatly. "If Stanton is right and what happened a little while ago was because we shifted back in time for a moment, then we have to face another possibility. Even if the boat were a safe place to be, where would we go? Mr. Stanton, do you know which direction Miami is?"

"No," Stanton confessed. "But when the fog lifts—"

"It's not fog," Steve said. "And I think you suspect that. Nothing is right. The sky is wrong, the ocean is too flat, the color is all weird, and there is no horizon. Miami isn't out there. Nothing is out there."

There had been a scratching at the back of Stanton's conscious mind, like a cold dog at the back door of a warm house. He knew that everything he was seeing was beyond normal, but he had been working hard to convince himself that things were more normal than they were. It was time to open the door and let the pesky pooch in.

"Time travel is impossible," Steve said. "At least, practically it is. Theoretically, speed and gravity can alter time. Quantum physicists talk about subatomic particles moving through time, but people aren't subatomic, and any speed or gravitational force strong enough to bend time would pretty much destroy us."

"Where do you get all this stuff?" Tony asked. "You sound like my science teacher."

"I read *Scientific American*," Steve said. "Science is the only thing I do well. Everything else I screw up."

"You're no screw-up," Stanton said. "Right now I'm pretty sure you're a genius."

"Wait, wait, wait," Tenny said. "I don't follow. If time travel is impossible, then what are we doing on a century-old battleship?"

"We're not in the past," Stanton explained. "And Steve is suggesting that we're not in the present either. We're—"

"Someplace in between," Steve said.

"But we saw sailors, heard the engines," Tenny complained. "Richie said he saw smoke and the ship's wake."

"The sailors were transparent . . . ghostly," Stanton said. "That's because we didn't really go back in time—not fully, anyway. They saw us, too, but I bet they saw us the same way we saw them."

"Like ghosts?" Tenny said.

"Exactly," Steve said.

"The more we go back, the less substantial we will seem to them, and the more substantial they will appear to us." Stanton pinched the bridge of his nose. "You're right, Tony—this stuff cramps the brain."

"Except we can't really go back," Steve said. "At least not fully. If we do, we cease to exist. We can't exist outside our own time. The more in touch we become with the past, the less . . . substantial we will be."

"There's a cheery thought," Richie said.

"This is stuff for theoretical physicists," Steve said with a shake of the head, "not high school students like me. I could be all wet on this stuff."

"Well, we have to do something," Tenny said. "If Steve is right and the *Archer* slips back to its own time, then what becomes of us? We become their ghosts?"

Stanton looked back at the boat deck, uncertain what to do. He wished he were like the heroes in novels and movies. They always knew the right thing to do. But life was more complex than that. If he called for the lowering of the boat, he could get everyone off the ship, but the danger might be greater. If the boat went back to the early 1900s, it would either take them with it or leave them floating in a flaccid ocean.

Before he could speak, something caught his attention. It was subtle and unobtrusive at first, just enough to alert him. He looked down at his feet. They felt funny. A vibration, soft as a cat's purr, rose from the deck and through the nonskid soles of his shoes.

"Oh no," Stanton said to himself. He snapped his head up, looking at the tall smokestacks that rose majestically from the superstructure. A mist was forming at the funnels, a condensation darker than fog, and it was becoming thicker with each second that ticked by. Looking skyward, he saw the white cottage cheese melting away. He looked over the stern. The inky dark waters were lightening to a blue.

"Um, Skipper," Richie said. "I think we have a problem."

Stanton looked at the cable lifeline that rose from the deck and surrounded the ship. It was meant to keep sailors from falling overboard. It was a safety measure but Stanton saw it differently. If they started sliding backward like they did before, they would hit the cables with more force than any naval engineer could have anticipated. The rail would do fine, Stanton knew; it was the human body that would receive the damage. That thought was compounded by the fear that one or more of them might slip over the side and fall into the churning cauldron of seawater whipped into a deadly froth by four gigantic, triple-bladed screw propellers.

Disaster was a second away.

The faint smell of coal assaulted Stanton's nose. The change was about to happen and there was no way he could stop it.

"Run!" he snapped loudly, pointing ahead. "Forward! Everyone! Run, run, run! Get as far forward as you can." Fear sickened him. His spine felt like an icicle, his stomach like a vat of heated acid. His heart couldn't decide whether to beat wildly or seize up. It tried both. "Go, go, go!"

There was no discussion, no questions were asked—the others had sensed it, too. The girls were the first to spin on their heels and run. Even Mary, weakened by illness, lost no time in fleeing forward. Tenny followed immediately behind them. Stanton grabbed Steve, spun him around, and gave him a push forward. "Go, boy, go! You too, Tony!" But Tony hung back just a step, as did Richie. Less than two seconds passed before the group was running for their lives.

Stanton lingered a moment longer, wanting to be the last in line, hoping that his body might serve as a cushion for any who slid back when the shift came. He had no idea if it would work that way, but he had no time to reason it through. If it might work, it was worth trying.

Sound began to replace the dull, muted condition they had endured since the storm. A quick glance up revealed that the smoke from the stacks had darkened another shade and—

Thunder cracked with a concussive force that sounded like a bomb going off between Stanton's ears. Gravity seemed to lose its grip as he rose in the air and felt himself slipping back at a speed that seemed impossible. He reached forward . . . stretched . . . clawed . . . at nothing. Stanton was a dry oak leaf in a hurricane.

The light changed . . . strobes pulsed . . . flickered . . . unending flashes of lightning in his eyes.

"Oh, Lord, no . . ."

Apart

Something hit him in the back of the knees and Stanton flipped backward. Pain fired up his torso with such intensity, he felt as if he were being electrocuted. His feet flew skyward and then over. As he completed the forced somersault, Stanton saw the blue-green ocean directly below him—an ocean topped with the angry froth of salt water churned into a deadly, roiling mass by propellers designed to push a twenty-thousand-ton battleship through open ocean. His body wouldn't be noticed by the machinery.

He stretched out his hand in a desperate attempt to grab something, anything. As he felt himself begin to fall, something filled his palm—something narrow and cold. It was the upper cable of the ship's lifeline. Stanton's hand closed like a clamp. He felt the skin of his hand tear as he made his last and only effort to save his life. His backward flight stopped abruptly and his body swung forward again and his hip hit the edge of the deck. The impact felt like someone had taken a sledgehammer to his body.

His hand slipped and Stanton began to fall again, but another cable was just a foot below and he managed to seize it. He wasted no time in bringing his other hand up—taking hold of the only thing that separated him from death.

He hung for a moment, trying to force his lungs to breathe, demanding that the pain which scalded every nerve would cease. Hitting the lifeline, then swinging into the hull like a wrecking ball, had forced his strength from him. Determination . . . will and determination kept his hands from releasing their grip. That and the scorching fear he felt for the others. What had happened to them? Reluctantly he looked to the starboard waters, fearing that he would see Jamie or Steve or one of the others floating by, their arms reaching toward him, pleading for help he could not provide. But he saw nothing in the water.

The strength in Stanton's arms began to wane, to evaporate under the stress of holding his weight. Blood from his right hand trickled down his arm, staining his shirt. He tried to pull himself up but he was too damaged, too worn. He kicked and pulled but while he was able to lift himself some, he couldn't bring enough of his body up to throw a leg over the side.

Spots, like black flies, filled his vision. His head bobbed and Stanton knew what was happening—he was passing out. "Well, Lord," he prayed. "Somehow I didn't see it happening like this. Help the others and—"

He heard a thud, then a sliding noise. Suddenly he saw a face coming toward him. It took a moment for him to realize it was the face of Tony, who was sliding along the deck on his stomach. He was headed straight for Stanton. If he hit him, there would be no hanging on.

Tony's slide ended as his head slipped beneath the bottom cable. Arms, strong arms, encircled Stanton.

"Gotcha," Tony said.

A second later Stanton felt Tony's hands take hold of his belt. "Hang on, Skipper," he said.

"Skipper?" Stanton gasped. "That's the first time you've called me Skipper." He strained to get the words out.

"Yeah, I'm a bundle of warmth," Tony said. "Stay still." Tony began to reposition himself, awkwardly pulling his knees under him while keeping a tight grip on Stanton's belt. "Here's what we're going to do." His voice was strained by the awkward position. "On three, I'm going to lift you and you're going to pull. Move your hands up to the next cable. Got it?"

Stanton looked up. The distance to the upper cable was just a foot but it looked like a mile. "I don't know, Tony. I'm losing my grip as it is."

"It's time you trusted me, Stanton," Tony said. "I'm not going to argue. On three." Tony didn't wait for a response; he counted and counted quickly. Before he had finished saying three, Stanton felt himself moving up with surprising speed.

"Got it."

"Can you hang on by yourself for a second?"

"Yeah."

Tony let go, slipped from beneath the bottom cable, then sprang to his feet. He bent over the top cable, reaching down with his right hand and grabbing Stanton's belt once more. "Again on three," he said but this time he didn't count. He just said three and Stanton moved up again, high enough for his feet to touch the deck. Less than a second later he was standing on the deck, with just the lifeline separating him from safety. Tony let go for a moment, then grabbed the front of Stanton's shirt. "I got ya. Start climbing."

Stanton did, putting his left foot on the bottom cable and throwing his right leg over the top. A second later he was standing on the firm, wood-covered deck. The fact that the deck pitched and rolled didn't bother him. Considering what he had been "standing" on a moment before, the rolling deck seemed rock-solid. Placing his left hand on Tony's shoulder, he said, "You are a blessing from God. I owe you one . . . a big one."

Tony collapsed.

N
Λ

Richie was lying facedown, trying to make sense of his situation. His head hurt and his mind was a cobweb of confusion. He had opened his eyes for a moment but saw little more than the dark steel that pressed against his cheek. It was cold and was sucking the heat from his body.

Steel? Cold? Pain?

Moments ran into each other and slowly his thoughts began to form a recognizable picture. Last he remembered, he was running from something or to something. The others were ahead of him and someone was behind him.

Someone? Someone important. An image came to mind. A middle-aged man with an air of authority about him. He was yelling, "Run!"

Stanton! As if someone had thrown a switch, all the divergent thoughts that had been floating in his brain like fireflies in the forest coalesced into a single bright light of understanding. The events, the fears, the uncertainties, the mysteries were not the fodder of dreams; they were facts—facts he had lived through.

Rolling over, Richie sat up. The act made his head throb and he expected an artery to give way at any moment. He rubbed the back of his neck and his temples. Blinking several times, he cleared his eyes, then took in his surroundings. The light was dim, different than it was a few moments earlier, before the sounds, the light, the sudden, irresistible movement. He had been on deck running toward the bow when everything went loud, then dark. The next thing he knew, he was facedown in the heat of the room—

Heat?

Richie looked around at his surroundings. Moving his head hurt, but the pain was secondary to the confusion he felt. He was in a room filled with noise and heat. His back was to a bulkhead and before him was a jungle of metal ducts, ladders, elevated walkways, pipes, and machinery he couldn't easily identify. The air was thick with the smell of oil, the heat of machinery, and the noise of steam.

Then there were voices. "I just checked it."

"Check it again, boy; the captain is pushing us hard and these boilers are new. If one of them gives way, Cookie will be serving us up as lobsters."

He didn't recognize the voices. Standing, he staggered for a moment and noticed that the deck was moving. It had happened again—the very thing Stanton feared. But how did he end up here in the . . . the . . . He looked around again and took a guess: the boiler room. Stanton had said that these old ships were steam-powered. Coal-fired, steam-driven. But the boiler room would have to be low in the belly of the ship. He had been on the upper deck, the open-air deck, not in the interior.

Straining his still-staggering mind, Richie tried to put the pieces together. On the deck one moment, in the boiler room the next. And where were the others? They had all been going the same direction at the same time.

"She reads fine," came the first voice.

"Let's make sure it stays that way," the words were brusque but then softened with pride. "She's humming fine. Those engineer boys cobbled this together in short order, but they sure made it right. If anybody wants to mix it up with us, they will find more than they bargained for."

The voices were strained, shouted to overcome the ambient machine noise. Richie followed them and found a small gathering of sailors, men standing near a series of gauges. He counted six men. There may have been more spread throughout the room; Richie had no way of knowing. He hesitated, then walked toward them.

"Um . . . hello." Richie waited for a response. He waited in vain. Perhaps, he thought, they couldn't hear him. He shouted, "Excuse me, who is in charge here?"

Nothing. One of the men turned and walked toward Richie. "I know I'm not supposed to be here," Richie said, "but—"

The man walked by him as if he weren't there. Richie recalled the discussion on deck and what Steve had suggested. The young genius was right.

Richie was invisible.

Darkness. Abject blackness. Pungent, oily smell. Hard metal.

Tenny lay in a fetal position, legs pulled tightly to her chest, head cranked forward, her chin just inches from her knees. Her eyes were open but the blackness was as abysmal as when they had been shut.

She waited.

She listened.

She shuddered. Why was she so cold?

Releasing the stranglehold she had on her legs, she tentatively extended a foot, wondering what it would touch. It touched something hard, unmoving. Retracting her leg, she sat up cautiously and was relieved that her head did not find something sharp and hard.

She wondered if she had gone blind. It had been her greatest fear as a child. In sixth grade a blind student joined her class. His unseeing gaze had frightened her, and the thought of losing her eyes had kept her up at night for a week and peppered her dreams when finally she did sleep.

Now she sat in the blackest place she had ever been, and wondered if it was the world around her that was black or if something had happened to her vision. Her back hurt, she felt bruised in several places, but her eyes felt normal. Of course, she had no idea what blindness felt like.

She crossed her legs and used what senses were working to assess her situation. It was a reasonable, logical thing to do. Reason and logic had to be coaxed to the front of her mind, and they had to pass the screaming fear and doubt that stood in the way like an agitated crowd. Panic pressed in upon her and she wanted to cry out, to scream for help, but discipline was a better tool. Tenny forced the hot emotions to the back of her mind and let them simmer.

"Hello?" she whispered. No one responded. Her voice sounded odd. "Hello," she said louder and was surprised to hear it come back to her a half beat later.

For a moment she wondered if she had died. Maybe this was the other side of life: cold, hard, lonely. "No," Tenny said to herself. Hell isn't made of metal. She had to be somewhere on the ship. "Anyone there?" This time her voice was strong. No answer came.

"Captain Stanton?" Nothing. "Richie?" More nothing.

She sighed and fought terror-churned nausea. Slowly she raised a hand over her head and felt nothing. Then she extended her arms to her sides and turned her torso back and forth as much as physically possible. There was nothing in front of her but she did feel the metal wall behind her. Shifting her position so she could better reach the wall, she ran her right hand along its smooth surface. Hard and cold, but that was to be expected on a battleship.

Keeping her hand in contact with the wall, she worked her way to her feet, thankful that she didn't smash into anything. "Okay, girl, keep your head in the game." She wondered what had happened to the others and she was filled with apprehension. She knew they wouldn't abandon her; certainly Stanton and Richie wouldn't, and she doubted the girls would. Other thoughts percolated in her mind. How had she come to be in the dark? On deck one moment, semiconscious in utter blackness the next—how could that be? But she chastised herself. "Find out where you are first, then figure out how you got here."

She was now facing the wall, both hands gently placed on the smooth surface. She took a step to the left, then another. The wall was curved, bowing toward her. That surprised her. Methodically she took several more side steps, her hands tracing the curved surface. She stopped when the texture of the wall changed. Her left hand felt a small rise on the surface. The rise had bumps—evenly spaced bumps. "Rivets," she said to herself. The rise was a joint strap binding two surfaces together.

A few more steps and Tenny had an idea where she was. She must still be on the ship, and the only place she could think of that had such a uniformly curved wall was inside one of the barbettes, the cylindrical turrets in which the large guns were located.

"Now that's deductive reasoning," she told herself. "But it doesn't change anything. You're still talking to yourself in the dark."

She took consolation in one thought. The gun turrets were meant to be manned. That much she knew about old battleships. And if they were meant to be manned, then there had to be an access point, a hatch or door. All she needed to do was find it.

N
ʌ

Jamie opened her eyes in darkness and her mind flooded with confusion. She was sitting awkwardly on what felt like a slope of rocks. How she had come to be seated in such a fashion was beyond her. She recalled Stanton yelling, "Run!" and run she had. Why he would shout such a warning was unknown, but she had come to know that he was not a man to play practical jokes. If he felt they should run, then she would do so without question. So far he had been serious, caring, and up front.

Everything she had seen and experienced since the sudden onset of the storm confused her beyond words. She had nothing but questions and fears. The questions she kept to herself and the fears she kept tucked away out of sight. Her nickname at school was the Ice Maiden—hard and cold. Few warmed up to her and she warmed up to no one.

Keep to yourself. Be self-reliant. Avoid attachments. That was how to fend off emotional disaster. Let no one into your life and no one could hurt you. At least no one you cared about. What others called her didn't matter and even when it did, she had become expert in squelching those feelings, freeze-drying them under the icy blast of apathy.

The strategy had worked well enough so far, but this situation was different. It was one thing to keep fellow students at arm's length and push away caring parents; it was quite another to find yourself . . . well, wherever she was.

Now, that was a question. Where was she exactly? And how did she come to be sitting in the dark?

Muffled sounds reverberated around her. The air was cool. And she was sitting on something—something uncomfortable. Shifting her weight, Jamie noticed that the rocky surface beneath her shifted too. Placing a hand beside her, she touched something hard and about the size of a baseball. With both hands she felt along the surface, and everywhere she touched she found the same thing: baseball-sized rocks. That didn't make sense.

She tried to pick one up. It wouldn't budge. It felt odd—slightly flaky. She leaned over and sniffed. The slope was pungent.

Taking a deep breath, she immediately coughed. Something powdery was in the air and it stuck in her nostrils and in her throat. Jamie had no idea where she was or how she got there, but she did know it was time to leave. She tried to stand but her footing gave way and she flopped backward, landing flat on her back. She gritted her teeth more out of frustration than out of pain. No one had been around to see her fall but she felt embarrassed nonetheless. Embarrassment was normal for her, though she struggled to never let it show. She cast the image of a resolved, self-satisfied young woman—both qualities she lacked.

Scrambling to her feet, she tried to stand again but was rewarded with the same inglorious plunge to the rocky slope. She swore loudly and her words came back to her in a cold echo.

A light went on and Jamie froze at the sudden illumination. The light stung her eyes and she blinked furiously against the abrupt but welcome intrusion. Now she could see, but it took a moment for her mind to comprehend the images her eyes were sending. She was facing up a black, rocky slope that rose to meet a steel wall about eight feet away. The rocks now made sense. They weren't ordinary rocks; they were lumps of coal, millions of lumps of coal, one piled upon another until they made the incline of a small mountain.

"Oh, yuck," she said, standing. "Double yuck. Serious yuck."

When they first saw the *Archer*, Stanton had said something about the ship being steam-powered. This must be where they kept the coal to heat the boilers. It was a dark place, even with the electric light burning.

The sound of metal hitting metal rebounded through the bunker. Jamie jumped a foot and slipped again, falling face forward into the coal. Immediately she rolled over on her back and tried to determine where the loud retort had come from. There was another noise of metal against metal, but unlike the first, which came like a cannon shot, this new sound persisted. A second later Jamie knew she was listening to metal wheels on a metal track. Glancing down at the floor, at the place where the slope of coal met the horizontal surface, she saw a narrow set of tracks similar to those she had seen as a child when her parents took her to the park to ride the kiddy train. These tracks led to a door that hung open on large hinges. That must have been what she heard, she decided—the door opening and slamming against the metal wall.

Voices. Unfamiliar voices. Jamie's heart jumped and began to pound as if trying to break free from its rib cage prison.

"Me back aches," she heard. "New ship, new captain, new adventure, an' me stuck down in Hades itself, pushing coal like me grandfather did in the mines."

"Stop the bellyaching," another voice said. "This ain't no mine and you ain't no coal miner. This here coal keeps us off the streets. You want to go back to picking pockets in London?"

The voices were weighted with an accent which Jamie recognized as British. The first man's accent was different from the second's, but she had heard both types on television.

"It was cleaner work, weren't it?"

"This is important work. When the kaiser rises up and thumbs his nose at king and homeland, I want to be there. If that means shuttling coal, then I'll shuttle coal."

The men to whom the voices belonged passed through the door, pushing a metal cart along the rails. The metal wheels protested mildly but moved evenly along the tracks. The cart was round on the bottom and looked as if it could be tipped on end to unload its cargo. They stopped at the foot of the coal slope, picked up shovels, and began loading the cart with the black fuel.

"Well, ain't you the loyal one. Maybe King Eddie will have you over for tea soon."

"King Edward is a good man, and you'd do well to remember that," the second man snapped.

"Aye, Your Majesty." The first man stopped shoveling and gave an exaggerated bow.

The men wore dark-blue pants and white T-shirts. Coal dust covered them from head to foot.

Jamie was paralyzed by shock. These were the first people she had seen since coming aboard the battleship. How would these strangers respond to seeing a young woman sitting on their coal pile, or coal mound, or whatever they called it?

She waited for their response but they seemed not to have seen her. It was time to take the initiative. "Um . . . excuse me." Her voiced seemed hollow but certainly loud enough to be heard, yet neither man responded. "Uh . . . guys . . . up here." She gave a little wave.

Neither man changed. Both loaded a shovel with coal and dropped it in the cart.

Jamie's frustration grew, and when frustrated she became sarcastic. "I say, ol' bean, might I have a moment of your time? Chaps? Lads? There's a girl in your coal."

Nothing. She was tempted to hurl a piece of coal at them and tried again to pick up a lump, but it was as immovable as if it had been glued in place.

"That's enough," man number one said. "The skid is full."

"Just a couple more," his partner replied and shoveled two more spadefuls of the black material. "There 'tis. Just the job."

He stuck his shovel in the mound and took hold of the cart—the skid, as the first man called it—and began to push.

"Come on, guys, you're giving me a complex," Jamie said.

The first man rounded the little trolley and began to push.

Jamie was suddenly filled with terror. If they left, they would certainly close the door and turn off the light. She would be locked alone in the bunker. Starting forward, she began to work her way down the black slope. "Wait for me, guys! Don't leave me here."

The moment her feet met the solid deck, she was in a run, squeezing through the door a few moments before one of the sailors turned to close it.

For the moment she was free—lost and confused, but free.

N
⋏

Swaying.

Rocking.

Swinging.

Steve felt sick. He recognized the nausea. It was the same sensation he had felt during the storm: the burning in the gut and the undeniable desire to empty the contents of his stomach. Before opening his eyes, he fought to push the queasiness down. He had tossed his cookies more times in the storm than he had in his entire life. His abdominal muscles still ached from the previous episodes. He had no desire to start down that path again.

After taking several deep breaths, he willed himself to consider his surroundings. He was seated on a hard surface and leaning back against something that seemed to rock and pitch. It felt round against his back, as if he were leaning against a huge tree.

Still fighting off the nausea, he placed his head between his raised knees. He opened his eyes and saw his feet with their Nike sport shoes. Below his feet was a metal deck. The deck seemed to be moving. He raised his head and saw a guardrail a few feet before him, a guardrail that rocked and swayed. That puzzled him, but what was beyond the guardrail terrified him.

"Whoa!" he shouted and pushed himself back against the support behind him. Between the rails he could see the ocean and the horizon. The horizon was distant, as it should be, but the ocean was down—far down.

Steve snapped his head around and saw that the guardrail circled the small platform upon which he sat. He wasn't on the main deck anymore. He was much higher. Steeling his courage, Steve stood on wobbly legs and took hold of the top of the guardrail, squeezing it with such intensity that he felt he would break his own fingers.

He looked down. The deck he had been running on a moment before was down there—forty feet or more down there. Obsidian smoke poured from the two stacks below him. Behind the ship ran the white, snakelike wake. Turning his attention forward, Steve saw white spray fan into the air from the bow, which was cutting through swells as if they were imaginary—and with every swell came the pendular sway of the mast.

The fact was obvious. Steve was standing on a narrow platform at the top of the tripod mast that rose from the deck of the battleship and into the sky.

"How did I get here?" he asked and then sank back to the small deck. "I hate this. I really, really hate this."

N
Λ

Cold. So very, very cold. Dark, so abysmally dark. Movement, left and right, up and down. Mary hugged herself, trying to hold in what little heat remained in her thin body. Her jaw ached from clenching her teeth to cease the endless chatter. Her body shook, trembled, quivered. The outside cold was seeping in through her pores, threatening to conquer every ounce of heat.

A dim light burned overhead, holding back the darkness as a cracked dam held back rising waters. The light was a naked bulb with a wire-mesh frame around it. Shadows were everywhere, counterbalanced with weak streams of illumination that appeared like spokes on the wood-decked floor.

Mary patted her arms and bounced from one foot to the other. She wore a pair of baggy jeans and the same powder blue T-shirt she had donned earlier that day. On her feet were thin canvas shoes. She wore no socks. She was not dressed for bitter cold. And the cold was consuming her, eating at her like flesh-digesting bacteria. She doubted she could live much longer in this place. It was too cold and she was far too weak; she had endured too much already. Death was stalking her, hiding in one of the many shadows, waiting like a leopard in a tree ready to pounce on the first weak animal to come by.

Despondency covered her, her spirit bending under the weight of it. Death was near, but was that so bad? she wondered. What did she have to live for? This trip? It had been a nightmare from the moment she stepped foot on the catamaran. Should she struggle to survive so she could return home? Return to the place that had stripped her of all dignity? Could she face a mother who refused to see the crime, or face a father who spoiled the very meaning of the word *parent?* He was a soulless man, consumed by self and kept alive by an evil that demanded the sacrifice of others. Maybe freezing to death wasn't so bad.

As tempting as death was, she couldn't bring herself to surrender, not yet. She had to live on. She didn't know why. She could picture no reason to continue living, but a flame of hope flickered deep inside her, in a place only she knew about. A secret place.

Frosty mist poured from her mouth with every breath, rising slightly, then disappearing as if it were too cold to survive. Mary looked around and saw that she was surrounded by death. Flesh hung from hooks or rested on metal shelves. She knew nothing of ships, especially century-old battleships, but she did know what a freezer was. Meat, cow and pig, hung in ghoulish ornamentation from the metal ceiling.

"Meat locker," she said. The term sounded right. Somehow she had been transported from the main deck into this place. She didn't remember the transference, but she did recall opening her eyes and finding herself lying under a gutted and skinned side of beef.

She had screamed before she realized what she was looking at. *No reason to be afraid of a butchered cow,* she told herself. At least no reason she could think of.

The refrigerated room was large. Stanton had said something about seven hundred or more crewmen—a crew that size required a lot of food. The deck pitched and shifted. She knew the battleship was under way. Oddly, the motion no longer bothered her. For that matter, neither did her stomach. The chronic pain she had experienced on the *Tern About* seemed to have diminished. She had no explanation for it but was glad to be rid of the burning ache.

It was time to get out, Mary decided. Death might be welcome but this was no way to go. Forcing her mind to think about something other than the bitter cold, she walked to the closest wall. There had to be a door somewhere. All she had to do was pick a place to start and follow the wall until she found what she was looking for.

Tucking her hands under her armpits, she fought the impulse to drop to the floor in a pile of shuddering flesh. "Door," she said aloud. "Door ... door ... there has to be a door." Moving through the red and white carcasses, being careful not to touch the metal shelves that might suck the heat from her body like a vacuum cleaner, Mary pushed on. Step followed forced step. Her body ached from the unrelenting shivering but she forced it from her mind. One thing she had noticed about Stanton, Richie, and Tenny that was different from the kids her age: the more dangerous the situation, the calmer they became, the more focused their minds. They must know something she didn't. Still, it was a behavior worth emulating.

Every step came harder, as if her feet were freezing to the wood slats beneath them. Her muscles were slow to respond, and she knew that the death-leopard was patiently waiting until the right moment to spring, claws and teeth flashing in the dim light.

She took another step and wondered: if she died here, what would happen to her body? The whole slipping-between-times thing was beyond her understanding. She was not stupid. In fact, she knew herself to be unusually bright—not that it mattered to anyone. But science was not her strong suit. She had no interest in it. History was more her style. Living in the past, after all, was much easier than living in the present. Perhaps she would die and her body would go back to her time. Perhaps not. Who knew? Who could know?

The journey around the room continued. One short, staggering stride followed another in uncertain footing. Her bones now ached but still she walked the room's perimeter. The room was large but it had its limits. It was a matter of endurance. There was a door; all she had to do was find it.

Fifteen steps later she did. It was a gloriously ugly affair—a gray steel slab with rounded corners—but it looked beautiful to Mary. Her steps came quicker, enlivened by the hope of warmth that lay beyond the steel. She reached the door and studied it for a second, looking for a doorknob. Instead of a knob she found a simple lever. It was wrapped with strands of thin rope.

She took the handle in hand and pushed down. It didn't move. She tried again but the handle seemed locked in place. Her heart skipped several beats. She pulled up on the handle but it refused to budge. No matter which way she tried to move the latch, it remained immobile. There was no give at all. It was as if its internal mechanism had been welded.

"No," she whispered. "Come on . . . come on!" She put her other hand on it and pulled up with all her strength, then pushed with all her weight, but the rope-clad handle remained locked in position. Mary stepped back and kicked at it in frustration but only achieved pain for her efforts.

"No," she said, choking back the sobs she knew were bound to erupt. "No, please . . . no."

She stepped back until stopped by a pendulous side of beef. Folding her arms in front of her in a vain attempt to fend off the icy fingers of cold, Mary dropped to her knees and bent over. "Please, God . . . please, please, please . . ."

John

The noise was almost deafening. John, who had the moment before been standing next to jail cells, was back in the mess space, surrounded by long wooden tables and benches. Men dressed in blue uniforms and white T-shirts sat at the tables eating sausage and potatoes. They ate with a wild abandon, as if this were the first meal they had seen in the last week. It took a moment for John to realize what they were eating; his initial perspective was skewed because they appeared to be upside down. Instead of being in the very aft part of the ship, he was pressed against a cold bulkhead, feet directed at the ceiling, his back against the wall, and his head and shoulders on the deck. It was as if someone had picked him up by the feet and dropped him on his head. It felt that way too. Since he had no memory of how he got in that position, he assumed he must have passed out.

Seeing several hundred sailors seated around tables chewing loudly and joking between bites made John scramble to his feet, brushing himself off and straightening his clothes. What would he say? How would he explain his presence on the ship? He steeled himself for their quick approach and certain questions.

None came.

Man, he thought, *these guys really like their food.* Looking to his left, he saw the door he had passed through before. Slowly he inched toward it, when someone stepped in from the other side. It was the black-haired sailor. His cheek was still red where the older man had popped him.

"Hey, Weed, did you do a proper job on them bogs?"

John looked toward the voice. It was the man who had been giving the orders. He wasn't eating with the rest of the men. John assumed he was some type of officer and probably ate with those of similar rank.

"I did," the teenager said. There was an air of defiance in his voice.

"Remember what I said, boy. If they ain't as clean as the king's own dishes, then you'll be eatin' out of 'em."

"I remember," was all he said.

The bigger man studied him for a moment. John assumed the younger should address the older by some term of rank, but clearly it wasn't coming. "You're useless, Weed, ain't nothing but a bloomin' big girl's blouse."

John was confused, first by the fact that no one seemed to take notice of him. Last time, the black-haired teenager saw him and even winked. Now he and the scores of other sailors acted as if John didn't exist. He was also confused by what he was hearing. Was "weed" the boy's name or an insult? Context helped him understand that a "bog" was a vulgar word for toilet or urinal. What was meant by "big girl's blouse" was a mystery, but judging by the laughter that followed the comment and by the boy's expression, it wasn't a compliment.

The tormentor studied the boy for a moment, then shook his head. "Well, off you go, lad. Get your grub. Your mum ain't here to fix it for you."

More laughter.

Weed started forward, passing near one of the tables. A foot shot out in a well-timed and successful effort to trip the boy. He crashed down, his head bouncing off the deck. Laughter exploded through the mess area. Weed sat up and rubbed his forehead. John could see a dark, purplish knot forming just above his right eye. Amazingly, the boy said nothing, but John could see the jaw tense and the eyes change. He knew confined fury when he saw it. He had lived with it ever since he entered his teens.

"What's a matter, Weed?" the offending sailor said. "No sea legs yet?" The new tormentor couldn't be much older than Weed but he was much larger. John could see that even though the sailor remained glued to his seat.

The laughter reverberated in the large steel hall in a cacophonous crescendo. John pitied the boy, which was quite a feat, since he seldom pitied anyone other than himself.

"Captain on deck!" someone shouted.

The laughter died immediately. Even the echoes seemed to die in place. The hilarity was replaced by the mass confusion of sailors struggling to get to their feet. No words were spoken. The room was suddenly filled with silence.

John watched as a man he judged to be in his early forties walked in. His back was so straight that John wondered if an iron pipe had replaced the officer's spine. The captain's uniform hung on his stout body as if it had grown there, as if it were part of his anatomy. His eyes were dark, hard, and cold, but his face, expressionless as it was, gave off an air of kindness.

The captain walked to where the one everyone called Weed was seated on the deck. Unlike the others, he had not come to his feet when the captain entered. The officer studied him for a moment.

"Take a bit of a fall, did we, son?" the captain said. His words were formal, devoid of emotion.

John saw Weed cut his eyes toward the sailor who tripped him, then back to the captain. "Yes sir. Clumsy of me." He struggled to his feet. No one made a move to help him. He swayed for a moment in counterpoint to the moving deck.

"Accident, was it, son? Or did you have help?" The captain looked from Weed to the sailor who had tripped him. The sailor blanched.

"Accident, Captain. I'm still adjusting to the ship's movement."

"It takes time, son." He was speaking to Weed but his eyes were fixed on the prankster. John saw the captain's lower lip pucker in and out two or three times; then he snapped a question at the sailor, who stood at rigid attention. His words came out like the crack of a whip. "What's your name, sailor?"

He was caught off guard. "Um . . . my name, sir? Um . . ."

"You do have a name, don't you, boy?"

"Sir, of course, yes sir. Thomas, sir. My name is Reginald Thomas. My father is—"

"Your father?" the captain snapped. "Is your father on this ship, Thomas?"

"Um, no sir. I only meant—"

"I don't give a fig who your father is, boy. If he's not on this ship, then I don't need to know him. Unless, of course, you're trying to impress me or curry favor with me. Is that what you're trying to do?"

"No sir. It never entered my mind," the sailor shot back, his eyes fixed straight ahead.

"Do you like serving on this ship, Thomas?"

"Yes sir. She's a fine ship. It is my honor to be numbered in her crew . . . sir."

"Spot on, sailor. It is your honor. This is the newest, most modern ship in the Royal Navy—but it still has a yardarm, Thomas. Do you understand my meaning?"

"I do, sir. The captain's meaning is very clear, sir." He seemed to melt like a candle under a blow-dryer.

The captain nodded and turned his attention back to Weed. "That's quite a goose egg on your noggin, son. You'd better get to sick bay and let the doctor have a look at it."

"Yes sir," Weed said.

"Maybe young Thomas here should accompany you."

"No sir," Weed said quickly. "I know where it is."

The captain studied him for a moment, then looked around the mess bay. It seemed to John that the room had just gotten much colder. "Very well," he said at last. "Carry on."

The captain strode away with determined strides. No one moved for several moments; then Weed started to leave. A hand shot out and grabbed his arm. It was Thomas.

"I'll get you for this," he said through clenched teeth. Now that Thomas was standing near Weed, John could see that the tormentor stood a good foot taller and weighed thirty pounds more.

"Wanna have a go, Reggie?" Weed said. "In the mood for a bit of a row? I'm here. Go ahead, take a poke."

Thomas's free hand clenched into a fist and John was certain the smaller Weed was about to get a faceful of knuckles, when a voice split the tension.

"Weed!" It was the large man who had decked the boy earlier. "You heard the captain. Get your sorry carcass to sick bay."

Weed yanked his arm from the grasp of his tormentor and walked away.

John ran after him.

N
∧

"Tony. Tony." Stanton slapped the boy lightly on the cheek. "Come on, son. Wake up."

Tony groaned and opened his eyes. He blinked several times, then asked, "What happened?"

Stanton smiled. "First you saved my bacon. Next you passed out. You okay?"

"I think so." He sat up and shook his head. "That was weird."

"Everything is weird. Think you can stand?"

"Yeah. Sure. Why not?"

"No need to be macho around me," Stanton said. "If it weren't for you, I'd be fish chum."

Shaking his head again, Tony replied, "Oh yeah . . . that. You owe me a pizza."

"I owe you a whole bunch more than that. Any idea why you fainted?"

"Women faint, boss. Men pass out."

"Right. Silly me. Any idea why you passed out?"

Tony rubbed the back of his head. "We were running forward, and then the next thing I know, I'm sitting with my back to that round gun thing there and the back of my head feels like a cracked egg. I jumped up and started looking for everyone else. I saw your hands on the lifeline."

"I'm glad you did," Stanton said. "Turn around."

"Why?"

"I want to look at the back of your head."

"I'm fine," Tony objected.

"Yeah, well, I'm going to look, and if you try and stop me, I'll tell everyone you fainted."

"You call that gratitude?"

Tony turned and Stanton studied the back of the boy's head. There was no blood but there was a raised area in the scalp. Placing his hands on Tony's shoulders, Stanton turned him around and looked in his eyes. "Pupils are equal. How's your vision?"

"I still see you and this boat. Despite that, my vision is fine."

Stanton laughed. "But you only see one of me, right?"

"Thankfully." Tony pulled from Stanton's grasp. "I'm fine. Really. I just bumped my head and got the wind knocked out of me."

"You got the wind knocked out of you? Maybe I should—"

Tony raised his hands as if to fend off Stanton. "I'm okay, man. Leave it alone."

"Okay," Stanton agreed. He paused, then said, "Thanks."

"Yeah, yeah, you said that. Where are the others?"

Stanton looked around. "I don't know. I don't understand what happened." He looked at the sky and the water. "Clearly we slipped back again, but this time it's lasting a lot longer."

The sound of metal hitting metal caught their attention. It sounded as if it came from the side of the ship. Stanton stepped to the starboard lifeline and looked over the side.

"What is it?" Tony asked.

"It looks like one of the square ports has been opened." Suddenly a man's head and upper torso appeared. He was holding a large metal bucket, which he turned upside down. Garbage, carried by the wind, flew aft and fell to the churning ocean a few moments later. The man withdrew the bucket, reached around, grabbed a handle on the square steel door, and slammed it shut with a loud clang.

"Ironic, isn't it?" Tony said. "You, Mr. Naval History, are standing on a hundred-year-old ship and the first thing you see is someone taking out the garbage. You must be in total awe."

"Were you born this cynical or did you have to work on it?"

Tony shrugged. "We each have our art."

Stanton was bothered. "He looked very real. Not ghostly."

"Yeah, so?"

"Before when we saw crew, they appeared insubstantial, translucent, ghostly. The man we just saw looked as solid as either of us. That means we've come all the way back."

"That little nerd Steve said that if we came all the way back, we would cease to exist. Looks like he was wrong."

"Good thing for us, but he may be only partly wrong. We need to find the others."

"Where do we look?"

"Everywhere," Stanton replied. "Let's move forward. I was in danger; the others may be also." An unspoken prayer bubbled from his heart as he began to jog. *Lord, help us. Help me help the others—*

"Look up," a voice from above said. Stanton's mind came to an abrupt stop. Had he just heard a voice from heaven? "Look up," the voice said. Stanton's eyes popped open and he raised his gaze skyward. The distant voice spoke to him again. "Captain Stanton. Up here."

"What?" he mumbled. Then he saw someone waving his arms—someone on the searchlight platform two-thirds of the way up the tripod mast. It was Steve. "Steve? Is that you?"

"What's he doing up there?" Tony asked, then quickly added, "I know, I know. What are any of us doing here?"

"How do I get down?" Steve called.

Stanton had no idea.

N
Λ

Steve was stretching every fiber of his courage just looking over the side of the platform. He was relieved to see Stanton and Tony. That was the good news. The bad news was that he was still high up the main mast, standing on a platform that seemed too narrow and certainly moved too much. Dizziness threatened his stability and weakened his legs, but he fought it off. He had to. Allowing himself to be incapacitated now would only make things worse.

Now that he had Stanton's attention, he felt a little better, but relief would only come once he was off the mast and back on the wide main deck. Behind him, on the port side of the mast, was a Jacob's ladder—a ladder whose rungs were held in place by rope—but it only went up to the platform above. He had no idea what that platform was, and he had no desire to climb the wobbly, wiggly ladder to find out. The direction he wanted to go was down, and he wanted to do it as safely as possible.

Steve had spent the last five minutes assessing his situation and fighting nausea. The ship's movement was magnified tenfold where he was. There was little to see on the platform itself. A large searchlight was fixed to a stanchion at the front of the platform. Two hatches were situated in the deck. Since there was a searchlight, someone had to be able to operate it, and that meant some sailor would have to climb up to the platform to do the work. He wasn't sure what they paid sailors in those days, but it wasn't enough.

The hatches were the most logical choice and Steve wasted no time in trying them out, but no matter how hard he pulled, neither would budge. He could see no locks or any other device to keep the hatches clamped down so tight. As far as he could see, they should open easily. His guess was that there was a ladder inside the metal mast—otherwise why have the hatches at all? Guessing was good but it did nothing to help him pry open the hatches.

The idea must have occurred to Stanton too, for he called up that very suggestion.

"They won't open," Steve shouted down. "It's like they're welded shut."

Stanton told him to hold on and then he and Tony disappeared for a few moments. When they came back, Stanton shouted, "There's an access door down here but it won't budge either."

Previously, Steve had thought they might be slipping back and forth in time. It was a ludicrous idea but the only one that explained the facts. If that were the case, if people could go back in time, then there was the danger of changing something that would forever alter the future. Some thinkers reasoned that nature would never allow such a thing to take place, that if a person could travel back in time, they would be unable to alter anything.

At first Steve had assumed that the time traveler would simply cease to exist. That's what he had told the others but there was another possibility. They might be able to go back but they wouldn't be able to interact with the environment. If that were true, it would explain why he couldn't open the hatches. They weren't welded or even locked in the normal sense of the word. They were locked by time.

An idea occurred to Steve. He turned to the Jacob's ladder and studied it. It looked frail and flimsy, merely two ropes separated by wood rungs. Steve had to test his theory. Their survival depended on knowing as much about their environment as possible. He steeled his jaw and forced his acrophobia to one corner of his mind. Stepping to the back of the platform and to the thick mast, Steve leaned over the rail and stretched out his right hand to grab the ladder.

He felt sick. Things began to spin but he ignored it. This would only take a moment.

The ladder was out of reach.

"Oh, come on," he said to himself. "The ladder is here for a reason. There has to be a way of reaching it." He took a step back and studied the situation. There was a way to reach it. All he had to do was climb through the cross members of the guardrail, hang over the edge with the pitching ship four or five stories below, and take hold of the ladder. Simple, really.

"Yeah, keep telling yourself that," he said aloud. "Okay, the sooner you do this, the sooner you can say it's done." Odd, Steve thought. That was something his mother said. Steve stepped on the lower rail and tentatively swung his right foot over the top. He was now straddling the safety rail, with the platform on his left and a lot of open air on his right. Cautiously and while holding tightly with both hands, he brought his left leg over so both feet were now on the "wrong" side of the rail.

His teeth chattered in fear, his stomach flipped repeatedly, and his palms began to sweat. "Just like on the jungle gyms at school when you were little," he told himself. That's what the part of his mind associated with fiction said. His rational mind reminded him that a fall from an elementary school jungle gym was all of five feet and onto soft sand. If he fell here, his plunge would be well over forty feet and there was the hard steel roof of the ship's superstructure to break it—and every bone he had.

"Slow and steady," he reminded himself. Turning sideways, he let go with his right hand while tightening the grip of his left. He could feel the perspiration being squeezed from beneath his palm and fingers.

The ladder hung just three feet away. It should be easy to reach. His fingers touched the ladder. It felt cold. It felt stiff. A rope ladder should move but this felt . . . odd, inflexible.

"Just as I thought," Steve said. He felt a surprising measure of pride. Then he felt his hand slip from the guardrail.

Steve started down.

N

Λ

"What's he think he's doing?" Tony asked. "The little twerp is going to get himself killed."

"Steve, stay on the platform," Stanton shouted.

Steve fell.

"No!" Stanton screamed. His eyes slammed shut involuntarily, not wanting to see the boy's body bouncing off the steel.

"He's okay," Tony said, pumping his fist in the air. "The idiot is okay."

Stanton forced his eyes open to see Steve hanging on the unmoving ladder. "Thank God," Stanton said. "Thank God."

The relief was only momentary. Steve jerked against the ladder as if trying to break it free from its supports.

"What's the nerd doing?" Tony asked.

"Wait a second," Stanton said, "why isn't the ladder moving?"

"Who cares? It saved Steve's life. Isn't that enough?"

"It's a Jacob's ladder, Tony—a rope ladder. It should be bouncing all over the place, but it's not."

"Now you're thinking, Steve," Tony said. "Get back on the platform, buddy."

Steve was reaching back to the guardrail and had it in his grasp a moment later. With relief Stanton watched as Steve scuttled over the rail and back onto the platform. He disappeared from sight for a moment, then appeared at the rail's edge. "Did you see that? Do you know what that means?"

"It means you lost your mind?" Tony answered loudly.

"Yeah, buddy," Stanton shouted. "I know what it means. Sit tight."

"Okay," Tony said, "I think I've missed something."

"We all have," Stanton said. "We all have."

Jamie followed the two sailors as they pushed the skid along its tracks. They were filthy, dusted in a black film of coal dust.

"Come on, guys," she said. "Talk to me."

There was no response. It was the third such request that Jamie had made and she was becoming angry at being ignored. "Hey, I'm talking to you, buddy." She poked one man in the arm. He gave no indication of her touch, but Jamie felt she had just poked the side of a car door. The man's shoulder didn't have the expected give of flesh and muscle. It gave not at all. The fabric of the uniform felt like steel, and the arm beneath it felt as malleable as a stone.

"This can't be," she said. She watched them move. Every step was fluid, every motion exactly what she expected a human to look like when walking. Someone with inflexible limbs shouldn't be able to move at all, but here they were, pushing a cart full of coal down a track, walking like normal people.

Normal people? Was that the problem? Maybe it was she who wasn't normal. She stopped and held out her hands. They looked the same. Felt the same. Clean, positive flesh tones and—wait. Her hands should be black with coal dust. After all, she had been sitting on a pile of coal just a few moments before. The sailors were covered in the stuff. Why were her hands clean? She looked at her clothing and shoes, all of which were dust free.

"I'm dead," she said. "That's why they can't see me. That's why the coal doesn't stick to me. I'm dead. I'm a ghost. Won't that mess up Stanton's ordered little world."

N
⋀

Tenny had found the door. She had methodically worked her way around the barbette, her hands tracing the curved metal shell. Since she had encountered fewer obstacles than expected, she concluded she was not in the turret area, the place where the twelve-inch guns were located. While she had never been inside such a place, not even on a modern warship, it took little deductive reasoning to know there must not be much room in the actual gun quarter. Each turret held not one but a pair of massive cannons. Judging from the barrels exposed beyond the turret, and allowing for the necessary equipment to raise, lower, load, and clear the guns, she should have bumped into them by now.

The open space in which she had felt along like a blind woman on a moonless night told her she had to be one or two levels below the guns. It must take many men, she thought, to lift the shells and firing powder to be loaded into the breeches of the hungry guns. What was the firing powder called again? She tried to recall her naval history. Stanton would know. That man seemed to know everything.

Cordite. That was it. Cordite. The ship was from the decade of the 1900s. It was around that time, maybe the late 1890s, that black powder was replaced by cordite, a material that was more stable and gave off less smoke. A detached piece of trivia from one of her history classes at the academy came floating into her mind like a child's helium balloon. The Spanish-American War was the last major conflict in which black powder was used. That would have been—she thought for a moment—1898.

Not that any of that mattered. She was still locked in the cylindrical room. Finding the door had not helped her out. No matter how hard she tried, she could not get the door to budge. She needed a different approach and needed it soon. Not prone to claustrophobia, she felt nonetheless that the darkness was thickening, making it hard to breathe. She knew it was her imagination, but being deprived of any light was unsettling. Tenny had never realized how black darkness could be. Even on the darkest nights, there always seemed to be some light somewhere: stars in the heavens or distant houses. Here there was no light at all.

Leaning against the smooth surface next to the door, she forced her mind to settle, to focus, to plan. It was no easy task, because the longer she stayed in the stygian gloom, the more her thoughts became unruly, wanting to pull away from logic and embrace panic. At times her thoughts were like cats on leashes, an impossible pairing.

"Sooner or later someone is going to come in here," she told herself. At least she hoped so. She had yet to see another soul or hear even a muted, distant voice. The only indication she had that the ship had come alive was the unending movement of the deck. Earlier the ship was as still as if it had been mounted to a concrete foundation. Now it pitched and rolled rhythmically. From that she assumed, at least hoped, that there were now crew members aboard who might let her out.

Of course, there was Stanton and Richie. They wouldn't leave her behind—not that they had anyplace to go. That was assuming they were unharmed.

Tenny had never felt so alone.

Her choices were few. She could sit by the door and wait for someone else to open it, or she could try to find another way out. Never a patient woman, she decided on the latter.

Now she was faced with another decision. In her previous exploration she had come across a ladder, easily identifiable by its shape and construction. She had no idea where the ladder went. She had followed the vertical supports down and discovered a manhole where the deck and ladder met. It made sense. Crew members would have to move up and down the decks while in the barbette. Firing twelve-inch guns was not a job for a single man. Shells had to be moved from their storage places to the guns above.

Above. Tenny gave the direction some thought, wishing she had paid more attention to the turrets when she was on deck. Of course, they had had other things on their minds at the time. She tried to call up an image of what she had seen, like a person removing a photo from an album. She could see the exterior of the gunhouse, with its two thick barrels projecting menacingly out of the steel skin. The housing had several sharp angles where armor plating met armor plating. Three rounded structures were forward on the gunhouse, and Tenny assumed they were either ventilation ports or, more likely, sighting hoods, a place where the gunners could see their target, making adjustments as the gunnery spotters directed them and—

That would mean there were openings. At the very least there might be some light, something to thin the blackness. It was settled. She would move up.

Being more familiar with her environment, albeit just by touch, Tenny made her way to the ladder as quickly as caution would allow. She found it easily enough and looked up. A faint glow trickled down the opening in the ceiling above. That was all she needed. Putting foot to rung and hand to rail, Tenny began her ascent, moving slowly, fearing an unseen sharp projection that might easily be avoided in light but might inflict a wound in the dark.

Every step was made as tentatively as if a snake were coiled around the next rung. Slowly Tenny took one step at a time. Finally her head passed through the manhole of the deck above and her eyes were greeted with sweet light, dim and diffused, but lovely light nonetheless. Encouraged, Tenny took the last few rungs, forcing herself to maintain the guarded pace.

This room was far more crowded than the one below, dominated as it was by the massive guns she knew were there. Light came from the three sighting hoods on the gunhouse roof and from the space around the barrels where they passed through the armor plating. The place was filled with levers, handles, and hand wheels, used for things she could only guess at. Speculating might be fun ... at another time ... in another place ... under different circumstances. What she wanted now was out.

Her heart picked up its pace in anticipation of leaving behind the metal tomb and being reborn into light and fresh air. To the back was a door. Working her way around stools and other gunner paraphernalia, Tenny made her way to the door, grabbed the handle, and tried to turn it. The handle refused to budge. It moved not at all, not even a slight wiggle. Despair started to rain on her optimism. She looked up and saw a hatch in the roof and a ladder leading to it. She was up the ladder a few seconds later but had no more luck with the overhead hatch than she had with the door.

Descending again, she pounded her hands on the ladder's rungs. "Let . . . me . . . out." Several deep breaths later she turned and looked at the sighting hoods. Light trickled in through the three hoods, but it came through narrow slits that served as windows. Too small to use as an exit, she decided. "There must be a way out."

Then she saw it. "Of course," she said and began to move forward in the gunhouse, to where the gun barrels projected out into the open air. The guns were designed to be raised and lowered to adjust for distance. That meant the guns protruded through a slot in the armor plating—a large slot.

The guns took up most of the available space, but because they rested parallel to the deck, a space existed above the barrels. A person—a small person like Tenny—could work their way through the opening and outside the gunhouse. All she had to do was mount one of the guns, shinny along its long barrel, and squeeze through the open space. It was going to be a tight squeeze and there was a chance she wouldn't fit or would even become stuck.

It was a chance she was willing to take.

N
Λ

Mary Moss longed to sleep. The cold of the freezer was invading through her clothing, pressing through her pores. Her muscles ached from uncomfortable shivering and she felt faint. The shivering was slowing. At first she was grateful, and then she realized the meaning of it. Her energy was flagging, her body too tired even to shiver. There was a limit to what a body could do; hers was close to its limit.

At first the thought of dying frightened her, but now it seemed a welcome release. Never had she felt such discomfort. Never had she so despaired of seeing another day. It was hopeless. She had even prayed. It was all she had. She prayed. She begged God. She made promises, but the door remained shut and immovable.

Still on her knees, her body pulled into a tight ball to save every ounce of heat, Mary gave up. There was nothing left to do but die—to fall to her side and surrender to the assaulting, unrelenting cold.

There was a pop.

An infusion of light.

Warmth rolled over her in a wave.

Her thoughts moved at glacial speeds. Mary tried to understand what was happening but her brain was sluggish. Opening her eyes, she saw a pair of shoes walk by.

In an agonizing effort Mary straightened herself. Every joint seemed frozen. A man dressed in white had walked in, passed her, and advanced toward one of the shelves. Struggling to her feet, Mary turned toward him and said, "Help," but where she had meant a cry, she got only a whisper.

"Lamb chops," the man said. "That'll make the old man happy."

He turned and Mary realized he was headed for the door that led from the freezer to the outside. She wobbled on unsteady feet and turned to see a glorious white light pouring through the opening. *The door is open*, she thought. *Finally it is open. The door!*

The man passed her, heading for the opening.

"Wait," Mary said. "What about me?"

He gave no response. *The door. The door. The door!* Her mind was screaming. She watched as the man turned to shut the heavy metal slab, when her chilled brain realized what was before her: one chance of survival. If that door closed, she wouldn't survive the next half hour.

Willing, commanding, demanding that her legs move, M&M started forward. Every step was a work of Herculean effort, but she fought through the despair, pushed back the pain. The door was only three or four steps away but the distance seemed end-less. The man in white switched the paper-wrapped package he had retrieved from one hand to the other and reached for the door.

"No, no, no!" Mary cried out. This time the whisper roared, but the man acted as if he were deaf. He then lifted his head and stared right at her. He gave no sign of seeing Mary as she stum-bled forward, leaping the last step.

She tumbled to the deck outside the freezer and rolled past the man's feet. She rolled twice and rested on her back, looking up at a man who did not see her.

The fall sent shock waves of pain through nerves made sensi-tive by exposure to unbearable cold. She cried out and a sob erupted from her lips.

The man walked off, tossing the package from one hand to the other. He began to whistle.

Dark Plans

"Man, I thought I had it bad," John said as he trotted to catch up with the boy everyone called Weed. "I gotta love the way you didn't give in. Never show them you care, right? Hey, right?"

Weed sped his way along, moving at just short of a trot. He had marched through the mess area and into a large expanse John was already familiar with. Racks of canvas bags filled the open space. Weed took no note of them. His head was down and John could see the tension in his neck.

"Come on, buddy," John pleaded. "I'm on your side. Talk to me." The dark-haired, victimized teenager gave no sign of hearing anything John was saying. In a desperate effort to get noticed, John raced ahead and stood in Weed's path, his arms extended, intent on taking him by the shoulders until he acknowledged his existence. "I can be as stubborn as you, pal."

Weed continued forward, never slowing. John grabbed the boy by his uniformed arms. "Slow down for a sec—what the . . ."

John was moving back at the same rate Weed was advancing. The sneakers on John's feet slid across the metal decking as if someone had poured a thick layer of oil on the surface. John dug in his heels but nothing changed. Weed walked, pushing John backward as if he weren't there. John's mind began to spin wildly.

"This ain't possible," he said. "How are you doing this?"

John released the boy and quickly stepped to the side. He lifted his left foot and examined the sole of the sneaker but saw nothing to explain what he had just experienced. He did the same with his right shoe. "This is whacked." He raced after Weed, who rounded a corner and slipped through a door. John charged after him.

He was in a room that was three times as wide as it was deep. To his left, near the far wall, were two rows of beds. In the middle of the space was a large table with benches on either side. A bathtub was tucked in a corner.

"Can I help you?" a tall, thin man with a beaklike nose asked.

"Captain ordered me to sick bay, Doc," Weed said.

"And just why would he ... Oh, I see." The doctor walked over to the boy. "How'd you come to have such a fine knot on the head?"

"I fell and hit me head on the deck."

"Yeah, with some help," John said. No one responded to him.

"Fell, did ya? All by yourself?"

"Yes."

"I don't think you're that clumsy, boy. And I'm pretty sure this didn't come from a fall to the deck." He pressed the bruise on Weed's cheek. Weed flinched but said nothing. "Who did that to you?"

"It's me own fault," Weed said. "Just a fall. Nothin' more."

The doctor sighed. "Tell me who hit you, boy. I'll have him in front of the captain before he can make up an excuse."

"I said it's me own fault, Doc. That's all there is to it."

Another sigh from the doctor. "There's a difference between loyalty and stupidity, son."

"I'm sure I wouldn't know, sir."

"Very well." The doctor looked in Weed's eyes and ears. "Any double vision, ringing in the ears, that sort of thing?"

"No."

"There's not much to be done, then," the doctor said. "You're going to be sporting a bit of a black eye for a time. The knot on your head is about as big as it's going to get, but it will be sore. If anything changes, come see me. For now, no binnacle list for you."

"I'm not looking to be relieved of duty. Am I dismissed?" Weed asked.

The doctor studied him for a moment. "Revenge never works in the navy. You know that, don't you?"

"Yes sir."

"I don't think you do," the doctor stated. "Carry on. Try and stay out of trouble."

Weed turned and marched out of the sick bay with the same intensity, now heading toward the ship's bow. John followed close behind. "Why are you protecting those guys? They've got judgment coming to 'em. You don't owe them anything. Trust me, I know."

Weed gave no sign of hearing him. He marched on, head down, avoiding eye contact with every sailor he saw. John dodged each crewman. Once he cut it too close and his shoulder collided with a middle-aged crewman with a pockmarked face. It was more a glancing touch than a collision but it was enough to spin John on his heels.

Although he couldn't explain what was happening to him, he was smart enough to assess the situation. No matter how much he spoke, no matter what antics he invoked, no one noticed him. He was fully and completely invisible to them. That was a fact that brought him some satisfaction. An invisible man could have some real fun. But he also learned to stay out of the way of others.

Weed worked his way forward through the ship until he came to a ladderway. He looked down the descending steps and then started down, his feet hitting the rungs in rapid fashion. It reminded John of a tap dancer.

"Hey, slow down," John said but got the usual no response. John followed after him but was slower. He had to hustle at the bottom to catch up and when he did, he saw Weed starting down another ladder. John kept up the chase.

John's breath was coming hard and he felt as if he had just run a mile. By his count they had descended three decks. They were now in a hot, loud room. John could see men shoveling coal into some kind of furnace. Weed paid no attention to the room or to the men. Clearly, he had a destination in mind. He moved forward of the ladder and into an enclosed space. John had to race behind him to beat the closing door.

Something was different about this room. John had noticed many smells since coming to in the mess area. He had smelled the sausage and potatoes in the mess hall, the acrid aroma of coal in the boiler room, but this place was worse. The smell not only assaulted his nose but burned his eyes. "Whoa, what is that? This place reeks."

A man who appeared a good ten years older than Weed glanced up from a paper he held in his hand. "You're early. Aren't you supposed to be in mess right now?"

"Not hungry," Weed said. "I want to be ready for the drill."

"Strength comes from eating, lad," the man said. He sounded Irish. "You're no good to me if you faint from hunger."

"I don't faint," Weed shot back.

"Is that a fact, now? Well, you just be sure you don't or it will be both our hides."

"Can I check my station?"

"The drill is more than an hour away, lad. Come back in thirty minutes. That's when your shift begins."

"I'm here now. It can't hurt for me to check my station. This is the first full gun test. I want to be perfect."

"Can't fault you for that," the man said. John assumed the older man was one of Weed's superiors. "I hear you got tagged to clean the aft heads. Did your mouth get you in trouble?"

"I didn't do nothin' wrong. I was mindin' me own business, I was."

"That, my young friend, is the navy way. We mind everyone else's business. You getting assigned to this new ship on your very first cruise, well, that makes people think your uncle is passing favors your way. Folk don't much like that. Makes 'em feel . . . inferior. I'm assuming the urinals shine."

"They do," was all John said.

"That mouse you got under your eye, boy—that a gift from anybody I know?"

"I fell."

"Fell down, did ya?" The man shook his head in disbelief. "I'll say one thing for ya, ya know how to take a beating."

"Can I check my station?" Weed pressed.

"You can do more than that, lad." The man approached and held out the paper he had been holding. John could see a list of items and numbers written beside them. "I need to spend some quality time in the head. You can double-check my inventory. After the drill, we will need to give an accurate account of the charges used, so count good, lad."

Weed took the list but didn't look at it. The man studied him for a moment. "You all right, boy?"

"Yes. Fine."

"You sure? You don't look fine."

"I'm positive."

"Well then, I'm off. Back soon." Then he exited the room at a near trot.

"I hope he makes it in time," John said. He returned his attention to Weed just in time to see him drop the paper on the deck. He placed a foot on the document and ground it on the metal until the paper tore. "Sheesh, you're just asking for trouble. Even I know when to back off."

Weed walked around a wide cylindrical object that reached from deck to ceiling. At first John assumed it to be a large support column. As he followed Weed around it, he saw that it had a door in the side. It looked like a small elevator. Too small for a man but big enough to send packages up and down. Weed paid it no attention. Instead he approached a side door and opened it. A strong, pungent odor rolled out of the adjoining room.

"Man, that stinks," John said.

Weed left the door open and John could see that it was designed to be locked open as well as closed. He followed the sailor inside and saw stacks of cloth-covered cylinders. They were piled in rows, one neatly set atop another.

"Man, it smells like gunpowder in here . . . oh, I get it. This is where you keep the stuff for big guns. Impressive. I bet you could do some real damage with this stuff."

Weed leaned against one of the supporting shelves and lowered his head. He stuck his hands in his pockets, then slowly removed a small folding knife. John watched as Weed pulled out the blade and studied it for a moment. The blade glinted in the artificial light. A second later Weed lifted his head and John could see tears streaming down his face. The sailor let his head roll back. Then his eyes rolled back.

"You're freaking me out here," John said, not expecting Weed to hear.

A few seconds later Weed took a strong grip on the knife, raised it above his head, then brought it down in a vicious arc. John jumped back, thinking Weed was trying to dig the knife into his own leg, but the blade missed the boy's limb and plunged into one of the sacks. Weed twisted it, turned it, then worked it back and forth, cutting a line across the bag. Dark powder poured out.

Weed was just beginning. He stabbed another bag, then another. More and more powder flowed, creating small mountains of black on the deck. He cut ten containers, then slowly closed the knife and returned it to his pocket.

He reached into his other pocket and removed a small box— a box of matches.

"Whoa, man. What are you doing? Stop. Stop!"

Weed raised a match, studied it for a moment, then smiled. "Maybe revenge does work."

N
⋀

Richie was as relieved as he was puzzled when he found an open hatch to the main deck, the one he had first stepped foot on when he climbed the torpedo net boom. That seemed a year and a half ago but it had been less than a day—at least as far as he could figure. Best he could tell, day meant something different here. He had worked his way up from the boiler room, assuming that the natural place for the others to go was the original meeting place. He would at least start there. It was faster than trying to search the whole ship, especially when one couldn't open a door or hatch.

That bothered him. He sensed his own physicality. He had touched himself, pinched himself, and everything seemed normal—except no one could see him or hear him, and while he could touch everything he saw, he could move nothing. It was as if everything had been welded in place. But the sailors he saw going about their business were able to do everything he couldn't. He shook his head and put the puzzle behind him. He would wrestle with those questions later. The first thing he had to do was find Stanton and the others.

He had come out on the starboard side of the main deck. The meeting place was on the port side, meaning Richie had to jog around the superstructure. After being in the confined belly of the battleship, he was glad for the freedom of movement. He trotted with purpose, feeling that time was somehow running out. He had no evidence to base that fear on, but it seemed nonetheless real.

As he rounded the forward bulkhead, he heard his name called. He stopped and spun around, looking for the caller.

"Richie!" Tenny was moving his way fast. When she was three feet away, she launched herself at him, wrapping her arms around his neck. He caught her around the waist and they held each other for a moment. "Boy, am I glad to see you."

"Likewise," Richie said with genuine affection. "Where have you been?"

"I was trapped in one of the gunhouses," she explained. "It was black as tar in there. I had to feel my way around and when I found a door, I couldn't open it. I thought I was going to be stuck in there forever." She explained how she had escaped.

"You're a genius, girl. Are you hurt?"

"Bruised, but that's it. How about you?"

"I'm okay. I woke up in the boiler room."

"Richie . . . the sailors . . . they're . . . they're . . ."

"Not responsive," he said, completing her thought. "I think we're invisible to them. They can't hear us. They have no idea we're here. If we are here."

"What do you mean?"

"It's this whole thing with the doors and hatches not opening. I know they work, because the crew can open and close them.

But I can't. That means the problem must be with me . . . I mean with us."

"How?"

"Who knows? The academy didn't cover this kind of situation. We'll have to figure it out later. Right now let's find the others."

"I was heading to our original rendezvous spot," Tenny said. "That's the logical place for everyone to meet."

"Ditto," Richie said. "Let's do it."

Rounding the superstructure, they saw Stanton and Tony in the distance. "Thank God," Richie said. He had been in a steady state of prayer since coming to in the boiler room. "Captain," Richie called. He felt no hesitation in shouting. None of the crew he had met had responded to anything verbal.

Stanton turned and his face lit up with a wide smile. Tenny and Richie raced forward, dodging crewmen who moved along the deck, oblivious to the pair. Again Tenny launched herself, nearly knocking Stanton over. Once he released her, she embraced Tony.

"Is everyone all right?" Stanton asked.

"Confused and sore but ready for duty," Richie answered. "Where are the others?"

Stanton looked up at the mast. "Steve's up there," he said. "I don't know about the others."

"What's he doing up there?" Richie craned his neck and saw Steve pacing around the spotlight deck.

"He's up there for the same reason I was hanging off the stern looking down at four angry props." Stanton brought him up to date and Richie did the same. "More important than how he got up there is, how do we get him down? He's tried the manhole hatches but they won't budge. I'm certain there's a ladder in the main mast, but it's useless if he can't get those hatches open."

"What we need is for a crewman to open a hatch," Richie said. "But I don't know how to do that. I think he's stuck."

"I don't think he likes heights," Tony said. "He's looking pretty squirrelly."

"Take it easy, buddy," Richie called up to Steve. "We'll figure it out."

"I have an idea," Steve shouted back. "But it's pretty crazy."

"What?"

"Let me think about it; then I'll let you know." Steve stepped back, out of sight.

"You don't think he'd do anything stupid, do you?" Tenny asked.

"He's pretty level-headed," Stanton said. "I think we can trust his judgment."

A moment later Steve reappeared, crawled up on the guardrail, bent over, worked at something, then stepped off into thin air.

Richie could hear him scream.

N
Λ

"This is the dumbest thing you've ever done," Steve said to himself. He had thought it through, reasoned it out, weighed the odds; still, he was scared beyond words.

He was standing on the pitching guardrail, one leg over the top, the other fixed to the aft edge of the platform. Just below the platform was a pulley and a pair of metal cables. The cables led from the pulley, which was fixed to the back of the main mast, to another pulley set on the end of a large boom that extended horizontally a few feet above one of the upper decks of the superstructure. He estimated that the cables ran at a fifty-degree angle. Pretty steep.

In principle his idea was sound; in practice it was madness, but Steve knew he would never get off the elevated platform unless a crewman came up through a manhole and was kind enough to leave it open for him. The odds of both things happening were abysmal. It was time to face his fears and take charge of his situation. Good thoughts. Strong thoughts. Then why was he so scared?

The answer was apparent: to make his plan work, he had to climb the rail and lean over into the open air, reaching down to the metal cables. Nothing could be more foolish.

Steve reached.

The real problem, he knew, would be in his ability to hold on to a cable that was certain to cut the tender flesh of his hand. So he had to hold on with something else. That something, he decided, would be his belt. It was leather and less likely to shred than human skin. Still, once the descent began, there was a chance that the cable could cut through the leather band. It certainly would if he let himself slide freely. Friction alone would destroy the belt. His descent would have to be controlled. If he could keep himself from freewheeling down, then he should be able to settle on the boom. From there his fall would be less than six feet or so. And if he were cautious, he might, just might, not fall at all.

Removing his belt, he leaned over the cables and, holding himself in place with a leg wrapped around the guardrail, swung the buckle end at the lower of the two cables. It was important that he work his way down on the lower cable, not the higher. If he hooked onto the top cable, then the belt would not only rub against it but rub against the lower line as well, making two points of contact—two points of breakage.

"This is stupid. I'm an idiot. I should be locked up in a nuthouse. Just forget it, Steve; it can't be done."

He swung the belt with one hand and grabbed the end as it came up the other side of the cable. Miraculously, he caught it the first time. He was grateful. The awkward way he had to support himself was making his legs burn with the fire of fatigue. He didn't have the time and strength to make repeated attempts.

Fastening the belt into a loop, he looked at the cable he planned to slowly work his way down, shifting the belt from time to time to avoid wear in just one spot, wear that would break the belt and send him plummeting to his death.

"Don't look down," he told himself. "Just focus on the cable and everything—"

He felt his foot slip, followed by a sudden plunge.

He heard himself screaming.

N
Λ

The slide was too fast and instinctively Steve kicked his legs, raising them as high as he could, trying to get the soles of his sneakers on the cable to brake his speed. But each kick just added momentum to the already breakneck descent.

Down, down. Steve knew it could not be more than a few seconds, but each second lasted an eternity. He kicked. He slid. He screamed.

He looked up, expecting to see leather, heated by friction, cut in two, sending him dropping like a bowling ball to the deck. It took one of the eternal seconds for Steve to realize that he wasn't riding on the leather band of the belt but on the buckle—the metal buckle. Shooting a glance down, he saw the thick derrick patiently waiting for his impact. He had no doubt who would win in that meeting.

With less than a second to go, Steve tried again to get a foot on the thick cable in a last-ditch effort to slow his descent. Success!

The soft rubber sole of his sneaker slid along the cable. The cable ate away at the shoe. He felt his slide slow … slow … slow. His foot slipped but now he was only a few feet above the metal boom. He prepared for impact, hoping his legs would be strong enough to hold him and prevent him from tumbling end over end.

Steve hit the boom so hard that his teeth hurt, but by holding on to the belt above his head, he was able to use his legs as shock absorbers. Pain rifled up his hips, back, and arms. Dark spots began to float before his eyes. It took a moment for him to realize he was standing on the boom, still clutching the belt.

Slowly he eased himself down until he straddled the eighteen-inch-thick derrick. Releasing the belt, Steve leaned forward and hugged the beam, his arms and legs wrapped around the tubular arm. He couldn't breathe and his heart was a machine gun.

The deck was ten feet below him, too far to jump. Slowly he inched backward like a caterpillar—compressing himself, then working his legs back. Foot after foot, he worked his way down the sixty-foot-long boom toward the base of the tripod mast. Once there, he could shinny down the boom's vertical support. That was his theory.

He heard footfalls. "Steve … Steve."

Hands grabbed him and helped him to the deck. Through bleary eyes Steve saw the concerned face of J. D. Stanton. Next to him were Richie, Tenny, and Tony. "Hi, you guys. I thought I'd drop in."

"That was the dumbest thing I've ever witnessed," Stanton said, but there was only relief in his voice. Steve stood on his wobbly legs.

Tony was about to explode. "That was … that was … the coolest thing I've ever seen. You da' man, baby. You da' man!" Tony hugged Steve and lifted him from the deck. "Anybody picks on you, they answer to me. Man, that was way over the top."

"Um, thanks, Tony," Steve said. His legs were shaking, his heart skipping, his stomach knotting. He turned to Stanton. "Did you see the cable?"

"I saw the whole thing," Stanton said. "I thought I was going to need CPR."

"No problem, Skipper," Richie said. "Tony will give you mouth-to-mouth."

"Not me," Tony shot back. "I'll be sure to wave goodbye."

"Wait a minute," Steve said. "I mean, did you see what the cable did?"

"I didn't see it do anything," Stanton admitted.

"That's the point," Steve explained. "I'm not a big guy but I weigh enough to make the cable bend some. It didn't budge. Not a millimeter of deflection."

"Meaning?" Tony asked.

"I was wrong about us not being able to exist in the past," Steve said, his breath coming back to him. "I mean, here we are talking, so I got that part wrong, but not by much. I couldn't open either of the hatches in the platform up there. I'll bet you guys have tried to open a door or move something and it wouldn't budge. Right?"

"Right," Stanton said and filled him in on what Richie and Tenny had experienced and on his inability to open the hatchway at the bottom of the main mast. "I think I know where you're going with this. We don't cease to exist in the past but we can't affect the past."

"Exactly. We can see it, move in it, but can't change any of it. We can't open a door, can't blow out a candle, can't do anything. Several physicists have suggested this. They say that nature has safeguards against anything from the future changing anything in the past."

"Then why are we here?" Stanton said, more to himself than to the others.

"Who knows?" Tony said. "It's some kinda accident or cosmic joke."

Stanton shook his head. "I don't think so. I think we're here for a purpose."

"Like what?" Tony asked. "To see a miracle or something?"

"No," Stanton said. "I think we may be the miracle."

Emergency Bells

J amie moved carefully through the companionways. Already she had learned that it didn't pay to talk to anyone. They weren't listening. They were robots which had not been programmed to acknowledge anyone other than their own kind. She had made the mistake of bumping into one of the blue-uniformed creatures that looked so human, and found herself flat on her fanny, her head spinning as if it had been a bus that hit her instead of some young sailor.

Now she moved with greater caution, avoiding all contact by pressing herself to the wall or scampering out of the way. Her life had been difficult and unhappy until this trip. Now it was bizarre. A part of her—a very large part of her—wanted to find a corner, collapse into its shadows, and weep. But there was another part of her, a part she had had no idea existed. It gave her strength, put steel in her spine, and helped her take the next step when she was ready to quit.

Despite her newfound strength, Jamie was confused. She was lost. All she knew was that she had been in a room full of coal, a room filled with big boilers and dirty sailors with big shovels and coal dust clinging to them like paint. That work looked miserable.

Many of the crew looked her age, yet their eyes were older, their mouths drawn by the difficult work they did.

Where was she? She had followed various corridors, climbed up and down ladders, and peeked in nearly every door that stood open. Where were the others? Worry began to work in her gut. It was an unfamiliar feeling. That place was usually occupied by anger and bitterness. But now she nurtured a fear that her travel companions might be hurt. Why should she care? They were nothing to her.

"Forget them," she said to herself. She couldn't. Push their faces, their names, out of her mind. Use them to get back to Miami, then walk away without a word. For years she could dismiss any person she wished. It was a practiced art. So why couldn't she dismiss Stanton and the others? "I must be getting soft. That's the last thing I need."

Jamie stepped aside to let another sailor pass, then rounded yet another corner.

She screamed.

Another scream.

Jamie took several steps back, then stopped. Before her was a young woman, hunched and shivering. Brown hair hung straight down like strings. "Mary? What happened to you?" Jamie approached her.

"Cold. Lost. So lost." M&M began to cry. Jamie waited for a smart remark to load itself from her vast arsenal of criticisms. None came. The armory was empty.

She wrapped her arms around Mary. Sobs from the deepest area of Mary's soul rolled from her. Jamie pulled her close, willing the warmth of her own body to be transferred into Mary's. Mary shivered from cold, shook from despair.

A moment later Jamie traveled a path she had not visited since she was a child. She began to cry. Sob joined sob and the two girls supported one another as unseeing crewmen passed them without the slightest glance.

"I'm here now, Mary. I'm here. I won't let anything happen to you."

The weeping continued.

Two hearts fragmented in a moment—a second later the healing began.

"I admire your style," John said, "but this is extreme, dude. I mean, we're talking serious flash burn." He was staring at Weed, who stood alone in an aisle surrounded by explosives. In his hand was a wood match, the head of it set against the strike plate. John could see the muscle in the crewman's hand tense.

"I know you can't hear me, but you really need to think twice about this."

Weed began to mumble.

"Time for me to leave," John said to himself.

The mumbling caught his attention. It was familiar.

"Water. The deep. Wants me. Loves me. No one else. Death loves me. Death loves me. I should have jumped when I had a chance. Afraid. Too scared. Should have stepped overboard. Peace in the dark. Comfort in the cold."

John froze. The words were similar to what he had been hearing. Words offering peace, acceptance, in exchange for his life. The words had been soothing, comforting, persuasive. He had agreed to the trip because he had a plan. All his life no one paid him notice. He was driftwood in his family, in his school. He was the rat in the pantry that caused everyone to recoil and throw out anything it might have touched. His life had no meaning. His life had no purpose. He had nothing to offer.

Death was good.

Death would settle it all. That would show them. His mom and dad would be standing around an empty grave, without even a body to bury. That would teach them. And if they criticized him, why should he care? He wouldn't be able to hear them. Death had no ears. Death had no feelings.

He had planned to slip overboard when the opportunity was right, when the others slept or were distracted. He had taken great satisfaction in picturing them searching the yacht, calling his name. It had been comical.

The voices promised him that. Death was the answer. No one got out of this life alive; it was all just a matter of time, a function of hours, days, and years. Sooner or later everyone became worm food. Why should he wait?

This boy understood. He heard the same voices—the sweet, friendly voices.

"Painless," Weed said. "They'll be sorry. I got me pride. I got me rights. They picked the wrong lad to torment. Fire. Boom. Heat. Boom. Peace. Painless. Death is the answer. No one leaves this life alive. Why wait?"

"Hey, you been reading my mind, buddy. You just got more imagination than me. You're more inventive."

The voices were returning. They were bringing clarity.

The darkness will come. The peaceful darkness. Pain will be gone; the fear will evaporate under the steady heat of death. It won't take long. The others don't understand. Can't understand. It is beyond their comprehension. They can only see the end. It is the beginning that matters. The beginning of nothingness . . . blessed nothingness.

"The beginning of nothingness," John said.

"The beginning of nothingness," Weed said.

"Blessed nothingness," they said in unison.

Do it.

A different voice. No, the same voice but a different sound. The voices had always been in his head. Now it was in his ear.

Do it. Blessed nothingness.

"Do it," John mimicked. Why not? Sudden death by explosion was as good as any other. His limbs would be torn from his body, his flesh vaporized. It would be quick. It would be merciful. It would be majestic. John held out his arms and threw his head back. "Do it. Do it. Do it."

The chant was hypnotic. So much so that he barely heard the string of obscenities from behind him.

"Have you taken leave of your senses, lad? You'll kill everyone on board. You'll sink us for sure."

John turned to see the man who had handed the paper to Weed. His face was as white as eggshell, his eyes as wide as quarters.

"Stay back," Weed shouted.

"Okay, okay, take it easy, lad," the man said. "Anything you say. You're in charge, chum."

"I ain't your chum. I never have been. I'm no one's chum. No one."

"That's telling 'em, buddy," John said. "What did this guy ever do for you?"

"Steady on, lad. Steady on. What do you want me to do?"

"Die with me," Weed said.

"Great comeback, dude," John said with a laugh. "Die with me. I like it."

"No need to be rash, son. Maybe I should get the captain."

"Get the captain," Weed agreed.

"I will. I will. Just don't do nothin' until he gets here."

"Hurry," Weed intoned just above a whisper and returned his attention to the match. His hand was a tremulous mass. John was sure his shakes would be enough to strike the match's head into a blaze.

"Blessed nothingness," Weed said.

"Yeah, baby, blessed nothingness," John agreed.

N

Λ

The hunt had begun. Stanton led the group, moving as fast as he could across crowded decks and through companionways made narrow by sailors who were unknowing juggernauts, each capable of inflicting a wounding blow, perhaps even a deadly one, without ever knowing that a collision had occurred.

Stanton and the others were hamstrung. When they first stepped foot on the wood deck of the *Archer*, they had had full reign of the vessel. Nothing was hidden from them. Every door opened, every hatch swung on its metal hinges. They lacked power but were at least free to move. Now they could only progress through open areas. At times Stanton was tempted to dash through a door that was slowly closing, but he resisted. A closing metal door was no danger in a normal world, but here it could be a crushing press, capable of breaking bones or squeezing the life out of any one of his crew unfortunate enough to be caught between door edge and doorjamb. The picture was disturbingly ugly and Stanton used his sense of urgency to push the garish image out of his mind.

He had missing people to worry about. Jamie, M&M, and John were still gone. He had to get them back. Assuming they were still alive. They had to be alive. He refused to entertain any other possibility.

The easiest place to search was the superstructure: the bridge and the flying deck. Ladders and stairs made access easy, and the missing kids were just as likely to be up as down. Steve's escapade on the spotlight platform was proof of that. Starting high had the advantage of organization. In a maze it made more sense to place a hand on one wall and follow it until it ultimately led to the exit. A person might travel a much longer distance, meet many dead ends, but finding the exit was guaranteed.

They arrived on the navigation deck and found half a dozen people. A young sailor stood ramrod straight at the wheel. Junior officers gazed at the horizon. A man Stanton was certain was the captain stood near the center of the windowed front wall. A stiff breeze whipped around the bridge's open ends, making it a wind tunnel of cold air. No one on deck seemed to mind.

"How's she handling now?" the captain asked.

"Beautifully," the steersman said. "She's a beast at slow speeds, but the faster she goes, the more gentle she becomes."

"I heard the same of the *Dreadnought*," the captain said. "Slow-speed maneuverability is crucial. We'll drill on that tomorrow. I want all bridge officers up to snuff on this."

Normally, Stanton would have given a year's salary to sit in the background and listen to the discussion. For a historian, to hear the bridge conversation while a ship like the *Archer* was undergoing sea trials would be invaluable and like Christmas to a child. But this was not a normal situation. Stanton quickly looked through the windows of the captain's ready room and the chart room, both places he had been before. He saw no sign of his missing charges.

"Let's go—"

"Captain! Captain!" A man, winded by his dash to the bridge, burst onto the deck.

"Easy, man," the captain said. "Chilton, isn't it?"

"Yes sir," the man said. "We have a problem. A big problem. The ship is in danger."

"Steady on," the captain said evenly. "Take a breath."

The man did. "It's Weed, sir. I mean Roberts … everyone calls him Weed …"

"I'm familiar with the lad," the captain said.

"He's all off, sir. Loony. He's in the cordite room. Powder everywhere and a match in his hand."

"Which powder room?" The captain acted as if he had been informed that his ship had a scratch in the paint.

"Amidships, sir. The big one."

"I see. Do you know what he wants?"

"Wants, sir?"

"No man threatens to blow up a ship without wanting something."

Several other officers had gathered around the captain.

"Emergency bells, sir?" the youngest officer asked.

"By no means, Mr. Clancy. That might set him off."

"Begging the captain's pardon, but it sounds like young Roberts is going to set us off. There is enough powder to send us to the bottom in short order."

"I am aware of the danger," the captain said smoothly. He lowered his head in thought. "Very well, then. We send a message. Order the wireless office to get off a quick dispatch. We abandon ship. Quietly, gentlemen. Quietly as a cat. I don't want young Roberts to know what we're doing. He may see his opportunity slipping away. Am I understood, gentlemen?"

"Aye, sir," came a reply in unison.

"Get what help you need but keep it on the QT. Off with the lot of you."

"Orders, sir?" It was the helmsman.

"Steady as you go, son. Any change now might be enough to upset the boy's apple cart. I will be leaving the bridge. You will be on your own for a while."

Stanton could see the terror on the young sailor's face. "But sir—"

"I'm sorry, son, but I have a visit to make. Try not to hit anything. Think you can do that?"

The young man straightened his spine. "Aye, sir. I won't let you down."

The captain gave a confident nod and marched from the navigation deck. He gave every sign of being calm, even cold, in the face of burning danger, but Stanton got a good look at his eyes. The man was terrified.

"You don't suppose—," Richie began.

"That John is somehow connected?" Stanton closed his eyes. Everything in him wanted to say no, to say that John was just a little misguided and greatly misunderstood. But somehow he knew that would the greatest understatement of this century—and his own.

⋏

Jamie held M&M for long minutes, letting her weep as if it could remove the poison in her soul. She held her. Rocked her. Stroked her hair. No words were exchanged. None would suffice. A different communication was required, a knitting of damaged spirits. M&M was the abused teen, fearful of all around her, the one who downplayed herself at every turn: dowdy clothes, dour expression, whispery voice, and avoidance—always avoidance. Jamie was the tough girl, the "I'm more trouble than you can handle" woman, brash, snotty, difficult at all times. Where M&M avoided people, Jamie drove them away. Different technique, same result.

"We have to go," Jamie said.

"Okay." Mary sniffed, then wiped her nose with the heel of her hand.

"Feel better?" Jamie asked softly.

"Yeah. I'm warmer. I thought I was going to die."

"I'm starting to think Stanton is right," Jamie said. "Someone seems to be looking out for us."

"You mean God?"

"I don't know," Jamie said. "I don't know anything about God, just that we're not on speaking terms. Still, it seems right."

"Maybe God got us into all this. Maybe we should be blaming him."

"Maybe," Jamie said. "Maybe. Let's go."

"Where?"

"I don't know," Jamie admitted. "I can get lost in the mall. If I ever went to the mall."

"Up," Mary said. "Too many people down here. Mr. Stanton would want us to go up, to the place where we first came on board. That's what he would do."

"He's a smart man," Jamie said.

"Nice too. I think he really cares about us."

"Yeah, maybe he does." Jamie released M&M but took her hand. "I bet he's looking for us right now. Let's find a ladder."

A crewman scooted past them, then another. Jamie pulled M&M back and pressed her against the wall. "Watch these guys. They knock you over with a touch. I think they're aliens or robots or something."

"They look human."

"Looks can be deceiving," Jamie said. "Trust me, they're not normal."

"They're in a hurry. They weren't moving this fast before."

"Yeah, something's up."

A sprinting sailor clipped Jamie's shoulder and she went spinning to the deck.

"Jamie!"

Jamie looked up and saw several more crewmen charging her way like buffalo in a stampede. Jamie staggered to her feet and raced to the wall, pressing herself to the partition. The line of sailors grew and the passageway was filling.

"Something's wrong," Jamie said. "They look afraid."

"What could scare sailors?" M&M asked. "War?"

"I don't know, but I bet they know the way up. Can you run?"

"Yes, I think so."

"Okay, we're gonna run with them, but don't let them run over you. Okay?"

M&M took a deep breath. "Okay."

"Let's go."

Jamie took Mary by the hand and started off, trying to stay as far from the others as possible but still see where they were going.

From the Depths

Following the *Archer*'s captain was like running an obstacle course. The man moved with driven purpose, leaving Stanton and the others to do their best to keep up. It wasn't that the skipper was moving so quickly, as much as it was the danger ordinary objects presented. A wad of paper or a cigarette butt was a potential tripping hazard, and every crewman was a linebacker capable of flooring anyone of Stanton's team who came in contact. One thing, however, worked to their advantage. As the captain worked against the rising flow of his crew, who were making ready to abandon ship, the streaming crowd of sailors parted before him like the ocean before the prow of the ship. No one bumped shoulders with the captain.

As the captain approached one of the ladderways, an officer cried out, "Make way, lads. Captain on deck." As if by magic, the worried sailors divided like the Red Sea before Moses.

Stanton was conflicted. His first impulse was to order Richie to keep the others topside and abandon ship with the crew, but Stanton had no idea how that would work. Although he didn't understand the physics of the problem, he knew that if an *Archer* crewman did as little as sit on Tony or Steve or anyone else from

Stanton's time, it could injure them, maybe even kill them. Being on a crowded lifeboat might be more dangerous than staying on the ship. Besides, he had to deal with John. At the moment he had no facts to indicate that John was somehow involved, but his intuition was sounding emergency bells all its own. If John was somehow connected, then maybe one of them could reach him.

They descended several decks, staying as close to the captain as possible. He knew where he was going; Stanton could only guess. Better to follow than foolishly run ahead.

The captain moved at a good clip, not trotting but not strolling. Stanton knew what he was doing. He must appear calm at all costs. A ship's crew took their cues from their leaders, especially from the captain. If the sailors saw their top officer running wild-eyed through the dim interior, it might heighten the barely contained panic.

Step followed purposeful step and Stanton stayed close on the man's heels. The deeper they descended, the fewer of the crew they saw. At one of the boiler rooms the captain turned right. An open door stood before him. Stanton peered over the man's shoulder and saw a large room with a wide cylindrical column spanning floor to ceiling. It took only a moment for Stanton to recognize it as the hoist that would transfer shells and cordite charges to the gunhouses on the upper deck. They had arrived at the scene.

As they crossed into the large room, Stanton could see a man standing at another door, his attention fixed through the opening. He was speaking and the terror in his voice was evident. "... we can talk about this." It was the sailor who brought the report to the captain. He must have run ahead.

"Ain't nothing to talk about," a voice said from the room. Stanton assumed it was the voice of the man called Roberts.

"That's right," another voice said with enthusiasm. This voice Stanton recognized, and he wished he hadn't. It was John. "Blessed nothingness. Remember blessed nothingness."

"But—," the crewman began, then stopped when he caught sight of the captain. "Captain Burke is here."

"Burke," Richie whispered. Stanton turned to see him just over his shoulder. The others waited outside the first door. "At least we have a name for the skipper."

The frightened crewman approached Burke. "I've done my best, sir. He won't listen to reason. Frankly, I think he's well off his rocker. If he lights that match, sir, we are well and truly sunk."

"Thank you," Burke said calmly but in a whisper. "You're dismissed. Please abandon ship with the others."

"But sir, this is my station. I should stay with you."

"That's very noble but you have your orders."

"But sir—" Burke looked hard at the man and Stanton saw him wither. "Aye, sir." The sailor turned toward the first door and hustled out. Stanton and Richie backpedaled to avoid a collision.

Burke inhaled deeply, then released a steady stream of air between his pursed lips. It was the first sign of tension Stanton had seen in the man. Burke took three steps forward and turned to face the explosives-filled room. Stanton and Richie followed.

"Young Mr. Roberts," Burke said with formality.

"Captain," Roberts replied with a slight nod.

"Roberts?" It was John. Stanton could see his back. He was facing Roberts. "Roberts? I thought your name was Weed."

"How's the head, son? Did you check it at sick bay as I ordered?"

The man is incredible, Stanton thought. *Ice water in his veins.*

"Aye," Roberts said. "But the doc said I was fine. Just a good-size knot on me noggin."

"Glad to hear it, Roberts."

"You might as well call me Weed, sir. Everyone else does."

"Weed is an insult, son. I don't insult my crew."

"Your crew don't seem to mind doing it."

"They will now, son. I'll make sure of it," Burke said.

Roberts laughed. "No need, Cap. I plan on taking care of that for you. No need to say thanks."

Stanton was about to call out to John when he heard the sound of running footsteps. He turned to see several crewmen powering through the door. Again he and Richie struggled to get out of the way. Each sailor carried an antique-looking rifle. Stanton had to remind himself that the weapons were new and modern for the time. The lead sailor held up a hand and walked in the open space slowly, like a cat hunting a bird. Quietly he racked the rifle's bolt action, then nodded to the captain, who gave no sign of noticing them.

The intent was clear. Upon the captain's order the sailor would step forward and fire a round into Roberts, most likely a head shot.

"Young Roberts," the captain said. "You have my attention, sir. What can I do for you?"

"Nothing, Captain. Not a bloomin' thing. We all die today. Blessed nothingness, Cap. Blessed nothingness."

"I don't understand, Roberts. Have I mistreated you?"

"You? No sir. Not you. But your crew has. Every day and in every way. I'm tired of the abuse. I'm tired of the jokes. I'm tired of the names. I didn't ask to be here. I didn't ask to be assigned to this ship. That was my uncle's doing, none of mine. Do you hear me?"

"Indeed I do, son."

"I'm not your son," Roberts snapped.

"You're on my ship, Roberts. I see all my crew as family. Some behave and others, like those who have tormented you, misbehave."

Richie leaned close to Stanton, shielding his words, not from Burke and his crew but from John. "Do you think this is the reason we're here? Is this the miracle you were talking about?"

"Seems likely," Stanton whispered. "I'm just at a loss for what to do."

"You're not alone," Richie said. "I'm fresh out of ideas. I suppose we could charge in there and take John by force."

Stanton shook his head. "Captain Burke is in the doorway. There's not enough room around him and we can't move him—not in this world."

"Captain Stanton," a voice said behind him. It was Steve. "You know, if that sailor there fires the gun and the bullet hits John, he's a dead man. We can't change things here, can't move objects or people, but they can have an effect on us."

Stanton glanced down at his wounded palm, where the metal lifeline had dug into the flesh, leaving a wide gash.

"I know," Stanton said. The hard truth had already occurred to him.

"One other thing," Steve said. "Tony saw the girls. They were running with the sailors. Tenny and he went after them. They're going to bring them back."

"Find them," Stanton said. "Tell them not to come back. Lead them to the stern of the ship. If he detonates the cordite, it will split the ship in two. It'll go down in minutes. You may have to dive into the ocean. It's a bad choice at the speed we're going, but it's the only choice."

"Got it," Steve said with courage beyond his years.

A kid like that deserves a long life, Stanton thought. *They all do.*

"I thought I recognized that voice."

Stanton snapped his head around. John was looking right at him. He had an odd, evil smirk pasted on his face. "You found me, Captain. I'm impressed."

"John, we need your help."

"I'm not interested in helping you," John snapped. "I'm interested in helping me."

"By dying?" Richie asked.

"Absolutely, Richie Rich. Spot on, as these guys would say. Blessed nothingness, man. Blessed nothingness."

"Blessed nothingness," Roberts said.

Burke replied, "There's no such thing, son."

"I think there is," Roberts said.

"Confusing, isn't it, Captain?" John said. "Conversation on conversation. They can't hear us or see us, but we sure can see them. And this is worth seeing." He paused and looked at Roberts. "He's gonna do it, you know. He really is."

"I think you're right," Stanton said. "We have to stop him."

"Stop him? Stop him?" John laughed loudly. "You can't stop him. You know that. We can't do anything to these guys. We're observers, Stanton. We just get to sit in the stands."

"John—"

"Don't interrupt me," John shot back. Then he calmed himself. "I've been thinking, Captain. I'm capable of that, you know. Everyone thinks I'm as dumb as a brick, but I'm smart enough to figure some of this out. You said this ship was only a rumor, built at the same time as that other ship but in a different shipyard. What was the name of that other boat?"

"HMS *Dreadnought*."

"*Dreadnought . . . Dreadnought.*" John chuckled. "Does that make this the *Dead-nought?* Get it? I think this ship became a rumor because Weed here—I mean Roberts—dropped the match. Kaboom!" He shouted the last word, waving his arms. "That might be embarrassing, right? A brand-new ship explodes for no reason. I don't think the Brits would let that kind of information out. Am I right?"

"That's my take on it," Stanton said.

"I'm glad you agree."

Burke's words caught Stanton's attention for a moment. "We need to talk, son. This isn't the way to handle things."

"Not proper, what?" Roberts said, mocking Burke's accent.

Stanton forced his attention back to John. "John, why do you suppose we're here?" he asked calmly.

"Because Roberts is about to blow this ship in half."

"That's not what I mean. Why are we here on this ship?"

"How should I know? I'm no . . . Wait. You think it's some kinda miracle, don't you?"

"Yes, I think there's a purpose to it. I think we're here to stop what happened a hundred years ago."

"You mean God sent us back? Boy, did he pick the wrong team."

"I don't think he did, John. I really don't. I think he chose the perfect team and the perfect person. We are here for a reason."

"Why doesn't God just work some miracle? He's in the miracle business, right?"

Stanton could see that John was getting more irritated. He was thankful that the boy couldn't strike a match of his own.

"Hand me the matches, son," Burke said. "No need for this to end this way. Hand me the matches and we'll call it a day." The captain took a step forward, further blocking the door.

"*Back*," Roberts said. "I'm going to torch this place. I really will." Burke froze.

"Persistent, isn't he?" John said. "You gotta admire that. The dude's got guts."

"John, you have to help," Stanton said.

"There's nothing I can do, and nothing I would do if I could. I'm ready for death, Stanton. I've had it. I know this kid behind me. He may have lived a century before me but I know him. We're two of a kind. We're twins. Everyone hates him; everyone hates me."

"That's not true, John."

"Oh, stop! Please stop with the Mr. Rogers talk. It turns my stomach. At least I can own up to my problems. At least I can see the world as it is. I want to die, Stanton. Can't you get that? I want to die. I'm tired of the name-calling. I'm tired of being the outcast. I'm tired of these voices in my head." He rapped his skull with his knuckles.

"Voices?" Stanton said.

"I came on this trip to die. The voices said I could slip over the side of the yacht at night. No one would miss me. I'd sink into the blessed nothingness. Just me and the water and death."

"Why didn't you do it?" Stanton asked.

"I don't know ... I chickened out. But I'm not going to chicken out this time. I'm staying here until Weed lights the match. Boom, baby!"

"You didn't slip over the side," Stanton said, "because you didn't want to die. The voices are wrong, John. They're very wrong."

"They're in my head!" John shouted. "Always in my head. Always talking. Always saying things. They're real, I tell you. Real."

"The voices," Roberts said. "They tell me this is the only way out. The only way out."

Burke said, "The voices are lying, Roberts. I want you to listen to my voice."

"Spooky, ain't it?" John said. "It's like we're psychic twins or something."

"Captain Burke is right," Stanton said. "Don't listen to the voices. Listen to your soul. That's the real you."

"I don't believe in souls, or God or heaven or hell," John argued. "There's nothing to listen to."

"It's there," Stanton said. "You can feel it. God is speaking to you."

"I said I don't believe in God! It's not possible."

"Is it possible that we're standing on this ship decades before any of us was born?"

"So . . . so what? Are you saying that God sent us all back here so you could . . . could save my life?"

"No," Stanton said. "I believe God sent us back here so you could save our lives."

"What?" John shook his head. "Nah, I'm not buying that."

"I am," Stanton said. "You're the one who understands this kid better than anyone else does. You know what he's thinking, what he's feeling. He hears the same voices you do."

"I don't care. I want to die." John paused, then took a deep breath. "You'd better get out of here. The kid is really going to do this. You stand a better chance up on deck."

"I'm not going anywhere," Richie interjected. "I'm going to die with you."

"You're an idiot," John said.

"Yeah, I know, but we started on this trip together; we finish it together. I'm staying right here."

"Me too," Stanton was surprised to hear Steve's voice. "You go, I go."

"That goes for me too." It was Tony.

"And me," Tenny added.

"Me too," Jamie and M&M added.

Stanton looked at Steve. "I thought I told you to lead everyone topside."

"You did," Steve said. "We had a different idea. You can court-martial us if you want, but we're staying."

Stanton felt something catch in his throat. He turned back to John. "We're not leaving you, John."

John opened his mouth to speak but nothing came out.

Filling the silence, Stanton said, "You're the man here, John. I'm telling you, God did not send me back. He sent you back. *You* need to stop Roberts."

"How? There's nothing I can do. You can only resist the voices so long. Roberts doesn't have any strength left. His life is over, and that means ours are over too."

"Will your family miss you?" Roberts asked Burke.

"I suppose so," Burke replied.

"No one's going to miss the likes of me," Roberts said. "No one at all."

There was a soft crackling sound and the air was filled with the smell of sulfur. Roberts had lit the match.

Chaos ensued. Burke stepped back and the sailor with the rifle stepped into his place, raising the weapon to his shoulder.

The match dropped.

The gun fired.

Stanton held his breath. Then he saw it: John had flung himself forward, his hands held out as if he were diving to catch a football.

The match fell into John's hand.

The pain was beyond description. John had no idea why he did it, but something deep inside, in a place he hadn't known existed, broke, and suddenly nothing mattered more than catching the flickering flame of the match.

He saw Roberts strike it.

He saw Roberts drop it.

And John dove toward the young sailor's feet, arms extended. The match fell in his open hand, but instead of being a light piece of wood with a small flame, it felt as if it weighed a thousand pounds, and the fire burned like a blowtorch.

The match, against all logic, drove John's hand down, toward the deck, toward the pile of explosive cordite that had run from the punctured containers. It was agony. It was a bit of hell held in his hand. The fire was too hot, the weight unimaginably great.

The back of John's hand touched the cordite and he steeled himself for the explosion, but no explosion came. The match continued bearing down like a powerful pneumatic press and John screamed from the agony of it. He felt the bones in his hand splintering. His vision darkened.

He felt something else: the impact of a body on the deck next to him, and something grabbing at his hand. Suddenly the weight was gone. John opened his eyes and saw Captain Burke lying on his side next to John, the match in his hands, his fingers pinching the head that had a moment before been burning.

John rolled over on his back and looked up to see Stanton and the others, pale with fright. A second beat went by in slow motion.

There was another sound. It was Roberts. "Me shoulder. You shot me in me shoulder."

The sailor who had fired the round advanced, rifle in hand. Burke rolled on his back and bellowed, "Stow that weapon. Another shot in here could set it all off." The sailor stepped back but another entered, his hands empty of a weapon.

"Watch it," the sailor shouted, then charged, leaping over the prone captain and John. He landed on Roberts. "Let me see them hands, boy," the sailor snapped.

"Me shoulder," Roberts whined. "Something's broke in me shoulder."

"Got them," the sailor said, holding up a box of matches.

Burke struggled to his feet and so did John, who staggered out of the room. "My hand. It crushed my hand."

"You did it, John!" Stanton said. "You really did it. You saved over seven hundred lives."

"My hand," was all John could say.

"Everyone out," Stanton ordered. "This place is going to be packed with people. If we don't want to get smashed, we need to leave."

John looked at the faces of the others. Each wore a smile that communicated more than words.

N
Λ

Captain Burke had ordered the area secured until the explosive material was cleaned up, posting a guard by the door. "Get him to sick bay," he said, motioning to Roberts. "I want two guards on him at all times. No one is to touch him but the doctor. Understand? There is to be no crew access to him."

Burke exited the loading area and moved briskly to the nearest ladderway, ordering all sailors he saw back to their stations. "All is well, lads," he told them.

Once the tide of exodus was stemmed, Stanton led his party up the stairs toward the main deck. "What will the captain do?" Jamie asked.

"Reverse the order to abandon ship," Stanton explained. "I doubt anyone got off board. We're still moving too fast. Dropping lifeboats at speed is tricky at best, disastrous at worst."

"Then why did he tell the sailor at the steering wheel to keep the speed up?" Tony wondered.

Stanton led them up one of the curved stairways. One more level and they'd be on the main deck, breathing fresh air and able to stand out of the way of the many sailors still hustling about their business. "He was between a rock and a hard place. If he had cut the engines, Roberts might have realized that his captain was calling for the crew to abandon ship, and ignited the cordite. Captain Burke was buying time for his crew. A brave and smart man. I'd be honored to serve with him."

"If we don't get back to our own time, you may have the opportunity," Tony quipped.

John was silent. Stanton had positioned him in front and kept a hand on the young man every step he took. "How's the hand, John?"

"It hurts bad. It's killing me."

"I'll look at it when we're on deck and out of the way of the crew."

"Okay," John said softly. "I'm pretty sure it will still be hurting then."

"You're my hero, son. You knew what might happen, what pain there might be, and you dove for the thing anyway."

"It was more stupid than brave."

Stanton knew he was being modest. He also knew John was in agony. "Call it whatever you want, but I admire it and will never forget it."

Bolting through the last hatch and onto the open deck, Stanton felt the sun on his skin, the salty wind in his hair, and was nearly overcome with gratitude. "Everyone aft," he said. "Stay away from the crew. They're still a danger to us."

Several okays were uttered. Once at the stern, the very place where he nearly plunged into the churning propeller wash, Stanton pulled his crew together. He studied John's hand. It looked bad. The area where the match had touched his hand—a match that couldn't have weighed an ounce—was still depressed and red. Blisters had formed over much of his palm.

The others crowded in to see.

"Yeow," Steve said. "That looks like it might hurt a little."

"I was stupid to be down there," John said. "I just felt . . . felt that he was like me."

"I'm glad you were there," Tony said. "You saved us all, buddy." He stepped forward. "Sorry for being such a mouth around you. I didn't help things any."

"Forget it," John said.

"We're not forgetting anything," Jamie said. "We helped make your life miserable. I was miserable, so I thought I'd share it with everyone else. Seeing these guys makes me realize my life isn't all that tough."

"Life is always tough," Stanton said. "More for some than for others, but it's pretty much the same thing."

"Wait," Tenny snapped. "Anyone else feel that?"

Stanton looked down at the deck and up at the superstructure. Lifeboats hung from their davits. Some hung over the side of the ship, ready to be launched. "The captain's slowing the ship. It looks like he's coming about. I wonder if a boat got in the water. I bet he's going back to pick up—"

Home

J. D. Stanton was standing at the bow of the *Archer*, staring forward into the curtain of mist he had come to hate. The ship was dead in the water, unmoving, like a dead whale.

Then it hit him—they had been standing on the stern, not the bow. He turned and found himself alone. "Not again," he said to himself.

A moment later one of the doors to the superstructure opened and Tenny walked out. Seeing Stanton, she started in his direction.

"Hey, up here." Tenny stopped and turned. Stanton looked up and saw motion on the wing of the navigation deck. It was Steve. "At least I'm not on the mast. I'll be right down."

"I'll join you," came another voice from overhead. Stanton had to move forward before he saw Richie standing on the pinnace, which was still hanging from its davits.

Tenny joined Stanton and moaned, "I'm getting a little tired of this people-shuffling thing."

"You and me both," Stanton said. "You okay?"

"Yeah, the transition seemed easier this time."

Another door opened and a confused Tony appeared from within the superstructure. He made his way to Stanton and

Tenny. "A room with a bunch of old urinals," he said with disgust. "Why can't I land in the captain's quarters or something?"

"Any new bruises?" Stanton asked.

"Not this time."

Soon Mary, Jamie, and John found them. To Stanton's quizzical look they each described where they had just been.

"Some kinda kitchen," Jamie said. "And no cracks about a woman's place."

"Hammocks," Mary said. "A big room with row upon row of hammocks."

"Crew's quarters," Stanton explained. "What about you, John?"

"Engine room, I think. Lots of ducts, pipes, and something that looked like a big motor."

"Great," Tony said. "I get the toilet room and John gets the only thing on the boat I'd be interested in."

"There's more," John said. "Look." He held up his damaged hand. It showed no sign of injury.

Stanton examined it closely. "Good as new."

"How can that be?" Jamie asked.

"The injury happened in the past—nearly a hundred years ago." He looked at his own hand. The torn flesh was whole, pink, and healthy. "Apparently, what happened then doesn't carry over to the now."

Steve and Richie appeared and the conversation turned excited. They had just survived destruction and come through unscathed. It was too much to believe but not too much to celebrate. The joy ended when Mary moaned and doubled over. Jamie was by her side a second later. Tenny joined her.

"What is it?" Jamie asked.

"I feel bad. Real bad. My stomach."

Tenny laid a hand on her forehead and frowned. She knelt, slipped a hand under M&M's shirt, then retracted it a few seconds later. Looking at Stanton, she said a single word. "Hot."

"The reverse must also be true," Steve said. "Yours and John's injuries remained in the past. M&M's illness remained in the present."

"So we still have a problem," Stanton said.

"Look," Richie shouted, pointing. "It's the Zodiac."

Stanton turned to see the dinghy floating thirty yards off the port side. "It must not have floated very far after coming loose."

"Wait here," Richie said and ran to the stern. He sprinted back. "The *Tern About* is about a hundred yards astern. We can paddle to it easily."

"Something is changing," John said. "The mist is thinning. And look—the sky is looking more like normal."

"Does that mean we're going back to where we just came from?" Jamie asked, the fear dripping from her words.

"No, it doesn't," Richie said flatly. He kicked his shoes off and stripped his T-shirt away. "I'll be back."

"What are you doing?" Tony asked.

"Just don't go anyplace without me." Richie stepped to the lifeline, climbed between the cables, steadied himself, and then jumped off the edge. A splash followed and the group pressed to the lifeline. Richie was already swimming for all he was worth; one powerful stroke after another pounded the water.

Stanton watched with admiration and concern as Richie made his way to the Zodiac and kick-crawled his way aboard. Stanton expected to see a paddle hitting the water, but Richie shuffled his way to the back of the craft. A moment later a coughing sound came from the motor.

Cheers were sent skyward.

The engine died. A moment later it came back to life, sounding stronger than before and more musical than any mechanical device Stanton had ever heard. It resonated like a fine orchestra.

N
Λ

It was cramped aboard the Zodiac, but no one wanted to spend another moment on the battleship, nor did it seem wise. Stanton had no idea what would happen to it. Everything seemed to be returning to normal: the sky, the water, even the engine on the dinghy. Although loaded to the maximum, the Zodiac responded well, and Richie guided it through the waters, noting that the ocean was picking up "a little chop."

Despite being battered and broken, the *Tern About* looked as good to Stanton as it had the moment he first laid eyes on her. He was the first aboard and John was the second. Together they helped the others up and over the transom. Once the last foot touched the teak deck, Stanton was at the navigation center. He flipped on the radio.

It came to life.

Stanton keyed the mic. "Mayday, Mayday. Miami Coast Guard, this is the *Tern About*. We have an emergency to declare." He released the key and waited. Static.

The others joined him in the salon. No one spoke.

"Miami Coast Guard, this is the pleasure craft *Tern About*. We have an emergency on board." Again he released the key. A long minute passed. Stanton raised the microphone to his lips, then stopped. The static had changed.

"*Tern About, Tern About*, this is Miami Coast Guard. Please state your emergency and your location."

Silence hung heavy in the air, then dissolved in a blast of cheers.

Stanton flipped on the switch for the GPS tracking. It came on immediately, giving their exact position. He turned to his crew. "Folks, we're going home."

Six Months Later

Y ou shouldn't have done this," Mary said. "This had to cost you a bundle."

"I'm not paying for it," Stanton said. "Richie's father is."

They were standing at the bottom of a metal gangplank that led from a wood pier up to the starboard side of HMS *Archer*. The Portsmouth, Hampshire, fog had given way to a bright morning, allowing the sun to rain down yellow light on the English port.

"I didn't think you'd survive telling him about the damage to his boat," John said. He stuck his hands into the pockets of his jeans. There was a hint of teasing in his voice but nothing acerbic. His wisecracks no longer came with barbs.

"Neither did I," Richie said. "Captain Stanton went to see him and convinced him it wasn't our fault. I'm not sure he believes what we told him but that's understandable. Insurance paid for everything and the *Tern About* looks as good as new."

"I had to tell him," Stanton explained. "His boat was wrecked. He deserved the truth and I'm not comfortable lying. Other than my wife, I haven't mentioned it to anyone. Not many would believe it. Besides, it would change nothing." There had been no formal agreement to keep the events secret, yet each had told Stanton they had kept mum. It seemed wise and Stanton found some relief in that knowledge.

Jamie laughed. "I don't believe it and I lived it." Jamie seemed a little thinner and a little taller. Her eyes were bright and her smile quick. "I keep telling Mary this was all just a dream."

"It wasn't a dream," Mary said. She had gained several needed pounds, and the hair she once hid behind was now short and dyed red. "I have the appendectomy scar to prove it."

Stanton had lost more than a few hours' sleep over Mary. She had been airlifted from the *Tern About* by the Coast Guard and flown to Miami. An hour later she was having surgery. A very inflamed appendix was removed. "It could have gone at any time," the doctors said. The doctors had more to say. The large bruise on her stomach caught their attention, and Child Protective Services was called in. Mary faced many questions, her abusive father many more. A trial put him behind bars and he was dishonorably discharged from the navy. Now Mary and her mother received regular counseling and were slowly overcoming the emotional scars.

"Wow," Tenny said. "I can't believe we're in England. More importantly, I can't believe we're going back on the *Archer*."

"So much for it being a rumor," Steve said. He had grown six inches in the last six months. He was no longer the smallest of the group. "When we set sail, she wasn't a floating museum."

"No," Stanton said. "She was at the bottom of the ocean, put there by young Roberts."

"Begging your pardon, Captain," a proper British voice said behind him. "I believe you're mistaken. You are Captain J. D. Stanton, aren't you?"

Stanton turned. "I am," he said, feeling suspicious of the gray-haired man in the dark-blue suit. "And you are . . ."

"Oh, terribly sorry. I'm Commander Julius Burke, Royal Navy retired. I'm the new director of the museum." He extended his hand. Stanton took it and gave it a hearty shake. "Do you know an Admiral Kaster?"

"I do."

"Ah, just so. He phoned me last week and told me of your little excursion here. Wondered if I might give you a bit of a personal tour, as it were. I am of course honored to do so. First, I must correct you. As you can see, *Archer* is in fine shape. She was never damaged, not even in the war years—World War I, of course."

"Of course," Stanton said with a smile. "I'm curious, Commander. You said your name was Burke?"

"Yes indeed. My grandfather was *Archer*'s first captain. He served aboard her for many years. Passed on quite a tale or two, he did." He looked at the others. "And who do we have here?"

Stanton made introductions and handshakes were exchanged. "Well," Burke said, "I suppose you would like to go aboard. Please stay with me," he said as he started up the gangplank. "She's a beauty but it's easy to get lost inside."

"Boy, he's got that right," John said. The others laughed.

"I'm sorry, what was that?" Burke asked.

"Nothing," Stanton said. "Just some youthful humor." He put his hand on John's shoulder and gave it a squeeze.

"We should have left our initials," Tony said. Tony looked the same, spoke the same, but his tone had quieted. He had learned something about himself and about others. Friendship was possible with people vastly different from him.

The group had become friends. They lived in different cities but email and Instant Messaging kept them in touch. Stanton stayed in the loop as well. Over the months, he had shared his faith with each of them, Tenny included. Steve had been the first to respond, Tenny soon after. Jamie had embraced the gospel with a surprising zeal. Tony and John were still uncertain but they were at least listening and asking questions. That was all Stanton could ask for. Mary remained quiet about all things personal, but Stanton could see a difference. He hoped that one day soon she would open like the flower she was. Until then Stanton would continue to pray.

John had proved surprising in several ways. The voices that had haunted him in the past no longer came to his mind. He told Stanton their assault became stronger once they set sail. He had truly decided to kill himself, but the right opportunity never presented itself. That and he was afraid to die. Stanton couldn't prove it, but the image he had seen, as well as the crewman who had so frightened Mary, were somehow associated with the voices—how was a mystery.

Other mysteries plagued Stanton. He had yet to figure out why Mary saw crewmen on the *Archer* before anyone else, or how she could see them with the ship slipping—at least partially—back into its own time.

Steve summed it up best: "When you start messing with time, nothing makes sense. All bets are off."

Stanton yearned for all the answers, but he had lived long enough to know that life wasn't like a movie, in which everything could be summed up in a five-minute denouement. Perhaps that was the way God intended it. Wondering, searching, and contemplating were all wonderful exercises for the mind. They were also powerful calisthenics for the soul.

"Oh, I should mention," Commander Burke said with a broad smile, "some say this ship is haunted."

"Haunted?" Richie said.

"Oh yes. My grandfather told me that during the *Archer*'s sea trials, several crewmen claimed to have seen ghosts. And these weren't just ordinary sailors. One was a bridge officer who claimed to see two ghosts on the boat deck. Another was the ship's doctor and his aide. Said several ghosts had run roughshod through the dispensary."

"Pretty strange," Richie said with a knowing smirk.

"I should say," Burke replied. "The strangest account came from the chaplain, of all people. He said his Bible closed all on its own. So do be careful. You never know who you're going to meet on the *Archer.*"

"Amen," said Stanton.

Afterword

Portions of this book are rooted in the new genre of "alternate history," in which historical principles and events are altered slightly to bring about a different present. HMS *Archer* is a fictional ship. Although the Royal Navy has had ships by that name, the *Archer* that appears in these pages is purely fictional. The *Dreadnought*, however, was a real vessel that forever changed the way naval architects designed ships. The fictional *Archer* is based on the very real *Dreadnought*.

Alton Gansky

What Sinister Secret Lies Hidden in the Town of Roanoke II?

Vanished

Alton Gansky

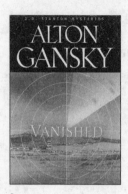

How did the entire population of this desert military instillation simply disappear? High-level Pentagon orders call J. D. Stanton, retired navy captain, back to active duty to investigate. Heading a crack team of military, government, and scientific experts, Stanton faces a bewildering scenario. Food still on dinner plates, gas nozzles still in the fuel ports of cars at the filling station . . . Whatever happened took the people of Roanoke II completely by surprise. But took them where?

Softcover: 978-0-310-22003-9

A Story of Faith, Courage, and Determination in
the Face of Unexpected and Unknown Evil

A Ship Possessed

Alton Gansky

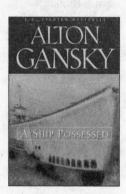

An American World War II submarine has come home over fifty years after she was presumed lost in the Atlantic. Now her dark gray hulk lies embedded in the sand of a San Diego beach. The submarine is in the wrong ocean, her crew is missing . . . And her half-century absence is a mystery that's about to deepen. Something is inside of the submarine—something unexpected and terrible. The task of solving the mystery surrounding a ship possessed falls to J. D. Stanton. What he is about to encounter will challenge his training, his wits, and his faith.

Softcover: 978-0-310-21944-6

Share Your Thoughts

With the Author: Your comments will be forwarded to
the author when you send them to *zauthor@zondervan.com*.

With Zondervan: Submit your review of this book
by writing to *zreview@zondervan.com*.

Free Online Resources at

www.zondervan.com/hello

 Zondervan AuthorTracker: Be notified whenever your
favorite authors publish new books, go on tour, or post
an update about what's happening in their lives.

 Daily Bible Verses and Devotions: Enrich your life
with daily Bible verses or devotions that help you start
every morning focused on God.

 Free Email Publications: Sign up for newsletters on
fiction, Christian living, church ministry, parenting, and
more.

 Zondervan Bible Search: Find and compare
Bible passages in a variety of translations at
www.zondervanbiblesearch.com.

 Other Benefits: Register yourself to receive online
benefits like coupons and special offers, or to participate
in research.